Praise for *The Seven*

'There are moments thro~~ughout this~~ ~~novel~~ that will long remain with me, searing and stark images that are indelibly etched in my memory.'

Anne Williams, Being Anne Book Blogger

'A really compelling and thought-provoking read. I could hardly put it down.'

R.E. Hodges, Author

'Jan Harvey's novel takes the form of a deftly signposted double narrative, moving back and forth across two time scales with ease.'

Jan Lee, Oxford Times

'It kept me awake until the small hours of the morning, something I haven't done for years. Many congratulations to the author for her considerable literary skills.'

Jane Bwye, Book Blogger, Book and Me.

'Tell it well and end with a totally surprising mystery, as Jan Harvey did, and you get a fine book which deserves all the success of which a debut novelist dreams.'

Bill Larkworthy, Author

'Jan Harvey has a way of writing with deep emotion and rich description while still allowing for the story to flow well and with ease.'

Sarah Swan, Sarah's Vignettes Book Blogger

'We cannot and will not stop talking about this book because it's just wonderful. Set in WW2 Paris and modern day Oxfordshire, this is a gripping tale of love and turmoil. A must read for historical fiction lovers.'

Madhatter, Bookshop

'Quite simply, I couldn't put this book down.'

Courtney Stuart, Reviewer

The Slow Death of Maxwell Carrick

Jan Harvey

Matador
9 Priory Business Park,
Wistow Road, Kibworth Beauchamp,
Leicestershire. LE8 0RX
Tel: 0116 279 2299
Email: books@troubador.co.uk
Web: www.troubador.co.uk/matador
Twitter: @matadorbooks

ISBN 978 1789015 850

British Library Cataloguing in Publication Data.
A catalogue record for this book is available from the British Library.

Printed and bound in the UK by TJ International, Padstow, Cornwall
Typeset in 11pt Minion Pro by Troubador Publishing Ltd, Leicester, UK

Matador is an imprint of Troubador Publishing Ltd

*This book is dedicated to the memory
of my best friend.*

Nancy, I wish you were here to read it.

My Infelice's face, her brow, her eye,
The dimple on her cheek; and such sweet skill
Hath from the cunning workman's pencil flown,
These lips look fresh and lovely as her own.
False colours last after the true be dead.
Of all the roses grafted on her cheeks,
Of all the graces dancing in her eyes,
Of all the music set upon her tongue,
Of all that was past woman's excellence
In her white bosom; look, a painted board
Circumscribes all.

Thomas Middleton

1

'Speech!' my deputy, Bob, shouted and the rest of the team joined him in a rowdy chorus. They had festooned the meeting room in pale blue, my favourite colour. There were balloons, banners and a large cake in the centre of the meeting room table with the words "Happy Retirement" piped on it. I shook my head in disbelief, I hadn't intended to leave like this, a few drinks down at the Eagle and Child maybe, but that was all I'd really banked on.

Someone handed me champagne in a plastic flute and as I cleared my throat I was fighting back the tears.

'Thank you, all of you, I wasn't expecting any of this.' I was very touched. 'I really mean it, you have all been marvellous to work with and I am honoured to have known you.' I held up my glass, as the froth poured over the rim. 'Here's to the best team an editor could wish for.'

That was autumn last year, the end of my career in publishing. I was scrap-heaped at sixty and, in all honesty, I didn't know where to turn or what to do with myself. Steve, my husband, was still teaching and loving it, but I was scratching about the house, alone all day, with only my thoughts for company.

Most women my age have the distraction of

grandchildren, but that was never going to happen with Sarah still single, on her way to forty, and no sign of a long-term relationship. I fleetingly toyed with the idea of getting a dog, but the whole thing didn't really appeal and, besides, we had our geriatric cat to consider. I mulled it over with my friend Becky in a small café just off St.Giles a month later.

'Martha, there must be something you'd enjoy doing.' She said this as she over-stirred the cream into her coffee and, even though she was my closest friend, I knew she was frustrated with me. After all, I had my freedom while she was still chained to a desk.

'I'd like to do yoga, maybe, or perhaps something arty? Learn to watercolour or something? Oh I don't know, I should really tackle the garden, I suppose.' I sighed more heavily than I intended to.

'So it's the plank, painting or potting then.' Becky was incredulous. 'Are you really telling me that, although you've known you were going to retire for over a year, you hadn't thought of something to do with yourself?' How could she understand? Becky's job was a bind, something to be endured, whereas I had always been absorbed with my career. I had thoroughly enjoyed it. 'What about writing? You love Italy, why not think about writing a book on say Florence or Rome, you've been to both places so often?'

'I don't know, editing magazines is one thing but a book, that's a huge undertaking and I–'

'And you have plenty of time to do it,' she cut in. 'Martha, can I be really frank with you?' I nodded. I was pressing my fingers to my lips, struggling to contain my feelings. 'I can't believe you because, in all honesty, I'd love the opportunity to do anything I wanted to and if I'm really truthful, I'm deadly jealous of you. I simply cannot believe you don't feel the same way.'

The café was filling up steadily, it was lunchtime, Becky's lunch hour. We ordered a cheese and onion toastie each, but I was sitting looking at mine blankly, while Becky devoured hers. I didn't feel hungry at all. Maybe this was depression. Whatever it was, I was feeling pretty low.

'Look, why don't you go through your village magazine tonight, see what's on in your neighbourhood. I bet there's something in there to interest you.' Becky was being kind, I understood that, but was I really reduced to looking for ideas in the local rag? I'd never so much as glanced at the magazine before. Steve always read it and told me the abstract empty names of the recent dead, and I knew none of them.

'You've heard of this chap, Sidney Purge,' he would say. 'He used to mow the playing field and the village green on a little blue tractor, lovely man.'

'Nope,' I replied shaking my head. When would I have seen Sidney Anyone cutting the grass in the village? I was never here. I used to get up at six every morning and battle with the traffic into Oxford to reach my desk by half eight and I rarely made it home before seven thirty.

When I browsed through the village magazine it was, as I expected it would be, a very amateur lick and stick affair. There was a plant sale coming up on the green, the fête in August was looking for volunteers and the church was going to be reordered, whatever that meant. I flicked through it: deceased people, three men one woman; two marriages and a christening, and a lost cat called Barney. Eventually a small advert on the inside back cover drew me in. It was very badly typeset, with a blurred image of the old prebend at the top.

Can You Help?

The Village History Group is looking for assistance in compiling and editing a book about local history. We need someone to help us with this exciting project.
If you can spare a few hours a week, please call 993875.

No email address.

Steve was nonchalant.

'It's up to you, sweetheart. I think you'd enjoy it.' He was speaking from behind a towering pile of homework. 'Anything to stop you moping around.'

'Moping?' I repeated after him.

'Well, yes, you have been… a bit. I think it would be nice for you to get your teeth into something, a project would give you focus.'

'I can't see me working with a bunch of local yokels on a book, can you?'

'Local yokels?' He snorted. 'We live in the Oxfordshire Cotswolds surrounded by overpaid stockbrokers and fat cat industrialists. I'm not sure I've ever seen either a local or a yokel. Martha, you need to get a grip and do something.'

He was right of course, it was what I needed and I had earned the brusque tone in his voice. It would keep me occupied and I had exactly the right skills, so I picked up the phone, took a deep breath, and tapped the number into it.

Tom Williams was an earnest young man with a goatee beard and dark eyes. 'How absolutely wonderful of you to agree to help us.' He was gripping my hand in a firm handshake. 'Do come in. The committee is in the living room.'

It was a tall Georgian house on the main road with highly polished flagstones running the length of the long hall. We turned into the lounge where the carpet was a sumptuous grey and gold that blended with the old gold of the sofa. It was all very tasteful.

The owner of the house was an imposing woman. Tall and slim, she wore an expensive gold rope chain necklace that hung flatly on her chest. Her name was Camilla Crocket, very Agatha Christie.

'My dear, it is a delight to meet you. I think we all feel much enthused that our little advert has trawled such a magnificent catch. You really are an answer to our prayers.'

'Well, I hope I can be of help,' I told her. I felt rather like a fish out of water, trawled or otherwise.

A short, bald man with pince-nez spectacles was next.

'I'm Roger Hughes, I have a background in publishing myself,' he told me with great earnest. I nodded kindly and asked him what he meant. 'I used to proofread for a friend of mine, John Darke-Taylor. Do you know him?'

I shook my head.

'I'm afraid not.'

'Oh well, he's very big in my church, a quite famous anthropologist, very clever indeed. He is an expert in–'

'And I'm Angela Gattis,' said an older lady, who stepped pointedly in front of Roger, stopping him in full flow. 'I chair our little group.' She had a gentle rise and fall to her accent. 'Yes, I'm American,' she said with a wry smile. 'And before you ask, I'm from Ohio.' She had the skin and hair of a woman half her age though she was at least eighty. 'Welcome to our group, Martha, and thank you for answering the plea we sent out. We sure do need your help.'

They poured a cup of tea for me and offered a biscuit. I took one out of politeness because they had obviously bought a selection pack in my honour.

'So what would you like me to do?' I asked. 'What exactly is the project?'

'If you don't mind we do need to have a formal session first,' Camilla said as she leaned across and picked up a large gardening book. On top of it was an A4 sheet of paper; a typed agenda, typewriter-typed.

It was stultifyingly boring, they laboured over every point and I helped myself to another biscuit just to break the monotony. I kept asking myself what on earth I was doing there. Roger, it transpired, was a detail man and liked to dot the I's and cross the 'T's. Camilla liked to write everything down in a tight, laborious script and Angela liked to talk and talk. Tom, was earnestly silent, listening in rapt attention to everything and smiling nervously at me when he caught my eye.

When I thought I couldn't go on any longer, when another subsection would have sent me screaming for the door, they turned their attention to me.

'Thank you so much for bearing with us Martha,' Camilla said with barely concealed excitement. 'This is where you come in.'

Tom picked up two lever-arch folders and placed them on the coffee table, and I took one and opened it. It contained plastic ring files, each with a sticker and a reference number written neatly on the front. Inside each were sheets of typed articles, pictures, the odd newspaper cutting, and a variety of scribbled notes. As far as I could tell they, individually, covered a different subject.

'Roger has referenced each file, as you can see,' said Angela, pointing at the labels. 'We have divided it into twenty chapters.' I nodded as Roger leaned forward and explained his referencing system, and I looked interested so as not to appear rude, which seemed to please him enormously.

As soon as I could find the right moment, I said: 'And you want to publish a coffee table book, I understand?'

'Oh yes, that's the idea,' said Camilla enthusiastically. 'It is to be called "Curs, Cowards and Conundrums," my husband, Gerald, came up with that.'

'And does it apply?' I asked.

'Does what apply?' she looked at me askance.

'Who are the curs and cowards?'

'They're all in there,' said Angela, pointing at the file

with a boney finger. 'Sure are some stories for you in that lot, honey. They're very entertaining.'

'And all from around here, in the village?'

'In this area, but there are two or three village stories that will make your hair curl.' She laughed and they all joined in with her. 'Honey, you won't believe what these villagers got up to!'

2

Inevitably, the subject turned to Cécile Roussell as I knew it would. There was an intrigue and excitement in his voice, something quite unfamiliar in George.

'I'm expecting her at four,' he told me.

A glance at the mantle clock told me it was almost three.

'And has she made contact with you since you received her letter?'

'She confirmed the timing of her visit by telephone yesterday,' he replied.

'And she said nothing further?' I enquired. 'Nothing more about Henry?'

'No.' George shook his head forlornly and I felt a real concern for my dear old friend, he had looked so down of late.

'And how do you feel, old chap? I mean about her, about all of this.'

'I shall have to wait and see, Carrick, but I can tell you I am both eager and filled with great trepidation about meeting this woman.' He offered me a cigarette, which I

9

accepted. As he held up the large onyx lighter, I noted the tremor in his hands.

'Are you quite well, George?'

'What? Yes, yes, I'm fine… Well, apart from the hip of course, still hurts, probably always will, but I have to admit Carrick this has weighed heavily on my mind in the past week. It's all so very unexpected.'

'She has merely asked if she might visit to see Lapston, am I correct?' I was running over old ground; we had already discussed this and he didn't reply. His eyebrows were knotted together deep in thought. 'George, may I see the letter?'

'What? Yes.' He was very distracted and I watched as he moved stiffly across to the bureau and retrieved the envelope from one of the pigeonholes. He handed it to me and I could see it was a six and two registered envelope franked in Oxford. The letter itself was in French, short and to the point, the hand typical of the French style. When I had read it. I looked up at George and I noticed, for the first time, the touch of grey at his temples and the weathering of a face that only grief can bring upon a man.

'It looks from this that she may not speak English; she has chosen to write in French,' I observed. 'Perhaps not educated to a sufficient level?'

'The French have never made much of an effort in that quarter.' His eyes narrowed as he drew on his cigarette. 'No clues to be drawn from it, I fear.'

'As you say, she simply wants to see the house where her beloved Henri lived.' I concurred. 'Hardly an onerous demand, I would suggest.'

'Can't help feeling a bit concerned about it, Carrick. This is the last person to see Henry alive, my only link to him in Paris.' George fiddled with his ear, a familiar trait of his when nervous.

'I'm sure there will be others shortly, comrades in arms and all that. They might seek you out and there'll be some sort of recognition to come I'm certain of it and then all the associated rigmarole.'

'I know, but this is a much deeper level than that old man, this is a woman who was very much... shall we say "attached." Oh, and going back to what you said just a moment ago, she does speak English and quite well it seems. You forget I have spoken with her by telephone.'

I felt a little foolish. 'Absolutely. For a moment it slipped my mind. I wouldn't make a very good Holmes, would I?' His smile, in response to my joke, was unconvincing. 'Would you like something to help relax you a little, a brandy perhaps?' I offered.

'No, no, absolutely fine, just a bit on edge, that's all.'

'And what of Alice?' I felt the familiar tug inside me when I spoke her name but I quieted it, told myself to put away foolish things, the time had passed.

'She's been away and returns from Scotland today. She knows about the letter of course but, like me, is about as surprised as one can be.'

Grant, the butler, appeared at the door a little after four.

'Sir, Madame Roussell has arrived.' I noted that George immediately straightened up and was nervously fiddling with his sleeve, something that was so unlike him.

'Very well, Grant,' he said. 'See Madame Roussell into the lounge.' He threw me a look that suggested he was about to ride into battle, so much so, I almost felt like wishing him luck. Poor George, he was never one for complications or affiliations. The war had turned all of our lives upside down, comrades, friends, servants everybody. I had lost my own flat in Mayfair in the bombing, and of course I will carry with me, probably for the rest of my life, the scars of battle, most of them unseen yet ever present.

George asked me to accompany him as he met Madame Roussell and that did surprise me, but I complied gladly because I felt I could offer him support if it were so needed.

As we walked through the great hall from the library, I could feel the chill of the English autumn evening closing in, but the days were long gone when George would order a fire to be lit in the hall. It felt too cold, but what was to be done about it?

In the lounge a golden shaft of light from the tallest window was falling on the rug, bringing out the crimson and deepest blue in the elaborate dragons woven into it. It highlighted the top of the tie back sofa and then fell upon the carved wood of the great oak fireplace. In the centre of this perfect tableau, with her delicate frame outlined in gold, was the most beautiful creature I had ever seen.

3

'Martha, what are you doing?' Steve was standing in the kitchen doorway, his hair a mess around a creased, sleepy face. I was sitting at the kitchen table with the contents of one of the ring files spread out in front of me.

'Oh Steve, I didn't want to wake you. Go back to bed, love.' He walked over to the sink and filled a glass with water. I could tell just by the way he walked that he was irritated with me. 'Did you know about the ship, the St. Scillian?' I tried to appeal to his better nature.

He came across and looked sleepily over my shoulder where I had a grainy photograph of a sailing ship in front of me. The same image was also on the screen of my iPad.

'It caught fire going around the Cape of Good Hope on the way to New Zealand. A whole family from this village were on board, twenty-nine of them, can you believe it? Grandparents, aunts, uncles, children, even a babe in arms.' I swept the screen of my iPad with my finger. 'Look here, it says two lifeboats were launched, but one was lost in a storm, the other was found by another vessel four days later. There were only five men left alive. They had been reduced to drinking the blood and eating the livers of their dead companions.' A shiver ran up my spine.

'Any other time, darling. I'd be glad to chat all night to you about historical doings, but it's two in the morning.' Steve chided. 'I think you should come to bed. I thought this little project might keep you occupied, but not consumed.' He was right and I stood up stiffly, realising suddenly just how cold my feet were. I clicked off the light, leaving my project behind me spread across the table.

When I awoke, Steve had left for work. I couldn't remember the last time that had happened. I went down to the kitchen and noticed immediately that he had swept all of my research materials to one side so he could eat his cereal and read the paper. Both the bowl and paper were still there. I suspected he had been running late and I suddenly felt absurdly guilty. I cleared his things away and as I placed his bowl in the dishwasher, I found his note by the kettle.

"Morning night owl! I've resorted to a note to talk to you and I'm wondering if this might become our new way of communicating? That Scillian ship is quite a well-known event in the village, there's a memorial on the green. Love, S x"

The memorial was a small stone obelisk, with tiny rosettes of rust all over an iron plaque: "In memory of those who perished seeking a new beginning, may God take them unto Him." There was a long list of names with ages ranging from seventy years to three months. I touched the top of the monument, I felt somehow compelled to. Cars passed by on the road, but I stayed silent for a brief moment then stepped back.

I was standing in the corner of the village green under a copper beech and looking across to the church. The grass was newly mown, the scent pungent around me, it always reminded me of school. There was a large blue clock on the church and as the long hand ticked on to twelve, a single bell chimed the hour. Ten o'clock. I decided to walk down towards it pushing my hands deep into my pockets; it was a sharp, cold day.

The church path was quiet, a woman walking a fluffed up Pekinese nodded a hello to me as we passed each other. She was wrapped in a fur hat and scarf yet behind her the cemetery was bursting with daffodils and crocuses.

I carried on past the village hall and up the lane to the meadows. At times like this I did wish I had a dog because it felt strangely conspicuous to be walking alone. The blood was pumping through my veins as I strode along to where the footpath narrowed to a single track as it crossed the river via a wooden bridge.

The big house was in ruins behind tall Cotswold Stone walls. While I'd always known it was there, I'd never really taken a good look at it. I scaled a mound of grass on the riverbank, but all I could see was the tops of boarded-up windows of the ground floor. It was a big, solid building with a skirting wall and large lawns dominated by two huge cedar trees. I found myself strangely drawn to it and walked across the narrow footbridge in an attempt to find a path to take me up to the main gates.

'I'm afraid you're wasting your time.' It was a voice from behind me and, as I turned around, I saw it belonged to a tall man out walking with a large black dog. I headed back towards him along the thin footpath and over the bridge.

'I was wondering where the gates are.'

'Over the other side. You have to come at it from the northeast and it's quite a long driveway. Here you'll end up in a bog and may easily get stuck.' He smiled kindly. 'Unless of course someone like me comes along to rescue you.'

He had a friendly, open face with collar length dark hair that was greying slightly. I reckoned that he was somewhere near my age, perhaps younger. He was clean-shaven and had the healthy skin of a walker. As I approached, his dog charged towards me then leapt up, almost bending in two with excitement as I tried to push it away.

'Scooter stop it, stay down!' The man was shouting, but the dog was wilfully ignoring him. 'I'm sorry. He's a flat-coated retriever. They love people unconditionally, but they don't understand that not all people love them back.'

'It's okay. I was brought up with dogs, retrievers actually flat-coats seem to be a very friendly breed.' Scooter was licking my hand and then he was sort of sucking on my arm. I was glad I was wearing an old coat.

'I'm Rory, I live up at Sarsten.' We shook hands, though it seemed a very formal thing to do in the middle of the countryside, then I realised that he was some way from home.

'Martha Nelson.' When I told him my name I nearly said 'editor', an automatic throwback to my working life. As I checked myself, Rory must have noticed something in my expression.

'If you'd ever like to go inside the house I can let you in, I have a key.'

That took me a little by surprise. 'Oh, I wasn't going to, that is I just wanted to, I …'

'Don't worry everyone wants to go and take a peek, the owner doesn't mind. As long as you don't sue him if a beam drops on your head.' Rory stroked the top of Scooter's head and the dog looked honoured to be sitting there beside his master. 'The owner hopes that one day someone will see it, fall in love and buy it, but it's a money pit if ever there was one.'

'Who owns it?' I asked.

'A guy called Keith, or as we all know him, Kipper Pike, an old boy builder who lived in this area for a long while. Then his wife inherited a house in Hampshire and a fortune to boot. He tried to sell Lapston Manor, but with the slump and everything, no one's been interested. The problem is over half the grounds are on a flood plain and the other half contains a quite substantial building, a big levelling job. No builder wants an investment of that kind, but it'll soon be time: things are on the up again.'

'And how do you know Kipper Pike?'

'I'm a landscape gardener. I've worked on one or two of his projects.'

'You're a long way from home,' I said. 'Sarsten's miles away.'

'By road, yes, but on foot under three miles as the crow flies. There's a bridleway that connects our manor house with this one, a carriage drive at one time. I would suggest. Are you local?'

'Yes, I've lived here nearly three years now. My husband and I live on the rise of the hill, the last house on the Swinford Road, where all the accidents happen because people drive too fast round the blind bend.'

'I know exactly where you mean. That bad, is it?'

'One, two every six months, and lots of near misses, but the council won't do anything about it. At the very least we need a slow sign.'

'Council's don't have money for anything these days I'm afraid.' He was right, the number of potholes everywhere was testament to that. 'I haven't seen you around these parts before. Are you enjoying a day off?' He had the lovely easy manner of a man who liked to chat, not a bit like Steve.

'No, no, I'm retired. I was a magazine editor in Oxford for over thirty years.' I felt the familiar knot of pain as I used the word "retired." 'Talking of which, one of our titles was Land magazine, you might know it.'

'I do, I was featured in it, July last year. Isn't that funny? It's a small world.'

Scooter had sneaked off, and the sudden loud splash of him diving off the bank into the river made us both start. Rory ran a few paces but came back, head shaking. 'He's fine. He loves swimming and this part's safe. Just round the bend there's a fast current, I won't let him swim up there.' Until that point, we hadn't caught each other's eye, we'd mostly been looking out towards the manor's imposing walls and when we did I felt stupidly shy and looked away too soon.

'Well, I must go,' I told him. 'I've got work to do, a project I'm just getting my teeth into.'

'Me too, back to the shackles of the computer.' He turned away and whistled for Scooter. There was a lot of splashing then I could see the long black body pulling itself up the steep, slippery bank behind a willow tree. 'Here, Scooter! Come on, boy,' Rory whistled between his teeth. 'Come on, Goofy.' Scooter was lolloping towards him, ears flapping and a huge stick, even possibly a bit of fencing, in his mouth. I waved and watched them walking away together along the edge of the field towards the Kings Stanley Lane. Rory turned and from about ten yards, shouted; 'I'm the Mill House, Sarsten, if you ever want to look inside. Bye.'

I dug my hands into my pockets again and walked away. Deep inside me, my stomach did an unexpected somersault and my step had more spring in it as I headed home.

4

I did think that George might slip me a sidelong glance, but he was too much of a gentleman, I should have known that. He walked over to the lady and shook her by the hand with great warmth.

'Madame Roussell, may I welcome you to Lapston. I am honoured you have decided to pay us a visit.' He beckoned me over from where I was still standing, just inside the door, and introduced me. 'This is my oldest friend, Maxwell Carrick.' She was intoxicating, truly, as indeed many French women are. A tall svelte figure, she looked immaculate in a tailored blue two-piece suit with a fox fur wrapped around her shoulders. Her hair was rolled back à la mode and on her head, she wore a hat with a fine netting around the brim. As I moved forward. she offered her gloved hand.

'Please, gentlemen,' she said with only a mere hint of an accent. 'Do call me Cécile, let us not stand on guard.' I thought it delightful that her expression wasn't quite right, it was endearing.

'Cécile, we are both delighted to make your acquaintance and even more so given that you knew my brother Henry so well.' George indicated that she should sit down and when she was seated, I saw the pained expression in her face.

She clasped her hands together.

'Ah Henri,' she said and I noticed, because she was using the French version of his name, her accent was more obvious to the ear. I could see that it flustered George a little and, as a diversion, he turned to Grant to order tea.

'How long had you known my brother, Cécile?' He asked taking a seat opposite her.

'Barely eight months,' she replied with a deep sigh. 'He and I were not, it seems, meant to be.'

'How terribly sad for you both.' George looked completely lost for a moment and I almost stepped in, but he rallied and said, 'Where did you meet each other?'

'In a small café in the Latin Quarter, it is one of my hauntings.' There was a rather strange moment whilst George and I simultaneously changed the word from hauntings to haunts in our minds, but it would have been impolite to correct her.

'And did you know he was English? I mean, were you part of his work over there?' I asked. She turned to me, regarding me I think for the first time, and instinctively I straightened my back as if our headmaster had just walked in.

'No, of course not, he was how you say, under cover. I did not realise until the very end.'

'Really?' George cut in before I could speak. 'How impressive. His French must have been faultless, but there again he was always extremely fond of languages and particularly French, such a musical sound to the ear.'

'He spoke it beautifully, very well indeed.' She sighed. 'I am not sure I can return the pleasure with how I speak English.' Cécile was peeling off her gloves, her hands delicate and long fingered, nails done in the French Manicure that I knew Alice so admired. She glanced up at me through her long lashes; her eyes large and hazel were absolutely distracting.

'Well, whatever else, I am so very glad that you were able to bring him such happiness in his final days. Tell me, if you would, what was the date he died? I fear no one has been able to tell me, and for some reason, I feel it is very important that I know.'

'It was the twelfth of August.' She spoke in a low voice and looked down at the gloves that were lying across her lap.

The irony was not lost on us; it was Sir Reginald's birthday. He had always referred to it as The Glorious Twelfth because it was the first day of the grouse too. The Glorious Twelfth. We would never be able to forget the date of Henry's death.

George was looking for a distraction, had we pondered on that date for long we might both have been overcome and made to look foolish, but thankfully, there is something bewitching about a French woman that her English counterpart has never matched, and we were both rather in awe. Our focus returned soon enough to our lovely guest. George leaned over the coffee table and picked up a decorated chinoiserie box, opening its fine enamelled lid.

'Would you care for a cigarette, Madame?'

'Thank you.' She reached out with delicate fingers to

take one. George placed the box back in its allotted space on the wide walnut coffee table where it disappeared amongst ornaments, leather bound magazine covers and crystal ashtrays. He flicked up the flame of the lighter and she leaned into it, the cigarette between her lips. I sat, stupidly silent, simply gazing at her.

'I must thank you most sincerely, Cécile, for making the effort to introduce yourself whilst you are visiting England,' said George. 'You must have more interesting diversions in Oxford to keep you occupied.'

Cécile tapped her cigarette into the nearest ashtray. 'I wanted to see Lapston Manor, to take a look for myself at the house where Henri lived. I felt it was very important to me.'

'Of course, of course. This must be most distressing for you and as I said on the telephone, anything I can do to help.' A sadness clouded George's face. 'It has been a terrible loss for us all.' There was a moment of reverence for the duality of their loss and she looked away, towards the fireplace, whilst she gathered her thoughts.

'But how wonderful that you are in Oxford and so close,' said George.

'Henri always promised he would have brought me to Lapston,' she said, looking terribly pained. It was obvious that she was deeply troubled and I was certain George was about to say something when, just at that moment, the double doors opened and Grant returned with the tea trolley. He served us all before quietly withdrawing and closing the doors behind him.

Cécile sipped the tea, she took it without milk, then

she looked around at the lounge taking in the faded opulence, and I was moved by how very vulnerable she looked as she did so. She was, no doubt, imagining what it would have been like to live here with Henry, to set up home in this fine English house together. I think both George and I thought, for one ghastly moment, she might even start to shed a tear. I even ran my fingers across the handkerchief in my breast pocket in readiness.

'I understand, from what you told me over the telephone, that you were not wishing to intrude, but I insisted because Henry had showed intentions towards you and, if you will excuse me for being so bold, one could never fault his taste.' For one dreadful moment, I thought George was about to espouse his well-worn theory that a man with an eye for a horse of good conformation had, almost inevitably, an eye for a beautiful woman too. It was something he was fond of saying so I interjected, fearing that it might be somewhat lost in translation.

'Are you staying in Oxford long?' I asked.

She was about to take a sip of tea, the cup suspended in mid-air.

'I will be moving on,' Cécile replied. 'I have accomplished my task in seeing where Henri lived.' She lifted the delicate china cup to her lips and dipped those entrancing eyes in doing so. She was a fine looking woman, demure, a delicate chin, neck and tantalising lips, and I could fully understand what Henry was doing courting her. I was about to suggest that she might enjoy a trip to Stow, and perhaps a spot of luncheon the following day, when George stepped into the breach.

'I am delighted that you have come to visit our home. May I offer you dinner tonight, then you can see the house properly tomorrow and we can take a walk around the grounds? I presume you are staying locally.'

'I have a room at The Crown Inn,' she replied. 'It is very comfortable and I have made a reservation to take dinner there this night, I feel I must not trespass any further on your kindness.'

'My dear, I insist, I won't hear of it. You must stay here tonight at the very least. Let me send for your things. Alice will be home just after six and I know she wants to meet you. I won't hear another word about The Crown. I will settle your account if you are agreeable, and you shall dine with us. In that way I can hear more from you about Henry, I owe you and him that much at least. You are our only link to him in the past eight months. Perhaps you will oblige us with sharing some of your memories, as I am sure it would sustain Alice in her grief, as well as Carrick here, and of course myself. I fear my sister, in particular, has taken this all very badly indeed.'

'Well, George, if you are sure, I would not wish to impose, but I should like to tell you very much of Henri and our brief time in Paris together.' Cécile placed her cup on the coffee table and smiled. George and I saw the relief in her eyes and knew instinctively that by being at Lapston, she felt closer to Henry. It was a good thing he was doing, a very good thing, I concurred entirely.

5

The second plastic folder contained a list of notices and fines imposed on villagers in the nineteenth century for wrongdoings. One man had been fined a penny for letting his cow run loose on market day, another a shilling for causing an "affray."

A fine riding horse was for sale on one faded poster and on another a corn mill to let, the advert read: "Presently possessed by Mr F Timms to be shown to interested parties at Whitsunday, 1877. Offers may be made to Robert Steurt of Sarsten till eleventh November next."

I put them to one side. Maybe a chapter towards the end could bring together little snippets of information like these, but chapter two needed something with more meat. The third bag covered the First World War and the loss of three handsome young men, from the same family, who were killed in battle. There was a picture of them on horseback, ready for action in their neat uniforms, leather bands across their chests. One of the horses had moved its head and it was a blur, but the faces of the men sitting astride them were proud with anticipation writ large on their fresh young faces.

I imagined the person who took their photograph, their father perhaps, pressing the shutter and not knowing he was taking the photograph of his three boys for the last time. They were so young, so much potential. I turned it over and there was a handwritten caption on the back; 'James, Arthur and Lindo, 1914.'

Heartbreaking.

Camilla had written the article in her neat rounded handwriting. It hadn't been typed up so I had trouble reading it, but I picked out the salient points. James was the oldest, just twenty. Arthur and Lindo were eighteen-year-old twins. They belonged to a family of gentleman farmers and had volunteered for service on the same day. James was killed early in the proceedings, but the twins had made it through two years being killed on the Somme in June 1916. Other members of our village died there too: George Crakey; Rupert Holder; Thomas Eyre; Harold Murray, the list went on, all of them in their teens or early twenties. I moved on, I wasn't in the mood for such sadness. I would come back to it later.

The next file was thin and had only a few contents. There was a picture of young woman in jodhpurs and riding boots, her knees drawn to her chest as she sat on a flight of stone steps. Behind her were the grandiose porch and great door of a large house. Above it, carved into the stone, were two shields to each side of a cross that was set above them on the apex of two sweeping inverted arches.

I flipped it over and, on the reverse, it said simply: 'Alice, Lapston, Autumn 1944.' She was a very pretty young lady with dark hair framing a heart-shaped face, but it was her smiling eyes that sparkled, and I guessed that whoever took the photograph had made her laugh. There were handwritten bills from a butcher's shop and a haberdashery store, amongst others, all made out to Lapston Manor.

At the bottom was a postcard depicting a beautiful honey-stoned house with two cedar trees on an emerald lawn. I instantly recognised it as the same house I'd seen over the wall the day before. There were high rising chimneys, an impressive front porch and large windows spaced evenly across its broad elevation. It all helped to make the house quite imposing and gave it an almost symmetrical beauty.

Angela had written about the house on a sheet of thin foolscap paper.

"Lapston was the 'gentle retreat' of Lord and Lady Aaron, built in 1751 of the Georgian style. Used as a weekend and holiday home, the Aarons had other houses in London and a hunting lodge in Sussex. In the early eighteenth century, the Lord Charles David Aaron was made Ambassador to Paris and came across a fine townhouse on the Seine in the process of being demolished. He bought many architectural pieces and had them grafted onto his own house. The treasures included a very fine stained-glass window, which was incorporated into the morning room.

"The Aaron family sold their summer retreat in 1904, when it was bought by a family from London, once again to be used as a country home. The Amsherst family were, originally, from Scotland, but moved south and took residence in London (Cadogan Square). They were wealthy from their interests overseas, and for the first half of the twentieth century the house was alive with life and colour, entertaining the nobility and wealthy of Europe. The fortunes of the family changed during the Second World War and the Amsherst family lost the house in 1945, some believe owing to a debt, but this has never been verified. The locals were convinced that there was an untimely death and it fell into the hands of a woman by the name of Roussell who later sold it to Les Fils du Cœur Pur Saint François (The Sons of the Pure Heart of Saint Francis) when it became a children's convalescent home.

"In 1957, there was a small fire in the west wing of the house and in the aftermath, many of the architectural fittings were removed. It was, almost overnight, reduced to a shadow of its former self and was bought for a song by a local builder in 1977. It stands today a relic of England's glorious past, like many other once graceful stately homes."

That was all there was. I tapped "Lapston Manor" into the search engine on my iPad and a short paragraph came up, much the same sort of thing but less detailed. I had a notebook in my handbag and scribbled down a few words.

I was intrigued and then I remembered Rory and his offer. I felt a really strong desire to see into the house so I could imagine it entertaining all those notable people. It was silly really because I'd never given it a moment's thought when Steve and I walked that way on the odd Sunday morning.

I made myself a cup of tea, and while I was hugging the mug and mulling it over, the phone rang. It was Angela.

'I'm just phoning to see how you're getting on with our exciting little project.' She had a singsong voice. 'Found the curs yet, honey?'

'I've reached the Lapston Manor section and I read what you wrote,' I told her.

'Intrigued?'

'I have to say I am, I'll admit it's had a sad ending,' I told her. 'Such a lovely place.'

'It sure was, honey. They sure wrecked it after those priests left, everyone in the village took something. You know the little cottage on the corner opposite the pub? It's the one with the two bay trees each side of the front door.'

'Yes.'

'They have a rather eye-catching square of carved stone in the front wall. It says 1751, and beneath the numerals is the maxim 'In faith, love' and if you look carefully, a feather. Well, it's from the house.'

'I'll have to take a look next time I'm passing.' I was trying to picture the cottage she was talking about more clearly in my mind's eye.

'It's quite visible from the road and there are many bits and pieces all over the village, that is if you know what you are looking for.'

'What about the "untimely death" you refer to in your article?' I asked.

'Well, that depends who you talk to, an old lady like me with an interest in history who tries to stick to the facts or the gossip mongers who like a good yarn.' She was laughing. 'You have to choose for yourself who to believe.'

'But what do you know about it?' I asked.

'I'm afraid I don't know enough to go into much detail but the house suddenly changed hands and no one knows why.'

'Are we talking foul deeds, do you think?'

'Honey, I have no idea. I was told by a villager, who is long gone, Seth Miller, that people had suspected something because suddenly there was an upheaval and all the family were gone. Seth was the gardener's help and he was let go without rhyme or reason. In fact, he told me all the staff were.'

'Who was it who died?'

'I'm afraid no one knows. Seth told me it changed everything and the house passed to a woman called Roussell, one can only imagine that she was a distant relative. I'd love to know more but I've researched everything I can about it and you have it there. I really do wish I had more answers.'

I found myself thinking exactly the same thing.

6

Alice clasped both of my hands in hers tightly and kissed me. She looked lovely in a plaid coat and fur-trimmed hat.

'Carrick, darling, I am so glad you are here. Do say that you are staying for my birthday.'

'I wouldn't miss it for the world. It's not every year a beautiful lady turns twenty five,' I told her.

'You flatter me, Carrick, I'm getting old.' She smoothed down her hair in the hall mirror and pinched her cheeks to give them colour. When she glanced at me, she had those kind expressive eyes, large and round, that charmed me still.

'You will never be old to me.' I let Grant help her out of her coat then I took her arm and we walked together to the library. A fire was roaring, and George was standing before it, looking down on the rising flames.

'Darling!' Alice left my arm to go and kiss her brother, her long dark hair catching the light of the blaze. 'How are you? I hope everything went well.' George brightened visibly on seeing her and she received one of his bear hugs. 'Well, I am simply dying to know all about her, what was she like?'

'I presume you mean Madame Roussell,' George said teasing her.

'George, stop it, you are trying to torment me, just spill the beans, you know I can't wait to hear all.'

'She is a very charming woman, elegant, beautiful and speaks perfect English.' George turned to me. 'Very striking, eh, Carrick?'

'She's a very pleasant lady,' I said gingerly, I didn't want to upset Alice. 'Typically French,' I added, as if that might help.

'Where is she staying, at The Crown? I want to walk over and see her tomorrow.'

'She was,' I told Alice, with one eye on George who looked immensely pleased with himself. 'However, she is now staying here, at your brother's behest.'

Alice turned from me to George, her eyes widening in surprise. 'Really? Where is she, the blue guest room?'

'No, she asked for Henry's room,' George replied. 'And I didn't see there was any harm in the request, even if it failed to impress Mrs Hall.' Alice raised her eyebrows because, like me, she had doubts about the suitability of such an arrangement, but neither of us wanted to upset the applecart so we stood down.

'Should I go and see her, welcome her?'

'No Alice, darling, Cécile said she was going to have a rest; the journey was arduous. She came over on a refugee boat and it was not at all pleasant for her, people were mixed. She stayed in Oxford for a couple of days. It was noisy and she has not slept well. We suggested she join us for cocktails at seven thirty.'

There was the trace of a pout on Alice's lips, but she quickly relented. George was lighting a cigarette and he offered us both one, but Alice refused, saying she was very tired after her journey and would go for a rest herself.

'Mouse,' said George, using the family's pet name. 'Don't overdo it with questions will you, especially about Henry. She does look very distressed.'

Alice's face darkened. 'I'm not insensitive, George, but I do need to know, I think we all do.' She cast me one of her looks and I knew I was fully expected to support her.

'It is quite possible that we may find out more than we wish to know, Mouse.' George sighed heavily. 'And we simply must not cause Madame any further pain, it would be heartless.'

Alice took her leave, her demeanour altered already. The few days in Scotland were over for her, and the harsh reality of our loss was once again in our midst.

'So what do you make of Madame Roussell, old man?' George asked as the doors closed behind Alice. 'I have to admit I do feel a lack of connection. She knew Henry at the end whereas I have not seen him for the best part of a year.' He sat back down heavily on the sofa, I saw him wince, his hip was obviously paining him. 'I still can't believe he's gone, Carrick. I went into his room yesterday to tell him some trifle that had occurred to me; nearly broke my heart when I realised I should never see him in there again, never sit and talk with him, share a problem. That's why I thought her being in there might bring it to life again, fill the void.'

'But so soon, George, I can't say I entirely agree. It's not as if we know her well, nor even at all.' I spoke to him with an expected honesty. He and I were at school together and that is where we became the best of friends. I was his confidante and proud to be so. He had always known that I would never deliberately upset him but, on this occasion, he didn't reply and, more than that, he looked away from me to the flames of the fire and the words were left hanging in the air between us.

As the mantel clock chimed six, I was grateful to have the chance to slip away and change for dinner so I took my leave.

In my bedroom, I laid out my own clothes, gone were the days of the valet. The requirement for a dinner suit was also a thing of the past and I think we all missed the formal and long mourned for days at Lapston. I fear George's father, Sir Reginald, would have turned in his grave if he knew of its decline. Sadly the war had left us no luxuries save for the relative peace and quiet of the countryside hidden away in an old house that had once, so rumour has it, been visited by old Kaiser Bill himself. The irony of that was not lost on any of us.

In my bedroom, I studied my face in the mirror and realised how tired I looked, the skin under my eyes was dark, my complexion sallow. Losing my own home was one thing, and I would somehow resolve matters in that quarter, but what I lacked now was an interest. I needed to hunt again perhaps, to find a distraction and, it was clear to me, I was seeking the love of a good woman. It even occurred to me that, perhaps, I was ready to settle down and think about children.

In recent weeks I had felt the need for stability, my

wilder days were behind me and I had begun to realise that I found no joy in my club nor in my very occasional visits to the houses of my friends. Everything was so very dull. How terribly spoilt it all was, everything tinged with loss, tragedy and heartbreak.

The unhappy period before this war had been one of belt tightening, but one always hoped that fourteen-eighteen really had ended it all. We had all been convinced that we would soon be back to some sort of normality until this abominable Austrian (for God's sake, we once thought him comical) had undone everything we held dear.

I removed my shirt and ran a finger across my chest; the scar was still livid, but not so crimson in colour. It was my eyes, with the deadness behind them, that told me the damage was still there. It was as powerful as ever, crouching in the dark corners of my mind, waiting until I could no longer contain it.

A light rapping noise broke into my thoughts. I pulled on my dressing gown and opened the door. It was Cécile. She was standing in front of me in a black cocktail dress that fitted sheath-like over her slim frame. She had swept her hair back and on each side, she wore a delicate diamanté pin. Her lips were scarlet; the oval eyes pencilled black. I looked at the pale rise and fall of her décolletage where lay a necklace, a delicate chain with a single silver feather on it.

'Carrick, please forgive me, I saw you walking to your room, I don't know where anyone else is to ask.' She was demure, her accent more noticeable with her voice low.

'Is there something wrong?'

'I just wondered if I am wearing quite the correct thing?' She smoothed down the dress with her hands. I noticed how flat her stomach was, how narrow the hips. 'I have no idea of what is appropriate in England, in Paris we have lost our way in fashion for some time.'

'You look perfect, my dear,' I told her. 'And, if you allow me, I will change swiftly and then come to collect you and escort you down to dinner.'

'Would you?' She seemed genuinely touched by my offer.

'Of course, I should be honoured.' Her eyes met mine fleetingly and I saw a brightness that was so very opposite to my own. All at once, I realised there was nothing I would like better in the world than to walk down the wide stairs of Lapston Manor with the beautiful Cécile Roussell on my arm.

7

'Bob, it's Martha.'

'Hello there. How are you?' I was standing by the window, the rain was spitting against the glass, the sky bruised and purple. Bob's voice was warm in the chill of the dining room; it was lovely to hear it, like sipping a hot chocolate.

'I'm fine, Bob; enjoying being a free spirit.' I wasn't sounding convincing and I knew it. I wanted to be back with him, helping me to work out the content of our next issue. 'I've got a little project to work on, a book, hopefully about the village.'

'Oh, I am pleased. I shall look forward to seeing it.'

'I'm calling about that, Bob. I wonder if you could do me a favour?'

'Anything, Martha, fire away.'

'Could you ask Polly to send me a back issue of Land? June/July.'

'Yes of course.'

'And, would you ask the editorial team of Home if the magazine has ever featured a Lapston Manor? There might be a record, before we digitised, somewhere. I haven't seen anything in my time, but I need info to pad out a chapter for the book.'

'Of course. Happy to.' Bob was always cheerful and very helpful, and I knew he would come up with the goods.

'Thank you, I really appreciate it. Give my love to Frances. We'll invite you over to dinner soon.' I found I was shaking when I pressed the red button. I could picture them all, as I stood gazing at the floor, working in the buzz of the office, the meetings, the colours, the tick tick sound of typing and emails pinging. I missed it so much.

I sat back at the table and reached for the fifth file. It was a fascinating read about the policing of the village. A cottage halfway down the sleepy old High Street had been the local police station and its neighbour, now covered in a deep crimson Virginia creeper in the autumn, was once the library. Nowadays the lorries thundered past them on an A road and sleepy was the last word you would use. There was a sample of crimes committed in the eighteenth century. "1791 Burglary of silver ornaments from a house in Meadow Lane. 1723 Stolen one loaf, punishment flogging: James Polder aged eleven." Then there was the twentieth century by comparison; "A bag of coal stolen from the merchant's truck; a racing dog missing; a bike stolen from outside the saddlers, now recovered."

There was the story of three Edwards brothers, who were caught stealing from "The Manor." The police had been tipped off and laid in wait by the window where the men had entered the property. As the threesome jumped out there had been a scuffle and one of the brothers had been knocked out, and later died. It was nineteen twenty-one, the manor was unnamed, I wondered if it was Lapston.

I read through some more articles and the time passed very quickly. The rain was battering against the glass doors of the dining room, a real squall. So much for little April showers. The next file was a thick one dealing with the church, which dated back to the twelfth century, and the Prebend House, where the Cannon had lived as part of his stipend. A short write up said: "The earliest known part of the present buildings are the two pilasters which formed part of the twelfth century granary, and in the graveyard between the two, many of the residents of the village are buried, including the famous cellist, Dame Margaret Dean."

When the rain cleared, I took a walk down to the church, with a view to looking at the Prebend House. St Judes was quite beautiful. The shingle path led to the front door, which was heavy and hard to open. Inside it, the air was chilly, the smell musty and damp, not a building that was heated very often. I had never been in before and I certainly recognised myself as part of the problem of dwindling worshippers, but Steve and I had never bought into the concept of God.

There were various memorial stones on the walls around me, and I walked along the length of them looking for a mention of Lapston. I found the granite tomb in the south transept, the place where the "Amsherst family of Lapston Manor" was interred: "Sir Reginald and Lady Augusta who left two sons and one daughter." Their names were carved into a marble plaque at the foot of the plinth and on top was a wreath of flowers, the petals delicately carved. I touched the cold stone and looked around the walls. There was no further mention of the family, no remembrance for the children.

A blast of music made me jump out of my skin. I stepped back into the nave as, without warning, Frank Sinatra was blasting out from all the speakers. "And now the end is near; And so I face the final curtain; My friend, I'll say it clear –" It stopped, the needle was scraping across vinyl, when did I last hear that sound? I couldn't recall. "But then again too few to mention, I did what I had to do."

It stopped dead and the silence was deafening. I peered around the column in front of me and saw the silhouette of a man in the anteroom at the back of the church. He was on his knees and fiddling with an old record player. As I attempted to leave unnoticed, he saw me and quickly stood up.

'Oh dear me, I do apologise. So sorry, I didn't see you there!' He was a tall, slim man of about forty. He had salt and pepper hair, which although receding from his brow, was full at the sides. 'How awful for you. I hope you weren't deep in prayer; that's why they call it the Devil's music, you know.' He looked both flustered and amused in equal measure. 'I'm so sorry.'

'You're absolutely fine,' I reassured him. 'I was only looking around, I haven't been in the church before.'

'Well, that's a fine welcome I gave you. I am sorry, I was testing out the old sound system.' He pointed towards the record player. 'Funeral, tomorrow, they want

Frank to accompany the coffin out. I'm afraid I find it poor taste, the vicar has to walk ceremoniously down the aisle to that.'

I was imagining the sight. I felt for the vicar and could imagine an elderly man trying to remain po-faced as the record player crackled into action.

'It must be difficult for him.'

'Her, she's a she.'

'Oh, a lady.'

'Yes, Reverend Sonia. She started here three months ago. We've been vicarless for almost a year, but the last one left under a bit of a cloud, you see.'

I leaned in. 'A bad cloud?' The journalist in me had her ears pricked.

'Oh yes, he made a bit of a mess of things and disappeared completely for the whole Christmas period without a by your leave. I take it you're not local or you'd be up to speed on this?'

'Oh no, I am. That is, we've lived here in the village for three years, but we're not religious.'

'Ah, that explains it, I wondered why I'd never seen you around. I'm Simon Young, I sort of look after the church for my sins, as you might say.' He raised his eyebrows and smiled. I told him my name and explained that I was recently retired and had started to see more of the area now that I had nothing to do.

'That is, it's not like I'm idle,' I said. 'I'm actually working on a book about the village.' I was validating my existence again.

'History group?'

'Yes, that's right.'

'This is Camilla Crocket's Cowards and Conundrums, isn't it?' he said.

I suddenly realised it was all Cs. 'Yes, she likes her C words!' I replied.

His eyebrows rose again towards his vanishing hair and we both burst out laughing. 'Would you like a cup of tea? I have no milk though I'm afraid.'

'I'd love one.' I followed him into the small kitchenette tucked away behind a screen.

The kettle was soon bubbling loudly as Simon searched in the fridge.

'No I'm sorry, no milk. Would you prefer a coffee?'

'Coffee would be great and actually, I take it without anyway, so that's perfect.'

We sat on the back pew, hands wrapped around the warm mugs. The nave stretched out before us to the chancel where two stunning floral arrangements, in white and pastel blue, stood each side of a rich crimson carpet.

'Is it a local person tomorrow?' I asked.

'Yes, lovely man, Charles Bury. He celebrated his seventy-eighth birthday last week. His wife Muriel and he met here in the village and have lived here all their lives. He had a very sad early life; he was brought up at the Children's Home.'

'Lapston?'

'Yes, that's right. It was a sad place. Muriel was telling me that he suffered greatly there. He was taken there because he was ill and they kept him in because they said

43

his parents were too poor to look after him. Muriel says he never talks, that is, talked about it, but he had terrible things done to him, from all accounts.'

A shiver ran through me. 'Poor man. It doesn't bear thinking about with what we all know now.'

'Terrible.' There was a pause and it felt a little awkward.

'And Lapston. I've been reading about it. Do you know anything about a death up there?' I asked.

'You mean one of the children?'

'No, before that time, the Amshersts?'

'Oh, yes, they are buried here. Weren't you looking at their tomb just before?'

'Yes, but there was only Sir Reginald and his wife, not the children.'

'I don't know for certain but the children died elsewhere, I think. I really have no idea, I'm sorry. I know that there were three children, two were called George and Anne I think.'

'Alice,' I corrected him.

'Alice, that's right, she was a lovely person apparently. She was part of the Auxiliary Territorial Service, the ATS, as a subaltern, just like the Queen, during the war. She could strip an engine and that's where she learned to drive. You see they had chauffeurs before the war, but the family's fortunes hit the rocks shortly after and they were reduced to just a few staff, and one man who looked after the garden and drove them around when they needed him. He died the month I came to live in the village, Jim Ogden, lovely man, very humble by all accounts.'

'So what happened to the family? It all seems a little unclear?'

'I don't have any idea. They were very withdrawn, they lost the heir to the house and after that, life at Lapston was very quiet. Certainly the annual ball had long stopped and I think they used to attend the tiny church in the grounds rather than come into the village. They only had a small number of staff; there were the two I knew of, Jim of course, and the gardener's boy, Seth.'

'Yes, I've heard about Seth. It seems that the whole demise of the Amshersts is shrouded in mystery, and perhaps deliberately so?'

'Possibly, the village has its secrets, quite a sprinkling of them.' Simon was enjoying himself. It occurred to me that perhaps he had quite a lonely life and a conversation was very welcome because he was very easy to talk to. 'Did you know about our monk?'

'Monk?'

'Oh yes, he was a young postulant during the Reformation. He hid from the Reformers in The Crown while they sacked the church. The villagers disguised him and took him back into the church where he hid in a tiny room above the porch for months. The Reformers came back and failed to spot the tiny door in the wall because it was partly concealed behind a tapestry. That's it there.' Simon pointed to a narrow wooden door beside the entrance. 'Would you like to see it?'

'Oh yes please.'

Simon fetched a ring with a number of keys on it and selected a large one, very old and rusty with a thick barrel.

He pulled the tapestry to one side, sliding it along a metal pole and revealed a narrow, wooden door set into the stone.

'Follow me,' he said. 'Do mind the steps, they are very precarious.' The staircase was almost vertical and very narrow. I'm not brilliant with tight spaces and I felt my throat constricting a little.

'Are you okay?' He asked as I reached the top of the stairwell.

'Yes, I just get a bit claustrophobic, it's fine though.'

'This is the room; not much to see but this little window looks over the porch. It's a sort of priest hole. Legend has it there is a tunnel from the church that leads to a concealed exit, which is how the young man escaped, but I see no evidence of it. To be honest, every old building in the country thrives on the intrigue of their priest holes, which means just about every sixteenth century laundry cupboard you come across must, at one time or another, have been used to secrete a clergyman.'

The room was no more than two metres square and the ceiling was low. There was a shelf cut into the wall and on it a faded picture of a blond Jesus with a star halo, in a tatty frame. 'Goodness, you'd never guess this room was here, would you.'

'No, and can you imagine being in here for months so no one could give you away?'

'What happened to him?'

'They got him and killed him just outside the church gate. They say he walks from the church to The Crown each year on the anniversary of the day he died.'

'Have you seen him?'

'No, I'm not a ghost type, much too level-headed.' He winked. 'But there are lots of villagers who swear they've seen him. Personally I would suggest that they're all the ones on the way home from The Crown!' I laughed with him but, as I took another look around the room, a wave of dizziness was coming over me.

'I'll have to go back down,' I said. 'But thanks for showing it to me, I appreciate it.'

We were back in the main church a few seconds later; the half a dozen steps we climbed down were very tricky because they were so steep.

'Any time,' Simon pulled opened the heavy church door for me. 'Are you all right? Would you like me to walk you home?'

'No, no I'm fine. I'm much better now, I just don't like tight spaces that's all.'

'Well, it's been lovely chatting, if you ever want to drop in again, feel free. I'm always here pottering or repairing and I'm one of the campanologists too, so if you hear the bells that's me as well!'

'Thank you, I might well pop in to say hello and, please, if you remember or find anything out about the Amshersts could you let me know? I live up at the villas, where the accidents always happen on the bend.'

'I know the ones, are you on the left or the right?'

'Right.'

'If I come across anything I'll certainly let you know. Take care, Martha.'

As I walked down the wide flagstone path through the

gravestones with worn away inscriptions, the sun burst out and the grass around me shone a bright emerald green. I looked down at the road where the young monk had met his death and then back up at the room over the porch. The tiny window was barely noticeable, only a slither of the sun's reflection gave any impression it was there at all.

8

We were the first in the lounge and I poured us both a drink. Cécile wandered over to the tall windows at the far end of the room. Long tendrils of evening light, bright as marigolds, were moving across the knot garden.

'What a beautiful sight,' she said, sitting on the window seat. 'The garden has been designed for this time of day, has it not?'

'George's father loved horticulture,' I told her as I passed her drink to her.

'Horti-culture? I don't understand, I'm afraid.'

'Gardens,' I explained. 'He loved gardens and he had this knot garden designed in nineteen twenty-eight. He dedicated it to his wife Augusta – there is an 'A' at the heart of it, shaped from the hedging.'

'Were they lovely people? You speak of them very fondly.'

She was still staring out of the window, exquisitely beautiful.

'They were the very best of people and therefore good parents, and both George and Alice are exceptionally decent and honest people, brought up in the best of ways. Everything they are came from the guidance of Sir Reginald and Augusta.'

'They had beautiful names too. Augusta is so very... how do you say? Graceful.'

Cécile sipped her drink and looked up at me, the soft light playing on her skin. I felt a connection with her, an appreciation of beauty that we so obviously shared. 'And how do you know George and Alice?'

I was at school with Henry and George,' I told her. 'George and I were both in the first year together. We found ourselves in a rather strict Scottish school, many miles from home. My father, because of his business interests abroad, could not visit me and so, eventually, I came to spend my exeats and holidays here. I was company for George on the long journey home.' She was listening intently. 'I have been the beneficiary of a family life only through the kindness of these people.'

'Then you have had more than me, I think,' she replied.

'You have no family?'

'Not now. I lost my parents when I was a small child to La Grippe, I was lucky to have escaped it myself.' She ran a finger down the edge of the curtain, turning her attention from me, steeling herself against the sad memories.

'We all were. Spanish Flu ravaged through the country taking even our most healthy young people, with no mercy. We lost school friends. It was truly miserable and all after the suffering of the war to boot.'

'And, were you in France like Henri?'

'Not like Henry. He was incredibly intelligent and very brave. Only the best were selected to work behind enemy lines like him. I was with the Royal Horse Artillery, in Italy.'

'On horses?'

'Not since thirty three – tanks.'

She was concentrating, her lips pursed. 'Tell me of Henri.'

'Henry was with the Parachute Regiment before he was seconded. He was the brains of the family, the one set to carry on Sir Reginald's role in the business.' I suddenly had to pause for a second and gather my thoughts because I couldn't speak about him yet without feeling a sharp lump in my throat. She touched my forearm lightly and I looked down into those melancholic eyes of hers, the nod of her head so slight that it was barely imperceptible, but she was telling me that she understood. We all shared the burden of loss. 'Henry was a pretty incredible man, a born leader and someone who I would describe as unstoppable but then, I suspect you knew that.'

She was listening carefully taking in my words. 'Yes, I agree. And George?'

'Ah, George is the soft centre, the heart of the family. He is kind and generous; old-fashioned in many ways. He was always going to be "the spare" who went into the church, but of course the war denied us all our callings.'

'And what would you have been, Carrick?'

'My father was a Foreign Envoy in India. I should have liked to follow him but he, well, he met a new woman – his now wife – over there.' It was then that my voice did weaken, something to do with the condition I fear, a ball of regret and anger in my belly that will never be unravelled.

'I am very sad for you, Carrick, I can see that your life has been unhappy.'

'Please don't get me wrong, Cécile, I have had a wonderful life here at Lapston, I will be forever indebted to the Amshersts and would defend them to the death if it were required.'

I looked down at the base of her throat and the silver necklace. 'That piece you are wearing, it is a feather?'

She reached up and touched it, running a delicate finger over it. 'Yes.'

'The family emblem is a feather,' I told her.

For a moment I could not tell what she was thinking, she looked lost for words, then she said rather despondently; 'Yes, I know... My dearest Henri gave it to me.'

I reached out and took hold of her fingers to reassure her that I shared her pain. The look she gave me spoke of an understanding between us, but she had to let go of my hand abruptly because, at that second, the door opened and George and Alice swept in.

Alice's eyes were aflame with excitement as she rushed up to Cécile and kissed her on both cheeks. 'I am absolutely delighted to meet you, Madame Roussell. I am so thrilled that you knew Henry and have kindly accepted our invitation to stay. I'm simply dying to hear all about him in Paris.'

Cécile, who had smiled as she greeted Alice, was changed instantly, her expression clouded over, on hearing Henry's name. 'I am happy to tell you, but please understand that it is très difficile; it is hard for me to talk about him too much.'

'Come, come,' said George. 'Alice, as I said earlier, we must not force ourselves upon Madame Roussell. Let us not talk of those matters until we are all good and ready. I see Carrick has made you a drink, Cécile, may I top you up?'

'Oh no thank you,' she replied. She was facing George and Alice, standing by my side, and I felt I could not move, that she already depended upon me even for the short time we had known each other. She turned to Alice. 'Please, my dear, do call me Cécile or I will not feel at comfort.'

'Yes of course, I would like us to be the best of friends, Cécile. Please come and sit down next to me. I so want to know about la vie de Paris.' Cécile duly took a seat beside Alice and, as I was able to see the two women side-by-side for the first time, it struck me how very different they were. Alice had selected a blue dress. I had seen it many times before, with some lace at her throat. It was pleasant enough, but she looked too young and gauche in it. I did wish, very unkindly I'm afraid, that she would make an increased effort to look more sophisticated.

She broke away from her conversation with Cécile, as if she knew I was considering her, and smiled warmly before turning back. All at once, I realised she was speaking French and Cécile was obviously charmed by her thoughtfulness. I watched them together, so different and yet both beautiful each in their own way. There was a soft roundness in Alice's face next to the high arch of Cécile's cheeks and long neck, the English rose versus the elegant fleur de lys of France.

'George, Cécile loves gardens. You must let her look at Daddy's designs for the knot garden after dinner. It will mean so much more to her when she sees it in the morning.' She turned to Cécile. 'Daddy was simply amazing. He put in the lavender walk too. It was always a great shame for him that the rest of the grounds were sold off, but the previous residents needed the money.'

It occurred to me, given what I knew, that this might sadly soon be the case for the current residents and I noticed that George steadfastly avoided looking in my direction.

'I would be delighted to show them,' he said. 'I will have Grant bring them to the lounge after dinner.'

The dinner gong sounded and we each escorted a lady to the dining room on our arm. George, as was right, walked alongside Cécile, but I felt a little disappointed even so. 'She is so lovely, Carrick,' Alice whispered, pressing herself into my side. 'I really like her. I can see why Henry loved her so much.'

'We are lucky she had the desire to seek us out. I am hoping it will help us all come to terms with his loss,' I replied.

We were sitting at one end of the table, the fire crackling in the grate. Grant was serving with the help of Lizzie, Mrs Hall's kitchen maid. It was embarrassing for George to have such a significantly reduced staff and I felt for him, for even if he had had a choice, there were no longer people willing to work as staff, particularly women.

'Before the war began, we had footmen and more staff, but times have changed, Cécile, you find us much reduced in means and I apologise,' he said. Alice glanced at me a little nervously. We both found George's statement surprisingly frank, but then he was a completely open and honest man – we should not have expected anything less.

'It is of no matter,' Cécile replied. 'We are all affected in this way; I have no maid at home, but I am certain matters will resolve themselves, in time.'

'I fear for the outcome of the war,' said George. 'I still hold out all optimism that we will defeat the Hun, but with so many of us injured, with no money left in the country's war chest I do fear that we are going to be up against it.'

'We have all fought so dashed hard, everyone of us,' I added addressing no one in particular, but there was the briefest pause during which I noticed Alice and George exchanged a look. It was transitory and, if I had not known them so well, I would have missed it.

'But the Allies have just taken Brussels and Antwerp,' said Alice enthusiastically. 'We have secured France. Hitler is surely on the back foot?' She was doing her best to lift our spirits.

'The fighting is one thing, Mouse dear, but I do feel a deep concern about the aftermath,' George continued. 'Over fifty per cent of our workforce is engaged in the war effort and we have nothing to offer them because the industries, on which we built our wealth, no longer exist.' He leaned back so that Grant could pour him a glass of wine, a rich ruby red in colour. 'We need a government that can lead us out of the war and put the "Great" back in Britain. We are losing the Empire, and if we borrow from America, which is being mooted at Westminster, we will be in debt for a very long time to come.' Then abruptly he changed tack. 'But this is no talk for ladies, Carrick, enough now. Let us make a toast to "absent friends." He held up his wine glass, the light of the candles reflecting brightly in the crystal.

'George where did you get this beautiful wine?' asked Alice.

'Madame Roussell brought it for us, from Paris.' Our eyes turned to her as one and, although it was not our intention, I think we made her a little uncomfortable.

'Then I suggest a toast to Madame Roussell,' I offered and as soon as Grant had charged my glass, George, Alice and I raised our glasses and I watched with pleasure as Cécile accepted our acknowledgement of her kindness. She dipped her head to us and her eyes expressed her gratitude. The wine was a beautiful, warm and well-rounded Haut-Médoc.

'The Germans hoarded the wines they stole from we Parisians,' Cécile explained. 'It wasn't so long after The Liberation that they were being sent around again. I can tell you, for example, they found eleven thousand cigars in just one vault. I managed to obtain a few bottles. I hope it is to your taste.'

'Oh my dear, it is a very great treat for us. How extremely kind of you.' George was almost moved to tears. None of us had seen such a bottle of wine for many months. He held his glass high and beaming, he quipped; 'I suggest we all sip with infrequency!'

As the soup arrived, a paltry vegetable which I felt lacked salt, we talked of those things we had had before rationing and what we missed most of all. I longed for roast pork. We had pig clubs in the village, of course, but it was still a rare treat. George missed his fine wines and Swiss chocolate.

'What is Paris like, now it is no longer occupied?' I asked Cécile.

'It is like a bird that has broken her wings; she is unable to fly but is instead eating anything thrown to her. It is a very distressed and sad city. They chopped down trees that had lined the streets for hundreds of years, so that they were lying across the road to make, how do you say, defence?'

'Barricades,' I said.

'Yes, barricades, and there is nothing to eat, not enough, but it feels worse here and I am grateful that you have let me share in your food tonight.'

'Being in the countryside, we have access to more,' said Alice. 'It is those in the city I feel for. It's not easy is it, Carrick?'

I shook my head. 'People have nothing, and I have no idea how we shall ever recover from the damage and destruction.' All of us sat silently for a second or two before Alice spoke up again.

'Come on now, we said we would talk of lighter things. What of Scotland, no one has even asked me how everyone is up there.' And so we progressed through a conversation about the Scottish Amshersts, who as usual, were in rude health and not suffering nearly as much as we.

'I have venison, smoked fish, shortbread and whisky for my party; they sent me home with a hamper,' Alice announced brightly. 'And my gift was a new wrap, and, in the clan tartan too.'

'They really are so very kind. I will telephone Douglas in the morning and tell him how much we appreciate it.' George looked terribly pleased.

'Oh George, you must tell them about Cécile too. Perhaps we could take her up to visit them on my next leave?' Alice was then struck with a sudden thought. 'Oh Cécile, it has just occurred to me… Say you will stay for my birthday. It's next Wednesday, but we are having a party on Saturday night, a few hunting friends and some girlfriends of mine. Do say you'll stay.'

'I am afraid that will not be possible. I must not outstay my welcome. I feel I would be taking advantage.' Cécile looked bashful and a little embarrassed.

'You would be most welcome, my dear,' George said kindly. 'I insist that you at least think about it. What say you, Carrick?'

'I would be delighted if you would stay,' I replied with complete honestly, for I could see myself taking her for a walk around the village, getting to know her better, being her confidante and friend.

'Then we are all three agreed,' said Alice. It was obvious that she was overjoyed.

It could have been different. Alice might not have invited her to stay, George may have thought of a reason why it was not possible. I could have argued some stance of disagreement, but none of that occurred and that is where it all began.

9

The magazine landed with a thud on our doormat a few days later. I tore open the wrapping and leafed through the magazine. There was a double page spread on him – Rory McBride, aged fifty-nine, a landscape architect and father of three, though now divorced. Helen Clark, the feature writer, had interviewed him. I sat down in my favourite old armchair by the window and began reading.

It was very interesting. Rory explained that he could design from scratch or redesign any outdoor space. He was responsible for the wild meadows at Eversham House and the Water Gardens at Lancester Hill House; both were pictured and looked stunning.

He had started his freelance business after his divorce and moved to Sarsten four years earlier. Rory was pictured at the bottom sitting on a low wall with Scooter, who was holding a trowel in his mouth.

At the bottom of the article, it said, "Rory is always looking for a special project that presents a challenge. He says, 'My favourite project was designing a walled garden in the Western Isles of Scotland. It was a pretty wild area and the client wanted a very static, regimented planting that carried the colours of the moorland outside into the interior. I planted Scotch roses, cardoons and foxgloves intermingled with a deep purple globe thistles. I've been back since and it really is stunning. The owner has cared for it very well and it is thriving.' Rory's next project is to design a clock face flowerbed for a former rectory near Moreton-in-Marsh."

I had almost finished reading when the phone rang, making me start. 'Mum, it's Sarah.'

'Sarah, how lovely. Where are you phoning from?'

'I'm in Warwick, at a work conference, and it's not exactly thrilling. They're going to merge with another company and I've got to get rid of the "dead wood." That's what they call their loyal staff. Irony is, I'm the last in and I'm going to be handling all the redundancies. It's going to be unpleasant and, plus, the other company hasn't got a very good reputation. Anyway, c'est la vie, I'm here now.'

'You'll do them proud, my love. They've got the best person for the job in you.'

'Thanks, Mum, I knew you'd say that. You are, after all, my number one fan.'

'No darling, that's your father!' I told her and she laughed.

'Okay number two fan. Anyway, it's not that I'm calling about. I'm going to ask you something and I need you to not say no straight away.'

I froze for a second because Sarah had always been extremely good at springing surprises and not always nice ones, like the time she asked if she could bring her miserable friend Anna home for the weekend. That had been a long and tortuous two days.

'I can't promise–' I faltered, and she didn't miss a beat.

'Mum, I think this is perfect for you. You remember Anna?'

My heart sank.

'Not again please. Remember when her boyfriend dumped her and you brought her home with you.'

'Oh you were both brilliant about it, Mum. That's why Anna thought of you.'

'Thought of me for what?'

'She married "the boyfriend" Frank, but they have split up after a year, he wanted her barefoot and pregnant in the kitchen knitting her own uterus and stuff, but she couldn't stand it.'

'Knitting her own what?' I chuckled because this was my funny and clever daughter to the hilt.

'They bought a puppy, a black labrador called Inca. She is beautiful and really well trained. You remember I told you Frank was a police dog handler for years?'

'Sarah, if you are asking what I think you're asking…'

'Mum, she's gorgeous. You'll fall in love with her.'

'The cat, I just know the cat wouldn't cope.' It was my first line of defence.

'Cassie is blind in one eye and deaf as a brick and she spends all her days in the spare room. She wouldn't even know there was a pup in the house.'

'How old is this pup?'

'Ten months. She's house-trained and very quiet. She's lived with two cats already.'

'I don't know, Sarah. Dad and I wanted a bit of freedom once Cassie goes.'

'I'd have her if you go away, I only live five minutes from work, so I could cope.'

I knew this had all been worked out way in advance of her ringing. It could have been worse we could have got Anna instead.

'I'll think about it, love. Let me talk to Dad.' I was stalling for time. As I turned back to the magazine, I saw Rory with Scooter and it occurred to me that maybe a dog would be a good idea. All at once, I could see myself walking her across the meadows by the river and I'd certainly appreciate the company in the house. As a girl, I'd had lots of dogs on the farm in Ormskirk, so maybe it was time.

10

The portraits of Sir Reginald and Augusta were looking down on us from the oak panelled walls of the dining room. I'd like to think they approved of us sitting at one end of the long dining table and conversing so merrily. I was seated beside Alice with my back warmed by the fire and opposite Cécile who was obviously enjoying our company.

The candles were cheap tallow and so they dripped thin pools of wax onto the cloth beneath the candelabra, but they made the evening more intimate and homely so no one was concerned. George was much cheered by the company and Alice was talking, for the first time in months, with levity in her voice. As for myself, I was watching Cécile. Her demeanour, at first withdrawn and preoccupied, now seemed to be transforming into the most pleasant of characters. What a happy band we made, for it was even possible to see the future with more hope, and I for one, felt sure that even my horizons were brighter.

We enjoyed a terrine of game, the rabbit and duck shot locally, and a very fine cauliflower cheese. Mrs Hall had done us proud, but then she always made an effort for a homecoming, and this was of course for Alice, her favourite.

It was Alice, much as I expected, who eventually broached the subject of Henry. We had been talking about insubstantial things, none of us wanting to return to the subject of the war or politics, when Alice asked Cécile how Henry had looked when they had met.

'Was he well? Was there enough in Paris to eat?'

'No, times were very hard for all of us,' said Cécile with a sigh. 'At the beginning the Nazis brought food into the country, I think they believed it would make us accept them more easily. In the early part of the occupation Paris was very much unchanged and people moved around freely, that is unless one caused trouble. They dealt with troublemakers tout de suite, you would say...'

'Immediately, or on the spot,' Alice suggested, beating me to it.

'Yes of course, immediately. It was not easy to avoid the re-tri-bution.' Cécile looked at me and I nodded to reassure her. She was so eloquent in English and then she would stumble, losing her confidence, but I admired her for making such an effort. 'We all saw things, from a distance, because it was dangerous to go too close. They would take people from the street, mostly men, and force them into trucks.'

'What happened to them?' Alice asked.

'They just disappeared. There were notice boards and bills posted everywhere saying: "Have you seen this person? Please help me find my husband, my boy." I used to thank God every day that I had no relatives to worry about, that my parents were already gone.'

'How awful.' George said with a grimace. 'And did none of them return?'

'Some, occasionally, and usually beaten how you English say "black and blue", they were sent back as a warning.'

'How did you survive it, the loss of your liberty and freedom?' I referred not to her alone, but to the Parisian in general.

'We had no choice, no escape. They were efficient and very ruthless, and in this way they had a lot of power.'

'And Henry?' Alice asked again.

'Henri was very quiet, moving about like he was invisible. If he saw anything happen, he would fade into the background, disappear like a magician's trick. I thought he was afraid, that he knew secrets and was frightened of discovery. I was not sure if he was working for the French or the Germans. It did not occur to me that he was English. When you are living in fear, the one thing you never do is ask questions of anyone. It was a rule that is not written.'

'When did you meet him?' Alice was fascinated, we all were, but she was leading the way. 'And where?'

'I used to stop often for a drink at a café in the Rue Saint-André des Arts and he was sometimes there, meeting someone or other in the back room. At first I saw him once or twice without saying anything, but then it was just after New Year and very cold. I was inside the café and the doors were all closed. I was very sad because I had lost a friend, a very dear friend, who had left Paris and I did not know where he had gone. I was all by myself, sitting with a glass of wine, somehow hoping Henri would come in and see me there. I thought he would be nice to talk to. Then the door opened and he came in and sat near me.'

The room was growing colder, the fire diminishing rapidly as we reached the end of our meal. I knew Grant would not put on more logs because the lounge would be ready for us.

'As I stood up,' she continued. 'I must have been clumsy and I knocked the table, the glass tumbled off and I looked around to see if the waiter had noticed. I felt a bit embarrassed. But it was Henri who stood up and asked me if I was all right and did I feel unwell? I remember most of all thinking that I could not place his accent, it was not Parisian. I presumed he was from Normandy, but I did not know for sure.

'I told him I was fine but only a bit clumsy and he pointed out that the tail of my fox fur had caused the problem, and then he said it should be shot and I pointed out that it already had been, and we found that funny so we laughed.'

'He had such a lovely laugh, don't you think?' said Alice.

'Wonderful,' Cécile replied. 'It would always cheer me up.'

'And then?' Alice was leaning forward, hanging on to every word.

'And then he asked if I would stay and have a drink with him, and I said yes and asked him where he was from.

He told me "here and there," and I didn't ask again because in those times everyone kept themselves to themselves.'

'What sort of things did you talk about?' asked George. 'It must have been so nice for him to be able to talk to a young lady.'

'Oh everything and nothing, as you do when you first meet someone. He was very good at talking about lots of things.'

'Was he?' I interjected. This I found most surprising. 'The Henry I knew was fairly quiet, a restrained sort of chap.'

'That's Paris for you,' said George. 'City of romance, and don't forget, old boy, Henry would have had no one to talk with day to day.'

Cécile was watching us converse, her eyes observing us intently.

'He was very interesting,' she said. 'He told me he had lived in Paris for some time and was a businessman.' She turned to look at George. 'I asked him about his business, but he told me it was confidential. I did not know at that time of course, but he was very secret.'

'Did you guess what he was?' I asked.

'Was?' Cécile looked puzzled.

'Did you know at that point that he was with the Secret Ops?'

'No, not until the end.' She suddenly looked terribly upset.

George stood up, sweeping his napkin from his lap as he did so. 'My dear, we have no wish whatsoever to distress you. Let us leave it there, there will be time enough over the coming days for you to tell us more. Let's withdraw to the lounge and I shall talk you through my father's designs for the knot garden.'

Cécile looked immensely grateful as George pulled her chair back for her, and Alice and I followed behind as we walked across to the lounge. It was always a beautiful room and that night never more so. Mrs Hall had laid out a tray of fresh coffee, a sight rarely seen at Lapston at that time, but it was obviously in honour of our French guest. It occurred to me that Mrs Hall had catered to the tastes of people from far and wide in her long service, so a single French woman would present no challenge, but I made a mental note to thank Mrs Hall when the moment next presented itself.

Whilst George and Alice took Cécile through the garden designs, I considered them, all three, from my place on the sofa. George had lost weight, his jacket hung loosely from his shoulders and there was something of a stoop to him. We were both only thirty-four, but he could have been mistaken for someone much older, and I suspected the same could be said of me too. Of the three of us Alice remained much the same, but without the girlish air we had loved so very much. No one could deny that she was indeed a pretty young woman, but she possessed nothing of the natural refinement of our guest. Cécile stood three or four inches above Alice's head, her frame altogether lighter, more chic.

They talked and pointed at the sketchbooks, and I could see the pages of intricate watercolours that I knew so well being turned through the gaps between their bodies.

How Sir Reginald would have loved to see them enjoying his work, he had taught me so much. I turned to the sofa opposite me and pictured them both there.

Sir Reginald had been an imposing figure and his wife, Augusta, a striking woman, a tall erect frame of such grace and beauty that I remained in awe until the day she died. They had loved me as a son, and I am happy to say I returned their affection. I found the company of my own father, by comparison, difficult and awkward during those rare times I saw him. My mother, being unknown to me because of her early death, was never referred to by either of us. I was sent to school at eight to board where I sought, in teachers and matrons, the love I so craved, but no one ever loved me truly, until I met the Amshersts.

It has often occurred to me, when I find myself dwelling on it, that I have never found love myself because of this lack of fondness and caring when I was so very young, and that is why I will always treasure the memory of Augusta and Reginald and the kindness they showed me.

'Carrick, dearest, you are floating away again.' Alice sat down beside me on the couch. 'Where do you go to, darling, I do wonder?'

'Here and there,' I replied, a little irritated by her interruption of my thoughts, I felt they were very much my own concern. She placed her hand over mine quite proprietarily. It annoyed me and doubly so because, at that very moment, Cécile turned towards us. I moved my hand away from under Alice's and reached for a coffee, leaving her puzzled. I knew this without looking at her, but it was no concern of mine.

'Carrick, you must tell me about your father and India. It is a long held dream of mine to go there.' Cécile took a place opposite me and I was delighted, once again, to be the subject of her attention even though there was little I could tell her about the sub-continent.

'I'm afraid I have never been,' I told her. I found myself frustrated when I couldn't expand on the subject and impress her. 'My father has never afforded me the opportunity to go, much as I would have loved to.' I sounded like a simpering fool and I saw the disappointment in her face. 'I'm afraid he was always moving around the country, which made family life very difficult.' She looked stymied. I scratched around for some way to entertain her further, but I couldn't think of a single thing to say, and was left stupidly tongue-tied.

George joined us and offered us all a cigarette. Real coffee and cigarettes! The last time I had this combination was in Monte Cassino. I found myself transported rapidly back to Italy and the happy faces of the people we liberated, the unsuppressed joy they felt in being freed. They had nothing yet they gave us everything they had: Coffee, cigarettes, tomatoes, a brace of pigeons and the wine they had saved for the day of liberation. The Jerries were defeated and we marched them through the streets, in their shame, jackets hanging open over grubby vests. Under those helmets were men who looked like accountants and librarians and young bewildered boys who had been forced to grow up too fast. All things considered, and in spite of everything they had done, we treated them well as prisoners of war because we didn't know then what we know now. I would have dashed every blasted head against the nearest rock if I had been party to the new intelligence. The eyes, the pleading eyes, the wretched dirty faces; the terrified women they had raped; the old men reduced to withered skin and bone; the children, pitifully thin infants with hollow, haunted eyes and the man hanging with piano wire around his neck, from a balcony. Evil, evil everywhere, terrible, terrible–'

'Carrick, Carrick!'

Alice's voice was wailing, screeching in my ear. 'Stop it,' I told her but she wasn't listening and her face was swimming before my eyes in and out of focus. I suddenly realised that I was leaning forward and my coffee cup was shaking in the saucer and it was so loud it was deafening. Everyone was staring at me.

'Carrick, old boy, come on now, it's all right.' I felt George's hand press down firmly on my shoulder. I hadn't even been aware that he had moved from the sofa. I breathed deeply from the centre of my chest as they had showed me in the nursing home, and when my vision cleared, for it had become blurred temporarily, the room came back to me, the colours were sharp once more and clear. I saw her face and it was full of alarm and pity at the same time. I dropped my eyes and drew in another deep breath. Then, because I was ashamed, I took my leave and wished them goodnight. I was abrupt and appeared ill mannered, and I knew it. Her eyes followed me out of the room as I departed, walking on shaky legs. As the door closed behind me, I heard her ask: 'Is it very bad?'

I gripped a tight hold of the newel post at the foot of the

staircase. The wide flight of steps rose in front of me, and all at once, they seemed to be the most insurmountable mountain imaginable. The feeling of solid wood under my hand was reassuring because my knees felt weak, as if they might easily cave in.

'May I assist you, sir?' It was Grant, appearing from the shadows in the hall. How long he had been there I could not tell, but I was very grateful to hear his voice.

'Yes, Grant, thank you. Would you give me a hand?'

I had known Grant for twenty years since the day he had joined the staff in London. I was unendingly grateful for the solid way he put my arm around his shoulder and the strength in him as he propped me up. Gone was any pretence that I was fit and well, but Grant would be completely confidential, I knew that. It would never be known that I was too weak to even mount the stairs, but what made me feel so very low was that I had let myself down in her eyes.

11

I had let Inca off the lead in the garden and she had come straight back when I called her. She had sat down in front of me proudly and took a gravy bone off me for her trouble. She had the sweetest disposition imaginable and had won me over completely from the start. I had also let her off the lead in the triangular paddock, an odd shaped patch of fenced land at the far end of the village inhabited, until recently, by an elderly donkey, and she had come straight back which convinced me that Inca was an angel.

Now I was slipping and sliding all over a wet muddy field that sloped down to a rambling brook, and shouting for my dog who was about to dive into the water. It was impossible to get a foothold on the greasy soil, even in my wellies. In the end, I had to give up, turn back and follow the path round the edge of the field instead. I could hear Inca splashing and frolicking and, basically, having a wonderful time, whilst I muttered and cursed under my breath about puppies, Sarah and Anna, and that no good ex-police dog handler husband of hers, Fred or Frank whatever he was called.

Suddenly there was long streak of black and a larger dog slid down the opposite bank and landed with a huge splash just where Inca was. I looked up and further along the footpath, the other side of a five bar gate, was Rory waving like an old friend.

'Hi Martha!' He was striding towards me, clearly unaware that Scooter and Inca were hidden from view and probably up to no good, or possibly Inca had been knocked over flat and was now drowning.

'Hi Rory, can you call Scooter?' I shouted. Rory looked puzzled but he whistled and immediately a huge dripping monster clambered up the side of the bank and came charging over to me. As Scooter arrived at my feet, he shook himself and covered me in dirty, freezing cold water.

'Scooter, come here,' Rory shouted, obviously annoyed, and as he did, so Inca appeared and galloped over to him. He caught her collar, and bending down, he led her over to me. She was shivering and I was covered in a spattering of mud, thanks to Scooter. I knew I looked a complete mess.

'Is this yours?' Rory asked, suppressing an ungentlemanly smile.

'Yes, she's called Inca. That is, we've got her on trial for a fortnight, but I think we're keeping her because Steve, my husband, adores her already.'

'And you don't?' Rory asked as I clipped on her lead.

'I did until right then, she just vamoosed, running like the wind, and there was not a thing I could do.'

'So Scooter actually saved the day then?' Rory was trying in vain to hold back a smile.

'Yes, good old Scooter,' I replied sarcastically, but the

tone in my voice was lost on the flat-coat who, without any warning, wheeled around in mid-air and knocked me off my feet. I remembered Inca pulling away from me and the grey clouds swirling above me, round in circles, as I landed flat on my back in the mud.

'Martha! No, Scooter, get away!'

Scooter was standing, looking down on me, ready to play with great gusto, whatever game this was. In the next second, Rory had replaced Scooter's face and, above him, only those high grey clouds.

'Are you okay?' He was holding my hand but, as I tried to sit up, he held me down with his hand on my shoulder. 'Just give yourself a minute,' he advised kindly. I had to lie there until the clouds stopped rotating. And then, when I was able to sit up, I felt absolutely winded. 'He hit you right in your stomach and you fell backwards, straight over. God I'm so sorry. He's a bad dog at times. It must be because of Inca. He doesn't know many other dogs.' Rory looked behind him and groaned. 'Don't look now, he's bonking Inca's head. Has she been done?'

'Yes,' I said, trying to regain my shattered equilibrium.

'Up you get then. I'm so sorry about this.' Rory put his arm under mine and heaved me up. My leg slipped on the mud and I felt truly humiliated and foolish. 'Come over here. There's a log we can sit on. I'm so sorry.' He led me gently by the arm and I sat down gratefully next to him as he produced a hip flask from his jacket pocket. He unscrewed the top and, offering it to me, said, 'I'm not sure there's anything left in there, but whatever there is, you're welcome to it. Do you feel okay?'

I nodded but, in truth, I felt quite sick and dizzy.

'You're probably feeling a bit woozy, but it will pass.'

'Where are they now?'

Rory looked up, squinting. 'About two hundred yards away, running in circles and Inca is chasing Scooter who, I freely admit, looks like a sideboard when he runs.'

I laughed and felt a bit better for it.

'I'd better walk you home,' he said.

'I'll be fine,' I replied, but I was still feeling a bit odd.

'No, it's no trouble and I can continue along the Oxfordshire Way from yours. It'll take me directly home.' I didn't have the strength to fight and I needed him to catch Inca too. As it was, they both came bounding towards us at that moment, and Rory had them on the lead in seconds.

He took them both in one hand and lent me his arm. It felt strong, muscular and reassuring, and I was grateful for it. He was much taller than me and so it felt odd walking with him as he coped with the two excited dogs, and I had to pull away.

As we passed the doctor's surgery, Rory asked if I needed to go in, but I was fine.

It took ten minutes to reach my house and by then, I was feeling much better. We talked only a little, mostly he was trying to navigate with Scooter and Inca pulling in two different directions.

'You'll have a coffee won't you?' I asked. It was the least I could do.

'I'd love one, but sit down I'll make it.' He made me

take a seat at the table whilst he found the coffee and filled the kettle. Scooter was lying on the kitchen doormat, tongue lolling out of his mouth, and opposite him, Inca was curled up in her basket by the Aga, fast asleep.

The book project was all over the place on the table, chairs and sideboard. 'It looks like you've been busy,' he said as he found a space for my cup.

'It's a book I'm editing for the local history group. I've made my way through half of it,' I told him.

Rory took a seat next to me. In front of him was a picture of a young man in an apron, standing outside a butcher's shop, sides of pork, pheasant and ducks hanging above his head.

'See that carved stone bull's head?' Rory pointed to the apex of the shop's roof. 'The shop's gone but the bull's head is still there. It's now part of a retirement complex.'

'Oh, that's interesting. I've never noticed it and I drive past there all the time.' We were leaning in, our heads close together and I could smell the outdoors on him, the pure scent of a fresh spring day. Without trying to be obvious, I pulled back a little, and he did too. At that second, something caught my eye. 'Don't look now, but Scooter is crawling across the kitchen on his elbows.'

'Scooter!' Rory reprimanded his dog without looking at him, and the black shape stood up, turned around, and went back to the mat. 'He scoots,' Rory explained. 'He was supposed to be a Jasper, but he had this commando move off to a tee since he was a pup, he thinks it makes him invisible.' He sipped his coffee. 'I am so sorry about what he did to you.'

'Don't worry, honestly, I'll be fine. It's more embarrassing when you're old and you fall over, isn't it?'

'You're not old,' he said and reached forward. I thought he was going to touch my cheek, but instead he pulled a stringy piece of grass out of my hair.

'I owe you for this,' he said, a curl in his lips. 'You could sue me, you know.'

'I could, but instead, may I ask you about Lapston Manor?'

'Yes, of course, goodness that lets me off lightly!'

'I've got to put together a couple of pages about its history, but what I've been given is pretty sketchy.'

'Well, if I can help you sure, but I don't know all that much.'

'It says it was built on the site of a building mentioned in the Doomsday Book.'

'Yes it was, it dates from 709, but I have no idea why it was such an accurate dating. It was a Saxon settlement. The manor had a half moat which has long gone and explains why the lower part is so boggy, I suspect.'

'And then what?'

'It was rebuilt and finished in sixteen hundred and three. The owner a Sir Corin Lockyear wanted his Queen, Elizabeth the first, to see it completed but she inconveniently died the same year.'

'That wasn't good timing then.'

'No, and he died three years after that, so the poor man, having taken twenty odd years to build his dream home, pegs it before the paint dries.'

'What a shame,' I said, smiling.

'Anyway, the Stantons inherited it and actually ran it into the ground; they lived in Hertfordshire and couldn't have cared less about it. The staff gradually drifted away and it fell into disrepair then it was knocked down. In the mid-eighteenth century, the Aarons bought the site and they built the new house with the intention of using it as a hunting lodge because it was so close to the Wychwood Forest. It was one of them who put the stained-glass window in the dining room.'

'From France?'

'I think so. It certainly had some French bits and bobs all over the place. The Amshersts then bought it. They were wealthy from business concerns here and there. I'm not sure but I was told it was investments and stuff. They sold it to the Catholic Church who ran it as a children's home.'

'I'm told bad things went on there,' I said.

'Yep, so legend has it and going on what we've learned of late I sort of have no doubt that they did.'

'And what about the French woman who was involved?'

'In what?'

'She inherited the house according to what I've read.'

'No idea,' he said, shaking his head, 'but I know someone who I think will know more, if it would help.'

'Who's that?'

'Norman Fry. His mother worked at the house a long time ago.'

12

I had not had nightmares, which surprised me. In fact I had slept surprisingly soundly and awoken late. One of the windows in my bedroom overlooked the knot garden and, from that direction, I heard the sound of talking right beneath it.

Her voice was musical, the sound of French to the ear so different from our own dreary tongue. They were talking, him pointing to aspects of the planting that were notable, and her listening intently, telling him how much she admired the layout and design. I viewed them from just behind my curtain so that if they had looked up, as the observed so often do, I could not be seen.

She was touching his arm, a light brushing of fingers here and perhaps an affectionate tap there. I felt something stir within me and I couldn't put a name to it at that time, but now I know to my shame that it was jealousy. I wanted to be down there, treading the paths alongside her. I was already yearning for her touch. She looked so slight next to George. The onset of middle age had thickened his midriff, the result of too little exercise. He had given up riding because of his hip and did not even take walks in the countryside any longer. They moved onwards, still speaking

French. I could only hear every other word and so I was unable to pick up on the thread of the conversation, but she was making him smile and, at one point, he laughed. I could see in that clear morning light the pale grey of his hair. How stealthily these things do creep up on one.

She then turned to him and they were speaking English, her gazing up into his face, he concentrated on hers. I looked away for it was like owning a jewel and having someone else breathe on it without permission.

I had intended to venture out and join them, but I faltered at the garden door in the lounge and turned back. I retreated to the hall where I could see Lizzie Fry and Mrs Hall clearing away the breakfast things – it was well after ten o'clock.

'Oh sir, we didn't realise you were down, would you like us to leave everything?' Mrs Hall was walking towards me, her eyes kind and understanding. She quickly reached the threshold of the dining room and looked terribly concerned for me.

'No thank you, Mrs Hall. I am not at all hungry. I will wait until luncheon,' I told her.

'Are you feeling better, sir?' She was wringing her hands in her apron in a quite agitated fashion, but I knew she did so because she cared very much. She had known me since I was eleven and had cuffed me around the ears often enough for one misdemeanour or another but, equally, she had bandaged my wounds after many a boyish tumble and sent me off again with a kind word. I replied that I was very well and would look forward to lunch. Lapston was very dear to me in so many ways.

I was about to turn away and take my leave by the front door for a walk when I heard Alice's voice. 'Hello Carrick. Are you quite better?'

She was tripping down the stairs lightly, the broad sweep of the staircase behind her, the very mountain I had been unable to climb last night. She was wearing a polo neck jumper, breeches and riding boots.

'I am, thank you, Mouse. I slept well.'

'I am so pleased, darling. I checked in on you before I went to bed and you were away with the fairies.'

I raised an eyebrow.

'I think maybe I should take to locking my door if you are to be creeping about in the night.' It came out with far more ugly sarcasm than I had intended and she looked suitably injured. 'Oh come now, Alice, I am only joking. You are like a sister to me and you know it. Thank you for caring.'

She bit her lip, something I had learned to associate with insecurity in her, and looking over her shoulder, spoke in a low voice. 'May I talk with you?'

I checked my watch and acted as if I had somewhere to be and could only spare her a few minutes. She ignored that and, placing her arm in mine, led me to the left of the stairs and out towards the garden room. The two cedar trees were standing splendidly on guard, the sweep of lawn beneath them immaculate, owing to the loving attention of Ogden.

'Are you riding out?' I asked.

'Yes, I thought so, I haven't seen Beau for ages. I suspect you won't join me, but Jester says he's ready when you are.'

'I hope you enjoy yourself,' I answered, avoiding the question. In times past, I would have joined her and relished her company but, all at once, my mind was elsewhere. We walked out onto the shingle path then she stopped outside the conservatory and turned to face me.

'Carrick, I'm just going to be direct with you.' She looked bold and I felt unsettled. 'I think you should obtain help, you should see somebody.'

'Alice I–'

'You are not well and I feel it really should be addressed and perhaps, if you would be agreeable, I would happily accompany you.'

There was such honesty and loving kindness in her eyes it made me feel exceptionally bad about what I said next. My mind was racing, the thoughts jumbled in my head, but one thing was clear to me: I didn't want her advice however well it was intended.

'Alice, frankly it is none of your business, please do not interfere; I will handle it in my own way, and in my own time.'

As I turned away, I knew I had left her speechless with my rudeness, her mouth had formed an 'O' and with her eyes wide in surprise, she looked completely lost for words. I flicked angrily at the head of a long leggy flower in the border and its petals showered onto the path in my wake.

13

The flowers were beautiful: freesias, yellow roses, pale green chrysanths and my favourites, Alstroemeria. I buried my nose in the bouquet, it was heavenly. The little card with them said: "I'm very sorry, I am a buffoon, Love from Scooter x."

'Who are they from?' asked Steve as he passed by me in the hall, looking over his half moon glasses.

'From the dog, the one that knocked me over,' I told him as I looked at the card again.

'I should think so. It needs to be kept on a lead if you ask me, you're lucky that you're not badly hurt.'

'Oh it's fine. He's a nice dog. The breed is like that apparently. Flat-coats are known as the Peter Pan amongst dogs because they never grow up.'

'And don't tell me the owner looks like Captain Hook.' He picked up the newspaper from beside the mat and opened it, immediately losing interest in me, and the flowers.

'Actually, he's very nice,' I said quietly into the blooms, but I knew he wasn't listening. I watched as he settled in his armchair, slippers on, Brian Matthew playing his sixties music on Radio Two with Inca lying contentedly at her master's feet. He was in his element: school; home; beer; occasional hill walks and Sarah's visits. He was looking for nothing more than that, whilst I was still fighting the strangest feeling of being dumped by life. I was an unwanted element, dispensed with and trying to find herself in a stupid village project, and I had begun to have real doubts that it could ever be a book. None of them had the first idea about producing it, let alone costing it and marketing the damn thing.

'Do you think it's got legs?' Camilla had asked in a long and tedious meeting the day before. 'Is it interesting enough?'

'In truth, it's not going to have a wide appeal,' I told them honestly. 'I'm afraid our village history is not all that fascinating to a wider world.'

'But what of our curs and cowards?' Angela looked quite put out.

'I've been through most of the chapters and they are very good–'

'But?' She cut me off.

'There needs to be more substance to it. Just recounting historical facts and the dates isn't quite enough for a coffee table book.'

Tom looked very disappointed. 'It's been a lot of work,' he said flatly.

'Oh I realise that,' I said. 'But, you see, it needs to be written in a way that engages people.' I was just being honest, but I could feel hackles rising around the room. 'What I'm saying is, for example, Lapston Manor, there is a hint of a mysterious death but there is no more on the matter.'

Angela tutted. 'Well, you can't make these things up, my dear. It has to be true.'

'I know,' I replied, gritting my teeth. 'I was just wondering if you could pad it out a bit here and there, perhaps take a look into some of the pieces you've written and put in some more information.'

'I don't know,' said Camilla curtly. 'I hope you realise this project does comprise a large body of work, carried out over many years.'

'Don't get me wrong I do understand that.' I felt like conceding but I couldn't put my name to something that wasn't of a professional standard. People seeing Martha Nelson on something would expect a certain level. Or was that then? Were those days over for me? 'Lapston Manor, for example, became a children's convalescent home, but there is nothing about that anywhere.'

'Oh it was all very secretive,' said Camilla. 'The children went home, or somewhere else and left the area, and the priests are long gone.'

'Except for Muriel Bury's husband,' I replied. 'He was in there. Could we for example, go and see her and ask her about it?'

They looked at one another blankly, the whole prospect seeming to confound them.

'I'm not sure that would be very appropriate, given her circumstances,' said Camilla, leaning back and folding her arms across her chest. She was obviously becoming annoyed and I was feeling distinctly uneasy.

'Not just now,' I said, 'but perhaps when she feels better.'

'I could talk to her daughter Debby,' said Tom. 'I went to school with her. She may know something and might broker the suggestion with Muriel for us.'

'What a shame I didn't think of it when Mr Bury was still alive,' said Angela, shaking her head. 'I saw him so often round and about and we would sometimes chat. I'm sure he would have told me a few things.'

'Actually, I think not,' Roger said. We all turned to him. 'I got the firm impression he was terribly disturbed by it and he refused to say anything.'

There was an uncomfortable silence.

'Okay, well perhaps that's not a good idea,' I said, giving in. 'However, there are other chapters we could develop a little. I'll look into the Lapston Manor death myself, but maybe you could all revisit those chapters that need more information.' There were a lot of disgruntled mutterings. 'I'll do a list of those that could benefit from being enhanced, and circulate it.'

'If you must dear, if you must,' sighed Camilla. I knew immediately none of them were onside, they were packing away notepads and there was the chink of teacups as they tidied up and then they resolutely wished me goodbye. It was definitely a goodbye, no au revoir implied at all.

14

I took the bus to Burford and attended to some business at my bank. I confess I was toying with the idea of leaving for Oxford that evening, but Alice would never have forgiven me. I loathed her idea of a party because, in the first part, I found too much noise difficult and secondly, the same old faces would bore me. Besides, I actually considered it in poor taste given that we had so recently lost Henry, but Alice had vigorously argued the point that we all needed cheering up.

I had already bought a gift for her, a beautiful brooch, which I had found in an antique shop in Oxford. It was a daisy, topaz in the centre surrounded by white-gold petals. It was a beautiful thing, delicate and very fine, and I was pleased with it. However, as I was passing the milliner's window a very attractive silk headscarf caught my eye. It was a cheap thing, but I knew she would like it and, in addition, it had a daisy pattern, which the woman in the shop pointed out to me, as she laid it over her fingers. The two, I surmised, would complement each other most favourably.

I was home for luncheon and making my way upstairs when I heard voices in the garden room. I leaned quite a way over the banister but couldn't see anyone through the open door.

'Careful or you may fall.' Cécile was standing above me on the landing. I looked up and met her gaze, then I carried on walking upwards and we met on the turn of the stairs. She was almost level with me, just one tread above me and, in truth, I should have stepped back because there was too little space between us, but I felt no inclination to do so.

'Did you enjoy the gardens?' I asked.

'Oh yes, they are very intricate and quite beautifully designed. I have been fortunate to see the gardens of Versailles and they are splendid, but this one at Lapston is so complicated and truly delightful; I shall never forget it.'

'And you have until next week to enjoy it,' I said. 'The lawns and most of the beds are stunning with their autumn colouring.'

'I have nothing but a window box of geraniums in my appartement,' she defaulted to the French pronunciation quite without noticing. I heard the trace of a sigh in her voice.

'Where is it?' I asked, still standing too close, but neither of us moved.

'In Saint Michel, in the Latin Quarter. In my street there is a tourelle which is quite, how do you say, notable. Do you know it?

'Should I?' I asked, staring into her eyes.

'It is quite a famous road, one of the oldest in the city, I believe.'

I was watching her lips as she spoke, the fullness of the

bottom one, the finest, pale hairs above them. I imagined the hair at the nape of her neck, the feeling of her skin, soft and smooth to the touch.

'Carrick,' she spoke my name and then again, 'Carrick.' And I realised I was in another world.

'I do apologise,' I said, my gaze set firmly on her mouth. I could not raise my eyes from those lips. She stepped down so that she was beside me on the same tread and raised a hand to my cheek. The touch was light as gossamer, but it sent an exquisite ache through me.

'You are still not feeling well, are you?'

'No, I'm absolutely fine, in fact I'm feeling much, much better.' Then, seizing my moment, I said, 'I wondered if I might take you out to dinner tonight?'

'That is very kind of you, Carrick, but I am already being taken out to dinner this evening. George asked me at breakfast.' She smiled and I saw in her a trace of sympathy that I did not appreciate.

'Very well, I'll see you in a few minutes for luncheon,' I retorted, continuing past her as she proceeded down the staircase. I stopped short of my door and instead, leaned over the balcony, just catching sight of the top of her head as she reached the bottom and made for the garden room.

All at once, and for the very first time, I experienced some very ill feelings towards my dearest and closest friend.

15

I had almost finished looking at the two folders, only three files remained. One was called "Sarsten, A Neighbouring Hamlet." Not the punchiest title I ever saw, I thought unkindly. I had been feeling quite touchy about the History Group. Camilla had called to say that they had held a sub-committee meeting which appeared to involve everyone except me and had decided that they wanted the content to stay very much as it was.

I was stuck then between two stools: the need to make the book professional and also meet their requirements which were very fact based and, if I'm very honest, boring. I should of course have kept my head down, made some editorial revisions, and then presented the galleys to them, convincing them that I'd hardly changed a word. Something told me though that such a plan would not have worked with such pedants.

I pulled out the article about Sarsten. It was written by Tom and had been typed, and even contained references, mid text, something usually added at the end.

"Sarsten is a tiny hamlet of workers' cottages and a former water mill, the wheel of which has long been lost. Sarsten House is the current home to a supermarket magnate and benefits from the largest parkland in the area. The owners do not like trespassers since two of the residents were involved in a high profile court case." This was exactly my point, the reader would want to know who those people were and pictures should be available if necessary. I had no idea to whom this referred and it annoyed me let alone any readers. I continued reading.

"Sarsten was the home of the Radcliffe-Earl family from seventeen fifty-one. It was built in the Georgian Style and is of the locally quarried sand stone. The orangery was one of the largest in England and was famous for its fruit tree collection during the early nineteenth century. The famous astrologer Miles Frim lived at the manor for a time, as did the author and historian Frederic Aynsley. They both rented the house from the Radcliffe-Earls."

There was a picture pinned between the two sheets of writing. It was a colour photocopy of the house, a very splendid place with tall windows, and its servants. There were at least fifty by my estimation. There was even a groom mounted on a large chestnut horse, its tail cruelly docked. The original picture had been black and white, but someone had carefully hand-tinted it. I carried on reading.

"Sarsten has always been a very busy and thriving house. The observatory built in the centre of the house used to draw many astronomers and physicists from all over the country. Sadly, it burned down in 1929, just as the Radcliffe-Earls made huge losses on the stock market in America, which meant they lacked the funds needed to rebuild it. The family moved out and the house has had a number of owners culminating with the present occupiers who bought it five years ago and who have restored much of the building and grounds.

NB Plans for a cross-country course for three-day-eventing have recently been submitted."

There was a planning application attached to the back.

This was another case of a story glossed over. Why did the observatory burn down? The same year as the family made losses? Did one of them go mad and try to set fire to the house?

It was time for a walk, I needed air, and although Inca and I had been round the block that morning, I wanted more space to think things through. I was pondering on where to go when the idea came into my head to drive to Sarsten and take a look at the village myself. I scooped up Inca's lead and called her from her bed. She came gladly, wagging her tail.

The settlement was tiny, just four small cottages lining the narrow lane that culminated in a dead end. There was a gatehouse, an octagonal affair with a studded door and old latticed windows. The mill was a four storey brick built monolith at the end of the lane. It was built low into the bank of the river which meant the ground floor could not be seen until I had parked the car and viewed it over the wall. The millrace was flowing fast beneath me, the water spewing up as it hit the outcrop of stone where once the wheel had been.

I turned to the left and saw the former miller's house

tucked behind a clump of ragged bushes on each side of a narrow gravelled path. Inca was pulling me towards it, sniffing the air and wagging her tail. I took a deep breath to quell the twist of reticence in my stomach, and followed the path. There was a small clearing to the front of the house, which had once been a modest cottage, but which now boasted a glass extension, overhanging the water below. I could see Rory working on a large computer, his profile catching the blue glare of the screen. At that moment he looked up and saw me. A big smile lit up his face and seconds later he was opening the front door.

'Stand back!' he shouted as a big black mass of fur cannonballed past me and bounced towards Inca. I fortunately managed to step to one side, which meant I narrowly missed being flattened again.

'Scooter, you thug.' Rory wasn't laughing. He pushed past me and tried to catch the hairy monster but Scooter was having none of it. He body-swerved and sidestepped like Barry John, and was soon playing tag with Inca whose lead was flying behind her. I hadn't even realised at that point that I'd let go of her.

'I'm sorry,' said Rory. 'I had him locked in the kitchen but he's started to work out how the latch works. I'm going to have to build something akin to Guantanamo for him.' He looked embarrassed as he motioned for me to come into his house whistling for the dogs. They raced over to us and barged past me into the house. 'You know the Crufts obedience class?'

'Yes.'

'I'm not entering him for it.'

'That's not exactly a news flash,' I said and we were both laughing as Rory pushed the kitchen door open for me. I unclipped Inca's lead and she went off around the kitchen nose to the floor sniffing for crumbs. Scooter sat waiting in the middle of the kitchen, one paw hovering in the air, his face full of expectation.

'He now expects a treat because he came back to the whistle,' said Rory shrugging. 'What a dog.'

He threw a gravy bone to each dog and they retreated to the far end of the kitchen and lay down together, Inca closing her eyes as Scooter licked her head. 'Like old friends,' said Rory. 'They make a cute couple.'

'They do.'

'It's so nice to see you. Does that mean Scoot's flowers have worked and we're forgiven?'

'Of course. All forgiven and almost forgotten.'

'Drink?'

'Tea?'

'Coming up, unless you'd like a glass of vino. It's nearly four and somewhere in the world a yardarm is being hoisted, or whatever one does with a yardarm, any idea?'

'I think you'll find the sun rises and not the yardarm itself.' I suppressed a smile because I realised immediately that he already knew that.

'Well, whatever it is, let's have a glass of wine just to celebrate its existence.' He was already uncorking a bottle of Sauvignon and, when he poured it, it glugged into the glasses. 'You can always walk home,' he said nonchalantly, 'or even stay over.'

I looked away because his comment made me feel

uncomfortable. I ran a finger along the edge of the kitchen work surface, trying to think of something to say whilst he was putting the bottle away in the fridge. To him it was nothing more than a quip.

'Remind me, how long have you lived here?' I asked.

He passed over my wine and opened up a bag of Doritos, emptying them into a very nice brown clay dish.

'It's a Bernard Leach. It should be in a display cabinet, but I like using it. That means it's beautiful and useful at the same time.' Rory led us through to the lounge and then stood to one side so I could take in the space before me. It was two rooms knocked into one, a large beam down the centre of the ceiling. The far end was dominated by a wide picture window and, as I moved forward, I could see that a quarter of the floor was glass too. It extended right over surging water in the river below.

'Coming up to five years, in answer to your question.' He watched me as I looked down at the water beneath my feet. 'This is the same river where I met you, the one next to Lapston.' He pointed at the deserted mill. 'They were still operating there until the late fifties.'

'So, why did it close?'

'The new mill by the station, that was opened in the sixties, all mod cons. They recently opened a very nice shop too, good bread.'

'I didn't realise. I'll have to take a look, I did see the sign going up.' I was feeling a little giddy looking down at the water, I wasn't sure I liked the sensation. 'I presume you don't suffer from vertigo,' I said.

'No, water's my thing, can you believe it living here?'

he replied. 'I love to look at it but I can't actually swim.' My mouth must have fallen open because immediately he added, 'I can paddle, I'm not hydrophobic or anything and I like to drink the stuff too. How about you?'

I was still marvelling at the fact I knew someone of his age who couldn't swim, but I answered, 'Claustrophobic.'

'I suppose we all have something. My mother is scared to death of sticky labels. Pittakionophobia.'

'Goodness. Does she still have it? How does she shop?' I asked.

'Badly!'

'Like the dog with no nose?' I was laughing and he was too, and when he smiled, his mouth was slightly crooked and his eyes lit up. He reminded me of Steve in a way, but Rory's skin was clear and healthy looking whereas Steve's suffered from being inside so much.

Rory took a seat on a comfortable looking couch and I chose a worn armchair that looked well-loved. 'What an unusual house. This glass extension really is quite something.'

'I wasn't sure at first, what with my water thing, but actually I think I might have done the same thing with the building. It would be a shame to be over the millrace and to be able to hear it but never see it.'

'I agree, but doesn't it make you want to wee all the time?'

He threw back his head laughing heartily. 'For the first three years yes, but now I'm used to it.' He sipped his wine and was watching me from over the rim of the glass, weighing me up. Already we were very relaxed in each other's company, I even felt like I'd known him a long time, like an old friend.

'So what are you doing up in my neck of the woods?' he asked.

'I was reading all about Sarsten House for my book project and thought I'd pop up and take a look. I've never even been down this lane.'

'No one comes down here unless they have a reason. There are no footpaths, all the land is privately owned. I'm allowed to walk on the old carriage drive, but that's because I'm well behaved. They don't know about Scoot's thuggish behaviour – yet.'

'Who owns it now?'

'You know that really cheap corner shop operation, Seven/Seven?'

'Yes, ages ago, in Oxford, on the Cowley Road and in Headington.'

'That's right,' he said. 'Turns out our Mr Seven/Seven sold out when the going was good and made himself a fortune. He's earned it mind; he started as a barrow boy in the East End.'

'Goodness.' I looked over my shoulder towards the iron gates, just visible between the trees. 'And he's applied for a three-day-event course recently?'

'Yeah, but he won't get it; there's one nearby already and the traffic would be congested on the main road. He'll probably have something else up his sleeve though.'

'What about the fire that burned down the observatory in 1929?'

'Insurance,' Rory replied in a very matter of fact way.

'They lost a fortune on the American stock exchange, he had an American wife, the family was almost bankrupt. Lord Radders thought he could solve all his problems by burning down the house and, because he loved that observatory so much, he thought it would hold more sway if a fire started there.'

'And did it work, did he get a payout?'

'Nope, they sussed him out and he was facing a long spell in the clink, but managed to get himself, and the family, away to the States and was never heard of again. His assets were seized and sold off – always painful – and I suspect he started over again, but I really have no idea. An English cut-glass accent always charms our American friends.'

'At last!' I said rather joyously. 'Something tasty for the history group's book, these stately homes seem to come with a whole host of stories don't they? I'm still working on this mysterious death at Lapston.'

'What do you know so far?'

'Not that much. I'm hoping that your Mr Fry might help me.'

'Ah yes, I called round a couple of days ago. Gladys Avery, his neighbour, told me that he's away for a couple of weeks. I'll let you know when he's back.'

'Rory, is there any chance of seeing Lapston?' I asked.

'Yes, of course. It's too late now the dusk is setting in and it would be dangerous to go in the dark, but how about next Monday at two? I'm going there anyway so I can pick you up.'

'That will be out of your way though, won't it?'

'No, I'll be coming back from Oxford, I've got a project over there.'

'Okay then,' I said, sipping the last of my wine. 'Two on Monday, but I'd better be going now.'

'Are you sure you won't have another?'

'No. I'm driving so I'd better not and anyway my husband will be home soon and he'll be wondering where I am.' Rory looked a bit disconsolate and I knew he'd hoped I'd stay longer.

'Okay, but come for a drink after Lapston on Monday. We can have a really good chat.'

I felt a prickling down my spine, a mixture of excitement, trepidation and something else, a thrill, deep inside me, of seeing him again.

16

Mrs Hall had gone to the trouble of making an omelette for lunch, the fruit of her beloved hencoop. I watched Cécile as she forked it into her mouth and I imagined her in her apartment, eating a simple meal such as this. Her apartment would be a sleek affair, elegant and fine, with red and blue furniture and tall windows that drenched the place with sunlight.

'George tells me you are going out to dinner tonight,' said Alice brightly.

'Yes, he wants me to see Burford; I understand it is very beautiful.'

'Oh, you will love it,' said Alice. 'It's your favourite place in the world, Carrick, isn't it?' I knew I sounded disagreeable when I replied that many places were to my taste and Burford was not particularly notable. Alice looked quite taken aback. I couldn't help it but there was a lack of warmth in my voice and she glanced sidelong at George who, in turn, looked a little uncomfortable.

'I think we shall dine at The Highway,' he said brightly and changed the subject. 'From all reports they have a very talented new chef who knows his way around a ration card.'

I glanced at Cécile. Did I detect unease in her? I couldn't tell.

Alice became quite subdued but it wasn't my concern. I was focused entirely on Cécile and asked her to tell me about the gardens of Versailles, somewhere I had planned to visit for many years. At length, she told us about the king and his intriguing hobbies and pastimes.

'In the middle of the seventeenth century, Louis, the Sun King, had a menagerie of ferocious beasts at Vincennes,' she told us. 'There were lions, tigers, and leopards all kept in cages around an amphitheatre where the king could entertain visitors with their battles. One ambassador, I forget which one, saw a fight to the death between a royal tiger and an elephant.'

'Oh my.' Alice pulled a face. 'That all sounds ghastly.'

The idea of keeping wild animals in small cages did nothing for me, but Versailles and the menagerie Cécile was describing so eloquently sounded quite remarkable. I wondered how our own very drear and dark Buckingham Palace might compare to such splendour.

Cécile addressed Alice with a calm, unwavering voice. 'It is no more ghastly I think than you in England getting on a horse, in a red jacket, to chase the deer or fox.' She sipped her water then looking across to George, she said, 'Do you not think so, George?'

'What? No, my dear, I should imagine it was to the taste of the people at the time.'

'As was the guillotine to the rabble on the Place de la Concorde, I have no doubt,' said Alice, a little fiercely.

'That was something that needed to be done,' Cécile

said, a chill in her voice. 'It is a poor country that is not freed from the shackles of an hereditary ruling family.'

'Our royal family is very important to us. The King and Queen have been stalwarts during these trying times,' Alice replied. 'And they do not rule us.'

'I think we are on dangerous territory, ladies. We must agree to disagree,' said George with a polite cough. 'And there's nothing wrong with that.'

It was only I who caught the look that Alice threw at Cécile and it was at once apparent that the façade of their friendship was suffering from a hairline crack.

I was sitting on the bench on the lower lawn some time later. The rushing flow of the water as it tumbled through rocks then swirled into the deepest fastest flowing part of the river was some fifty feet away, but still audible. Cécile was walking along the stony path that wound up from the calm square of the river that was sectioned off to form a bathing pool. I saw her coming long before she had seen me, and when she waved, I noticed that she picked up her pace.

She was wearing a greenish pencil skirt and a simple white blouse. They skimmed her body, making her look taller and even more elegant. I didn't stand as she approached and it gave her the option to walk past me with a nod should she so wish, but she didn't pass by. Instead, she took a seat next to me on the bench without a word and that is how we stayed for a short time.

'Carrick,' she said eventually, her voice quite soft. 'I feel that my presence here is causing something of a rift. I may be wrong but I do not wish to cause any upset. If I am in the way and causing any... difficulties then I will go at once.'

The thought was suddenly unbearable. 'Oh no, Madame, please do not think that way. If we have been unreasonable or unkind I must apologise most profusely.' I met her eyes, and hers, hazel flecked with brightest green, met mine.

'Are you sure?'

'Yes, yes, I assure you. I have been unwell and I think Alice, if that is to whom you are referring, is still grieving and has confused feelings. I can assure you that I am quite recovered.' I touched her hand to reassure her, her skin was soft, pale like oyster silk.

She didn't look away, indeed she held my gaze, giving me a stirring of hope. 'Then we will say no more of it,' she said, her voice still soft. I was drinking her in, the hand beneath my touch, the eyes, and the round fullness of her lips. I leaned in but she looked away and returned the hand to her lap. 'Please, tell me of Henri.'

I looked across the lawns, the lowest terrace falling away into a bank of lilies, their heads teetering towards going over. Below them, the great willows dangled their leafy fingers into the water, verdant after the summer's heat. For a moment, I saw him coming up from the pool; he was lean and long-limbed, his brown hair was cut short and turned black with damp from swimming. He had a unique easy gait as he came marching up the slope, his old cricket jumper rolled under his arm. He wore his tennis shirt a pale green and his slacks were cream. I saw him then as if he were right there before us, as if I might introduce him to Cécile for the very first time. He would have kissed her hand no doubt and made us laugh with some witticism or other.

'Henry was remarkable,' I told her. 'He was a truly remarkable person. For all that George is muscle and brawn, Henry was lean and athletic. It was like comparing a St. Bernard to a Wolfhound.' I was not too sure whether she understood my analogy. Did they have such dogs in Paris? I had my doubts, but I also had her attention.

'You knew him,' I continued. 'He was like no other man you could meet.'

She nodded. 'That is true.'

'He was equally at home with bat or ball, played winger in rugby, and was on the school team from the first year. George and I could never emulate him. Henry became head boy, whilst we never quite made the grade.'

'Grade? Pardon me, you are going too fast for me.'

'I'm sorry, we were not as good as him, pas aussi doué.' She followed my meaning. 'He was one of those few who are good at all things: maths; languages; sport but not, I am relieved to say, in art, thank goodness.'

'Why thank goodness?'

'I, for my sins, am the artist in the family.'

'I had no idea,' she said looking pleasantly surprised. It gladdened my heart that I should have found something that might impress her. 'Will you show me your artwork?'

'Yes. I, if you would like to see it, I should be delighted. I have a little studio in Oxford, though I have done nothing since I was called up, naturally, and I have somewhat lost my passion for it.'

'Oh you must go back to it,' she said and I felt something inside me uplifted by her voice. She had such a gentle feminine way about her that was very much at variance with her demeanour, very hard to put into words. 'What do you paint?'

'I paint landscapes in the main, and sometimes people.'

'And George?' she asked, swerving the subject away from me sooner than I expected.

'Ah, George, he is a faithful old dog, a very good man, and honest as the day is long. As I said before, Henry was such a shining light that I fear he left me, rather us, very much in the shade. Sir Reginald and Augusta loved us all very much, but there was a light in their eyes when Henry was about. I am just so very glad they did not live to hear word of his death.'

There was a moment's silence. We were both looking out towards the river. A faint whisper of a breeze lifted the scalloped collar of her blouse; it caught the corner of my eye.

'I would have liked to have known them,' Cécile said sadly. 'But now I have met you and George and dear, sweet Alice.' For some reason, I could not seem to make my thoughts align coherently. I was picturing the Amshersts, but a new life was opening up for me, a life I preferred and had always wanted. 'She loves you very much.'

I turned and looked at Cécile with astonishment: 'Who?'

'Alice, of course.'

I responded immediately. 'Alice!' I was completely taken aback. 'She may have done at one time, but I can assure you that she is over it. She is more of a sister to me, or a best friend.' I must have sounded terribly indignant, but Cécile was unmoved and, it appeared, somewhat amused at my reaction, her mouth twisted into a wry smile. 'She is just a girl,' I countered. 'I have known her since she was a mere babe in arms.'

'And so?'

'My taste is for sophisticated women,' I told her crossly. 'The war has altered us all and it forced all of us who went away to be more mature. They stuffed young men into uniforms and we grew up quickly, we had to. Now these childish things do nothing for me.'

'You would call love childish?' she retorted.

'Only in the context of being loved by someone too young and gauche for me,' I replied emphatically.

'You should take love where you can find it,' she said wisely. 'To be loved is to be. I am certain that it is one of life's great treasures to love and be loved.'

I knew she was talking about Henry, for I certainly couldn't be the object of her affections, but as she spoke, I felt a special bond between us. She was trying to establish whether or not I had someone else because she was attracted to me, of that I was certain. At that moment we shared something, it was right there above the river with the ghost of Henry watching over us and wishing us well. Yes, I believed most strongly he would wish us well.

17

Steve was poorly. He had phoned in sick, which was highly unusual. I sat on the side of the bed. He looked grey and drawn, and he had pulled the duvet up to his chin, yet he was shivering. I had made him a Lemsip, placing it on the bedside table next to him where he could reach it.

'I'm sorry,' he groaned. 'I hate being ill, and we've only just had the Easter holidays.'

'That was over month ago, and there is nothing you can do, my love, so just give in to it and get lots of sleep.' I kissed him on his clammy forehead and cupped his face in my hands. 'I'll make you a snack, if that's okay, then I'm popping out for an hour or two.' He looked a bit let down and it pinched my heart. 'I won't be out for long, I'm just going to look at Lapston Manor.'

'Who's taking you?'

'That nice chap I met out walking, the one with the big black dog.' Steve didn't say anything. He was always so reasonable and fair, and what did he need to be concerned about anyway?

'I don't want anything to eat,' he said wearily, turning over and pulling the bedclothes around him.

Half an hour later, I closed the door quietly as he slept, his head deep in his pillow. It wasn't the flu but whatever sort of bug it was, it was certainly making him very ill.

I stood outside our house, a little way down the road, telling myself that Rory could see me better there, and not that I was out of sight of our bedroom window.

He was driving a pickup, a big rusty white thing. I had to climb up and onto the seat. There was no sign of Scooter and I can't say I was disappointed.

'Hi Martha,' Rory said cheerfully. 'I'm so glad you can still make it.'

'I didn't take your number. My husband's poorly and I–'

'Do you want to cancel?' Rory asked, looking both concerned and terribly disappointed in equal measure.

'No, no, it's just that, Steve's asleep now, it's fine, honestly.'

'Okay, if you're sure?'

'Yes,' I said purposefully. 'I'm dying to see inside the house.'

'Don't be too let down when you get there though, will you? It's very run down.'

We drove down the High Street and up to the brow of the hill where we turned sharply left into a narrow leafy lane where a long line of plane trees stood like a guard of honour to each side.

'I had no idea about this little road.' I had always thought it led to a caravan site, but Rory explained that was in the next field along.

I was still struggling to get my bearings when we dipped down and then up again and a large field of sheep opened up to our right.

As we turned round the bend, we met with a sharp corner and there they were; the gates of Lapston. Tall and splendid, they towered over us.

Rory jumped out and unlocked the padlock on a heavy chain that held the gates together. They creaked open, heavy and unyielding, as he pushed them back, and in doing so, gave way to a long drive, its surface chipped and broken, weeds forcing themselves through every crack.

I watched Rory as he returned to the truck – he was looking thoughtful – then he saw me and smiled. He heaved himself into the truck, using the grab handle of the door.

'Ready?' he asked and I nodded, feeling stupidly excited. 'It gets really bumpy now so hold on to your hat.' He was right; the pick-up went down potholes and rose up on tarmac that had breached as if it had been in an earthquake. After five hundred yards, it became flatter, less difficult to drive over, but it still jolted us around.

'I need a four wheel drive to cope with my work,' Rory said as we lunged into a very large, long pothole, the car grumbled and thrust itself forward.

As we turned the corner, Rory stopped, and I felt an unexpected lurch of fear inside me. We were miles from anywhere and I was in a car with a man I barely knew at all. I suddenly felt oddly insecure because I hadn't thought it through. I must have been staring straight at him, as I weighed it all up in my mind, because I realised he was urging me to turn around and look over my left shoulder.

I followed the direction of his eyes and there it was, Lapston Manor. The sunlight was moving slowly across the expanse of green in front of us, almost as if it was coaxing us in. The grass, once I imagined an immaculate lawn, was no longer cared for and mown. Instead, it had become a wild meadow. Couch grass, docks and the skeletal remains of rough thistle had taken hold, and the new buds of unknown flowers were dotted here and there.

The house was double-fronted with a bay window to each side of the large porch. Her windows were tall, mullioned, and there were at least ten of them, all of them symmetrical, as were the high chimneystacks that I recognised from the photograph.

'Isn't she beautiful?'

'She certainly is. I've never seen a house quite like her, all the sills and little embellishments on the front are so minimal yet they catch the light.' I was in wonder at the sight before me.

'Let's go in,' Rory said, pressing his foot down on the accelerator. 'The drive narrowed considerably and became gravel that crunched and spat under the wheels.

We pulled up right outside the front door where we climbed down out of the pickup and stood on the wide apron of driveway. 'Turning circle for carriages.' Rory waved his hand in a circular motion as I stood looking around me and just at that moment, the sun broke through a cloud and the whole façade of the building was highlighted by the most theatrical afternoon light. The mullioned windows I had seen from the other side of the lawn were dead and dull hollows. The glass was long gone, half were boarded up, but the rich honeyed Cotswold stone had become warmer and more welcoming.

Rory had a huge key in his hand and we proceeded up three wide steps to the front porch. Just inside were low stone shelves for taking off boots or for depositing packages, and above the old heavy door was a carved portico.

'That's a pediment with a carved stone tympanum. There is a similar one at Eversham House, one of the Paris purchases.' Rory stood beside me, looking up. 'People often wrongly call this a portico.'

'Really?' I said, suitably chastened, and made a mental note for myself. He opened the old door, and tapered shafts of sunlight poured into the hall in front of us from hundreds of different holes in the roof, like a stage set lit from above. Before us, the majestic staircase rose up and fanned out on each side to a gallery above our heads.

To each side of us were double doors and the same again each side of the staircase at the rear of the hall. The doors at the rear were missing and so I could see the sunlight playing on the surface of the tiled floors beyond. For a second, I listened as if I might hear voices coming from the rooms, but there was nothing save for the creak of wood as the wind lifted the tiles above us.

Whilst I stood taking it all in Rory was silent next to me, but he was clearly delighted to see the awe and wonder in my face. Then the sunlight was gone, snatched from us by a cloud, and the house changed in an instant. It was dark and sad, the panelled walls smashed, broken or covered with green mould. The floor, of once immaculate black and white tiles, was pock marked and chipped but mostly hidden beneath rubble and discarded litter. The whole place was damp and forgotten, and I felt deeply troubled that something once so obviously grand was now broken, desolate and left simply to rot. There was evidence of rats too, telltale droppings and chewed things like wire and plastic. It smelt of old wood, damp cement and squalor, seedy and pungent in the back of my nose.

'Isn't it sad?' Rory sighed. 'So much life drained out of her and forty odd years of sadness behind her.'

'It is,' I agreed. 'What's in there?'

'Dining room,' said Rory. 'Come and take a look, though I warn you, the hall is by far the nicest part.'

He was right, the dining room, once a wooden panelled affair, was wrecked. The floor had been removed, the supporting joists, now exposed, were rotted and the spaces between filled with rubble. There was a wall-mounted sliding blackboard but someone had thrown a heavy object at it and it was split in two. I found myself moved because the whole atmosphere was so gloomy and depressing yet, through it all, I could see her as she once was.

We picked our way across to the lounge where Rory had trouble opening the large doors because a bird of considerable size, a black thing with huge wings, was blocking it from the other side. It was staring up at us with round glassy eyes as Rory kicked it away. Above us there was no ceiling, just a huge gaping space that spiralled up to a chequerboard of missing roof tiles. The lounge had two aspects: one to the front and the overgrown lawn, the other at the rear where a tall casement window towered above the remains of a window seat.

Rory would not go forward. 'The floor is rotten, we could go straight through,' he warned, catching hold of my arm protectively. 'Don't go any further, Martha.'

The room, I was certain, had once been beautiful, the cornices and ceiling at one time boasted exquisite plasterwork but, in more recent times, the interior of the house had been slowly deteriorating. An old iron bedframe was stowed against the wall and a white medical cabinet was lying on its back in the middle of the floor, its glass shattered. Around it was the debris and dirt of a building left to its own devices, destroyed stealthily by the elements. Everywhere ivy was creeping in through the cracks in the walls.

We left the lounge and walked around the edge of the hallway, where the floor looked at its most weight supporting then we headed towards the rear of the house. On the way Rory tapped on a single door and said, 'Drawing Room once upon a time, then an office. We can't go in there; the ceiling's caved in,' and then tapping on another, 'Kitchens.'

Then we were standing at the threshold of another room, its brightly lit interior was due to the row of ornate French doors leading to the garden. From there I could see the skeleton of a magnificent conservatory, the panes smashed or missing. The shards were lying like a bear trap across the floor, their deadly jagged points glinting as the sun, once again, came out and brightened up the whole place.

'This was a morning room, somewhere to go whilst the servants cleaned the house,' Rory told me. 'The floor's rotten here too, be careful. We can look at the conservatory from the lawn.'

We turned back, and I looked up at the staircase and the splendour of the gallery going around the space above me. There were empty doorways leading off it, the doors all missing and some of the walls were punched through whilst elsewhere wallpaper had curled and fallen away.

'Are the stairs safe?' I asked.

'They're stone so they are safe, but the landings would give way. The rafters have come down in many of the bedrooms; there are only a few remaining to hold up the roof.'

'Have you been up?'

'Yes, but you're not allowed to,' Rory said, his mouth set in a firm line, a smile at each corner.

'Why isn't it plastered all over with Health and Safety notices?'

'Because Kipper doesn't do Health and Safety. He's a bit old school.'

'It doesn't look like it has many visitors,' I said, turning back and looking towards the front door.

'It doesn't, those days of kids getting up to no good have gone. Social media and stranger danger has seen to all that and in various places he's put up cameras, all fake, but the kids don't know that. Also, if you look by the gate there's a sign saying dog patrols are frequent.'

'But they're not?'

'No, except for Scoot and me.'

'He'd knock anyone flying at twenty paces,' I said.

'This is true.'

'So why are you and Scooter up here so often? Are you Kipper's security?'

'No, we're up here for a whole different reason. Would you like to see it?'

'What?'

'Follow me.' He turned right and opened the door to the kitchen hallway. I followed him, though I had no idea where he was taking me.

18

Alice and I were seated at one corner of the small table in the morning room. We had started using it for informal meals during the war when only one or two of us were home. It was very rare that three of us had dined together because George and I were never there at the same time.

Alice was wearing a pale yellow dress, a pretty affair with a bow at the front and a simple white cardigan. She was in low spirits again, the brief excitement of Cécile's visit had given way to an overwhelming sadness, the unrelenting grief of losing Henry that had carved so deep into her soul. It blighted us all. It was like trying to run away but finding one's legs in treacle, like something in a nightmare, the pain always bound to catch us up.

'Is everything all right with you, Mouse?' I asked as I caught her gazing across the lawn.

She sighed heavily. 'I'm just wishing he was here, either with or without her, I wouldn't care which, but I so desperately want him back.'

I reached across and placed my hand on her arm. She still didn't look at me but I could see the swell of a tear on her lower eyelid, and I felt for my handkerchief, ready to pass it to her.

'I can't see life ever being any fun again without him,' she said. 'It simply won't be the same. Just imagine what Christmas and Easter will be like. We shall be so very dull and thinking of him all the time.'

'I am certain he would want us to carry on and make the best of it, old girl.'

Then I passed her the handkerchief as a tear rolled freely down her cheek. She apologised and I told her not to be silly and reassured her that we all felt deeply upset in spite of the brave faces we displayed to the world.

She sniffed and dabbed her eyes. 'That's why I wanted us to have a party,' she said sadly. 'Just to cheer us up a bit. God knows, but until now, when have we three been together for more than a day in the last four years?'

'It's a splendid idea and so very important that the world goes on, the world Henry gave his life for,' I said gently. 'I think a party is a capital idea.'

Of course, I was not being truthful, and thankfully just at that moment Mrs Hall arrived with our meal – a plate of rabbit stew with cauliflower cheese, last night's leftovers being used up.

'Thank you, Mrs Hall, and thank you for the coffee last night and the omelette today. I'm sure Madame Roussell appreciated your efforts to make her feel at home.' Mrs Hall looked very pleased and was, I noted, brimming with pride because I had passed comment on her thoughtfulness. She said thank you to me and that it had been her pleasure to cater for the French lady.

'You are a good man,' said Alice as Mrs Hall departed. 'I would never have noticed such things, I am such a goose.'

'A very lovely goose!' I told her, and gave her wrist a friendly squeeze.

'Thank you,' she giggled. Her mood was recovered and I was pleased, it would be a pleasant enough evening.

'What will you do now, Mouse? Now that the war is finally coming to an end?'

'I really have no idea, I can strip an engine, you know. I have muscles in my arms.' She bent her elbow to show me, the muscle was barely noticeable but I made approving noises. 'So a life of keeping house and knitting no longer appeals,' she told me. 'I might look at taking a job somewhere, but I really don't know.'

'I can see why you would want to do something different. A life at Lapston will seem very dull by comparison. I fear it will become tiresome for me in the long run.' I spoke truthfully. 'For the present, I am enjoying being returned safe and with those I love best.'

'You should come riding with me tomorrow,' said Alice. 'We could hack out, no more than a gentle walk until you feel fitter, it can only help.' Of course by fitter she meant the scars on my feet, but in particular my mental health. It seemed it was her current pet project to pester me about it. I stifled the unpleasant reply in my mind and instead poured us both some water.

'I will, I will come out with you,' I said at length. 'It would do me good.'

Alice was very pleased and we talked on matters of the house and the times we had taken tea with Augusta at this very table. She would relish telling us about her exotic orchids, now long since gone, and the gardens and how she and Sir Reginald had travelled and made acquaintances, through their love of horticulture, right across Europe.

'I am sure that you could find an interest if we called on some of those acquaintances,' Alice suggested. 'There will be a good deal to do to recover this country, you just have to look at the East End, the rebuilding there will take decades. They say the planners are already jostling for position.'

'If they bother,' I remarked. 'I'd be inclined to raze the last remaining buildings to the ground and build a big area of parkland, a memorial to those who were lost, a green haven in the city for people to enjoy.'

'I was talking to Johnny Gilder-Smith a couple of weeks ago and he told me the King and Queen were nearly killed when that bomb hit the Palace.'

'Oh I doubt it. They were in the underground shelter, according to The Times.' I had an unshakeable confidence in my chosen source of daily news.

'He said they were sitting by a window and were very nearly killed as it shattered. One of the footmen was very badly injured.'

'I think we might need to make allowances for Johnny's sense of drama and propensity for a good story,' I told her.

Her face clouded a little. 'Carrick, you always make fun of my friends. Johnny's not all that bad.'

'If you say so,' I said, laying my knife and fork down. 'At least he's still here, when so many of our dearest friends have gone.'

We were both silent, our thoughts returning all too quickly to Henry.

'I suppose you think Cécile is very lovely,' Alice said at length. I knew there was no malice in the statement because she was not capable of such things and I responded stating that I liked our new friend very much and found her quite charming. My companion shifted in her seat so that she was facing me more, then she leaned in slightly. 'I think so too, but I have to say…' She looked down and her voice trailed off.

'Have to say what?'

'I can't see her and Henry together, they just do not seem to be a couple.'

'Whatever do you mean?' I was quite astonished.

'I cannot accurately put it into words, but I always saw Henry with someone more colourful, less composed. Does that make sense?'

I regarded her as I let the words sink in. 'No, Alice, it does not. I think she is exactly his sort; refined, beautiful and très élégant.' I said the final two words in French for effect. Alice looked at me, her eyes round and filled with fascination.

'Why, Carrick, I do believe you are entranced by our French guest!'

'Don't be silly, Alice. Now you do sound like a goose,' I chided. It really was none of her business, and a step too far and, for her part, she looked suitably chastened and perhaps a little hurt too. 'That is simply not true.'

She bristled. 'Then that is a good thing because I think George has fallen for her hook, line and sinker.' I was incredulous, but she was quite obviously convinced in the matter. And then it dawned on me that she, with her female intuition, might even be onto something, and a cold shiver ran up the length of my spine, as the morning room suddenly grew inexplicably cold.

19

Rory and I were walking around to the rear of the house. The lawn there was a dry scrubby grass and patches of bald earth were like stepping stones scattered across it. They led to the high wall, and beyond it the river, and then my village.

'This was a camomile lawn back in the day and that collection of fallen down buildings and rubble over there was once the stable block. But it's been a long time since it was used for anything other than garden machinery and storing wood, the horses are long gone.' Rory walked round to a terrace in front of the lounge windows.

I stopped dead when I saw it.

The knot garden was about forty metres square, equal to the entire length of the house. The box hedges had been designed to form four right–angled corners. Four smaller sections sat within those and each one was an inverted semi-circle surrounding a central, circular bed. The box hedging in the middle of that had been carefully shaped into an "A". Inside all the gaps in the hedging were stunning white roses.

'Breathtaking eh?'

'It is beautiful, and so immaculate.'

'It's my dirty secret,' Rory said with a big grin. 'I sneak up here and maintain it. I cannot bear to think of it being lost like the house. I managed to recreate the "A" in the middle, "A" for Amshersts. I feel like I'm commemorating them, well in some small way.'

'Oh Rory, it is stunning, just amazing.' I moved across the border of lawn he so obviously cared for because it looked, for all the world, like it had been trimmed with nail scissors.

'I planted tea roses, for the summer, at the far end there on the terrace fencing, I'm pretty certain they would have been grown there before. Beautiful things. A French horticulturist, Francis Meilland, sent cuttings to friends right across Europe because he knew the Germans were about to invade. It was said that they were flown out of France on the last available plane. They have named it "Peace" since then.'

'How amazing.' It was a breathtaking sight, a sea of white constricted by neat green hedges. 'I think your garden is absolutely fabulous.'

'I hoped you'd like it,' Rory said happily. 'But I also sort of knew you would.'

'Why? I'm not a gardener. Put it this way, I'm not serious about it.'

'Yes, but you are an inquirer and you appreciate beauty.'

'That's the journo in me,' I said. 'What you mean is you think I'm nosey and like things ordered and well laid out.'

'A Virgo?'

'Cancer actually, but please tell me you don't believe in that rubbish.'

'I don't, but it's funny how you meet people and can almost guess their star sign. It dates back to the pagans and the other ancient long dead religions that worshipped the sun gods. We've moved on and of course hijacked it all for our more recent religions, but I often wonder how close they were to nature and whether they knew and understood so much more than we do.'

'I have to admit, standing here in the sun with the knot garden in front of me, I do wonder if we haven't lost an awful lot.' I was brushing my fingers on the soft petals of a rose; the scent was delightful.

'Trust me, we have,' he said earnestly. 'But have you noticed how nature quickly reclaims everything; the ivy has entered the house and will soon loosen the stones and take back to earth what came from earth?'

'Wow, that is deep,' I replied turning to the house. The façade was covered in ivy and clutches of weeds that spilled out of downpipes, broken sills and ran right along the base of the building. 'Isn't it terribly sad, the slow deterioration of a place that once was filled with life?'

'I think so,' said Rory, but he wasn't looking at the house, he was staring at me. I stole only the briefest glance at him, but he did not look away, instead it was me who turned away. 'I think you're like that too, Martha,' he said.

'An old house with weeds in my drainpipe?' I said in mock indignation.

'No, you are someone who was once full of life and now you are lost.'

I wasn't sure what to say. It felt like a make or break moment, and I decided I should speak guardedly. 'I have my project. It keeps me busy and don't forget, I'm now somewhat expert on the subject of my village.' I was being sarcastic because I was nowhere near being an expert.

'Which is good.' He was standing some four feet away, hands on his hips, elbows out. 'But you need something else in your life before your lights dim and the ivy does begin to grow.'

I felt truly indignant. 'I don't know how you've picked that up in the very short time we've known each other.'

'I realise I have only just got to know you and I don't want to be rude, but it does show. When I met you, you looked sad but still purposeful, since then all I see is someone who's...well, depleted.'

I was speechless. I might have taken that from Becky or Bob or, for goodness sake, Steve, but this was a stranger who I barely knew. Yet as I was standing there with him an emergent power, an energy was unifying us. Even in that brief time together, we had shared something tremendously special and that something was the dilapidated ruins of Lapston Manor and its enchanting secret garden.

20

I was up early. I had taken my sketchbook out and captured some loose drawings of the statues on the front lawn as they emerged from the morning mist. The house was like a ghost shrouded in a cloth of white, its walls shielding the ones I loved, and the one I dared to dream that I could love – if only George had not got himself in the way.

They had returned after eleven the night before. I heard them coming up to bed. He wished her a very good night and I listened to her footsteps as they passed my door. Did I imagine that they stopped? How I wished she had knocked for me, even just to say goodnight.

The sun was beginning to break through as I headed back, sketchbook under my arm and camera around my neck.

She was sitting on the front step, her hair pulled back into a ponytail, wearing a black jumper and breeches, knees tucked up, arms wrapped around them.

'Alice! Am I late? I thought we said ten.'

'We did. It is half past nine. I just wanted to see if you were aware of the time because I know that when you go off sketching you forget to eat, let alone ride out with your best girl.' She was smiling and she was so enchantingly pretty when she did so. I hadn't called her my "best girl" for a long while and it jolted me back to another time, another place.

'My very bossy girl,' I joked. 'How did I ever manage all those years away without you telling me what to do?' She tilted her head to one side and pulled a face. 'If your face sticks like that you'll blame me!' She looked so attractive in the morning light, I told her to pose so I could take her picture.

She pouted like a film star and I laughed. 'Come on now, be serious.'

'I can never be too serious around you,' she retorted, 'but if you don't want a pout, fair enough.' I clicked the shutter and knew it would be a lovely one. Alice loved riding and I was about to go out with her for the first time in a long while, her eyes sparkled.

'I'll be back in a jiffy. You go and saddle up and I'll be there in no time.'

I had forgotten what it was like to stand next to a horse, to look into those deep dark unfathomable eyes, the overwhelming calmness of them. Alice was quite right; this was therapy.

'Hello Jester, old man. I've missed you.' I rubbed my hand up and down his broad bay face and he nudged me as if to tell me to stop being so wet.

Alice was carrying my saddle over her arms, looking so petite behind it. I took it from her and threw it over Jester's broad back. He eyed me as I tightened the girth and I knew he was doing his old trick of blowing out. Alice was up on her thoroughbred, Beau, in a trice, and he was walking forward disobediently whilst she tightened her girth.

'Beau, behave, stand still,' she reprimanded. Then to me, she said, 'I've had a word with Jester and he says he's going to behave very well today, being as it is your first time back in the saddle.'

I led Jester to the mounting block. At almost seventeen hands, I needed the extra height it gave me. I gathered the reins, and when I looked up, Alice was really very jolly about it all. 'I am so very happy to have you come out with me. I have really missed this.'

My horse was rock solid. The old fellow knew his job, and even when Beau barged into him as we left the yard, he took the blow, staying square and solid underneath me. The trees had begun to mellow, the green leaves tipped with gold and red and, as the sunlight sparkled through them, it was all so beautiful. In front of us, magical patterns danced across roads and leaves frothed beneath our horses' feet. It may have been autumn but the world felt renewed after the dry dirt and depression of Sicily.

'I know what you are thinking,' Alice snapped me out of my reverie.

'And what would that be?'

'How glad you are that I talked you into this.'

I gave in completely and patted Jester's deep muscular neck.

'You are right, Mouse. It is the best thing I could have done.'

'I'm glad,' she said and, though I expected more from

her, she held back. I felt there was something she wanted to impart to me, but I'm afraid my moods had made her feel uncertain.

We hacked for well over four miles down the shaded lanes and, as we came back over Sarsten Hill and along the main road, Beau tiptoed around the "dig for victory" vegetable plots dug out of verges. The bird-deterring ribbons were blowing in the breeze and it unsettled him.

We came back down the lane to the river, and I even cantered Jester along the old carriage drive, much to Alice's delight. Jester did not cause me a minute's concern, even as Beau shot forward in reaction to the hollow squawking of a pheasant in the undergrowth.

We arrived back at the stable block in good spirits but, as I dismounted, the drop nearly finished off my feet. It was an intense pain, searing like lightning rods through my shins. I took a deep breath, knowing such a sharp pain was not good. The doctors had said things would improve, and I had been doing well, but the pain on landing was severe. I should not have jumped off, the mounting block was just a yard away. I held on to the stirrup leathers for a minute as the soreness rose through my thighs to my groin. It was my own stupid fault because I should have used the mounting block.

I glanced across at Alice who was oblivious as she led Beau back to his loose box. I rested my head against Jester's strong shoulder and took a deep breath.

There were lights flashing, the sound of bullets, the rounds firing inside my head. Beads of sweat gathered across my brow and I leaned further into my horse, the familiar warm sweat smell of him my comfort and he stood solidly supporting me. The firecrackers in my head were so very loud. They all were shouting, screaming. One man was rolling on the floor, hands clutching the bloody mess and spillage of his torn belly.

I pressed to the fur and rubbed my cheek into it. The neck muscle felt sure, rock solid against my forehead. He was standing still, he could have moved, but he didn't. He knew his job, the old schoolmaster.

He was the horse I'd been given on the morning of my twenty first birthday, my present from the Amshersts. I had hunted him, show-jumped, hacked him out more times than I can remember and now he was keeping me from keeling over. I reached up and patted him, then pushed myself away, but the world began to spin around me as I fought and tried hard to keep it all together.

'Carrick, darling, what's wrong?'

'I'm fine, Alice, please just leave me alone.' I was harsh with her and I even think I may have pushed her away. I'm not sure, I can't remember, for the next thing I knew I was waking up in my bed and Cécile Roussell was leaning over me and telling me I would be fine, that I must rest and that things would soon be better. I knew she meant us. We were going to be fine, things would be better because we would be together, very soon.

21

'He did what? He's an idiot!' Steve was very angry and he was levelling the most awful stare at me.

'It was all perfectly fine. He knows what he's doing.'

'Doing!' He mimicked. 'Doing! He took you into a derelict building, no hard hats, no regard for what might happen to you. He sounds like an idiot, don't you dare go there again.'

'Steve!' I fought back, which was so unlike me. 'Steve you don't own me, I can do what I like.'

He looked away, shaking his head in despair, then he came back at me. 'I don't own you, but I do worry about you. This man sounds like he doesn't know what's safe and what isn't. You mustn't go in there again. I forbid it.'

I bit on my lip, hard, it helped me to hold back and not say what I was thinking of saying because it would have been rude. How dare he? Forbid it! Who did he think he was, my father? How could he say those things about Rory who was just being nice to me? I went into the lounge and fiddled with the stuff on the coffee table, straightening the magazines and books, but before I'd finished, I returned to the kitchen and squaring up to my very imperious husband said, 'It's actually up to me what I do with my time, I have lots of it now and if I want to go exploring I'm perfectly all right to do so. If it were dangerous it would have security fencing and stuff around it.' I was just short of a foot stamp to emphasise my point, and a childish pout to boot.

'Martha,' said Steve, coughing and bending forward with the pain of it. 'I have no problem with anything you do, but I do wish you'd be sensible. You know what you're like; you love rooting around and exploring. It's the journo in you; I just don't want you to be a dead journo.' He did have a point; my wise, sensible maths teacher husband who lived in a logical world of black and white where everything had to be safety checked. He was right.

'Anyway, I'm going back to bed.' He coughed again. 'I feel crap.'

I poured myself a glass of wine and went back to the lounge to watch some television but I turned it off after the news, when the soap opera theme tune began. There was nothing on worth watching. I picked up the copy of Land magazine and, finding the article about Rory, I read it all over again. Steve had every right to be pissed off with me, and he wasn't well either.

After we'd seen the knot garden, I had gone back with Rory to his house for a cup of tea and, ostensibly, to let Scooter out, at least that's what I told myself. I was in a dreamlike state as I sat next to him in the front of his pickup, bathing in the glow of a lovely afternoon. He drove slowly, unlike Steve, and we took in everything around us:

the low-lying sun on the rolling hills that were crowned by the Wychwood Forest; the glint of the windows of the lone farmhouse on the top road surrounded by fields and high hedges.

'There is so much out here to take your breath away,' he said. 'The mists in the morning towards Kingham are just beautiful, I often get up early to photograph them.'

'You mentioned that in your article,' I said.

'Oh, so you've read it, know all about me eh?'

'I did, I obtained a back copy,' I told him. 'It was good.'

'I've got six copies, you should have just asked me.'

'Six?'

'Yeah, a couple of file copies to show clients, one for the coffee table which I keep placing on the top over and over again, and three more, one each for the kids. Not that any of them remembered to take their copy home with them.' He sounded quite flat about that.

'Tell me about them.'

'There are three.'

'So I gathered.'

'Amy, Jason and the baby, Emily.' He was obviously proud of them.

'How old?'

'Twenty, seventeen and fourteen.'

'What are they doing?'

'Uni, college and school, a very expensive school.'

'Ouch.'

'Exactly. That's three of them now and I'm still not sure I got anything like value for money.'

'And your ex?'

'She's a bit annoying.'

'They all are, aren't they?' I said, laughing.

'Yes, but she's annoyingly happy with a new man who the kids seem to adore. He's called Brett. Isn't that the most annoying bloody name for the man who stole your wife?'

'Yes,' I said, fighting back a smile. 'It is.'

'It's okay. You can laugh, if you like. I'm over it now, and plus, I've run out of pins.'

'Effigy?'

'Yes, and before you ask it didn't work. I used to have dreams of him suddenly keeling over clutching his heart and his balls, but that never happens in real life.'

I couldn't help myself; I roared laughing and he joined in so that, as we pulled up at the back of The Mill House, we were both still giggling like idiots.

He opened the front door and we both stood back whilst Scooter burst out, almost bending himself in two with his exuberance, his tail thumping against our legs.

Rory made tea and set a match to the fire he'd laid earlier.

The flames were soon roaring up the chimney and I was sitting on his worn leather sofa, hands wrapped around my mug. He came and sat down beside me and we watched the flames licking at the applewood logs.

'My final fire of spring,' he said. 'I just wanted one more before it warms up.'

I leaned back, my muscles relaxing into the leather. 'It's May and yet it's so cold.'

'I know, yet last week it was lovely.'

'Don't you find the seasons more unpredictable now?' I sipped my tea.

'I suspect that's been said every year since the year dot.'

I felt warm, suspended in a moment I could have bottled forever, like the Jim Croce song. "If I had time in a bottle..."

'Tell me about your husband,' Rory said after a while, he was relaxed and switched off.

'He's tall, has darkish hair, greying and its curly, not as much as it once was. He's got all his hair, like you, a good amount of it.'

'I'll take that as a compliment.'

'You may.'

'And?'

'Oh, yes, he's very straightforward, has a dry sense of humour. He doesn't do silly, he just doesn't get it. And he's terribly punctual and organised, more than me for sure. Oh, and he likes hill-walking, a bit of fishing from time to time, and the news.'

'What does he do for a living?'

'Maths teacher, he loves it. I can't think of anything more boring but he maintains that maths is the most beautiful thing in the world.'

'It can be,' said Rory, surprising me. 'It can be very beautiful, but I'm more of a trees in autumn, kingfishers, nude woman sort of a guy.' When I looked across at him he was raising an eyebrow and then he chuckled. 'But if maths is your thing...'

'It's not mine. I'd rather saw off an arm than do any maths. When I started out, I was a production assistant in a small publishing company in Carterton and I had to measure in points, picas and ems. I still don't know what I was doing–' I stopped talking, that silly memory of that first job brought me up short and, for a moment, I completely lost focus.

Rory reached across and put his hand on mine. I flinched and almost moved mine away, but something stopped me. He squeezed my hand. It was so small under his, and so pale, given the outdoor brown of his skin. He had hair on the back of his hand, like Steve's, but different, more dense.

'Martha.'

'Yes?'

'Find something that makes you happy.' I felt a knot rise in my throat and the sudden irrational feeing that I wanted to cry. 'Don't stay lost like this, find your truth.'

I wanted to turn and face him, to search in his eyes for the answers, but the prim and proper Martha took over. She leaned forward and placed her cup on the low coffee table then stood up. 'I think you'd better take me home,' I heard her say.

22

I could hear low voices: Alice and then a French accent, then Alice again.

'He's… the doctors said… long time…'

I strained to hear, without moving, so that I did not attract attention.

'Very difficult for you… will he never be able to…' It was her voice, more lovely for the softness in it.

'Cécile?' My voice was shredded, rasping, my mouth dry, and Alice was there immediately gently lifting my head and raising a glass of water to my lips.

'Cécile?' She was tender and caring as she let me sink back into the pillow.

'My darling, she is not here but she will be back soon, she and George have gone for a walk.'

I felt the wave of warmth overcome me, the need to sleep. Alice's fingers were on my forehead, cool. Her lips were moving, but I wasn't hearing anything. Then she was Cécile again, the refined features, the dark brown eyes, hazel, no not hazel, emerald. I sank into sleep and dreamed that I was back on Jester.

The sun was high, we were riding together kicking the horses on across bright green meadows and through sunlit groves and she was there, on Beau, Cécile, her hair streaming behind her as we galloped.

When I awoke again my room was empty, a half haze coming from the windows, the drapes not yet drawn. There were no lights on and no sound so, just for a minute or two, my mind had to adjust to where I was. I ran my hand over the cotton sheets and grasped the silk eiderdown. I was at home, at Lapston, I was safe. I flung back the covers and went to the mirror but what I saw made my stomach lurch. The man in the reflection was old and drawn, his skull visible under the skin, eyes bloodshot. I shook my head but he wouldn't go. He was staring at me with incredulity and a sense of horror too.

I went to my bathroom and switched on my shaving light. He was still there, grey and pathetic. I cleaned my teeth and washed my face, slicking back my hair with Brylcreem. As I stepped back, I thought I looked a little better but it was not a huge improvement; my eyes were still bloodshot. I changed into a fresh shirt and tie wondering who had undressed me and put me in bed – Grant more than likely.

The hall was dimly lit as if the whole house was playing dead to help me sleep. A crack of light from the library stretched across the tiled floor, and from somewhere I could hear muffled voices. I began my descent down the stairs, hearing the voices that were clearly coming from the direction of the lounge. Then Grant came out of the double doors, carrying a platter atop his fingers. He didn't see me, and I watched as he swept past to the kitchens.

As I stood outside the door, waiting for the moment when I should enter and not break rudely into the conversation, I heard George saying; 'Should I wake him?'

There was a short break before Alice replied, 'No, sleep will help him. Mummy always said if you need sleep your body will ask for it.'

Cécile spoke. 'It is so distressing to think that such a lovely man is suffering like that. I wonder how many more are the same?'

'Unfortunately it can't be helped, but it's over now and we must battle on. After all, we none of us have come through unscathed.' That was George.

'How is your hip now?' Alice asked.

'Oh no trouble, no trouble,' her brother replied. 'Been through a lot worse at school.' There was a chortle between Alice and George, then I heard George explaining our private school system to Cécile.

I stepped out of the shadows and into the room, which seemed extraordinarily bright. They all stood up as I entered, and Alice put her glass down and came toward me. She kissed me and drew me in. 'Carrick, I am so pleased to see you up. You've been asleep for hours, since you–'

'Yes, yes, Alice, thank you. I believe I must thank you too, Madame?'

Cécile looked a little surprised, but she nodded and smiled.

'Good to have you back, old boy.' George clapped me on the back. 'Sherry?'

'Yes please,' I said and, as we took our seats, Alice patted the place next to her and I knew what she was indicating, but I chose instead to sit beside Cécile.

'Are you feeling better?' Alice asked.

I informed her that I was. 'I should imagine all that exercise was too much, too soon.'

'That's what the doctor said, take it more slowly.' George handed me my drink. 'It doesn't do to go against medical advice, old man.'

I was irritated that they were talking about it because a man's health is, after all, his own affair. 'What time is it? I can't find my watch?'

'Oh, it is here.' Cécile stood up and moved across to an occasional table. 'Ogden brought it in. You must have dropped it on the lawn. We are lucky to have him.'

We? George did not so much as flinch and it passed Alice by too. We? She handed me the watch and I wrapped it around my wrist, but as I tried to fasten it, I was fumbling, the most frustrating long-term symptom of my condition.

'Here, let me,' she said and leaned down so that I was looking directly at her décolletage, her skin white as porcelain and the soft roundness of her breasts held fast in a black velvet bodice.

The watch was soon on. Her fingers being nimble and quick, made short work of it. She stood back and I saw her hips turning away from me, and the roundness of her derrière moving under the velvet. When she had gone, I found myself face to face with Alice and I saw in her a rather ugly female envy. Perhaps not quite, but certainly

141

she was unsettled by my closeness to Cécile. Was it my fault? I think not.

Alice was quiet at dinner whilst George, by comparison, was quite animated. 'Carrick, we walked down to the village at four and saw that big brute of a stag in the woods, he was standing there bold as you like, wasn't he, Cécile?'

'He was. I have never seen one that close, except in a zoo.'

'We should have a day's shooting, Carrick,' George suggested and ordinarily, and certainly before the war, I should have jumped at the chance to go deer stalking, but I had completely lost the heart for it.

'Maybe later in the winter,' I said dully, and Alice must have mouthed something at George for he changed course midstream.

'I was telling Cécile about the ball. Those days are long gone now but I remember, as a child, watching from the top of the stairs, the dancing in the dining room, the colour and the music, such a spectacle.'

'It was on the wane by the time I was born,' said Alice. 'I have always been rather miffed about that, but I suppose things will never be the same again.' She sighed.

There was a moment of stillness as Henry entered our hearts and left just as quickly. It would always be so; his ghost was something we had to accommodate from here on.

'I recall Christmas, all those candles in the windows and the snow, the people arriving in furs, the wreath Mrs Hall and I made for the front door. When the rationing is over, we should make every effort to bring back Christmas, it would be so very lovely,' said Alice. She was a little more cheerful for the thought of it.

'I'm just glad we three have made it through,' said George. 'I feel that every occasion we are together will be a very special one, to be savoured, and I am doubly glad to welcome Cécile to Lapston. Her coming here may have been under the saddest of circumstances but how very joyful it has been, for all of us. May I also be so bold as to say it has warmed my heart, in particular, to be able to meet the lady who won my brother's.'

I watched them both. She was looking at him demurely, he with something akin to self-satisfaction but when she turned away from him, it was me she looked at, the special regard you see only in the eyes of a companion of the heart.

23

'Hello Simon. What a surprise!' It was pouring down and standing on my doorstep, dripping wet, was Simon from the church.

'Hello Martha. I've brought something for you.'

'Come in.' I stepped back and ushered him into the hall.

'I say, what a lovely house,' he said as I helped him off with his drenched walking coat. 'It's what they call a villa, isn't it?'

'It is. Pass me your coat and I'll hang it in the utility room.' He followed me, a briefcase pressed to his chest as I sorted out the coat. 'What a foul day.'

'I know, but I had to be up this end to deliver the Parish newsletter. I once saw a postcard, you know, it had two pictures side by side, both the same cartoon of sheep huddled together in the rain. One caption read "Britain in the Winter," the other said "Britain in the Summer." I thought it was very funny.'

'And true!' I added. We made our way to the kitchen were I was cooking a batch of scones and the smell of them was divine. Over the past fortnight, I had discovered my inner Mary Berry, and Steve and I were both growing fat as I experimented with tray bakes and puddings.

'Can I do you a cup of tea and a scone?' I asked.

'Ooh, rather, I'm famished.' The ting of the bell was telling me the scones were ready and I lifted them out of the oven feeling outlandishly proud of myself even though my mother used to produce such things all the time.

'Maybe a new career is unfolding,' said Simon. 'Those look extremely good. I don't suppose I can interest you in running the church fête cake stall?'

'No, but you can interest me in making a cake for it,' I said kindly. 'I don't do anything related to religion.'

'Really? May I ask why?'

'Wars, famine, tsunamis, cruelty, sick children, you name it I cannot see that any loving God could allow those things to happen.'

'Yes, fair point, that is the standard non-believer's reply, I see it rather differently. You see, the whole God thing needs to be taken apart and reconstructed, oh that we were allowed to, but to me it means cohesion, community, helping those who are poorly or not well off. It helps those who have lost their way too, gives them a moral compass.' I placed the jam and cream on the table and poured hot water into the teapot to warm it. 'I think God is in here.' He patted his chest. 'If only people would seek to find it in themselves.'

'I think two thousand years of the beardy old man on the cloud has caused the problem,' I replied. 'I'd be much more open to your inner God theory, but that belies the need for organised religion, doesn't it?'

He nodded. 'Quite so, but what would happen to all the beautiful churches? I love the buildings, the sheer craftsmanship.' I piled the warm scones on a plate and put them in front of him, the smell was mouth-watering. 'Goodness,' he said, 'I called at just the right time, didn't I?'

We dived into them and they were delicious.

'Would you like to know a secret?'

'Go on,' he said, eyes alight.

'I've never made scones before.'

Then we were laughing and discussing the last series of the Bake Off like two old friends.

'Anyway, talking of old beautiful buildings as we were doing before your gorgeous scones, I have some thing to show you,' he said.

He lifted his briefcase up onto his knee and unclipped it.

'Look at this.' He passed me a blue plastic file. It was the front page of a newspaper, the local rag. "Priceless items stolen from Lapston Manor," the words big and bold. I looked up at the date, seventh of March 1921. Under the picture of the house, the same front door, was a three-column news piece.

"Three brothers were apprehended last night in the grounds of Lapston Manor by police officers who had lain in wait to apprehend the villains. The thieves resisted arrest and the youngest of them sustained a serious injury and is now under the care of the doctor. Charges have been brought against the burglars who are known to police as Thomas Edwards (20), Richard Edwards (18) and Harold Edwards (16) all of whom were found with silver and other stolen items of value in their possession."

I looked up at Simon who was watching my face for a reaction.

'Goodness. It was Lapston,' I said. 'I knew about this from the history group.'

"The owners of Lapston Manor were not present at the time but their butler, a Mr Fellowes, said he had been awoken by a strange sound at two o'clock which had set the dogs barking. The thieves had entered through an unsecured window in the library."

'Where did you get this?'

'Wouldn't you like to know?' said Simon mischievously. 'Actually, it was my very own mother, I was visiting her last Wednesday and we got onto you and your visit to the church and that you mentioned Lapston. Blow me if she didn't stand up, walk across the room, open up a drawer and produce this little lot!'

'Wow,' was all I could say.

'I know. It was the last thing I expected from dear old Mama. She had simply kept hold of them because they were connected to someone she knew, a lady called Sally Fitzgerald, daughter of the sister of the brothers. Does that make sense?'

'Yes, and again wow.'

'I know but that's not all. Look in there.' He pointed to the file lying beside me on the table. There was a small press cutting, about two inches square.

"A court in Moreton, Gloucestershire, today found Mr James Fellowes guilty of aiding and abetting a burglary on the sixth of March, 1921 at Lapston Manor. Mr Fellowes, an employee of the Amsherst family since 1910, confessed to police following questioning. Mr Fellowes will be sentenced in April, at a date and time yet to be confirmed."

'Well I never,' I said, holding the small piece of paper out in front of me. 'The butler did it in the library! May I keep these for a few days?'

'No need. I made copies on the vicar's photocopier.' Simon handed me an A4 envelope from his case. 'And before you ask, I've made a copy for our local history buffs too.'

'Oh well done, Simon.' It was to be my next question. 'I'm really grateful, in fact this earns you another scone.'

24

George was talking with great animation and I could only imagine that something had come over him. We were all struggling, each in our own way, with Henry's death and all of us were quietly mourning him, making mention of him at a suitable juncture, but none of us had yet thrown our heads back and roared with laughter. George was doing so now and I felt nothing but embarrassment for him and for the situation.

George and I were the closest of friends, but he had hardly spoken a word to me since Cécile had arrived. Granted, I had been confined, but there was a time when we sought each other out quite naturally for example, both reading the papers together in the morning room post breakfast or enjoying a cigar after dinner. These simple pleasures seemed to have been on the wane since Cécile had arrived.

'Are there still nine holes open at the club? I thought it might be nice to golf tomorrow, George.' I said this almost as an extension of my thoughts.

'What? Oh yes, that is no. I'm afraid I cannot, old chap.'

'What a shame,' I said through my teeth. 'What are you up to?'

'Why I am taking our delightful guest to meet the Fosters.'

'The Fosters?'

'Yes, I thought it would be a pleasant change of scenery and they should be delighted I'm sure to meet Cécile.'

Cécile was sipping her soup, her eyes not meeting mine. 'I should have thought the Fosters a little old hat,' I said sharply. 'Surely we have better acquaintances who would be, shall we say, of more interest.'

Alice, who had been extremely quiet until that point, put down her spoon and said, 'I think that is a little unfair, Carrick. Sir Gerald and Lady Beatrice are the most charming of couples and their house and particularly the gardens, are an absolute delight.' I felt slapped down, like an annoying spaniel. I continued with my soup.

George, who has never given any quarter to angry silence, stepped in. 'My dear, you will simply love the topiary gardens and they have a collection of rare ducks called Mandarins, they are charming little things.'

The Fosters' unending drivel about their birdlife was so dire I could think of nothing worse for Cécile, who had surely lived such a cosmopolitan life in the city.

'Do you like ducks?' I asked her impudently.

'I have nothing to say about them, except they taste very pleasing,' she replied and this made us all hoot, particularly George who seemed to find it extremely amusing. Perhaps, I thought, she has been able to lighten the atmosphere and good for her, given what she had been through.

It wasn't until after George and Alice had gone to bed that I found myself alone with Cécile. Dinner had been all prattle but, after dinner, we talked of the new way forward, how we each saw the future and what would happen to Churchill. Alice said there were rumours that he was very ill. George was fearful of further inheritance tax and the ramifications for the house. The plain truth was that we had nothing left to sell to maintain it, especially if any surprises were to come along. We had replaced our most expensive works of art with cheap copies, purchases made in Stow, or worse, my own paintings which all felt rather desperate. The silverware had survived the burglary in twenty-one, only to fall foul of inheritance tax when Sir Reginald passed away.

Cécile was beautiful in the lamplight as she stood by the piano, looking at a picture of a young Henry. She had her hair up in a chignon. It looked glossy and immaculate, so much so I wanted to reach out and touch it. She sipped a glass of water, her fingers enhanced by a glinting ring on her right hand, third finger.

'Are you not tired, Carrick?' she asked as she placed the photograph back into place.

'I've slept too much today to be tired.'

'Me too. That is I am not tired, the night is yet young.'

I stood up and moved towards her. That was my cue, the chance to talk to her more intimately, but she turned and walked away.

She moved over to the globe and gently pushed it so that it rotated under her hand. 'Tell me, Carrick, where have you been? In the world, I mean.'

I quickly moved to stand beside her, her hand lingering over Africa. 'I have been to Cape Town,' I told her. 'My father met me for a holiday there. I travelled out by boat with another family who were emigrating. I was eighteen.'

'And what was it like?'

'Cape Town?' I said, placing my finger alongside hers. 'It was very beautiful.' I was drinking in the fragrance she wore; I could smell roses.

'I have heard they have purple trees there. Someone, I forget who, once told me about them.'

'The Jacaranda trees,' I said, my voice still little more than a murmur.

She looked up at me, her eyes so warm, so honest, I could see everything in them, everything I needed to know.

'Are they as beautiful as my friend told me they are?' she asked softly. I was hypnotised by her lips, so full, a fresh application of red lipstick on them.

'They are.' I leaned in towards her. 'They are as beautiful as you are, Cécile.'

She moved away again, leaving me standing, teasing me. I could feel myself reacting to her. She was everything I had ever wanted in a woman. I followed her to the sofa and we sat down. At first I thought we might sit together but she placed herself at the near end of the couch, in front of the coffee table, and was therefore blocking my way, so that it would have been ungainly to try. Begrudgingly, I took a seat opposite.

'May I have a cigarette?' she asked. I told her sourly that the box was in front of her and then I thought better of myself, and relenting, I stood up to light it for her.

'I should like to return to Oxford on Sunday,' she said,

blowing the smoke into the air between us. I sat up, tapped the ash from my own cigarette, and immediately asked if I might escort her.

She looked at me, eyes half-closed behind the smoke, those terrifyingly attractive cats eyes that could fix on me and demand my attention. 'I should very much like you to escort me, Carrick, I shall look forward to travelling with you as I am not sure of myself in England.' A feeling came over me then such as I had never really known prior to that moment, not in all my life. I felt the first strands of the joy of love wrapping around my heart and pulling themselves tight. I knew that in Oxford I should have her all to myself.

25

I was determined to stay away from Rory. It had been nice, an interlude and a reminder of those first tentative steps of a relationship, of being fancied even, ridiculous as that might sound. However, I was sixty and laughter lines were appearing round my eyes, the skin was starting to crinkle under my chin.

Steve and I had been together forty-two years, a lifetime. I had met him at our local youth club, he a gangly youth who was good at pool, me a real sight with a beehive and thick black eye-liner. We'd passed the stage of lovemaking and become good companions, best friends. That's what I read everywhere; you just accept each other and rub along neither of you making overtures or silly declarations. I knew that whilst talk of future plans had diminished and Steve had become less outgoing over time, we were absolutely certain of each other.

When the envelope dropped on my mat, I knew it was from Rory. I went to the window and saw him striding down the hill, with Scooter straining on the leash. I tore the envelope open and saw it was a postcard.

"Meet me at the gates at four tomorrow."

No signature, just an instruction, something I wouldn't

have equated with him. I pressed the card to my lips and breathed in. I could smell him, the countryside, fresh air, earth.

Steve was at school. It had taken him so long to recover from the virus I had been worried. He had been very weakened by it and started talking of retiring and, to my dismay, of moving to Wales. I wrote a cheerful note, telling him I'd gone to look for a birthday card and a present for Becky in Chipping Norton. I had already bought both.

Rory was leaning against the four by four, his hands in his pockets and as I pulled up, he smiled.

'Hi,' he said as I climbed out of the car. 'Was I mysterious enough?'

'Very,' I heard whining and a repeated thumping sound from inside his car.

'Are you ready for the black bomber?'

I had on my old clothes and girding my loins, standing square on two feet as Rory opened the door of the pick up, I was prepared. Scooter launched himself from it like he'd been shot from a cannon. He was soon sucking my arm and then he bounded off as if he knew where we were going.

'Follow him,' Rory said, motioning me towards a narrow bridleway that led along the outside of the wall to the woods.

The tree cover was dense as we walked along a narrow path.

At the end was a low iron kissing-gate. Rory slipped through it then held it open for Scooter who bent his way around it like an eel.

'Kissing gate,' Rory said with a mischievous twinkle in his eye, as he held it from the other side for me to pass through. I went through it with a smile.

Suddenly, I realised we were in an overgrown graveyard, the tops of gravestones just visible in the long grass. The worn path turned a corner, and as we rounded it, we were standing in front of an old church. The stone porch was small with an old noticeboard to one side. It still displayed yellowing notices that were held in place with rusty drawing pins. Rory used a similar key to the one for the house and let us in. Scooter was made to sit and wait for us in the porch, though I did wonder how long that would last.

The church was tiny, with box pews, the walls whitewashed, the wood dark brown. A tiny spiral staircase led up from just inside the door to a gallery. There were marble plaques on the walls around us with worn inscriptions. The altar was simple, a wooden table covered in a blue cloth, mildewed and stained with white marks. The whole church was no more than twenty-five feet in length whilst to the right in the middle of a small organ chamber was a stone font.

An old organ with stops and yellow keys was in the corner, its wooden sides leaning up against it as if they had fallen off when it was moved. There was an oven or fireplace of some sort in the wall opposite and a table with faded leaflets pushed up against the wall. It smelt damp, sad and neglected, though not as bad as Lapston itself. I leaned against one of the pews, taking it in. 'So this was the church for the house?'

'Yes, the families from the house used it, and their servants, for weddings, funerals, christenings.'

'And when it was a children's home?'

'I'm not sure. I've been told they used the morning room because it once had a stained-glass window, but I don't know for sure.'

I bent down and picked up something from the floor. It was a peg doll, two eyes drawn on it and a little strand of red woollen hair. I smiled because I made one just like it when I was a little girl.

I looked back up at the gallery over the door and then again at the opposite end. There was no colourful stained glass, just diamond-shaped leaded lights, but all of them transparent. Outside, I could see the waving branches of a beech tree.

We left the church and locked it. Quite predictably, Scooter had moved, no doubt on his elbows, from the porch to the nearest gravestone, and looked suitably guilty when he was reprimanded. Rory pushed against the heavy wooden door, making sure it was firmly locked. 'There are so many churches being burgled and vandalised these days, I come down here a lot to check on it. I hope anyone coming here thinks they might be caught in the act.'

The tall skirting wall of the house was running the full length of the graveyard; its Cotswold stone tumbling over in places. It would soon come crashing down and then anyone could invade Lapston's privacy.

'Through here,' Rory said, ducking and edging past a yew tree that took up almost all the space between wall and church. I followed him, the needles of yew caught on my jacket.

At the other side of it, he was standing in the mottled shade, pointing towards a gate. It was a small archway through the wall, the gate solid and, I presumed, locked, but Rory clicked the handle and it opened. All at once, we were in the grounds of Lapston again, this time on the west side. A gravel path led us up steeply to the sound of rushing water. Twenty feet away, the river was gurgling and spluttering through a cordon of rocks, then it fanned out to be much broader like a sheet of gold as it caught the sun's rays. It was roughly a square, a man-made pool, and on it, two swans swam galleon like on the surface, unfazed by the two humans who were suddenly standing on the bank looking down on them.

Lapston rose above us, majestically, the early evening sun warming its buttery walls. We picked up another path that curved back on itself as it ascended through the long grass and at the top appeared a wooden bench. It was old, lichen encrusted on its wooden slats, but it was sturdy enough. We sat and watched as three ducks quacked overhead, one of them peeling off, urging the others to change direction.

'Thank you,' said Rory.

'For what?'

'For waking me up to the beauty of Lapston, and its gorgeous little church again. It's only when you show someone around that you really appreciate these things.'

'Thank you for showing me,' I said. 'I've really enjoyed seeing them.'

We sat for a while watching the evening light settle on the meadow across the river. There were flies cutting shapes out of the air, the evening balmy, a thin clean air all around us. I felt like I could sleep here and never want to wake up.

'How many people have sat here I wonder?' I said lazily.

'Hundreds I expect,' he said. He was leaning back face to the sun, eyes closed. He was so easy to be with, so relaxed, so not Steve.

I had to be heading back soon but this was one of the most peaceful places I had ever been. I stole a glance at my watch it was five fifteen.

'I must go,' I said.

'Why?'

'Steve will be back from school soon and I have a casserole planned for tonight and I haven't even chopped the onions.'

'Martha,' he said.

'Yes?'

'I want to make love to you.'

26

The guests were gathered in the lounge, music blaring from the gramophone, a Bing Crosby number, I forget which. Alice, in a beautiful white silk dress that I had never seen before, was in full flow and her friends were gathered around her in a group. The chatter was dominated by the hee-haw laugh of Gerald Caruthers, he with his flat feet. The other chinless wonders with their reserved occupations were in tails; white pressed shirts relics all, from a time so long ago when no one had a care.

'Carrick, how lovely to see you.' It was Dylis Fullerton-Jones, dressed in a frilled thing, consuming her, making her seem asinine and old-fashioned. I was already used to the simple lines and style of French couture.

'Good evening, Dillie. I trust you are well?'

'I'm very well, thank you, and you?' She had a shrill voice. It had always been extremely annoying. 'How lovely of you all to host a party for us. Alice looks frightfully well and, in spite of everything, happy. I was so terribly upset to hear about Henry.'

I thanked her for her condolences and was wondering what I might say next when Cécile entered the room on George's arm. She was so stately, so very chic, as she proceeded into the lounge and made her way towards Alice.

The music crackled to a finish, leaving a suspended silence around the room whilst everyone had turned to look at the two of them. George looked incredibly proud as he greeted Alice with a kiss and introduced Cécile to the waiting guests, and I noted that Alice too was thoroughly enjoying herself. Grant was pouring champagne, a small glass for everyone. He had raided the cellars and brought up two of the last remaining bottles. I knew he had kept them back especially for these birthday celebrations and for the day of victory.

George tapped his glass and the conversation ceased, an expectant silence.

'I would like to take this opportunity to thank you all for joining us at Lapston. What a joy it is to see you here to celebrate the twenty fifth birthday of my dearest sister, Alice. For the three of us it has been a dreadful year.' Here he nodded towards Alice then myself. 'But we have come through because we are so supporting of one another.

'I would also like to welcome Madame Cécile Roussell, who, in a very short time, has been a blessing to us. She has lifted our spirits and I know that Henry would have been absolutely delighted to see us enjoying each other's company.

'And now to Alice's present from me. A little early, sister, but this party was the perfect diversion to stop you prying.' There was a murmur of laughter in the room and

Alice protested, but she was shouted down. 'Grant, if you would.' I suddenly realised that Grant, Mrs Hall and Lizzie were standing by the door, all three grinning.

Grant disappeared for a second and when he came back he was holding something in his arms. Dillie was blocking my view so that I had to move for a better one. Alice cried out loud when the thing was passed to George. It solicited such a joyful response I guessed what it was; a small black labrador puppy. George kissed Alice on the forehead as he handed over the little chap who yawned and made a delightful squeak.

'Oh thank you, George. How simply wonderful, how truly wonderful.' She was crying with joy, wiping the tears away with the back of her hand. She pressed the dog's small round head to her cheek and the puppy closed one eye about to fall asleep, his pink belly full, fat and round.

'Our last dog died back in thirty nine and it simply didn't seem right to have one since, but I, for one, cannot go on any longer without a canine around the place.' George rested a hand most lovingly on Alice's shoulder as she hugged the little black body to her neck. It was a truly moving moment but when my eyes wandered to Cécile, I being the only one who was watching her, it surprised me that her face was so impassive. She was entirely unmoved by what was, without a doubt, a most touching scene.

She was unaware of me watching her and, from her lack of reaction, I could only presume she did not like dogs. Whatever it was, she was most clearly unresponsive.

I was about to move towards her when I saw her expression alter, as if a light had switched on inside, for her whole countenance changed. I followed the direction of her eyes and saw that George was beaming at her and she was returning the warmth in his eyes.

Dillie began talking again, the whine in her voice so immensely irritating, I listened only to every other word. Her fiancé was due back shortly on leave, from the RAF. 'When do you imagine it will be over, Carrick?' I wasn't listening to her, instead I was watching Cécile talking to George, her hand lightly placed on his forearm. They were merry, her eyes almost glittering. I swallowed hard. 'What do you think, Carrick?' the whining continued.

'I do beg your pardon, Dillie. I must see Grant about something.' I touched the back of her arm and left her standing, a champagne glass in her hand and absolutely dumbfounded.

I was outside gulping for air, it was very important not to succumb. If I focussed on the knot garden, the play of moonlight on its low hedges and the faded colours of the dying roses between them, if I could just focus, I told myself, just focus.

'Carrick.' I spun around, my heart skipping a beat, but it was only Alice. She stood behind me looking like an apparition, a spectre in her white silk dress.

'Alice. You made me start; I didn't expect you.'

'You thought I was our lady ghost?'

We used to invent ghosts as children, George and I, to frighten the life out of Alice. She was always incredibly unaffected in fact, on reflection, I think we scared ourselves more.

'Do you remember when you locked me in the secret cupboard in the attic so that I could watch her through the fretwork? Only you forgot I was up there and one of the maids had to come and find me. What was I, five?'

I nodded. 'Some such young, impressionable age,' I said as she moved towards me. 'I fear we were very cruel to you.'

'You could have damaged me psychologically for the rest of my life,' she replied.

The moon was high and a sliver of silver light touched her hair. In contrast, the glow from the lounge was poor since the dim out was still in force. She looked very pretty and so young.

'Instead, ironically, it was me,' I said.

She took my hand and held it in both of hers. I didn't remove it for it was comforting.

'Carrick, I have something to say, something I have been meaning to say for a very long time.'

'What is it?'

'In spring last year, you proposed to me,' she said. 'Do you remember?'

How could I forget, the embarrassment and awkwardness was seared into my mind. 'What of it?' I asked.

'Carrick, darling,' she continued. 'I want to tell you that I made a mistake; I refused you, it was foolish of me.'

'It's of no import,' I said stiffly.

'Oh, but it was because you stopped writing to me. I

know you were terribly hurt, I realise that now.'

I turned my face away and let go of her hand, unable to think of what to say next, but she filled that space for me.

'I want you to know, if you asked me again I would say yes, I wouldn't hesitate.'

'Mouse, I–'

She placed her fingers against my lips. 'Don't say anything, I don't want to rush you.' She took hold of my hands again. 'But I want you to know that, for my part, I love you and I always have. I was young and foolish in turning you down. I think we could be happy together, I am certain we could make each other happy. I know this now and I want to look after you. I–'

'Alice stop, stop this nonsense.' I stepped away angrily, shaking her off me. 'Stop it.'

She looked terribly confused and understandably quite alarmed. 'Carrick.' She grasped for my hands once more, but I pulled them away angrily.

'Stop it, Alice.' I put my head in my hands.

'Are you unwell, darling?'

'No, will you stop asking that, Alice. No!' I wheeled round, confronting her.

'Alice, I love someone else. You are too late. Please leave me alone.'

She was speechless, her hands dropping to her sides. For a moment, she was staring at me, an ugly frozen moment, her eyes searching mine for answers to impossible, unspeakable questions. Then she turned and walked away, the gravel crunching underfoot.

I waited five minutes, heat blazing through my body, and then I went back into the house and straight upstairs to my room.

I pulled out my suitcase and packed.

I would be leaving with Cécile as early as possible the next day.

27

'Rory, I–'

'Don't say no, please don't let me down.'

'I must go,' I said, but I didn't mean it and I didn't move an inch.

He shifted along the bench and sat next to me. Gently, he placed his arm around my shoulders and we sat staring across the meadows. A lone butterfly fluttered around us and was gone in an instant. I felt the weight of his arm, the arc of it around my shoulders.

Neither of us spoke.

The river was gushing between its banks. The old church, at the foot of the slope of tangled grasses, stood unmoved behind the crumbling wall, a keeper of secrets for all time. I didn't want this perfect moment to end. I sank back into him and he brushed my hair with his lips.

'I wouldn't make you do anything you didn't agree to. If this was the only moment I ever had with you I'd accept it,' he said softly.

'I couldn't do it to Steve,' I told Rory honestly. 'Not after all this time.'

'Have either of you ever been unfaithful?'

'No, it's never been anything other than him and me.'

Rory sighed, but didn't move. We sat together for ten or fifteen minutes, in absolute silence, and the thing that bothered me most was that I felt completely comfortable and secure in him, like nothing would or could ever come between us.

'I must go,' I said as a heron launched its lazy flapping wings into the sky, causing enough distraction to stir me to action. He removed his arm and we stood up, the sun's heat had warmed us both, the feeling of relaxation was hard to break.

Back at the gates, I watched Scooter leap into the four by four.

'I can't, Rory, I just can't, but if I could.'

'I know, you would. All the nice girls say that.' He slammed the door shut. 'Well, don't say I didn't ask politely.' He was such a kind and giving man.

I smiled and kissed him lightly on the cheek and he pulled me to him, resting his head on top of mine and his hug was strong, it consumed me and I couldn't pull away. There in the sanctuary of his body lay another way, a chance to change, move on, find a new me, but at what cost?'

'Don't mind me!' The voice was jovial but the shock of it, breaking in on us, took me completely by surprise.

It was Simon. He was wearing walking boots and a gilet and was holding a Nordic walking stick in each hand. He was almost upon us as I pulled away from Rory, my face scorched with embarrassment.

'Hello Martha. So sorry to interrupt a moment between you two. My only option was to go back in the other direction, but I need to use the footpath past the church, you see.' He held up his walking sticks as if he thought it might explain.

I stared at him searching for something to say. 'Hello Simon, I er, I...'

'You must be Martha's husband,' he said brightly. He freed a hand from the loop in his stick and moved forward extending it towards Rory.

This was a truly ghastly, awful moment, and if there was a God he was already paying me back for my adulterous thoughts. I ran through all the things I might say, all the lies I might come up with to convince Simon that I was not a cheating wife.

'We're actually good friends,' said Rory. 'I'm working on a project with Martha, the history group's book. Martha and I have just been exploring Lapston's old church.'

'Really,' Simon said, looking from Rory to me and then up at the gates behind us. I didn't dare look at him, I felt so ashamed.

Rory continued. 'We're old friends, Martha got me an article in Land magazine last year and I was delighted to repay the favour by showing her around. Have you seen the house?' He was so controlled and unfazed whilst I, at the same time, was beginning to tremble.

'No, I've never seen it,' Simon said, stepping back.

When I finally made eye contact with him, I could tell that he was weighing up the situation. I saw something in the look he gave me, a frozen stare matched by thin judgmental lips. 'Jolly good. Anyway, I must be off, I have to set the church up for the Evergreens tea party.' He pressed on, following the path below the one we'd taken to the church. He kept his head held erect and didn't look back. I knew he had seen through us.

'Oh my God.' I ran my hands through my hair. 'I can't believe it, of all the people, I hardly know anyone in the village and the one person I like and have only just met sees me out here with you. I just can't bloody believe it.'

'He won't say anything. His type never do.'

'You mean good honest people with morals.'

'Martha, you gave me a hug. We haven't broken any laws, we hugged.'

I walked towards my car, my mind racing, and as I opened the door, I said; 'I'm sorry, Rory, truly.' He didn't react, he just looked at me and I felt wretched. He was still standing, gazing after me as I did a three-point turn and drove away.

28

George looked over Cécile's shoulder at me, his expression forbidding. 'I had no idea you were going back to Oxford today, Carrick.'

'I'm sorry, old man, I thought I mentioned it,' I replied with insouciance. 'As it happens, it fits in well with Cécile's plans and I can escort her.'

'But what of Alice, will you be back in time for her birthday?'

'Yes, yes, of course,' I said, answering for both Cécile and myself. I saw her head move a little to the side, but she didn't turn to look directly at me.

'She is organising a special meal for us all.' He stepped forward and kissed Cécile on both cheeks. 'Please come back, my dear. We would love to have you representing Henry at the table.'

'Of course, George. It would be my honour. This is only au revoir,' She kissed him lightly on both cheeks. We climbed into the trap and, as Ogden flicked his whip over the cob's wide rump, I saw George look crestfallen, but it did not weigh heavily on me because it was the moment I felt I had taken charge of the situation.

The day was glorious, the dying days of summer giving way to a quite splendid autumn, and red and gold tipped leaves lined the fields of Oxfordshire as we passed through. The train journey was too short, too simple and I should have preferred to have been going further in her company. She asked me about my flat and Peterson, from whom I leased it, and I explained that he was still fighting in Normandy with the Grenadiers. We talked of Paris and London before the war and of her taste for escargots and my aversion to them. She was wearing a red jacket and a cheerful silk scarf knotted loosely around her neck. The spirit between us was light, the connection strong. From time to time, when she was looking elsewhere, I looked down at her legs. She wore stockings, unlike Alice, and I imagined running my fingers inside the band and rolling them down her thighs.

She marvelled at the spires rising up above us, and the beauty of the colleges with their immaculate emerald green quads. I smiled because this beautiful city suddenly seemed to be beckoning me onwards to a new life, a life with her, and I think she knew it too.

'Is your studio here in the centre?' We were standing at Carfax and I was about to ask her if she would like to meet for luncheon.

'No, it is just over Folly Bridge. Would you like to see it?'

'Yes, I would please.'

It warmed my heart to think she was so interested in my art and I instantly regretted my lack of recent work. My studio was on the southern bank of the river, tucked away behind a line of willow trees. The grass was wet with dew, and small droplets rolled over the tips of our shoes as we walked towards it. It was above a boathouse and there was a small lobby at the rear and a narrow flight of stairs that led up to the first floor. I led the way, still carrying her small valise. She followed, her footfall light on the steps behind me.

'Through here.' I pointed to the small studio. It was dominated by a large half-moon window that cast a good deal of light across my desk and easel, the very reason I had rented it in the first place.

The air in the room was stifling so I pushed open the roof light and the atmosphere lightened immediately. She removed her coat and laid it over the back of my chaise longue. My work was spread across various surfaces, the many sketches and watercolours I had completed over several years. The few that pleased me were framed on the wall.

Cécile lifted up a small watercolour and inspected it closely. 'Where is this?'

'That is the church at Lapston.'

'I thought so. George showed me around it. It is beautiful, Carrick, a fine piece of work.'

'Thank you.'

She moved across to my plan chest, the sketch on top was a nude, a pencil study from art college, I had been using as reference. 'And this?'

I stepped to her side. I could smell the roses on her skin again. She was wearing a light woollen sweater, cream in colour. I could see the strap of her brassiere through the weave. I wanted to lay my hand on her shoulder, feel it under my touch.

'That is something I did as a student.'

'It is masterful.' She turned towards me and I then was standing so close to her, I could feel her breath on my cheek. Her eyes were soft, drawing me to her. I lifted my hand to cup her chin, it felt natural and right but she moved to one side, away from me. 'I wonder if you might draw me, I would like a nude done.'

A lightning bolt of shock ran through me, the frisson of nerves seeming to swamp me for the moment. She was asking to be naked before me.

'I would… would love to,' I stammered. The deep surge of energy I had felt inside subsided, a warmth overtook me, for this was it, this was everything I had wished for.

'Then I will be here at ten,' she said calmly as she shrugged on her jacket. 'Would you please tell me how to find my hotel. It is not far from here I think?'

She was staying at The Angel Hotel on The High.

I insisted on walking her there and, as we arrived, the pavement was spattered with polka dots of warm rain.

I thought she might let me kiss her there and then, but we were in the street so when her lips brushed each cheek and she moved away from me, I simply said: 'Au revoir,' for the following day she would be all mine.

As I pulled away from her, I noticed a telephone box some sixty feet along the road, a blue Jaguar parked beside it. I felt so uplifted by my journey into Oxford, and my time in Cécile's company, that I wanted everyone to be happy, including Alice. I felt the urgent need to apologise to her but, as I was about to dial, my attention was attracted to a flash of red, in the corner of my eye, coming out of the hotel.

It was her, Cécile. She was standing looking away from me, her hand shielding her eyes. I pushed on the stiff door. It was obvious to me she was looking to see if I was still in the vicinity. I strode towards her, raising my hand so that she might see me as she turned around.

Then I halted, for a companion, a man of medium build wearing a trilby and tweed overcoat, was joining her. She kissed him on both cheeks and linked her arm with his. I watched them cross the road and both were running a little as the rain fell more heavily. I could smell the pavements, the sand in the concrete becoming wet beneath my feet, creating that uniquely English scent.

I think my hand may have still been raised in the air, ready to wave, as she turned the corner and disappeared, with him, into Turl Street.

29

I watched Steve as he sipped his wine. We were sitting in the garden, him reading a Stephen Hawking book, me with a women's magazine closed on my lap. I wanted him to ask me if I was okay, take some notice of me, just once tell me again that he loved me. Does this happen in marriage, especially a seasoned marriage, the passion replaced by a trusting companionship? I wanted to scream at him, "Steve, another man wants me, you must fight for me."

I constantly revisited every minute of the afternoon with Rory in my mind. The memory was glorious with colour, like a painting I could travel over, examining every tiny detail. The church; the narrow shingle path up from the river to the bench; the half hour or so sitting next to him; Scooter lying below us in the long grass, panting.

There was a bumblebee on the pot of flowers next to me. I could hear its angry buzzing as it tried to fly with its legs heavily laden with pollen. That was me; my burden being the life I had built with my husband, what would it be like, I wondered, to fly away?

It was a few days later, I saw Simon in the churchyard as I walked past with Inca. He was talking to a young couple and I guessed they were discussing their wedding plans. I nodded at him and he was about to acknowledge me but his face darkened, just a little, and he looked away. He knew.

I found every day away from Rory harder than the one before. I thought about everything else, cleaned the house, baked cakes, worked on the project, but my mind constantly returned to him. Each time I saw him, Lapston Manor and its secret and incredible knot garden.

'Have you found anything else about Lapston?' Angela Gattis and I were sitting in the front room of her little cottage. The curtains and sofa coverings were chintz and the carpet, threadbare in places, had seen long service. Her pretty rose tea set was very old, but by far the finest china I'd seen in a long time.

'My dear, they have found very little, nothing of note.' I passed her the photocopies Simon had given me.

'I have these.' I showed her.

She took them from me and, putting on her glasses, she read them slowly. I was very pleased with what I brought to the table, but she was distinctly unmoved.

'I had heard that about the butler,' she said. 'But the name Grant comes more to mind. I thought it was he who was investigated by the police, I must have got that wrong.'

'I wonder why you thought it was Grant and not Fellowes?'

'I don't know, let me think.' She stood up and walked over to a large antique chest of drawers, which stood proudly against the wall behind her. She pulled out a brown file, an old fashioned thing, and placed it on the coffee table between us. As she opened it, I saw the contents, a mixture of assorted notes and writings, all in her recognisable hand.

'Here it is.' She passed me a record card, a pink one, at the top was written Lapston Manor and then there were three paragraphs.

"Grant, James. Butler, Lapston Manor 1921-1944. Born in Kingston, Surrey.

"Started work as a hallboy at fourteen, trained at The Ritz arrived at Lapston in 1921.

"Grant was a corporal in the Home Guard in 1939 whilst three other inhabitants of the house included Major Henry Amsherst, Major George Amsherst and a family friend, resident at that time, Maxwell Carrick.

"Grant was dismissed from his post when ownership of the house was transferred."

Angela was reading the card alongside me. 'I can't believe I missed all that info, honey. We could put some more flesh on the Lapston bone with that.'

'I'll see what I can find out about Grant and the Amshersts. There might be something on Google about them.'

'On what?'

'Google, oh never mind.' I smiled inwardly. 'I bet I can find out a bit more now.'

'And don't forget this Carrick fellow,' she said, passing me the card and tapping her nail on the name. 'Here, take this, but let me have it back when you're done.'

I was walking home up Pudding Lane, a one-way street, when I heard a vehicle coming up behind me. When I turned, I saw him at the wheel of his pickup but he drove past and my heart, which had soared for a few tremulous seconds, sunk immediately. Then he stopped and backed up, so I picked up my pace and drew level with the driver's door. He looked so sad, so not himself. I wanted to reach out and squeeze his hand.

'How are you doing?' I asked.

'I'm fine. You?'

'Fine.'

'Don't suppose you've thought it over and have decided to give in to me?'

'No. That is, I've thought about it, of course, but no, Rory, I can't.'

He looked away, eyes focussed on the building site at the top of the road where men in hard hats walked backwards and forwards pushing wheelbarrows.

'That's a great shame, Martha, because I think we'd be good together, and you should know that I'm very good in bed.' He turned his head towards me as he said the last bit and I had to laugh.

'I'm sure you are.'

'Is it Scooter? Only I could pack his sandwiches in a road map and send him off somewhere.'

'No,' I replied kindly. 'It's not Scooter. I'm married. It's a small consideration, I know, but it means I'm prevented from hanky panky with other men.'

He looked away again and I flattered myself that, even though we were joking with each other, I was breaking his heart.

'You'd have to bring your own hanky, I only have panky at home.'

It was so silly. He was so very different from Steve, I laughed heartily. At that moment, a car came up the road and the driver sounded her horn crossly. I pulled away from the pick-up's window sharply .

'What's your number?'

'My mobile?'

'Landline, I can't remember mobile numbers.'

'832757.'

'I'll call you,' he said, releasing the handbrake. 'Norman Fry's home, saw him yesterday.' And then Rory was gone and I gave the driver of the car behind a killer stare for interrupting me while I was talking to the man I was falling in love with.

30

He is holding a knife to my throat. I have my eyes closed. No, they are open. I can see the blade and the fine edge of the black steel. It is cold and hard against my neck, he is slicing slowly, back and forth, making it unbearably painful, and I can taste the iron of the blood gurgling in my mouth. I try to scream but I can't make a sound.

And then, I realise it isn't me after all. I'm watching Collins, it's him not me. The Jerry has him by the hair, his neck is exposed, the white of his chest, the line of red where he is sunburnt, the sunburn is red, no the blood is red, he is red, he falls forward. I am still. I am waiting, my heart is beating, thumping in my chest, and it vibrates around my rib cage. Now he's coming for me and I can't free myself from under the iron bar, my feet, my feet. I scream. No one hears me. The flats are half empty, so many men away fighting, so much iron-tasting blood being shed everywhere.

I scramble to the kitchen for a glass of water.

I let it run over my hands, but there is no blood, just my fists curled into tight balls of anger.

I expected her to change her mind, but at ten I heard the light tapping on the door and she was standing there before me. She kissed me on both cheeks, taking in the gaunt tired expression on my face, no doubt. Sleep, after my nightmare, had proved impossible.

This time, I followed her up the steep stairs. She was wearing a high heel, the seam of her stockings running up the calf.

In my studio, I asked if she would like some tea. She declined.

'Where do you want me to sit, on here?' She pointed to the chaise longue I had dragged into the middle of the room. It was covered in a William Morris fabric, opulent and strong, cyan and magenta, to offset the white of her skin.

I nodded, unable to speak. I had not drawn a figure for over ten years. I even had doubts in my abilities, but I was determined. She took off her jacket and handed it to me, and I hung it on the back of my door. She said not a single word, in fact she had her back to me as she pulled the blouse out of her skirt and began to undo it. It shimmered as she shrugged it off and I caught hold of it before it dropped to the floor.

She was not wearing a brassiere. Her naked back was smooth, not a single blemish. She unzipped her skirt and it skimmed her legs as it fell off. I bent over and picked it up, placing both her blouse and skirt on the back of a chair. When I turned back to her she was rolling her stockings down her legs, her fingers under the band, her pale pink nail polish showing through the sheer fabric.

I felt a lightness in my head and a knot in my throat, all at once pleasurable, disturbing. I had never felt this way about any woman before. She was standing in front of me absolutely naked, her bottom pear-shaped, the light soft on her curves. She leaned over and straightened the fabric, so that it lay completely flat against the bed, then she turned around and sat on it, one arm draped over the higher end.

I had moved back behind my board and easel, the sight of her blocked from me whilst she adjusted herself. All at once, I was overcome with awkwardness, absurd as that might sound, but when I peered around the edge of the board, I saw not only the object of my study, but of all my desires.

I could not help my eye as it travelled over the long legs, the calves curved one upon the other, the thighs slender, the darkness of her, and the stomach flat, inverted and perfect between her hipbones. Then her breasts, full and round, the dark nipples erect under my gaze and finally, her eyes. They were not hers but instead the unconditional stare of the nude woman in "Le Déjeuner sur l'herbe." Challenging, unmoving and audacious. I had to shake myself out of my deepest thoughts when she asked, 'Will I do?'

'Yes.' I half croaked the word and without saying anything further, I picked up my pencil and began to work on the points of reference, skimming over the shapes she made. I could feel myself overcome with the desire to commit her to the paper before me, and with everything I had in me, I would make her mine, enjoy that delicate skin under my lips. The thought was filling me with an uncomfortable desire.

The drawing was a good one and as I stood back, for the first time in half an hour, she moved her head.

'Come and take a look,' I told her. She came to stand beside me so that if I looked down I could see the cleave of her breasts.

'It is good, Carrick, but my feet are too small.'

I was quite taken a back, criticism being the last thing I expected. 'I think they are fine,' I replied tersely.

However when she lay back down and I measured them with my pencil, arm held out straight, I could see that she was quite correct. I altered them, irritated with myself, but made a better job of it.

'All done,' I said and she stood up. I moved back so she could see for herself but she had picked up the blouse and was slipping it on. It fell over her form, lightly brushing the contours of her body.

'Would you like to take luncheon with me?' I asked tentatively as I saw an opportunity to take things further. After all, we had been intimate; she had been completely naked before me.

'No, thank you,' she said icily. 'I have a good deal to do, I will be eating later at my hotel.'

The rise of anger in me was almost uncontrollable, I found I was talking rapidly, unable to check myself.

'I saw you stepping out after I dropped you off yesterday,' I said.

It was clumsy and I sounded desperate and grasping.

'Pardon?'

'I said... I simply said that I saw you yesterday, you were meeting a gentleman and—'

'You are mistaken, Carrick,' she said bluntly.

'But your coat?' I said, scratching around for words.

'There is a woman in that hotel with one of a similar shade, now if you have finished, I must go.'

I stood back as she pressed past me, she didn't kiss me nor touch my hand.

Within seconds, she had closed the door behind her, and all that was left of her in the room was my drawing and that lingering scent of her French perfume.

31

I googled "James Grant butler" and all kinds of permutations of the name and title, but it was to no avail. I looked back at the card – Major Henry Amsherst. I entered his name in the search bar. One result:

"Major Henry Amsherst. Born 1907. Eldest son of Sir Reginald and Lady Augusta. A highly decorated British Army officer during the Second World War. He fought with the No. 4 Commando and French Resistance forces. Promoted to Special Operations Executive in late 1943. (Awarded the VC posthumously in 1945 for acts of outstanding bravery behind enemy lines.) Captured and tortured by the Gestapo in Paris, August 1944."

I looked for an image of him and found one, a handsome noble face. He was in uniform wearing a peaked cap, the picture sepia and very beautiful. He had the most enigmatic eyes. I found myself involuntarily touching the screen. He had such a kind face, but I found it chilling too, because he had been so young and to die like that it was unbearably sad.

My mobile buzzed so I closed my laptop and picked up the phone. 'Martha, it's Bob, how you doing?'

'Bob! How lovely to hear from you. I'm fine.'

'Have you found your groove?'

'My what?'

'Your "raison d'être" in retirement.'

I laughed. 'I have, Bob, I'm getting up to all sorts, including baking. Nothing like my mother or indeed my grandmother, I'm afraid, but I've had a couple of triumphs. It would appear that I'm very good at scones.'

'I have to say you have stunned me there,' he said. 'Way to go, Martha Berry.' I suddenly remembered how cheerful it was working in an office with all the good-natured banter. I swallowed hard. 'How can I help you, Bob?'

'Actually, it's me that is helping you.'

'Really?'

'Yes, we located an old back copy, very old, I'm talking 1961 here, of a magazine we no longer publish. It's called "Stately Homes" and in it there is an article on Lapston, its history and all that. I've photocopied it and I'll send it over to you.'

'Thank you, Bob, you're an angel.'

'You can pay me back with that dinner invite and I will look forward to pudding!'

I pressed the phone against my ear, as if it might bring me closer to Bob, to the office, to my former life but it was just cold and hard against my cheek. 'Will do, Bob, I really appreciate it. Thanks a million.'

He was gone and the room was empty, the clock ticking slowly in the corner and the hum of the washing machine going into spin cycle.

'Come on, Inca,' I said with great resolution. 'I need a walk. We're both getting tubby.' She came over to me, nails clicking on the wooden floor of the dining room. I rubbed her head and felt the soft velvety ears between my fingers.

'What do I do, Inca? Tell me, what do I do?'

32

It was late on Tuesday morning, I had spent the rest of Monday under a cloud. I was exhausted through lack of sleep and felt utterly dejected. The red coat was a mystery to me, but it was no mistake, I had clearly seen her, yet she had denied it.

I stepped out just before noon and was surprised to find it raining again, and quite heavily. I pulled my hat down and the collar of my raincoat up as I walked along the street.

I found myself standing opposite her hotel, drawn by a force to which I could put no name. I smoked a cigarette and then decided, much against my nature, to go in and see her uninvited. I would challenge her and tell her that I had not been mistaken. I would also declare myself to her. There was something very strong between us, some uncontainable passion, and I could barely conceal it.

As I strode in through the revolving doors, the doorman looked me up and down. I'd never been in The Angel before and was surprised to find it quite well appointed, with fresh flowers on a circular table in the middle of the reception hall.

'Yes, sir,' said the man behind a large oak desk. 'How may I help you?'

'I have come to see Madame Roussell. Please will you tell her I am here?'

He looked at me as if he didn't understand, then he turned to his register. He ran a finger down the page and then flipped it over and repeated the process.

'I cannot see a Madame Roussell registered with us, sir,' he said calmly, frustrating me.

'Come on, man,' I said with irritation. 'Check again.'

He repeated the process, even more slowly, and then shaking his head, and seeming to take a delight in the fact he had not been mistaken, he said, 'I am afraid, sir, that there is no Madame Roussell registered with us.' He closed the book firmly and rested his hands on top of it whilst levelling a rather disagreeable stare at me. I looked around at the dark wood and polished floors as if it might present me with some clue.

I turned on my heel and left the hotel. I scanned the street right and left, but where to now? I remembered the telephone box and strode along to it with great purpose. The Jaguar was still there, parked alongside. I dialled the operator and asked to be connected to Lapston.

Grant answered. 'Grant, could you let me speak to George please?'

'I'm afraid I cannot, sir. He has gone out for the day.'

'Alice?'

'Out riding, sir.'

'Very well. Would you ask George to telephone me at my flat.'

'Yes, sir.'

I placed the receiver on the cradle and stood thinking for a moment, trying to work it all out.

Later, at my club, I played a round of cards with an acquaintance, Giles Lewis. He worked for the War Office in some high capacity, all very secretive, but he knew of Henry and his work, this Lewis had let slip to me in an unguarded moment. I found myself staring at him as he held the cards close to his face, whilst carefully studying those I had laid down. I saw her, swimming before my eyes, the blended colours of her skin under the changing morning light. It was pale and white one minute, then rich in colour as the shaft of sunlight from the window moved across her.

'Your go, old man.'

'What?'

'Your turn, Carrick.'

I was back in the room in a trice.

Lewis's eyes were squinting as he drew on his cigar. I found I wanted to tell him everything, ask for his opinion on my situation.

'Lewis,' I said as I laid my card on top of his, 'what do you make of French women?'

'Whores most of them,' he said risibly. 'No sense of morals, gave themselves to the Germans, then the Americans, then it will be our boys without so much as a by your leave.' He puffed out a long cloud of smoke. 'You won't find better than a well-raised Deb if that is what you are after. Thinking of settling down, are we?'

'No, nothing of the sort,' I feigned a smile. 'Just met a Frenchwoman recently, can't fathom her out.'

'Have nothing to do with them I say, old boy.' He threw in his hand and I drew my winnings towards me.

'I think perhaps you are right,' I said. 'If only she were less bewitching, but she is a fascinating creature.'

'All the more reason to leave well alone, Carrick. One of my colleagues has met one, can't stop bleating on. He brought her back with him from Paris, besotted.'

I dealt the cards. If only I could forget her, not see her naked body every time I closed my eyes. The smell of her seemed to cling to me and I felt haunted.

She was haunting me.

'I'm back there myself in a fortnight,' said Lewis. 'I tried to absent myself claiming I was more useful in the Department here, but I was shouted down. They want to set up an Anglo-French agreement with the USA for a loan.'

'Now that we have reached the German border, how long before we can make certain of it all?' I asked.

'Not long now, old boy. Hold tight and find yourself a good English rose to marry. I say forget this woman and move on.'

I looked at the new fan of cards in my hand, a Queen and a Jack side by side. I threw them down on the table and told Lewis I was all in.

I needed to go home, have a whisky and an early night. Some part of me had to accept the fact that she was gone, lost to me, the dream had to be allowed to die. I felt a stab to my heart, but I told myself that it was the final pain caused to me by Cécile Roussell.

33

I was walking down to the river, the path threading through the meadows by the church. I threw sticks for Inca who, having made a great effort to run after them, never retrieved any. The sun was high in the sky and I could see a thin crescent moon too, a slice of silver in the blue. There was a sturdy wooden bridge over the river and Inca was clattering across it, bounding through the long grass in the field beyond. I stood, looking out across the brown water, watching it eddy around a stump of reeds.

'What a lovely dog.' It was Tom Williams, I hadn't noticed him coming through the field.

'Oh hi, Tom,' I replied, a little startled. 'Yes, she is lovely, new, Inca.'

'I'm not a dog person, but I know a nice one when I see one. How are you getting on?'

'You mean with the book?'

'Yes.'

'I have a few files to go through, full of little bits and pieces so I left them to the end.'

'Are you enjoying it?'

Inca returned. She had been in the river, upstream, and was wringing wet. She stopped and shook herself, the water spattering us both. I stepped back and Tom laughed as he brushed down his pale brown sweater, it was covered in black specks.

'I'm so sorry, she has no manners where shaking is concerned.'

'That's all right, it'll wash.'

There was a brief moment of silence and I had no idea what to say next. Tom was one of those people who waited for others to talk. He looked slightly awkward when, finally, he did speak.

'Martha, I wonder if I can have a word about the book?'

'Yes, of course.'

'It's just that the committee is a bit worried,' he said tentatively.

'About what?'

'It's just that they feel you have, shall we say, usurped the project.'

'Usurped,' I repeated after him. 'What on earth do you mean?'

'I'm afraid they think you are, shall we say, playing fast and loose with history?'

'What?' I was incredulous. 'Are you kidding me?'

'It's Camilla really, and Roger, Angela's much more easy going.' I noticed a quiver in Tom's voice, he was obviously very nervous. 'Please forgive me, and don't shoot me, I'm just the messenger. I–'

'You mean you've been sent to see me.'

'No, but I felt you should know in advance because most of the last meeting was about this and I simply didn't want you to go into it next week like Daniel into the lion's den.'

'Right,' I replied, not making any sense of it.

'I'm sorry if I've spoken out of turn.' His voice was still quite timorous, he was obviously uneasy.

'So do they want me to stop?'

'No, no, they just want it to be very factual, that's all.'

'Well, it's not my book,' I said, my ego bruised. 'What was said exactly?'

'Don't take this the wrong way but you were described as "very modern" and "lightweight." I knew I was giving him one of my dagger looks and it made him take a step backwards. 'Just so you know, it's not me who is saying that. Personally speaking Martha, you've been a breath of fresh air, but as you can imagine, they are very set in their ways, that's all.'

I stepped back, lost for words, feeling blindsided.

'Perhaps if you just toe the party line, Martha, and do as they ask but no more.'

I was absolutely crestfallen and so I called my dog to avoid eye contact with Tom, as an involuntary sense of rage was rising in me. I didn't dare give anything away so I made a fuss of Inca as she came trotting towards me, tongue lolling.

'Thanks for the heads up, Tom, I appreciate it,' I said as calmly as I could. I heaved Inca away from a scattering of sticks she was trying to reach and I was much too cross with her. I was jerking too hard on her lead and when I glanced up at Tom, who was staring at me, I felt awkward and cruel.

When I arrived home, I shut the door behind me and sobbed.

34

I had consumed too much alcohol. I let myself into the flat as the dawn chorus was underway and was trying numerous times to fit my latchkey in the lock. I fell onto the bed and woke up with a crashing headache at six, my mouth dry as dust.

I filled a glass until the water poured over the rim. I watched it gurgle down the plughole, trying not to think of the blood in Collins's throat, but my hand was shaking uncontrollably and suddenly the glass fell, shattering into the sink. I looked at the shards, the fine points that could so easily bring me to an early end. The clock ticked on steadily, water trickled in the pipes under the sink, and in the far distance a dog barked, the normal sounds of everyday life. I turned and walked away.

I awoke again at ten, my head thumping like a jackrabbit's leg. I had to travel over to Lapston, pull myself together and somehow rid myself of this dratted headache.

There were two presents on the side table; the daily maid had wrapped them very prettily for me, both the brooch and the scarf. It was Alice's birthday, her day. I had a duty to be with her, but the headache was unrelenting, a throb pulsed behind my left eye and, although my stomach was empty, I could not face food.

I arrived at Lapston at twelve. In spite of feeling so utterly wretched, the beauty of the house was not at all lost on me. The honey-coloured stone was almost the same colour as the gold autumn lawn. The horse's heads appeared over their half-doors and Jester kicked a hoof against his to attract my attention. I couldn't resist so I walked over to the stables and gave his nose a rub, faithful old man that he was.

'It's very good to have you home, sir,' Grant said kindly as he opened the door to me. I looked straight into his eyes, for he always provided a firm reassurance with his welcome. The old man he had replaced, Fellowes, had been so much colder. George's parents had been badly wounded by all that unpleasantness, but Grant's loyalty had proved invaluable. I had a great deal of time for him, as did George. The two were often to be found talking together and sharing a joke in these more relaxed times, it was something that would never have happened in Sir Reginald's day. Grant took my mackintosh and hat, telling me he would carry my suitcase upstairs and unpack it.

'Please do not trouble yourself, Grant,' I said. 'I'll take it, I'm sure you have much to do.'

'Very well, sir,' he said and withdrew. It was only fair on him that we now fended for ourselves. Very often we could see our former maids working the land in their corduroy breeches and thick woollen sweaters when we passed the fields around the house.

'Carrick!' It was George, coming down the staircase as fast as his hip would allow. 'I'm delighted to see you. Grant said you had telephoned yesterday when we were out.'

'Yes, I seem to keep missing you, old thing.'

'I was out with Alice. I promised I would treat her to the picture house. There is a new film, Double Indemnity, dashed good plot. Fred MacMurray and Barbara Stanwyck.'

'And where is our birthday girl?' I asked.

'She is out shopping with Cécile.'

'With Cécile?'

'Oh yes, she has been with us since Monday afternoon. Arrived just in time for afternoon tea, miserable wet day, mind.'

'I had no idea,' I said. My head was tightening with a searing pain around the temples as I spoke.

'Are you quite well, Carrick? You do look frightfully pale.'

'Bit of a late night last night, caught up with some old chums.' It was a lie of course, but he did not question me.

'Have a rest. I'll see you for dinner. I will be back by six.'

I lay on my bed, groaning, I had vomited as soon as I reached my room and the swill of whisky inside me made me feel wretched. I called for Grant and he fetched me some Angostura Bitters and a bread roll. I needed to mop up the alcohol in my stomach. I had asked for some coffee too but Mrs Hall had sent the message that there was none left and instead she had made mint tea with leaves from her herb garden.

I felt better at six. I had slept soundly but I found myself fixated on Cécile. I could not get her out of my mind, nor could I believe that between Sunday and that day, she had not made contact with me. She had Peterson's address, I had made sure of it, but it seems she had not given me a moment's thought in her plans to return to Lapston. I was confused and at a loss with what was running through my mind. The faint tap on the door came just as I was falling asleep. I expected that it would be Grant coming to straighten up my room for me and I realised it smelt quite awful. My suitcase was open at the end of the bed, the two presents lying on the top.

It was her.

I could hardly believe it, for she was standing there before me, her eyes searching mine under those lashes, just as before. Her lips were parted slightly, the teeth white. She looked so very beautiful.

'I just arrived back and heard from Grant that you have been unwell. I trust it is not the–'

'No, I have been under the weather,' I said. 'Some sort of chill, change of season, I expect.'

'I thought so, is there anything I can bring you?' She was charming, warm, caring, the French accent molten like caramel. I could not equate her with the creature who had been naked before me in my studio. In fact I felt ill at ease about it all and could find no words. She lowered her voice. 'I fear I have upset you.'

I had no idea what to think. I stammered a half-hearted reply before turning to see the present on top of my case.

'I have something for you.' I turned from the door,

suddenly anxious because she stepped inside my room. Could she smell the vomit? It didn't seem so; there was no reaction from her. In fact, she seemed to pay no heed to the state of the room at all.

'For me?' she said with surprise. I picked up one of the packages from my suitcase, wrapped in a thin pinkish paper, a small white bow on the top. I stood only inches away whilst she opened it, her neat red nails working at the bow deftly. She pulled out the daisy brooch. 'Why, Carrick, how beautiful, but why me? It is Alice's birthday.'

'I wanted you to have something, a gift from me,' I told her. 'And I have brought the drawing. I turned back to my suitcase and unhooked the false lid from where I produced the small marbled folio with the drawing inside. She took it from me, still holding the daisy in her hand.

'You are very kind.' She kissed me and I was lifted by the softness of her cheek brushing against mine and once again, I gave my sad and injured heart to her.

35

'Tell them where they can stick it,' Steve said when I told him about Tom. 'Honestly, you give people your time and hard bloody work and they snipe at you like this. It's not on. Tell them they can stick it where–'

'I can't, love,' I said truthfully. 'I'm enjoying finding out all this stuff about the village. Last night I was reading about a highwayman, Jed Sawyer. He escaped the law by making his horse jump the huge tollgate at the top of the hill. There's all kinds of things like that.'

'Yes, but I can't have you coming home crying.' Steve had a twitch under his eye, when he was angry it flickered beneath the skin.

'I was just feeling low,' I told him. 'I haven't been the same since I finished work, I really miss it.'

'Then tone it down a bit, do it exactly as they ask and sod the rest. Or write your own book, you're perfectly capable. You could write about that big house, tell its story right up until the present day and this fish chap. You never know where that might lead.'

'It's Kipper. He's a builder,' I said miserably. 'And I know I'm being silly.'

Steve circled me in his arms, his strength reassuring

and solid. I had no idea what had come over me but I had Steve, my rock, to turn to and that was all I needed.

'I felt so let down,' I whispered into his chest. 'All this work I've done making sure it's all readable and presented properly. It's the only thing that's kept me going since…' My voice drifted away.

'Make yourself a cup of tea, sit down with the paper and switch off from it all. We're talking first world problems here, not life and death, darling.'

The door banged shut as he left, his keys jingling in his hand – they gave him the freedom to a life outside. I sat looking out of the window, sipping herb tea and looking at the last blossoms of my raspberry bush before they finally fell into the gravel and their oblivion.

I was struggling. I had gone from editor to nonentity in just a few short months. I'd kept everything from Steve, but he had seen my unguarded moments and used words like moping and moody. That wasn't the half of it, inside I felt that any inner respect I had for myself had curled up like plastic in a fire, shrivelling from the outside in.

I shivered; it was cold again. The few weeks of warm weather had vanished and it was dark and cold under a sullen sky. There was a thump as the mail hit the mat, much earlier than usual and I went to collect it. I found Inca sniffing it suspiciously.

'Okay, good girl. I'm sure it's safe,' I told her.

It was an A4 envelope from Bob, the address written in his very scrawny writing. I spread the papers all over the table. The copies were good, finally it seemed someone in accounts had agreed to a new copier.

There were four pages, sepia and mono photos sat between closely set type. It's always remarkable to look back at handset type.

The article was written by a man of course, female journalists in the late fifties and early sixties still being a rare thing. His name was Michael Myere. The name rang a bell and I distantly recalled him coming in for a party to commemorate the firm's thirtieth anniversary. It would have been in the eighties. He was a stooped old man by then with a shock of white hair crowning a pink pate. He walked with a zimmer frame and had flecks of spittle in the corner of his mouth.

I shuddered. He must have been only seventy, maybe a touch over. I told myself not to think about it and, besides, fifty, they say, is the new forty.

The writing was terribly old school, even the word tomorrow was still hyphenated, "to-morrow."

"Lapston Manor, is a tribute to a lost age," it began and immediately it set out the list of forgotten fashions and customs from days gone by. I read down to the fourth paragraph, where the first mention of the owners came in. There were various stories and notes, and the reiteration of the rumour that Kaiser Wilhelm II had visited the house. There was also reference to the large number of French detailing dotted around the building.

Then it came to Sir Reginald and Lady Augusta who had purchased the house in 1904. They had three children: Henry, George and Alice. There was also a ward, a friend of the family. During the First World War, they had given the house to the army to use as an asylum for mentally ill soldiers. The family had moved to their house in London, returning in nineteen twenty, and finding that the house needed much work to restore it. Some of the soldiers who had been sheltered there were paid to redecorate and renew areas of the house and garden. Following a trip to California in the winter of 1933, Lady Augusta passed away of relapsing fever. Her husband died two years later.

I googled relapsing fever and it transpired that Lady Augusta had been bitten by a tick or louse, the poor thing. I was intrigued. This left Henry as the heir and no doubt George as the spare. Then Alice and the ward, I forgot his name. I wrote a question mark on my notepad.

Michael then talked about the house and the knot garden, which Sir Reginald had designed and made in 1930. He never lived to see it fully grown but its reputation as one of England's finest examples survived him:

"The family business, without Sir Reginald at the helm, suffered from his absence and from the onset of World War Two because all the men in the house joined up and even Alice took on work for the war effort. Many of the servants from Sir Reginald's time also left and the house was closed down, with only a housekeeper and gardener to look after it.

"George Amsherst opened the house again sometime in nineteen forty-three when he returned home injured and took up the family business. His portfolio included a small engineering company strategic to the later years of the war effort. By then, owing to lack of manpower and resources, the business had begun to fold and the decision was made to sell off all surrounding farmland. Finally, the family lost the house, and in spite of my best efforts I cannot find out why, but it was passed to a French owner who then quickly sold it to The Church of The Immaculate Heart. Lapston's sad decline included use as a children's nursing home, but it was abandoned in nineteen fifty-seven. The house is empty now, the contents stripped and all but a whisper of its former glory can be heard amongst its dark halls."

I looked at the images. There was a sepia picture of the house, arranged like the one of Sarsten House, but with only twenty or so servants standing outside. They included a very smart groom holding a good-looking grey horse.

There was another black and white photo of the ornate porch over the door. It was sharp and clear and I could see the carving on it. Inset pictures showed a stained-glass window in the morning room taken from different angles. The design was a swan swimming on a pool of bright water with the sun's rays pouring down on its snowy white back. It was absolutely beautiful. In the fourth picture Sir Reginald and Augusta sat in a very old car, he in a uniform with multiple medals across his chest, and she wearing a large ostrich feather hat.

I flipped the page back to look at the pictures on the first two pages of the article. One was of Lapston in its full glory, rich sandstone, tall windows, towering chimneys, all symmetrical and the immaculate gardens. The trimmed topiary and weed free shale were obviously very well maintained. The picture caption said "Lapston, 1931" and a small picture showed the knot garden just as it was with Rory maintaining it.

Rory.

The final picture, an old black and white one, soft in contrast, was of four people. They were standing on the steps of the house. The oldest was mid-thirties, a round faced man with a dash of grey hair, at least I presumed it was grey. In front of him stood a younger woman, her dark hair in a roll around her head, indicating that it was wartime. She looked terribly sad, almost lost.

Next to her was a rather good looking man with dark hair and he was smiling. Behind him stood a tall woman, her dress black velvet, a brooch on the strap, a flower of some sort. She had the most unforgiving eyes and I realised that she was looking straight out of the picture with a cold impenetrable stare, at me.

36

I was caught between two stools: the joy of seeing Cécile and the dread of seeing Alice, because I had upset her so. I was coming downstairs when I saw Cécile cross the hall and go into the library. Moments later, I heard the muffled sounds of her making a telephone call.

George was in the lounge, standing by the window overlooking the knot garden, a silhouette against the bright evening sun.

'I must apologise, George,' I said as cheerfully as I was able, whilst still experiencing the last vestiges of my headache. 'I missed lunch. I fear I do not have the stamina for drinking these days.'

George turned around, taken by surprise. 'Oh hello, Carrick, old man, what do you say? I do apologise I was lost in my thoughts.' He had a healthy colour to his cheeks and a sparkle in his eyes that I had not seen for a very long time. He clapped me on the back, just like the brother I knew him to be, I felt supported. I could easily have told him there and then my intentions towards Cécile and shared my joy and future hopes with him. He was, after all, my confidante and ally.

'I'm sorry,' I said, taking him up on his offer of a

cigarette. 'I've let the side down, I should have been in to see you all earlier.'

'It's of no consequence, old man. The ladies are somewhere abouts, dressing for dinner by now, I shouldn't wonder. It is so delightful that we have some life in the house at last.'

I poured myself a soda with ice as Alice joined us. She looked pretty with her hair up and curled on top of her head, quite the lady in fact but, in complete contrast to George, she looked pale and uneasy.

'Happy birthday, old thing,' I said giving her warm hug. I realised almost immediately that there was no reciprocation, her body felt slight and unyielding, gone was the enthusiasm of her arrival last week.

'Thank you,' she said coldly, stepping back, away from me and on towards George. She kissed him gently on the cheek. 'Thank you, George, for the puppy, he is adorable and so long overdue, the house needs some new energy about it.'

'When you think what we used to have before thirty nine, everything had to go, from Sylvester to Mrs Hall's chickens,' he said, shaking his head.

'Don't get maudlin now, George,' said Alice and, to her credit, she was lifting the tone once again. 'Old Sylvester had a long service and he was a wonderful hunter. You had him since you were fourteen or so didn't you?'

'Yes, he was a good old boy and he had a fine innings. You were six when we bought you that fat little pony, what was his name, Merryweather?'

'Merrylegs.'

'That was it, Merrylegs after the pony in Black Beauty.

208

You were mad for that book: you made me to read it over and over again to you, do you remember?'

'I do, and I would set up jumps for him on the lawn and our gardener would come after me with his broom shouting about hoof prints!' She had cheered up. Alice was never glum for long, but I noticed that she had yet to look me in the eye.

'What is all this merriment I hear?' Cécile was standing in the doorway, she was wearing the most beautiful dress. It was midnight blue with straps criss-crossing her chest. It clung to her frame, dramatically highlighting the slenderness of the figure beneath. On the bodice, of course, she wore the daisy. I recall walking towards her and kissing her, whispering into her ear that she looked absolutely beautiful, but again she failed to respond. Instead she went straight to Alice and wished her a happy birthday, then she stood beside George and I saw that he passed her a drink without looking at her.

Still, we made a happy band: Alice had softened and was more her old self; George in high spirits and I now felt quite well. They ribbed me about my hangover, but I took all the blows in good part. George had asked Grant to fetch the camera and we filed outside into the mellow autumn evening to have our picture taken.

Alice and I stood on the first step, George and Cécile on the next. I could feel her behind me, the scent, the nearness of her, her breath on my neck. Then she placed a hand on my shoulder and I melted. It was a sign: she was saying we were close, telling anyone who might see that photograph at some future date that we were a couple embarking on a lifetime together. I have never felt prouder than I was at that moment and Grant was capturing my happiness for eternity.

We walked into dinner, me arm in arm with Cécile. I had made sure of that on the pretext that it was Alice's evening and she should accompany her brother.

The first course was smoked salmon from Loch Fyne. We talked of many things and I promised to ride out with Alice again the following day. She, in turn, informed us that by the Friday she would be back in her barracks and not home again for some while. She had enjoyed a long leave because she had volunteered to go to France.

The venison was so delicious and such a rare treat that it was even possible to think of life after the war when such things would become normal again, part of the simple everyday life we craved.

As Grant leant down to remove my plate, I chanced to say to him that I hoped the staff were all going to be given some venison and whisky as part of Alice's birthday celebrations. I felt the great need to share my own happiness with everyone. Grant replied that he "thanked me very much for the kind thought."

That was the moment it turned.

I had, all evening been smiling and nodding towards Cécile. She was bewitching me, playing with me like a cat with a mouse. I was directly opposite her, the glint of the diamonds in her ears continuously reflecting the candlelight.

'Carrick, old chap,' said George, good affable generous George. 'I do wish you would hold off saying things like that to the staff.'

I stared in disbelief, as I was sure did Alice. I was seated beside her, but I could feel her tense up, her back stiffen.

'I beg your pardon?' I felt a chill of cold run through me whilst the hot tinge of embarrassment touched my cheeks. I looked from George to Cécile and saw that both were looking at me icily. I was quite wrong-footed, not knowing what to say next.

'I think it is up to me to give orders to Grant,' said George and then he picked up his glass and sipped from it, at the same time averting his gaze. I sat there frozen and unable to move whilst Alice shifted uneasily in her seat. Then, to her credit, she stepped in to defend me.

'George, darling, I do think that is rather a rude thing to say,' she ventured, she spoke gently, treading carefully. 'Carrick means well and there is, after all, plenty for everyone.'

'I am sure there is, Alice, but it is up to me, as master of the house, to say these things.'

There was an awkward silence as Grant, at that moment, re-entered the room. I wondered if he had heard anything, but his face was impassive as usual –butlers have a marvellous ability to avoid hearing things.

George cleared his throat. 'How was Oxford?'

'It was fine,' I replied stonily, my pride wounded. Alice stepped into the breach again and there was talk of the latest Food Ministry edicts, news from Westminster, and the hunt, would there be a return to more of it anytime soon? I did not participate because I was studying George and I saw then how much his manner had changed. I perceived a haughtiness about him, something had come over him and I was not entirely sure that I liked it. It had become obvious after I had taken Cécile away to Oxford.

We repaired to the lounge together where a roaring fire was awaiting us.

Alice touched my elbow. 'Do ignore George,' she whispered out of his hearing. 'He has become very pompous, for some reason, in the last few days.'

As she moved away to stand beside Cécile, I remembered her gift and left the room, gratefully I will admit, to fetch it. The rest of the house was uncommonly cold, the nights had drawn in and the frost had begun its nightly treachery.

When I returned to the hall, some five minutes later, I caught a glimpse of Grant by the kitchen door. The half-light caused by the blackout curtains meant I could not see with whom he was talking, but there was some sort of interaction afoot. The other person was tucked in behind the door of the morning room and, as I moved closer, there was a whispering of quick sharp words.

'Is all well, Grant?' I enquired. My voice sounded crystal clear in the empty hall. The door to the lounge was shut to retain heat, the light from under it a sharp line on the threshold and only the dimmest of lights were illuminated about the hall.

It was George who stepped out from the shadows. Grant backed away and left through the kitchen door without a word.

'Ah, Carrick, nothing to concern you,' said George

and he guided me, quite forcefully, by the elbow in the direction of the lounge.

'If I have upset matters with my comment about the venison, I am deeply sorry, George.'

'No, no, old boy, nothing like that, it's of no import. What have you got there? Ah, a present for Alice, how kind.'

We entered the lounge just as Alice was opening a gift from Cécile. It was a notebook with a French design on the cover with which Alice seemed very pleased. I handed her my gift and, as is the usual practice of women she was enchanted by the wrappings. I lit a cigarette and watched as she opened it, pulling out the scarf so that it billowed.

'Oh, Carrick, it is delightful, thank you.' She smiled and held it up against her face. 'I adore daisies.' I saw Cécile's hand go to the brooch where she ran a finger over it then glanced up at me, her face questioning; I smiled to reassure her.

Alice was opening another gift, from the staff. It was an ebony box covered in tiny diamonds of ivory, for keepsakes and such. Very charming.

'I am thinking that now is the perfect moment to announce my news,' said George, once Alice had finished fussing and had put the wrappings to one side. He was pouring us all a whisky, the colour of bracken on the Scottish moors in autumn. I could only wonder what this announcement could be, because he had said nothing of note in the past weeks.

He finished pouring and placed the decanter down. The silver tray rattled as he did so. He was obviously going to bring us good news and he was brim full with excitement. He took his place next to Cécile and I saw that she was looking down at her feet and obviously worrying. I strongly suspected that she was to be party to an announcement that involved only the family.

'I must apologise to Alice for intruding upon her birthday celebrations but I have some wonderful news to share with you.' George was looking immensely pleased with himself. 'As you know, there was a meeting of the party a fortnight since to discuss the by-election, and I am honoured to tell you that I have been voted as candidate for this constituency.'

Alice clapped her hands together. 'Oh George, what fun! I have always said if you did not go into the church you would make a fine Member of Parliament, I am delighted.'

'Well done, old man,' I said, raising my glass to him. 'They have made a damned good choice.' I waited for Cécile to add her own congratulations, but she was quiet and still looking down at the floor. She was embarrassed to be here, an outsider and I felt a tug of empathy because there have been times, particularly when I was younger, when I have felt exactly the same.

'And further, I have been giving much thought to my future career and could not be more delighted to tell you that I am not about to embark on this new chapter of my life alone. I have asked Cécile for her hand in marriage and she has agreed. I can proudly, yes most proudly, announce that this wonderful lady is to be my wife.'

37

Steve was holding a bunch of car keys in front of me. 'Happy Birthday!' He planted a kiss on my cheek then led me by the hand to the driveway.

'Oh Steve, it's lovely.' It was Volkswagen Polo, in metallic grey with cream leather seats. 'It's just lovely.'

'It's not new, a couple of years old, but not that many miles on the clock and just about anything's better than your old Honda, isn't it? Oh, and look, an added bonus...' He opened the driver's door and beckoned me over. 'Come and take a look at this.' He was very excited for me and put two hands on my shoulders as I leant into the car. The smell was lovely, fresh, clean not like my old jalopy. 'See, there.' He pointed at the dashboard.

'Satellite navigation!' I was so touched by his thoughtfulness because directions were not my strong suit.

'Yes, so you never need to get lost again,' he said joyfully. 'No more maps spread across bonnets for you.'

'Oh Steve, that's wonderful, thank you.'

He made me sit in the car and then he went round to the passenger side and climbed in next to me. 'How good is this? You can input a new destination here by clicking on these letters, or retrieve your old one by selecting this button and you can choose fastest route, a route avoiding motorways, or an economical route; good for saving fuel.'

I was watching him, his face was animated because he was so excited for me and I knew he would have stretched the budget to buy such a lovely car.

'Thank you,' I said. 'Thank you for being so kind.'

'It's my pleasure.' He kissed me again. 'Fancy a spin?' He was so pleased with himself.

'Why not?' I replied and he took me off to Stow and Moreton on a whim. Huge poppy fields flashed by and linseed too, a riot of primary colours in a lush green Cotswold countryside.

When we arrived home, we had laughed a lot, and he was going to the village shop for some fizz to celebrate my special day. As I opened the front door, my phone was ringing.

'Hi Martha, it's me.'

I knew his voice immediately. It sent a wave of warmth through my body. 'Hi Rory.'

'How are you?'

'I'm fine.'

'I'm just calling to let you know that Norman Fry is happy to meet with you on Tuesday afternoon. Would that suit you?'

I pretended to look through my diary, acting as if I was busy, as if this, us, was all very much a sideline.

'Er, yes, that looks fine.'

'Why don't you come here for two and we can have a cup of tea and a chat?'

I hesitated, the excuses were rushing into my mind, but I was ignoring them.

'That would be lovely.'

'Just a chat,' he said as if I needed reassurance.

'Yes,' I said wishing it were otherwise, foolishly wishing.

38

I felt sick, not the seesaw sickness of over excess, but the need to sit down, to clutch my stomach, to hold my guts in place. I held fast. George was beaming with self-satisfaction, his great round face the happiest I've ever seen it. I dared not look at Cécile. Alice had moved forward, offering her congratulations, whilst I was rooted to the spot, my throat knotted in constriction. I watched as Alice hugged them both but I could not hear what she was saying because there was a loud thrumming in my ears.

Alice then turned and was walking towards me. It was just a few short yards but she seemed to be travelling forever; as if we were both submerged in a pool. She raised her eyebrows to me, a private message of surprise written all over her face, then she was holding my hands, drawing me to the happy couple.

Then I was kissing Cécile, my eyes catching the sheen on the topaz at the centre of her brooch, it was so beautiful. The petals were enamelled and white, eight of them, so pretty. Alice loves daisies, I thought. It became a mantra repeating itself inside my head. George was clapping me on the back with his big bear paws.

There was a clinking of glasses, I have to presume I joined in, then words floated through my head, disjointed, surreal. "Parliament;" "Wedding;" "Small affair;" "Paris." Alice loves daisies.

I backed away when Grant came in and watched as George shared the news of the forthcoming nuptials. Grant's smile was forced and as he turned away, he glanced at me and I saw that his eyes were saying a thousand words, but his face was impassive, professional, betraying nothing.

I followed him out on some hastily made up pretext. He was walking at a march towards the kitchens through the dark hall.

'Grant.' When I called to him, he turned around, his face ghostly.

'Yes, sir?'

'I, I–' Frankly I had no idea what I was going to say. I wanted to ask him what he thought of this new turn of events and I felt the sudden need for an ally, but it was not etiquette.

'Is there something I can fetch for you, sir?'

'No, I… that is, I'm sure you are pleased about the new announcement, as indeed I am.'

'Yes, sir, very pleased.' His eyes told a different story.

'Only…' I moved alongside him, closer to the kitchen door. 'It was rather a shock for me.'

'Do you need something? Are you feeling unwell?'

'No, I, I–' I was stuttering like an old fool. I decided it was easier just to ask the question out loud. 'You seemed a little surprised, as indeed I was.'

'Yes I was, sir,' he said. 'Very surprised indeed. I'm afraid I will not be able to stay at Lapston now, I will have to find a new place of work.'

'Really?' I was stunned. 'Why? Was it something to do with the conversation in the hall?'

'Yes, sir, I'm afraid the new mistress would make life for me at Lapston untenable, I have made this clear to the Major.'

'Oh good God, Grant, you must reconsider; you are part of the furniture here, you have always have been.'

'Perhaps once, sir, but Madame Roussell has made it very clear to me that I must go, and I have no intention of outstaying my welcome.' With that, he bowed slightly and then turning away, walked towards the kitchen.

39

The doorbell rang. It was Becky with a bottle of red in one hand and bunch of pale lilac flowers in the other. 'Hi Becky, come on in.' I gave her a huge hug, I hadn't seen her for a long while.

'This can't go on, Martha. We used to meet once a week for lunch and now I don't see you in months.'

'I know, I can only apologise.' I did feel bad about it, but the time had just slipped away between my intentions and my acting on them. Steve was at parents' evening and then having a drink with some of his colleagues at the pub near the school, and I had called Becky at the last minute to see if she was free.

'How are things?' she asked.

'Oh just fine,' I replied.

'You're saying it I but your eyes aren't convincing me,' Becky said.

'How do you do that?'

'What?'

'See into my soul.'

'Heavens, Martha, you're like an open book, you always have been. You looked sad when I last saw you and you look even worse now, sort of dejected. Like you're pining or something.' Becky sipped her wine as I weighed it up in my mind. Could I tell her? She hardly knew Steve, surely she would take my side.

'Becky, can I tell you something in absolute confidence?'

'Of course you can. Oh my God, Martha, you're not ill are you?'

'No,' I replied, 'I'm not, but I might be going mad.' Even as I spoke those words I felt like I was betraying Steve, a low pain twisted in my stomach. 'I've met someone, a man, a very lovely man.'

Becky's eyes were like saucers. 'You've met someone… a man?'

I nodded.

'Who, where, when? Tell me.'

I felt so relieved that I let it all come out. At last I had someone in whom I could confide, but Becky's mouth dropped open in disbelief. When I was through, her total disapproval was obvious.

'This can't go on, you cannot betray Steve, you mustn't see this man anymore, it's far too dangerous.'

I don't know if I was looking for her approval or her acquiescence, but her flat refusal to hear me out, to let me explain my feelings, made me feel cheap. I was trying to defend something that was terribly wrong. I knew that and even as I did, I found myself imagining him there, right next to us on Steve's easy chair, his eyes on me, his body language telling me he wanted me. It was all I could do not to get up and go to this figment of him.

'You will kill this marriage of yours dead if you carry

on and you've been married for yonks,' Becky was saying. 'Forget this man, he's only attractive because you are vulnerable; you're bored and lonely on your own. Martha you're not listening are you?'

I wasn't listening; I was elsewhere, with him, on the bench at Lapston, on his sofa, standing looking over the river. All at once, I wanted desperately to be with him.

Becky tried to change the conversation, but it wasn't ever going to be the same again and I realised, with that slow churning pain in my stomach, that I wasn't going to be seeing her anymore, or at least not for a very long time. Not until I was out of danger with Rory, and it was danger, the danger of my own stupidity taking me over.

40

I do not know how I made it through the rest of the evening. I stayed outside the conversation, watching like a wolf at the mouth of a cave whilst the fire burned within. George outlined his key objectives as a member of parliament and, because it was a safe seat, it was unthinkable that he would not win. All the time I watched her, my sense of anger and betrayal quelled by the whisky and the cigarettes that I smoked incessantly.

At last, they left for a late night walk in the garden – the lovers. I was miserable, deeply wounded and very drunk.

'Oh Carrick!' Alice was beside me in a trice, her hand resting upon mine. 'Darling, I am so sorry. I know you thought yourself in love with her, but she really is not for you, she is not kind. She is not for George either and I must find some way to tell him. I'm afraid that he is mad with love for her and has been since that very first day.'

'Well, he might be, but he does not know her at all. He knows nothing of her.' I was slurring, I knew the drink had loosened my tongue. I should have taken more care. 'She already has a man in tow, I saw them together.'

'Really?' Alice leaned back, staring into my eyes. I might have been drunk but I had her attention.

'Yes really, the old fool, George. She is playing him like a cheap violin.'

'You are probably mistaken, Carrick, and anyway she is here now, she won't be seeing anyone else, they'll be together, more's the pity.'

I straightened up.

'You don't like her, do you?'

'That is a very strong way of putting it, Carrick. I hardly know her and she is to be my sister, but I would have picked someone... better for George.'

I lifted a finger and ran it along her jawbone, her skin so soft to the touch. 'Oh Mouse, you are such a balanced and reasonable person, such an antidote to me. I am a fool, a stupid fool.'

'You're not, darling. You have simply not been yourself in quite a while.'

'I have no idea who I am anymore.'

'You're my dearest friend, the kind, gentle friend who has been beside me for my whole life.' She was rubbing my shoulder in the most caring way. I raised my head to meet her eyes and saw her features melding together, her voice thrum, thrumming in my head, like a drum, like a volley from a machine gun and then everything went black.

The house was empty, or so it seemed, there was not a sound anywhere. It was eleven, the clock in the hall chiming icily in the stillness. I had mercifully escaped a hangover thanks to a large glass of water placed by my bed. I had downed it in one when I awoke in the night. Grant would have done that for me, he and George having

225

heaved my limp body up the stairs. It was with regretful shame that I gingerly stepped down the stairs, stopping at the turn of the landing.

Still there was silence.

Then the light sound of feet coming from the garden room and Cécile appeared. Grant had left the post on the salver in the hall, as he was wont to do when he was busy elsewhere. She picked up the wad of letters, reading the addresses as if she expected to see something. The third one caught her attention and she turned it over looking, I presumed, for a return address.

I knew that should she sense my presence, I would disturb her so I stood perfectly still. She pushed the letter deep into the pocket of her cardigan and walked to the library. I descended the stairs carefully, quietly stalking her as I would a lone stag. At the doorway, I peered in, keeping my body out of her line of sight. She was starting to open the envelope and I was intrigued, bewitched again by her for, even then, I could not take my eyes off her body, the lines and perfect shape of her.

'Carrick?'

I snapped out of my trance and dipped back behind the doorframe as if I could pretend I was not there.

'Is that you?'

I stepped forward like a schoolboy caught by a teacher smoking behind the cricket pavilion.

'Oh, yes, Cécile,' I said, stepping forward. 'I am very sorry. I didn't realise you were in there. I was looking for Grant.' I moved into the library. The letter was gone and her hands were empty.

'Perhaps you can help me?' she said calmly. 'I am looking for a book about the family history. George says there is one in here, but I cannot find it.'

I stepped towards the shelves and placed my hands on a red leather bound book. Pulling it out, I handed it to her. Her fingers wrapped around it, encircling the spine.

'The family dates back to the Huguenots. You'll find it all in there and how you will fit in.' I said the words unkindly and she knew it. She levelled her eyes at me. Those eyes, the clarity of them, the green overpowering the brown, feline.

'I presume you are not pleased by our announcement last night,' she said.

'I would say I was very much taken by surprise.' I edged towards a high-backed chair and perched on the arm. I lit a cigarette but I did not offer her one, the first and slightest way I had of not appeasing her. She noticed, I am sure, as I dragged deep and let a cloud of blue smoke come between us.

'So, you are to be mistress of Lapston,' I said, appearing calm whilst my heart beat against my chest like a bird's wings against the confines of its cage. 'Congratulations. It and George are both a good catch.'

She was looking at the book. It was open, balanced on her long fingers. 'Don't worry, Carrick, you have lost the battle, but not the war.'

I did not know to what she referred, but I could clearly see that she was laughing at me behind those cat's eyes. I drew again on my cigarette.

'You may think I don't understand you, imagine I

have not worked you out, but I have.' I felt my jaw stiffen, working against me.

'Really?'

'You posed for me, lay naked before me, what will George make of that, I wonder?' I thought for the split second that I had caught her off guard, that she had been hooked on my line, but she barely turned a hair.

'He already knows,' she said. She closed the book with a thud and walked towards me, my eyes level with her breasts. She was wearing a sheer blouse under the open cardigan, a thin sheer petticoat under that, her nipples hardened inside the soft rose printed fabric. I felt powerless before her.

'I gave him the drawing last night after we slept together in his bed. I was naked before him, it seemed the perfect moment to give him a lasting memento of the woman he will make love to for the rest of his life.'

I felt as if invisible strings were tied to my bones and that they were dragging me downwards to the polished oak floor, like Gulliver, overwhelmed by a thousand bonds.

'Nothing to say, Carrick?' I was silent, the bird breaking his wings inside me as it attempted to escape. 'No, I thought not. You thought you were going to have me did you not? You believed we would be the ones making love, my naked body under yours?'

She laughed, a dry sneer of a laugh. 'You are mad, Carrick, mad, and if you think you have any chance with me then you most certainly are. You cannot deny it; you are sick and broken, a sad remnant of what you once were.

It is an amour fou; you are insane. What do you think you could possibly offer me? Tell me.'

I could not meet her eyes. The bird was weak but I could feel the wings still pounding against the bottom of the cage.

'I will tell him.' I was speaking in a low tone. I could feel the beating like a pulse, the frustrated beating, the guns, a volley of machine gunfire. I put my hands to my head, cupping my ears.

'Tell him what?'

'I saw you in Oxford, with another man.'

'You were seeing things, Carrick, you are a sick and broken man, they all say it; you hear things, you see things all the time, don't you? You are not really sane are you? Look at you now, hands over your ears, blocking me out.'

'Grant!'

'Grant is gone, Carrick.' I looked up at her, hands even now over my ears, the beating, the repetitive beating pulse of the dying bird. 'No one is interested in anything you have to say anymore. Look at you, and you thought I could be associated with you, it's laughable. What chance does a sad wreck of a man like you have with anyone? Even Alice, poor desperate Alice.'

George was calling, his voice cutting through the sounds in my head, the room was going black then grey, gunfire all around me. There was Collins, his body slumped to one side, the Kraut, steel knife in his hand coming for me. I reached out to touch Cécile's blouse, pink roses swimming in and out of focus, my hand shaking.

She was gone.

It was George's hand on my shoulder, the heavy reassurance of it strong and substantial, reliably there for me.

'Come on now, old man. There now, Carrick.' His voice was gentle and he was pressing my head to his side, drawing me into him, holding me up.

She was gone.

'George, you cannot...' I said.

'Come on, old boy, there's a good chap.'

'You must not. Dangerous.'

'Not anymore, old boy, it's all over now.' He tightened his grip on my shoulder. 'Come on now, you have nothing to fear, nothing to fear.'

41

'You have nothing to fear,' said Rory, shaking his head and smiling. 'He's not here.' I was hesitating before I stepped over the threshold of his house.

'Where is he?' I asked, trying not to look as relieved as I felt.

'He's having a sabbatical at bad boys boarding school.'

'Really?'

'Yes. I'm going away tomorrow for a week or two so he's gone to his trainer's place while I'm away.' I wondered if he could tell how much my heart sank at the news that he would not be here. It turned out he could because he said straightaway, 'You look like you're going to miss me?'

I glanced at him for a second, endeavouring to give nothing away, but he was smiling. He knew.

He had tea and biscuits ready in the lounge. The fireplace looked dreary without a fire and the glass at the other end was wind-whipped with smears of dirt across it. Everything looked so much colder and dirtier this time – what did I expect of a man living on his own with a big, hairy dog who liked to swim a lot? I took a seat on his sofa, the leather was old and worn under my touch and when

I ran my hand across the surface, tiny bits of grit caught under my fingernails.

'How's Inca?' he asked as he joined me, passing me a mug of steaming tea.

'Oh she's lovely, very well-behaved.'

'Unlike certain other canines we could mention, eh?'

'Where are you going?' I asked, taking a sip of the hot tea.

'Spain. I'm being asked to landscape a holiday village in Almeria. It's where they filmed all the spaghetti westerns, apparently. So they tell me.'

'Clint Eastwood?'

'Yep, strange, isn't it? Of course it might not be true. The manager I met there before told me Walt Disney was born in the next town up the coast, but I looked him up and it said he came from Chicago.'

'I suspect it's a way of attracting tourists.'

'Martha, I'm sorry for what I said that time on the bench at Lapston. I should never have said it – it was impetuous of me and way out of order.'

I turned to face him. 'Please don't apologise, I can't tell you how much you boosted my ego. It's just that, well, I love my husband. He's an uncomplicated soul and he is grumpy, and I annoy him, but he's my simple, grumpy irritated old man.'

'How do you irritate him?'

'Oh, in ways many and varied. I was a workaholic that irritated him, then I retired and I became mopey and that irritated him. Then I really got into the book project and…'

'Don't tell me, that irritated him as well.'

I nodded. 'And I got told off for going to Lapston and not wearing a hard hat.'

'Really?'

'Yep.'

'Mind you, it is foolhardy, the house could have collapsed around our ears and who would have known we were there?'

'Simon.'

'Simon who?'

'The guy who saw us, you remember.'

'Oh Saint Simon of the High Morals,' Rory said with a smile.

I laughed. 'He's really lovely. Very kind. I made him scones.'

'Lucky old Simon, I've never been offered a scone.' Rory was pouting, mocking me, a shiver of excitement ran through me and I just hoped he couldn't see it.

'So what time are we seeing our Mr Fry?' I asked, changing the subject.

'As soon as we've had this – he said we could drop in any time to suit us.'

I stretched out my legs so that the toes of my shoes touched the underside of his coffee table and lay back into the couch. 'Isn't there something absolutely lovely about the sound of running water?'

'As long as I'm not in it I love it.'

'Did your not being able to swim come from something in your past?'

'I think so, I have vague memories of being in a swimming pool as a small child and not being able to get out. My mother was screaming. It was probably nothing, but when I go into water I just freeze, I can't move.'

'I was locked in my bedroom as a child. My father thought it was a good idea for some reason and then I was sick. I was only four and I couldn't get out. I was lying against the back of the door, sobbing and covered in vomit. That's why I'm hopeless around people who are ill,' I told him.

'We're a right pair, aren't we?' He lifted his hand and took a strand of my hair and placed it behind my ear. I felt a calmness run through me from head to toe, a feeling I had not experienced for a very long time. I could have stayed there, with him, for the rest of my life.

'Come on,' I said reluctantly. 'Let's go and see Norman Fry.'

42

Collins was slumped over, his throat cut, blood trickling over the folds of his jacket. I could see his legs twitching, like the frog's legs on the wire at school when we put a volt through them. Twitching, then stopping dead. Dead. My feet, the iron bar bearing down on them, the desert boots worn out, covered in Sicilian sand.

The knife was a heavy steel, black, and at the edge of it a ragged line of silver. Then he was falling, crashing down on top of me, his face registering shock, his eyes wide open as the blood sprayed across my sand-coloured uniform, ketchup from the nursery, my mother's face her eyes smiling, his weight crushing me, suffocating, his hair against my dry lips. He's heavy and the knife is splicing my skin beneath my jacket, the torn cotton starting to seep with blood. My blood.

'I am almost certain that it is brought on by stress,' I heard Alice say softly. 'He cannot help it. Yes, we asked him again and again to talk to someone, but he simply will not do it.'

'Let me take a look.'

It was the locum doctor, I'd never seen him before. Leaning over me, he pressed a cold stethoscope against my naked chest. He had large open pores on the end of his nose. The blankets were tightening across me, Mrs Hall was tucking me in, then there was a hand resting on my forehead. Cool.

'Mouse?'

'No, my love, it's Mrs Hall, now don't you worry at all. I'm here looking after you.'

'George.' My mouth was dry and she lifted my head letting me sip some water. The cold trickled down my throat, and then over my chin.

She mopped my damp skin with a flannel. 'Hush, rest now.'

I tried to focus on her, slowly realising that she was not Cécile, then I turned my head to the side and slept.

It was teatime before I emerged, the rain was driving down outside, hammering on the windows of the empty lounge, everywhere felt cold and still. I entered room after room looking for Alice, knowing that I sought comfort in her. For all at once, I knew she was my ally and so very important to me.

'Excuse me, sir, may I help you?' It was little Lizzie Fry, her maid's cap crooked on her head. 'Do you need anything?'

'Oh, Lizzie, I was looking for Miss Alice.'

'She's gone, sir, back to the Auxiliary, left an hour ago.'

My heart slumped. 'Is Grant here?'

'No, sir, he left this morning; Ogden took him to the station in the old trap.'

'Has he gone on an errand?'

'He's left us, sir, returned to London, says he's never coming back.'

All at once I recalled the whispered conversation and Grant's ghostly face in the half light of the hall.

'And where are the others?'

'They have gone to Stow, sir. I believe they are buying a ring for Madam.'

There was a blackness in my head, a void where the memories should be.

'I should like some tea, Lizzie, in the library.'

She bobbed and said, 'Very well, sir,' looking absolutely out of her depth, her small face uncertain.

In the library, I looked around for sight of the letter Cécile had been concealing, but nothing was disturbed. She had not put it in her pocket for I would have seen the outline of it. I was at a loss as I walked around and then it caught my eye, just a corner of the envelope, the stamp half hidden behind the mantle. The envelope had been inserted between the wall and wood in an effort to conceal it. I pressed my finger against the visible part of it, with a mind to easing it up and freeing it. It was clear that she had attempted to hide it, presuming that she could retrieve it later. As I pushed my finger against the wretched thing, it slipped away from me and dropped behind the wood. I crouched down and ran my fingers over the tiles that surrounded the hearth, it was somewhere behind them. I tried, knowing of course that I could do little to move the wooden mantle because it was stuck fast to the wall. The letter was gone.

'Is everything all right, sir?' It was Lizzie standing with a large tea tray, her eyes wide open watching me and wondering why I wanted to move the carved wooden fireplace.

'It's nothing to concern you. I dropped something behind the fireplace, it is not important.'

'Madam Roussell and the major have just arrived back, Mr Carrick. Shall I tell them you are in the library, sir?'

'Thank you, Lizzie,' I said, taking a seat in the plaid wingback chair. I steepled my fingers and rested my chin on them whilst I thought matters through. I was quite resolved to tell George he was making a huge mistake.

'Carrick, old man.' He entered the room on his own, arm outstretched to me in a friendly greeting. I stood up and shook his hand, beckoning him to sit down.

'I'm sorry about yesterday, George,' I said. 'I do feel much better today.'

'Good, good,' he said, lifting up the teapot and pouring himself a cup. I noticed Lizzie had set it for three. 'I'm sure you will soon be over this. It does not do to give in to it forever.'

I tilted my head, weighing the words up in my mind then I asked, 'Have you bought the ring?'

'What? Yes, Cécile wanted a new one. I offered Mother's but she said Alice should have it, and of course I agreed.'

'Of course she did,' I said, taking a sip of my tea. George was oblivious to the sarcasm in my voice, placing his cup down on the saucer and leaning forward.

'Thing is, old chap, one has to think to the future. These… episodes of yours, would it not be wise to address them sooner rather than later?'

'I will, George,' I replied, feeling more than a little embarrassed. I wanted to dwell on the subject of Cécile, but it occurred to me, all at once, that he was downplaying the extent of my problem and was even suggesting I could make myself better just by willing it to be so, if only that were the case. I studied his face then I realised he was waiting for me to continue. 'They said at the hospital that it would take time, I have to be patient, need rest and all that.'

'Yes, and this is all very well, but you see, life here at Lapston is about to change considerably. Cécile and I would very much like to embark on our new life together in peace and quiet, in other words, in private.'

I found myself gawping at him as I realised what he was inferring.

'Really? Is this Cécile's idea, George?'

'No, no, that is, if you think about it, it is simply what you would expect, old man. I'm not saying it has to be immediate.'

'It cannot be immediate, George. I have heard from Peterson and he is coming home.'

George raised an eyebrow, obviously miffed that I was unable to respond to his polite request at once.

It was me who leaned in next. 'George may I have a word with you?'

'About what, Carrick?'

'You and Cécile.' He looked unsure and so, I thought

unkindly, he should. 'I am going to be honest, George, I think you are making an enormous mistake. I think you are being fooled.'

'I beg your pardon?'

'I am telling you this for your own good, as your oldest and truest friend, I don't trust her.' The poor fool, he looked absolutely dejected, his face fell. I was telling him what he already knew. 'I am sorry,' I added, to lessen the blow.

'I find it very difficult to take this from you, Carrick,' he said, shaking his head. I hoped the expression on my face would tell him that I felt for him, that I really did want to protect him, and indeed Lapston too, and in fact all that I held so dear. He raised his eyes to meet mine. 'Do you really think I could rely on the judgment of someone who is mentally ill?'

I felt as if he had slapped me. I leant back against the chair, astonished and completely lost for words.

'George, that is hardly fair. I am talking about Cécile and the fact that she is not what she seems.'

'I do not know to what you refer,' he said starkly. 'I find her absolutely delightful as I did from the second I met her.'

'You have been made blind by love,' I said. 'If such strong emotion is what such a whirlwind affair can bring forth, personally I find it hard to believe.'

'We have spent far more time with each other than most before they announce such things, especially in a state of war. One has to make the most of things and seize the day.'

He was fighting back when I had expected him to roll over because he had always trusted my word above all things; I scrambled around for something to say.

'What of Grant? He told me last night that Cécile had told him to go and I believe he has now indeed departed.' Now George's face reddened. He ran a finger around the collar of his shirt as if it was too tight, something he did when he was wishing he were somewhere else.

'Grant is another matter. I do not wish to discuss it.'

'Really?'

'Yes.'

'She received a letter yesterday and hid it from you.' I indicated the direction with my head. 'It's there behind the wood of the fireplace.'

'How do you know?'

'I saw it. There was a small portion of it sticking out and I tried to retrieve it but instead dislodged it. She certainly didn't want you to see it.'

'See what?' It was Cécile, she was wearing a tweed suit, it was vaguely familiar.

'Carrick says you have concealed a letter dearest, in here.'

She remained cool, unmoved, her eyes never left mine. 'I did not conceal it, I left it on the mantel for you to read, George.' She walked to the fireplace. 'Where is it, Carrick?'

I knew then that she had been listening at the door.

'According to Carrick, it has fallen down the back there,' said George.

'What a shame. I will have to remember the contents.'

'Who was it from?' I asked, there was a tight knot of tension in my belly.

She sat down in the third armchair and calmly poured herself a cup of tea.

'I do not see that it is any concern of yours, Carrick,' she said, and George grunted an agreement without regarding me at all. I did not recognise him as my friend anymore. I felt the bile rising inside me. It was embarrassingly awkward, two against one. 'However, I will tell you that it was from my solicitor in Paris about my affairs, I must try to return soon to address some personal issues. Perhaps you feel you should accompany me, Carrick, to check on what transpires, it would appear that you do not think I am trustworthy?'

I was levelling a stare at her that was so fierce I felt I might scorch her with it. 'Who was the man in Oxford?' I asked maliciously. 'Who was he?'

'There was no "man." You have asked me this before Carrick and I told you then.'

'It was you, in a red jacket, the same jacket,' I insisted.

'No, it was not. It was a similar one, but of a quite different shade.'

'And your hotel, they did not know you when I came to call on you.'

She was cold as ice and the room itself was growing chillier by the minute with no Grant to light the fire. Who would do that now I wondered?

She spoke calmly and quietly. 'I was not staying at that hotel you simply presumed I was. I was actually there to–'

George, who up until that point had been staring at

the tea tray unmoved, took over. 'I will not have my fiancée interrogated like this,' he snapped. 'I have had enough and I must draw a line. Whatever Cécile was or was not doing in Oxford is no concern of yours or indeed mine.' He took a deep breath. 'Carrick, I must insist that you move out tonight for, as I was saying earlier, Cécile and I would like some time to ourselves.'

I looked from one to the other of them and stood up. I had obviously been the subject of discussions that had taken place elsewhere. I had nothing to say that would have made me look anything other than bitter. I walked to the door and took one last look at them both. She had her back to me. He was staring straight ahead, his face flushed with contained anger. There was my good friend George, to whom I had been only loyal and true for twenty-four years, and the woman who had come between us.

I heard her say, 'Well said, chéri.' She knew full well I could still hear her. 'It is long past the time for him to go – he has been taking from this family for too long.'

There was never more hatred in the bones of any man than I felt against that woman that day and, as I climbed those stairs for the last time as part of the Amsherst family, I vowed to God I would take my revenge on her.

43

Norman Fry lived in the most humble of cottages. The clay floor was covered in a worn rug, threadbare and dirty. In front of the large fireplace, which had been swept clean, there was a scruffy little dog. I could smell it from the second we entered the room.

The living room was small, two old armchairs and a narrow fold down table, with a single dining chair, almost filled it. There was a small television in the corner, the racing was on, the sound turned low so that the commentator's voice was a murmur.

Norman was a small man with a weather-beaten face and a burgundy nose, a drinker. He was wearing a three-piece tweed suit that had seen better days.

'Come on in and sit down.' He moved a tortoiseshell cat off the oldest and greyest armchair, I hadn't spotted it, such was its camouflage. 'Here you go, have Bess's chair.' He ushered me to the place where the cat had been, it was covered with fur. 'Can I get you some tea?'

'No thank you, Norman, we've just had one,' I replied quickly because I had just seen the state of the kitchen next door. Rory had taken a seat on the dining chair so that his back was to the window and the grey net curtains that sorely needed replacing.

'So Mr McBride tells me you would like to know a bit about my mother?'

'Yes please. I wondered if you could tell me about her time at Lapston?' I replied.

'Oh yes, now let me see, all in all, she was there for a couple of years, perhaps a tad longer. She did love it, worked for old Mrs Hall. What a lovely lady she was, full of kindness. My mum was a scullery maid at first and then a kitchen maid. She learned everything she knew from Mrs Hall, including how to bake. Oh yes, she was a fantastic baker, my mum.'

'What year did she join the staff?'

'When she was fourteen, so I would think it was nineteen forty-two or forty-three, somewhere about that time. She was in service like her mother and her mother before her.' He rested his hands over his old tweed waistcoat and sat back. 'Though they say my grandmother was of gypsy stock. That's why we have such dark hair, well I'm grey now of course, but I was once dark as a raven's back and I go brown very easily skin-wise too.'

'There was a butler, Grant,' I said, trying to make him focus on the house and its residents.

'Oh yes, Grant. He was with the family in London, back in the day. He had replaced that old con artist, Fellowes. Did you know about him being in league with the Edwards brothers? They tried to steal the silver, you know.' I nodded. 'Oh yes, they worked together to steal it. He was, by all accounts, a nasty piece of work, family couldn't see it in him, you see. Too nice.'

'What about Grant?' I asked.

'I have no idea, the only thing I know is that one day he was there the next he had gone. My mother was sweet on him, the older man. He was rather dashing, she said. She had her head full of Mr Grant, oh that's to be sure.'

'So he just went overnight?' asked Rory. 'Disappeared?'

'I think so, my mum never heard from him again, I suspect Mrs Hall would have told her if she had had any word from him.'

'And the parents were Reginald and Augusta?'

'Yes, lovely people, by all accounts but, you see my mum didn't know them, all she knew was they was very missed.' The dog raised its head and I could see its top jaw was longer than the bottom one. Its breathing was very laboured I guessed that it was very old. It returned to its slumbers and began a very loud nasal snore.

'That's Carrick,' Norman said with a smile.

'Carrick?' I said, my ears pricking up. 'Wasn't that the name of someone who lived at Lapston?'

'Yes, Mr Carrick, that's right. He was a cousin or something, always there my mum had a crush on him too, truth be told.' I smiled. 'He was a lovely man, very gentle and kind, and he always took time to thank Mrs Hall, and my mum, for whatever they did for them. That's why my mum liked him so much; he was a good man, a true old-fashioned gentleman.'

'And you say he was a cousin?'

'I think so,' said Norman, looking up as if he was

trawling his mind for more information. 'I may be wrong on that.'

'And there was Alice and George too?'

'Oh yes, for a long time, there were the three of them, three kids, happy as pigs in clover, thick as thieves. Then George met a woman called Russell.'

'Roussell,' I corrected him.

'No, Russell, I thought it was. I'm almost sure it was, my love. My mum saw her arrive you know, then without a by-your-leave, my old mum was sacked.'

'Really?'

'Yes she left the week after Grant.'

'Had your mum done something wrong?'

'No, she was very hurt by it and very angry. She was told to go and that was it, with no references too. Mrs Hall sorted them out for her with Mr Carrick.'

'This Madame Roussell owned the house after the Amshersts, didn't she?'

'I don't know, my love, you see my mum was on the outside after that. It was deserted until the priests came and then no one was allowed near. They made those poor boys work instead of having staff.'

'Weren't the boys ill?' I asked.

'No, love, that's what people called it. A hospital. But it was really an orphanage. I saw them when I was a little boy, used to go in through the gate by the church. They all looked so thin and wretched and they wrapped their arms round their poor sad selves, like they was always cold.'

'Poor little sods,' said Rory.

'Aye, poor things, no mums and dads, they were

247

evacuees whose mums and dads never came for them, so I was told and there was them that wouldn't behave with their village families.'

'What happened to the family?'

'The Amshersts? I can't tell you. My mum heard they had gone away, but I don't think it was good for them, they lost the house.'

'Was someone murdered, or killed?'

'Oh yes, that was a rumour going around that someone died. That French woman, she was the turning point. After that it was tragic.'

44

In my whole life, I never knew such pain as I did those following weeks. It was the most intense feeling of loneliness and of being entirely ostracised. I had also received word from Peterson that he was returning from Italy with a severe burn to his face and would need his flat. I did not say anything, for it was not for me to complain, his kindness in letting me use the place had been exemplary.

There was nothing for it; I took lodgings in Oxford, in a small arts and crafts house in Jericho, with a high-pitched roof and a garden that sloped gently down towards the canal. I gave up the lease on my studio and took a madman's delight in burning the paintings and drawings one by one. I watched as the flames caught and curled the edges, reducing them to shards of blackened paper. I thought that burning memories like that would ease my pain, but it did not.

Remarkably, I had had only a few attacks, none had been overwhelming and I had not blacked out. At one point, I found myself cowering in a corner of the bedroom of my new house in the middle of the night, but I recovered soon enough. I even told myself it was all related to Lapston and the unrequited love of... of her. What did she call it?

Amour fou; insane love and maybe she was right, maybe I was insane. They had both said it after all and neither of them had made any form of contact since I left Lapston, neither at the flat nor my club. It grieved me that George could forget me so easily.

I had been living for about a fortnight in Oxford when I met Dillie in Broad Street, she with the high-pitched whine to her voice that made my head ache. She had heard that George and his fiancée, the French lady she called her, (I did not remind her of the name) were in Scotland with Douglas and his family. In spite of it all, I felt the deepest wrench in my heart when I thought of George and how he had spoken to me, but I could not bring myself to think about her at all.

Dillie was wittering on about how lucky Scotland had been to escape the hardships of the war, when I cut across her and made it obvious that I was not listening to a word she was saying.

'Do you know if Alice is back at Lapston, by any chance?' I asked.

'No, no one is, save Mrs Hall, Ogden and the boy who does the horses.'

'Is it closed down?'

'I should imagine it might well be. Are you no longer staying there, Carrick?'

I did not wish to reply for fear I would become the subject of gossip. 'I have been busy with various affairs and have had no time to visit.'

'Have you moved here?' she asked, stepping closer, obviously intrigued. I moved back, away from her, just as a horse and cart pulled up beside us, the harness jingling. The smell reminded me of Jester. I shifted away to make room for the driver to place a nosebag over the animal's head.

We were standing nearer to the window of Blackwell's bookshop, Dillie even closer to me than before. 'We must meet up, Carrick.' She placed a small gloved hand on my arm. 'I would love to dine with you, perhaps in Little Clarendon Street one evening?'

The idea repelled me. Dillie was the last person in the world I wanted to spend an evening with. I mumbled some sort of excuse about being away for a while and vowed inwardly to avoid her at all costs. She looked hurt as she drew away but I could not have cared less. I realise now that I was hurting in extremis myself.

Alice could not have been more correct when she said that Christmas would never be the same again. No invitation came, nowhere to go, and no word from Lapston. I had written a letter to Mrs Hall enclosing my new calling card, the address of my new house printed on it. She had written a letter thanking me for it and telling me that George and Cécile had been invited to stay in Scotland for the festivities and that she should not be at all surprised, given the nature of recent conversations, if they did not look to settling there eventually. I recalled Sir Reginald's warm Edinburgh accent and his love of all things Scottish. What, I wondered, would he have made of George's poor choice in women?

Mrs Hall wrote further that Lizzie had been let go and needed a reference. I obliged, wondering at the same time, why George would not supply one, for surely Lizzie had done nothing wrong.

Although I had not seen them for two months, I still yearned for everything to be back to normal, for us all, yes even her if it had to be so, to be sitting around that fire in the lounge at Lapston, or in the dining room with the family portraits looking down upon us.

As the nights drew in and the temperature plummeted, I became low. I had written and telephoned Alice's barracks but she had not returned my letters or calls. There was nothing for it, I decided I would take the train to Cambridge and see her myself. She could not deny me in person, but even as I set about my plan, all thoughts of her troubled me. I had been a brute, very unkind, and I had delivered a low blow. It was little wonder that she would not reply to my messages and letters. I fully recognised that she deserved an apology.

The telegram arrived the same day, just as I closed the front door. I tipped the boy and he cycled off with a whistle.

As I tore the envelope open and read it, a Dakota thundered overhead, the low, throaty roar followed by its all-consuming shadow. Everything seemed to go dark, there was no movement or sound in the street, save for the omnipresent thrum of that plane.

"Alice killed Stop In France Stop Coming home Stop George."

When the plane had passed over, the world was still dark, the clouds grey, the road under my feet black as iron.

There was no colour, nothing, just a small monochrome world around me, and it was if there were no oxygen left for me to breathe.

45

'All our dogs were named after people from the big house,' Norman said, bending down stiffly to place a saucer of water by little Carrick. The poor thing looked at it, shivering, but choosing to leave it, he returned to his sleep. 'He's been a little bugger this one, quite an escape artist, but I love him. He's the last of the seven.'

I smiled to humour him, but really I wanted to get back to the mystery. 'And all are named after the residents of Lapston?' I asked patiently.

'Oh yes, he's the last. My mum named them all; Alice, Reggie, Gussie, Henry, Georgie and Carrick. After the first dog, a lab called Prince, there were two spaniels, Henry and Georgie, but the rest have been Heinz 57s. She loved her dogs, my mum. Hated cats, mind, couldn't stand them.'

'What happened after the French lady came on the scene?' I asked.

'Oh, well then, it was all very sad. You see, Mr. Carrick chose to move permanently to Oxford. His father came from the city originally. My mother never met the father of course, he was away all the time.' Norman settled back in his armchair. 'It was a rum do. Miss Alice was killed in Normandy. She was on a plane carrying medicines; they say she volunteered, even though she knew it would be dangerous. They could have a red cross on them if they was carrying just food, and stuff, but her plane was carrying ammo too. It was shot down and no one survived. It was a rum do. Such a lovely, lovely lady. I have a picture of her here.'

He stood up stiffly, a hand on his back. 'It's here somewhere... ah, there it is.' He picked up a small ornate frame. I recognised the smiling face, the bright eyes. Alice was sitting on a farm gate, younger than she had been in the previous photo I'd seen. Behind her was a horse standing in the sun, his eyes closed. She wasn't wearing riding gear, instead she wore a light coloured dress with a full skirt.

'How old was she when she died?'

'Twenty-five, too young. She was the second member of the family they lost to the war. Her brother Henry had already been killed in France. Both of them died there and they're buried out there, as far as we know. My mum was heartbroken. That's why we named the next pup Alice, you see, we'd got Prince from the big house and she was company for him. Prince and Princess Alice after the real Princess. Prince had been Miss Alice's dog, you see, but when she died... well, mum took him on, poor lad. Ogden was set to drown him, no one wanted him, that upset my mum something chronic.'

'Why didn't George keep him?' I asked.

'Oh he was in Scotland, or somewhere, didn't want a dog around.'

'Did he come back to Lapston?'

'I don't know, I really can't remember, but I would say not. The house was left empty and the next thing we heard was that Mrs Russell owned it.'

'What happened to George, and Carrick?'

'I think, no I can't remember anything about George.' Norman scratched his head. 'But Mr Carrick is still with us, he's in a home going towards London. He's not very well, but he's with us all right, must have reached his century by now. Would you like the address?'

I thought I was hearing things. It hadn't occurred to me that any of them were still alive. 'Yes, I would like it, how do you know about him?'

'He came back. He came to visit the house in the seventies. My mum opened the door and he was there, large as life and twice as handsome. He was a lovely man.'

'What was it like seeing him? Did you speak to him?'

'Oh yes, I showed him that picture of Miss Alice, and my mum had him stop for a cup of tea. It really upset him mind. They talked a good deal, I left them be. I had to go and work in The Crown; I did bar work in those days, you see.'

'What did he say to your mum?'

'Oh this and that. They talked about the house and he said he wanted to go up and see it again, but wanted to go alone. It was deserted, of course, by then. He left but he kept in touch by phone, the odd time.'

'Norman, thank you, you've been very helpful,' I said, standing up and taking him by the hand, his skin was rough and papery. The old eyes were rheumy and pale, but there was a twinkle in them.

'I never married,' he said, 'but if I did, I'd have married a pretty lady like you.'

I felt a knot of emotion rising in my throat and I turned to Rory who leaned across and patted the old man on the shoulder in turn. 'Thanks, Norman, I hope Carrick's okay,' he said kindly.

'Ah, he's old and creaky like me,' came the reply. 'But you two still have plenty of years ahead of you. I hope you'll be very happy together. You can tell when two people are meant to be together, and you're it.'

I turned to correct his assumption but Rory was between us, blocking the doorway, and the moment was lost.

'See,' said Rory as we walked on up the lane. 'Even old Norman is on my side.'

I didn't reply – because I didn't trust myself.

46

I arrived at Lapston at lunchtime on Christmas Eve. There was a heavy brooding sky in keeping with the dark thoughts in my head. Everything was my fault and I knew it. I will never be able to forget how I treated her and I will never forgive myself if I live to be a hundred.

As I passed through the huge iron gates, the lawn spread out before me a deep, viridian green and the house, with its frontage clad in ivy, sat low at the end of it as if it were hunkered down for winter. Mrs Hall answered the door. She was not the smart, cleanly presented Mrs Hall I knew, but a tired and drawn character more at home in a Dickens' novel, her eyes ringed in raw, red skin.

'Mr Carrick!' She looked so pleased to see me it near broke my heart. 'Oh Mr Carrick, I don't believe it. They didn't say you were coming.'

I embraced her; her bones were thin beneath her cardigan. For the first time ever, I noticed she was wearing trousers. She apologised and told me they were good for manual work, something forced on her since there were no other staff in the house.

'I should have gone with Lizzie,' she said as she led me into the chill of the hall. 'I should have gone, but Mr

George has me on a retainer and I couldn't face leaving you and, and, poor Al–' Mrs Hall began to cry, so I led her gently to the stairs where we sat side-by-side on the third step. The house seemed to creak and groan around us with no happy sounds to fill it and I knew, at that moment, that the conversations and laughter we had all shared were gone forever.

'When did you hear?' I asked. She had taken a lace handkerchief from her pocket and dabbed her eyes with it.

'Yesterday, just before midnight, Mr George rang. My legs gave way; I could not take it in, our beautiful girl, my darling Alice. I haven't stopped crying since, I didn't sleep at all.'

'And how did it happen, do you know?'

'He said she was flying over France in a plane taking supplies to a field hospital. I don't understand, Mr Carrick. It was carrying medicines. It would have had a red cross on it, yet they still shot it down.' Mrs Hall wept, her body wracked with huge sobs, the poor thing had been on her own since she received the news. I had my arm around her, although I was fighting back my own tears. 'All I want to know is do you think she died straight away? I couldn't stand the thought she was lying in some damp French field in pain, not my Alice.' Mrs Hall sobbed again.

'I'm practically certain it would have been instantaneous.' I lied because I too feared the worst. 'I'm sure it would have exploded as it hit the ground.'

We sat there the two of us, heads leaning together, and I realised in all my life Mrs Hall had been my one true mother, the one who loved us best.

'What time do you expect George and Madame Roussell?'

'Oh, I don't, Mr Carrick.' She sniffed. 'They were going to come back but then Madam Roussell pointed out there is nothing to come back for. Miss Alice will be buried over there and she felt it would be best for Mr George to be amongst his family and friends, in Scotland. I wasn't expecting anybody, especially not you.'

'Really?' I said, chewing over her words. Family and friends? Not a thought for me. 'Mrs Hall, what have you been doing here on your retainer?'

'Oh I look after everything now. I've put the house to bed, covered all the furniture with dustsheets, and I just live in the kitchen with only my hens to keep me company in the whole place. I had to give Lizzie the dog, Miss Alice's dog. I couldn't look after a young puppy, not at my age and with so much to do.'

I nodded thoughtfully. 'How would you like a house-keeping position in Oxford?'

She turned to look at me, her mouth dropping open in surprise. 'Do you know of someone who is looking?'

'Yes, that is I am, it is me. I need someone to keep house for me. I tried cooking and I find that I'm not very adept at it.' I managed a smile. God knows how.

'Oh Mr Carrick, I cannot tell you what that means to me. I would love to come and be your housekeeper, I have been so lonely here. I have not had the heart to tell Mr George, but since Mr Grant and Lizzie...'

'Then you will come home with me, and I say let us do it after some lunch, while the iron is hot, as they say.'

Anyone hearing the tone in my voice may have mistaken it as positive, but I was putting on a facade for the sake of Mrs Hall and for a moment she looked visibly brighter, but then her face dropped a little.

'But what about Mr George and–'

'You leave that to me, I shall write to them. They will receive the letter after Christmas and, by that time, you and I will be long gone. They deserve no better in my opinion.'

'Oh but–'

'Oh but nothing, Mrs Hall,' I told her, standing up. 'You and I will support each other.'

'My hens,' she said. She looked mortified at the thought of leaving them.

'Pack them in a crate and bring them with you. I have a coop in the garden, and a vegetable patch that needs some care and attention. Now, I must talk to Ogden, and of course Jim, about the horses.'

'Oh Mr Carrick, they've gone,' she said with alarm, palms pressed to the sides of her face.

'Gone?' my heart missed a beat. 'Gone where?'

'To the kennels. Madam Roussell telephoned on Tuesday and said arrangements had been made for them to go to the kennels – they've been destroyed.'

47

When he kissed me, it was so gentle that I felt only the finest brush of his lips on mine. I pressed my hands against his chest; it felt solid and real under my flattened palms. Then he leaned in and this time I could feel a pressure in his kiss and it spoke of the longing we had for each other.

A thousand feelings rushed through me. Nerves in my stomach somersaulted and sent shock waves through my body. He tasted so good, as if everything I had ever wanted was in front of me right then, everything I had ever dared to dream of.

I had a choice, step away or step right in. I placed my head against his cotton shirt and felt safe as he wrapped his arms around me.

'I must go,' I said, but I didn't move.

'Stay.'

'I can't, Rory. I must go, and I don't trust myself at all.' I expected one of his quips, but he was silent. I pulled away and refused to look at him as I searched in my bag for the car keys. I fumbled and dropped them, knowing that he was watching me. I could almost feel the ache in him. My stomach was churning with desire, something I had not felt in years.

'Bye, Rory,' I said, but when I glanced up at where he had been standing, he had turned and walked away.

48

I was seething with anger as I dialled the kennels. It was Hodgkins, the houndsman who answered, and when I heard his voice I could barely speak.

'Hodgkins, it's Maxwell Carrick here. Is it you who took our horses away?'

'Yes, sir, Mr Carrick. We came for them Tuesday as directed.'

'Are they... have you?'

'Oh no, Mr Carrick, I waited, you see. I said to Cyril and Jack, you remember Jack from Swinford? I said I wasn't at all sure about any of this, I hadn't heard from you or Miss Alice and, although it was on direct orders, I said no, I don't think we ought to do this. Not old Jester. You won the Berner's cup on him in thirty three, I said the old fellow deserves more respect than that.'

Tears welled up in my eyes.

'Oh thank God.' The relief flooded through me. 'Thank God you had the good sense. Where are they now?

'I have them here, we've got all these empty stables and only ten hounds we've got plenty of room.'

'And feed?'

'Yes, we've got enough for Jester and Miss Alice's Beau. Tell her he'll be just fine, we'll look after him.'

There was a long empty silence.

'Are you still there, sir?'

'Yes,' I replied weakly, I gathered everything about me and told him the news. 'I'm afraid Miss Alice has passed away, Hodgkins, she was killed in France.'

There was a stony silence, then I heard him take a deep breath. 'Not Miss Alice too, not her.'

'I'm afraid so.' I could barely speak. I knew the image of her was in his mind as it was in mine – those eyes, the sparkle in them. Neither of us said a word then, at length, I said, 'Hodgkins can you do me a favour? Will you take on Jim, our lad, to look after them? He knows them well and, until you hear from me, say nothing to Mr Amsherst about them. If any questions are asked, the horses belong to me. Send me your bill, I will forward my address, and make sure I pay the appropriate rate for Jim.'

'Yes I will, sir, I will look after them for you and Miss Alice even if she in't here no more. It's a scandal what she was proposing.'

'Who?'

'The French lady. She told us to bring them here. I tried to say it was up to their owners and she said they were a waste of money and that you and Miss Alice had moved on.'

'So it wasn't Major Amsherst who called you?'

'Oh no, sir, it was her. I asked to speak to him but she said I was being disrespectful. I was upset by that because I've always been very observant of my dues.'

'I apologise on their behalf,' I said, as the anger was rising inside me. 'I am very sorry for any inconvenience caused. Madame Roussell is French, from Paris, they are not known for their love of horses.'

'I heard they eat them over there, sir. Is it true?'

'I do believe it is.'

'Defies belief, Mr Carrick, how anyone can look a horse in the eye and think of eating it, I'll never understand, it would be like eating a loyal friend.'

'I'm indebted to you for what you have done, and tell anyone who is up to it that they can both be ridden out. So many people are missing their horses they might appreciate it and I'm afraid I can't ride for a while.'

'Will do, sir, and you can take it from me they will be well cared for, I'll speak to Jim directly.'

'Thank you.'

'And sir.'

'Yes?'

'Can I say that you're a very fair and good man. And I'm very sad about Miss Alice, we all will be in the village.'

'Thank you.'

49

Sarah was home for the weekend, she was full of news about her company and the redundancies and her plans for her holiday in Rhodes. She enthralled her father. I watched him gazing at her, chin resting on his hand, we both still marvelled that between us we had produced someone so amazing.

'So how are things here?' Finally she turned her attention to us and I took a seat beside her at the table. 'Still bored of being retired, Mum?'

'No, she isn't now,' Steve cut in. 'She's up to all sorts.'

I ignored him, he was trying to get Sarah on side and make fun of me. 'I've been working on a village book, the history group has asked me to edit it for them,' I told her.

'Work on it, edit it, give up all your time to it, but they won't respect you and listen to your advice. I don't know why your mum hasn't told them where to go, I would,' Steve chipped in.

'Thank you, Steve, that's not very helpful.' I chided him gently but there was an underlying tone that Sarah picked up on. Her eyes darted from him to me.

'What have they been saying?'

'Oh nothing, they're a bit stuck in their ways, a bit like your father,' I replied pointedly.

'Your mum's doing all this research and they don't appreciate it, they have no idea who they've got working for them. Ungrateful I call it,' said Steve.

Sarah turned to me. 'Is that true?'

'Sort of, but I'm having such a good time researching I really don't mind.'

'She's been climbing through old ruins with a mad old bloke who hasn't heard of Health and Safety.'

'He's not old and he's not mad!' I exclaimed, realising instantly that I was far too quick to defend him.

'How old is he then?'

'I don't know, about my age, perhaps a bit younger. He has three children, the oldest one is twenty.'

'Oh really,' said Steve. 'I thought he'd be a sort of David Bellamy character with sideburns and a woolly hat.'

Sarah snorted with laughter.

Suddenly, I felt wounded, stupid I know, but I didn't want Rory to be talked about like that.

'I'd like to meet him,' said Sarah.

'Well, you can't,' I said proprietarily. 'He's away, abroad, on a job.'

'What does he do?'

'Landscapes, a gardener, he designs gardens.'

'How lovely,' replied my daughter cheerfully. 'And you say he's single?'

'Sarah!'

'Oh Mum, I'm only asking. Single men over forty need to be logged and registered with the society for diminishing returns.' I must have looked shocked, because she quickly added. 'Mum, these days age is no barrier, I dated a sixty three year old last year.'

Steve looked horrified. "Sarah, I'm sixty four and I'm your dad.'

'And if something happened to Mum and a nice, attentive forty-four-year-old came along, you wouldn't kick her out of bed would you?'

I could see Steve mentally adding up the pros and cons in his mind.

'Excuse me, I'm still here,' I joked, and we all laughed.

'Right, I can't stay around here all day I have to tee off in half an hour,' Steve said as he stood up and kissed Sarah on the top of her blonde head. 'Find a nice forty-four-year-old to date and make sure you send him to me first to be vetted.' He stalked out, feeling in his pocket for his keys, then he groaned as he slung his golf bag over his shoulder and we heard the door being closed.

'Tell me about him,' said Sarah when he'd gone.
'Who?'
'This man.'
'Which man?
'The one you're in love with.'

50

Mrs Hall stood looking around my small lounge. She had slept on the short journey to Oxford, exhausted as she was, and we both arrived in Jericho feeling careworn and dejected. My house had some lovely features arched ceilings and the kitchen was almost hexagonal. It was rather rustic with an old range that I presumed had demised, for no effort of mine would light it.

The rear door opened onto a stone terrace and from there a long narrow garden fell away. Of course it was dark, so she could barely see anything at all.

'You can do anything you like with the gardens, obviously over half is vegetable beds, but there is a small upper lawn which catches the afternoon sun very well,' I told her.

'And my girls?'

'Ah, the hens. We'll pop them in the Anderson tonight and then we'll repair the coop tomorrow. It only needs the netting stretched back into place.'

'The house is very small, Mr Carrick. I shouldn't wonder if we don't trip over each other.'

'I think you'll find anything after Lapston is small,' I said in my most reassuring voice. 'Upstairs are two bedrooms of good size and a bathroom. You have a bed, an armchair and a fireplace with a good draw. It's cosy but serviceable, please do make it your own. Now, dear Mrs Hall, what do I pay you? I have no idea of such things.'

'Oh Mr Carrick, you have been so kind, I need only a small amount if you are letting me have bed and board and I promise in a few days it will look like a new pin in here.'

'Do I assume it doesn't quite look like a new pin at present?' I asked with a smile.

'It needs a woman's touch,' she said, rubbing a finger along a bookshelf and holding up a rather dusty fingertip. Of course what she said only served to make us both think of Alice. I could see Mrs Hall's face was about to crumple so I suggested we fetched the birds and took them down to the shelter.

Later on, we both sat, she nursing a drinking chocolate, me on the couch with a whisky, both tired but too afraid to go to bed because we were burdened with a grief so strong it was almost certain to consume us. The events of the day, I realised had been a diversion, and a good one at that.

'What happened to Grant?' I asked, staring into the flickering flames of the small fire.

'I have no idea. He was very angry when he left, he packed his things immediately and was gone. Such a lovely man. He went back to London – he said a friend of his needed help running a restaurant. It broke my heart to see him go, well it does doesn't it when you know someone so well?'

She paused momentarily. 'At least, I thought I knew him well...'

'What do you mean, Mrs Hall?'

'Oh I shouldn't say it really.'

'Tell me.'

'Well, he had struck up more of a friendship with Mr George, and I didn't think it was quite right for a man in his position. Sir Reginald would have put a stop to it, chatting with the staff in the library and such. They would discuss matters and then just tell me what had been decided. That was a bit upsetting – I did feel left out – but I cannot complain really because Mr Grant was a fair man with a good heart.'

'And Lizzie? You told me in your letter she left soon after.'

'She did, she was pushed out too.'

'Pushed?'

'Yes, by that woman, Madam Roussell. It was like having a cuckoo in the nest, forcing us all out.'

'Do you think she did it deliberately, I mean orchestrated it?'

'Normally I don't speak out of turn about anyone, but I didn't like that woman. I did everything I could to please her, made her French food and the like, but do you know she never once said a word of thanks.'

'Really?'

'I'm afraid not, and Mr George changed too. It was like he was under her spell and all so quickly. He became, I'd call it aloof, as if they were both better than anyone else. Then she was wearing Lady Augusta's clothes, helped herself to a blue evening gown and a very expensive tweed suit, she did.' I remembered the latter, in the library that terrible afternoon, the penny dropped. 'That's why Miss Alice left so soon, she couldn't stand it, and I told her we would all miss her, but she just said she had to go.'

I could have shared with her my deep misgivings about Alice, but even though we were closer than ever we had been, I couldn't say anything. It was as if all the words were stuck in my throat.

'Yet Cécile showed me such kindness when I, when I–'

'When you had your funny turns?'

'Yes,' I nodded.

'That was Alice,' she leaned forward. 'That was my Alice. She sat next to your bed. I covered her with a little blanket when she fell asleep.' Mrs Hall shook her head. 'She nursed you, Mr Carrick. That French woman never came near except if George asked after you, then she popped her head round the door.'

I tried to remember, but one image leached into another, dull shadows only, no clarity.

The mantel clock chimed midnight, a cold noise in the cosy room. It stirred us both.

'My dear Mrs Hall, I do believe it is Christmas Day.' I held up my glass in a half-hearted salute. 'To Alice, our darling Alice.' We turned back to the fire where the embers were slowly dying. The year was dying too, but inside both of us something was already dead.

51

'I have no idea what you mean,' I said, turning away from my daughter.

'Yes, you do. I can see it a mile off. Dad can't but let's face it he couldn't see it if it was written on the side of a bus and parked outside the window. I collected up the empty mugs and the basket full of left over croissant crumbs and took them into the kitchen but it was no good, she followed me. 'I could see it written all over your face, Mum.'

I turned back to face her, she was leaning against the Aga.

'I, I don't know what to d-do,' I said, tripping over my words like an idiot.

'How long?' All of a sudden she sounded accusatory, unpleasant.

I swallowed back the things I could have said. I wanted to snap her head off for talking to me in that tone, but more than that, I so wanted to explain how he made me feel, how much I yearned to be with him, how I couldn't go any further without causing pain to everyone, including her.

'It hasn't,' I replied, shaking my head. 'Nothing has happened.'

'How long have you known him?'

'Since early spring. He has this dog, you see, he knocked me over, and then there is Lapston.'

'The old house?'

'Yes, we, that is he, does the garden, the knot garden and he showed me.'

'Mum, you look absolutely terrified. I'm not going to say anything to Dad.'

I felt a strange kind of relief wash over me and I realised that my skin was tingling as my subconscious recalled Rory. That kiss. Even then, in front of my own daughter. My stomach churned and twisted, and I ran a hand through my hair wondering, as I did so, when had it become so thin? How on earth did he think I was attractive?

'Mum, you're not listening to me.' I realised she was right. 'You're not listening.'

'I'm sorry, darling, I'm just all over the place at the moment. It's very difficult.'

Sarah placed her hands on my shoulders, her head tilted slightly. When did she grow so tall, or was I shorter now? They say your backbone starts to crumble past sixty, don't they?

'Mum, you're going through a bad time, you've left work, you're feeling lonely then you've met this man and he's brought a bit of excitement in your life. You couldn't do that to Dad. He may be grumpy and boring now but you and him have history, a shared life, it's not worth throwing it all away.'

'That's what Becky said,' I told her.

'Then she's as sensible and mature as me.'

I placed a hand on my daughter's soft cheek. Her skin felt cool under my palm, the flawless complexion free of any signs of ageing.

'I know,' I said. 'I know, I could never hurt your dad.'

52

I woke up wringing wet, the sheets were wrapped around me and my right leg was hanging over the edge of the bed. I clasped my hand to my forehead; it had been a torrid and very real nightmare. I had been in the lounge at Lapston, I was miserable and overwhelmed with loss and then I saw Alice through the door. I fumbled in my pockets for a key and found one, but it didn't fit the lock. I pressed my hand against the glass hoping it would pass straight through, that I could control the subconscious thoughts myself, but the way was barred to me.

Outside the window, I could see Alice. She had a bonnet on with a scarf wrapped around it. She looked just like her mother, the same lovely face. I waved back and she beckoned me to come and join her in the knot garden. I began to cry, hot tears rolling down my face, and then she was turning and walking away, threading her way through the winding paths to the river and onto the long, flat field where the aeroplane wreckage lay strewn about her. Dead people lying like broken dolls in the muddy fields…

There was a light tapping on the door.

'Mr Carrick, is everything all right?' For one absurd second, my heart lifted and I thought it was her, Cécile, coming for me to take her down for dinner, me with her on my arm.

'I'm absolutely fine, Mrs Hall.' I shook the images from my head and downed the glass of water by my bed. 'I'll be ready for breakfast shortly.' I got a grip of myself. I had to go on, even if it were just for Mrs Hall's sake.

Indeed, the arrangement had been working very well. Mrs Hall had cleaned everywhere, washed my bedding, tidied the garden, and whenever I wanted it, she always managed to rustle up something to eat. My appetite, since Alice, was small and each day stretched into another, the gloom of darkness barely withdrawing before it began all over again. The hum of American planes rattled the house to the foundations at times, and outside the streets were dark and dreary.

In early January, I took the train into the city.

As I walked past the second-class carriages, I saw it was packed with people, like so many crates of chickens bound for market, bemused heads peering out through grimy windows.

It made sense for me to go up to London and oversee some business on behalf of my father. He had suggested, in his latest letter, that I might find employment in the war office, and I had to look willing. Mrs Hall had joined the local Women's Institute and was out more evenings than she was in. I was glad for her; she deserved better than the ghostly halls of Lapston. As for me, I missed it with every fibre of my being and, to make matters worse, George had made no contact with me. I had presumed that by snatching Mrs Hall from him, I might at least deserve some rebuke, but much worse was the silence and the very fact that he did not want to talk to me about Alice. I felt desolate for that reason, as if I had not only lost her, but him as well.

Between the latticed tape of carriage windows, I saw that London was grey and forlorn. It reminded me of the great flank of a dead whale I saw in a cove in Cornwall. The skin was slashed, the fibres of the flesh beneath it transparent, dull grey slits visible in the tough, limpet-clad skin. That was London now, a huge monster lying wounded and almost dead, the life draining out of her and made worse by the smog and the soulless winter. War had taken everything and was testing the very last of the British fighting spirit. In the back yards of dark terraced houses and the litter strewn streets were people with drawn ghostly faces. Women, old men and children, every one of them, shattered by loss, if not of loved ones, of their homes, their places of work or way of life.

Is this what Hitler had planned? To eradicate us, to raze our cities to the ground and then stick a flag in the rubble, his jack boot on our heads? It was madness from the start, pure madness begetting even more madness.

The train arrived at Paddington and the doors banged open accompanied by the hiss of the engine and then a cloud of steam surrounded me. As it cleared, I saw a familiar figure on the concourse. I stood on tiptoe to give me the advantage above the heads of my fellow passengers, but it was of no use. I quickened my pace, edging around a large group of children and their teacher, and caught again the sight of blond hair. Grant. He was walking quickly, nimbly passing through the American troops who huddled in groups waiting to board a train. I picked up my pace, half running and made after him.

He was striding most purposefully, with me some thirty feet behind him. As I left the shelter of the station the rain was like stair rods. I tried calling to him but he had his collar up, and unusually, no hat. It was obvious that he couldn't hear me.

I was almost upon him when he turned a sharp left into a building just off Conduit Place. It had a narrow frontage with a blue, anonymous looking front door and a window to one side, covered in criss-crossed tape just like the train. I stepped inside making the bell ring and brought in with me a cloud of wet air. It was an old shop and the display shelves and glass cabinets were all empty and covered with dust.

From behind a filthy curtain in the corner a man appeared, he was small with dark hair swept over a bald pate. His glasses being round and cheap made him look older than his years. He was looking very surprised to see me standing there, of that I was certain.

'May I help you, sir?' he asked.

I looked around me. There was no reason at all to explain my presence. I decided there was nothing for it, but to tell him the truth. 'I followed an acquaintance in here. I have not seen him for some time and, by chance, saw him again just now at the station.'

'An acquaintance, sir?'

'Yes, a Mr James Grant.'

He stood looking at me up and down. The steam was rising from my woollen coat, the room seemed to be filling with moisture from it.

'I'm afraid you are mistaken, sir. There is no Mr Grant here.'

He reminded me of the confounded little man at The Angel hotel.

'I have just walked in behind him and saw him enter.' I did not conceal the annoyance in my voice, but he merely met my words with silence. 'I insist that you tell Mr Grant I am here.'

'I cannot, sir, because he is not here.'

'What is this place?'

'It is my private business, sir,' he replied coldly. 'May I ask if you have been referred to me?'

'What on earth do you mean, are you a doctor or some such?'

'No, sir. Now, if I may ask you to leave, I would be very grateful; I am a very busy man.' He came from behind the counter and escorted me the two yards to the door and as I left he pushed it closed with great vigour.

I waited some ten minutes, on the other side of the road, in the shelter of a shop doorway, but no one came out. I spotted a workman, huddled under an oilskin on a bicycle, coming along the street. I stopped him and asked if he knew what the place was, but he said he did not and it was none of his business to tell me if he had known. I tried to give him a coin for his trouble and to tease some further information from him, but he shrugged me off.

That night I was in my hotel in Mayfair. It was surviving, but only just. Yards along the road my father's club had taken a direct hit. The whole atmosphere of the place had completely changed, I would have to describe it as a pervading weariness. The maître d'hôtel barely spoke, his face was haggard and his uniform looked shabby, echoing the mood of the place. Inside, I found Lewis back from France, his right hand bandaged, he was smoking a rather fine cigar with his left. I had asked him to meet me there.

'Carrick, old man,' he said. 'Take a pew.' I sat down beside him, knowing that he knew a little about everyone and a lot about the most important things. 'I haven't seen you since autumn. How is everyone at Lapston? I heard about Alice, dashed bad luck, a fine girl, looked just like her dear mother.'

'It is a huge loss for us,' I said, masking the deadened feelings inside me. There were many times in those dreadful days that I just wanted to explode with anger and this was one of them. I looked around at the men in their leather chairs surrounding me, wondering how many of them were experiencing the same thing.

'How is George?'

'He's fine, coping very well I expect. He is in Scotland currently.'

'Gone back already?'

I tilted my head. 'Already?'

'I had a drink with him at The Café Royal on Thursday.'

'You did?'

'Yes, he wanted to organise getting to France for him and a companion, knew I could pull some strings and all that.' I was completely wrong-footed and quite taken by surprise.

'Where was he staying?' I asked as calmly as possible.

'The Cumberland, I think, no The Strand, that's it.'

'He wanted to go to Paris. I told him he stood no chance, only top brass and civil servants higher than me could pull that off, but I could find some method of transport that would get him within shouting distance.'

'A companion?'

'Yes, he was taking a lady friend with him, apparently all very hush, hush. I would have thought he'd have told you, Carrick.'

'Yes, yes, I must apologise, it slipped my mind, when is he going?'

'Next week, all things being equal, I still have some calls to make.'

'Could you do the same for me?' I asked, as a waiter placed my whisky in front of me.

'What's all this about needing to get to Paris?' Lewis exhaled a smoke circle that rose between us, I watched as it dispersed. 'Suddenly everyone wants to go, it's a mess, lawless.'

'I have some urgent business to undertake for my father, he would like it addressed as soon as possible,' I lied.

'That doesn't cut any ice, I'm afraid, old man. The opportunities are very slim, but I will see what I can do.

Your father and I go back a long way and he pulled the odd string for me in times past, if you know what I mean. In early February a lot of my colleagues are going to and fro in an effort to make sense of it all. Maybe I could rope you in. The Yanks are working with us now.'

'Do you have any positions?'

'In Paris?'

'No, in the Ministry?'

At first, he looked at me askance then, leaning forward, he tapped the ash from his cigar into the ashtray. 'We're running a pretty tight ship just now and, I would imagine that will be the case for the foreseeable future.'

He and I both knew he was stalling; he had the influence to find me something if he so wished. He heaved a big sigh, and shifted in his chair. 'I think you should give it some time, old man,' he said. 'After all it's taxing work. One would have to be on full form, if you understand my meaning.'

I sipped my whisky and ended the conversation with Lewis when it was appropriate and not so that he would think I was using him. As I stood up to leave he suddenly recalled our last meeting.

'How did it go with your French lady?'

I was surprised he remembered.

'Not well, she left me for someone else, quite unceremoniously, I'm afraid.'

'Told you so. Same for my friend, you remember? All ended in tears there too, took him for everything and vanished.'

'Perhaps you are right Lewis, we should stick with our

English Roses.' I left him sitting there as an air-raid siren ground into action and with his presumption that I was off to a shelter, I walked though the pitch black streets, the spotlights scanning the sky above me, not caring if I lived or died.

53

I held the letter at arm's length and squinted; I needed new glasses. Norman's writing was entirely in capitals and his spelling was very poor. He had written out the address for the nursing home and telephone number, and then closed by wishing both Rory and me well for the future. A frisson of wretched guilt forked through me.

When I got home, I inputted the address into the contacts on my phone and then screwed up the letter. I even placed it inside another bit of rubbish to make sure it remained hidden in the bin, like a true deceiver.

It was a day or two before I dialled the number because I had to summon up the nerve.

'Lady Cormer House.' The receptionist's voice was friendly enough. I took a deep breath and asked if I might be put through to a Mr Carrick.

'You can leave a message for Mr Carrick, she said, but he won't take calls I'm afraid, he's quite hard of hearing. Would you like me to do that for you?'

I felt uncertain. Why did I want to speak to him? My journalistic instincts? Answers to burning questions? Did I need to know anything at all? Enough to talk to a complete stranger, one who may very well resent my visit?

'Hello, are you still there?'

'Yes, yes I am. Would you mind asking Mr Carrick if I could visit him to enquire about his time at Lapston Manor in Oxfordshire? He doesn't know me, but I'm working on a book about the history of the village, my village, the village where he lived for some time.' There was silence and I presumed she was writing. 'Please tell him that I'd be very grateful for his help, but if he is not up for a visit I would understand.'

'Oh he loves visitors, especially of the animal kind, if you have a dog please bring him with you. He asked for a horse to visit for his ninety-fifth birthday, that was a hoot.'

'I have a dog, Inca, I'll bring her with me,' I told the receptionist. She was proving to be a real help.

'Great, I'll pop this message down to him and explain it all. Your name is?'

'Martha, Martha Nelson.' I gave her my number and a thrill passed through me as I hit the red button on my phone; the old thrill of following a lead and going after a story.

It was back, the feeling I'd lost.

54

I spoke to Douglas from the telephone box at the end of my street that night, as always he was wonderfully warm and kindly towards me.

'They left last week, Carrick. Did George not tell you? Marriage plans. They want to be married in the south as soon as possible.

'Not Paris?'

'No, Cécile has friends who own a chateau in The Loire. They have a church in the grounds which she has set her heart on.' I fumbled for my next sentence.

'How is George?'

'Fine, fine. He seemed very happy, and of course she is such a lovely thing, I can't help but feel Henry's loss is his gain, terrible as that sounds.'

'Did they say when they would be returning to Lapston?'

'No, next is Paris to sort out some financial affairs and then who knows. They are talking about Switzerland for a honeymoon – you know they have friends in Geneva, don't you?' There was a moment of silence then with the tone of his voice lowered, he said, 'So how are you, old man? Any better?'

'Me?' I coughed a little, cleared my throat. 'I'm fine. I've moved into a house in Oxford for the time being. I will send you my new address.' There was another pause as if he was thinking how to couch his words to best effect.

'Cécile was telling us about it, about you, Carrick. She seemed very concerned, George too. Is there anything I can do? You do know you are always welcome here, some fine Scottish air in your lungs would do you the world of good.'

I wasn't listening, I was wondering what she had told him, what extent of my personal affairs she had sought to share. I saw her gathered with everyone in the grand hall for cocktails, mesmerising them as she told of my problem and how she had nursed me and worried about me. No doubt she told them everything except how she saw to it that I was removed from Lapston, like an unwanted dog, just like Alice's poor Prince.

Alice.

'Do you know what is happening about Alice? I was wondering what has happened to her... to her–'

I felt a pressure in my head, like a hand pressing on the back of my skull; it was always the same when I thought about her.

'She was buried over there, they sent a letter and George and Cécile are going to visit the grave after they marry. I thought–' He stopped speaking and I wondered what he was holding off from telling me. 'Cécile said she would write to you and let you know.'

'She would be unaware that I was living at my new address, I suspect. The letter is probably with Peterson at his flat.'

'How is he?'

'Badly burnt they say, in the face, but coping, somehow. I haven't seen him yet. He has sent word that visitors should stay clear for a while and his mother is there. She was a nurse – best of care and all that.' There was an ebb and flow of feelings awash inside me. I wanted to travel to this church in the gardens of this friend's chateau and take George to one side. I wanted to tell him he was making a mighty mistake because I didn't trust the woman and never would. I also wanted to walk away, go through the pain of being separated from my life at Lapston and start again. I was being torn in two different directions.

Before the conversation ended, Douglas said: 'Take care, Carrick. Do look after yourself.'

I wrote to my father that afternoon and expressed a wish to visit him, I thought some distance could only help, different circuit, new faces etc. As I handed the letter to the post office clerk I regretted it instantly; I was running away from me, my own worst enemy was in fact me.

'Why Mr Carrick, you poor thing, you looked drained.' Mrs Hall rested a hand on my forehead like a fussing mother hen. I tried to evade her attentions but she was eying me suspiciously. 'Come and have a drinking chocolate and sit yourself down, I don't like the colour of you.'

In those dark days, I only ever felt completely at rest in my armchair, one foot on the stool, the fire lit before me.

'Mr Peterson's mother called round at midday. I didn't know who she was, but she's a nice lady, we had a lovely chat.' Mrs Hall placed a cup in front of me on a low table and handed me a half dozen letters, then sat back in her own chair. 'I was out in the garden seeing to the girls and she gave me these, they had gone to the flat of course.'

I sorted through them. There were bills and the like, but nothing from Scotland, no contact from either of them. I determined to forget them and put them out of my mind.

'Mr Carrick, my love, are you quite yourself? You look grey around the gills to me.'

'I'm fine, Mrs Hall,' I replied. 'I have much on my mind, not least worrying about what to do next. I am afraid that I have met with something of a void, I fear the world is falling apart around us.'

She put down the knitting that she had pulled out of her basket and then she looked into my eyes. I saw in her such reassurance and support that I felt humbled. 'Let it go, son.'

I didn't look up at her, I couldn't. My face was set rigid trying to fend back tears.

'Let it go. Her. Him. Everything. You cannot go on like this, my love, you deserve better. No one can live with ghosts, just let them go.'

I began to sob and she moved across and held me, my head resting on her bosom, my face shrouded in hot tears.

55

The letter sat on the palm of his hand, in a tight scrunched up ball.

'What's this?'

I stared at it, lost for words.

'It...it's a letter.'

'Who's Norman?' Steve's face was stern, his jaw set.

'It's an old chap from Sarsten. He's been helping me with my research on Lapston.'

'And why does he wish you and this Rory person a happy future together?'

'It's nothing, he misunderstood, he's very old.' I felt sick and my stomach was twisting into a spasm. Steve opened the letter and spread it out on the kitchen counter, its tiny wrinkles like mountains and river valleys. 'Why have you got it?'

'I was doing the recycling and, as usual, you'd put things in the wrong bins. It was hidden inside another piece of rubbish. Hidden.'

'Steve, it really is nothing. I didn't want you to be upset; I knew you could read it two ways, I–'

'Two ways?' His voice was raised now. 'Martha, I've been watching all this very carefully, you know, I'm not stupid.' I tried to break in, tell him there was nothing to see, nothing to know. 'I see the daydreaming and the look on your face when you talk about him, I'm not as thick as you think I am.'

'Steve,' my stomach turned over, churning. 'Steve, there's nothing, nothing has happened.'

'Let's hope so, because I'll tell you now, for free, any man who messes with my wife will pay a heavy price. I don't do sharing.'

He screwed up the paper and, then unbelievably, he threw it at me. I was standing by the back door, I still had a pair of secateurs in my hands because I had been pruning in the garden. The little ball of paper hit me and fell to the floor.

I was staring down at it as he stalked off, his feet a heavy thumping on the stairs. The bedroom door banged and the house fell into silence.

Inca crawled out from her basket, moving long and low with only the slightest wag of her black tail. Gently, she picked up the letter and took it back to her bed where she began to shred it.

I could have taken any amount of shouting, but the letter being thrown at me stung in more ways than I could explain.

I fell into the old kitchen chair and I wept.

PART TWO

56

I saw him in my dream.

He was beckoning me to come to him, standing by our bench. Lapston was rising up behind him, but not as she is now because her windows were all there, glinting in the shimmering morning sun, her paintwork fresh and new. I wanted to go but my legs were heavy, they would not move. I felt hot tears on my face, rolling down my cheeks into my ears. I shouted his name, but I couldn't make a sound because my mouth was so dry; I had no voice.

I opened my eyes. The blue light of dawn was creeping in at the curtain edges. Next to me Steve was sleeping soundly, the rise and fall of his breath reassuring and normal.

But it was no longer normal. We were no longer us. An icy chill existed between us, words unspoken, his lack of trust in me misplaced, yet so virulent.

I slid out of bed and went downstairs to make myself a cup of tea.

The light streamed through the French doors and dust motes floated in front of my eyes. I checked my phone, it was seven o'clock and, as I brushed my thumb across its surface, I wondered if I should call Rory, although I had no idea if he was back from Spain or not.

When I finally met Mr. Carrick he was smaller than I had imagined and his room looked vast around him. He was sitting in an upright armchair his hands flat on the armrests and he was staring out of the window at a squirrel that was busy raiding the bird table outside.

'Mr Carrick?' I stepped into his line of sight, my hand extending in greeting. His eyes were pale grey, unfocussed. 'Martha Nelson. I arranged to see you earlier this week.'

'Yes,' he looked uncertain, as if it meant nothing to him.

'Is it all right if I speak to you?'

'Did you bring your dog?' he asked, as if all at once he'd remembered who I was. 'They said you would bring your dog.'

I was relieved he had remembered the arrangement, but I hadn't been able to bring Inca. Steve was taking her for a walk with a friend of his over to the Black Mountains, a once a year arrangement they had. I felt bad about it when I replied that I had left her behind. The old man's eyes dropped back to his hands in disappointment. He was fiddling with a piece of linen. It looked like a fragment of an old cushion.

'I'm sorry,' I said. 'I would have brought her if I could.'

'No matter, I like animals, that's all. I miss them more than anything else in here.' The room was soulless, no personal possessions at all, the pictures on the walls were replicated all around the rest of the building.

'May I sit down?'

'Yes, if you like.' I took a seat on the chair beside his bed. 'Who are you here to see?' I sighed, this clearly had not been worth the effort.

'You, Mr Carrick. My name's Martha. I wanted to ask you about Lapston.'

He stopped fiddling and looked up at me, his eyes were watery and opaque. 'I can't see you very well. I used to paint, but I can't anymore.' Then he held up the little strand of cloth. 'That's why I fiddle, keeps my fingers occupied.' He had a look about him of resigned boredom. 'I like a dog, labradors and spaniels, soft ears, nice to feel.'

'Did you have dogs at Lapston?' I asked, trying again to bring him back to the subject.

'Oh yes, lots of them, gun dogs, house dogs, collies on the farm too. And horses, my Jester and Alice's Beau. She loved horses, my Alice.'

'I've seen a picture of her, she was very lovely.'

'Oh she was beautiful.' Whilst he spoke, he shook his head regretfully. 'Beautiful, a really special lady, she was spirited, yet gentle as a lamb.'

'Were you cousins, or related in some way?'

He looked lost for a moment, then he shook his head again. 'No, but we were nearly married, you know. I asked her but she said no, she should have said yes, but she said no and it broke my heart.'

'I am sorry.'

'What's a nice young lady like you got to be sorry about?'

I had the most intense and stupid urge to cry right there in his room with only his rhythmic breath and the gentle tick of a clock to break the silence.

'You're quite a sad one aren't you, my love?' A stupid, uncontrolled tear rolled out of my eye then ran down my cheek and I fumbled in my bag for a tissue to wipe it away.

'Have you come looking for answers?' he asked. It was as if he understood everything despite knowing nothing. 'I've been there, you know, still am in many ways.' He leaned forward and placed a shaky hand on my arm. 'It gets better; you learn to live with it, the guilt. I did.'

'What gets better?' I asked, my journalist's interest was gone. I was just a woman chatting to a sweet old man.

'When you lose your old life, everything you hold dear, miss those chances… and mistakes you made.' He tapped his nose. 'When you realise it's not enough, not enough.' He was rambling and I couldn't follow him. He leaned back and began to fiddle again.

'Why did it all end for the family at Lapston?' I asked him. By then I was not hopeful of receiving a lucid reply. 'Why did they all leave?'

He didn't say anything, instead he stared out into space. I looked around the room and it was then I noticed a black and white photograph of a horse on his sideboard.

'Is that Jester?' I asked and it seemed the name brought him back to me.

'Yes, that's my old boy, I still miss him.' He turned from looking at the picture and back to me. He had once been handsome, his cheeks were fine, the hair now white was still long at the back and his skin was barely wrinkled, just the odd blemish.

'I loved them all, you know, the only family I ever had. I would have had summer after summer with nameless, unmemorable guardians if they had not made me part of the family and all because George invited me back for one Easter holiday. I would have had no one, no place to call my home.'

'Were you an orphan?'

'No, my dear. I lost my mother but my father was still alive until I was sixty. Turns out the men in our family are long-lived, it was just the women they wore down.'

He was still resting a hand on my arm quite comfortably, the backs of them age spotted, the fingers were long.

'Where was your father?'

'India with his new woman. I met her once, went out there, she couldn't stand me and I couldn't stand her. It's very hard to know that a parent cares nothing for you, but that's what I had to come to terms with. But then I had Mrs Hall, she loved me.' He sighed. 'She was the housekeeper, a darling, and she took care of me at Lapston, then in Jericho.'

I realised we were back on Lapston and used it to my advantage.

'So, why did you all leave so suddenly and why was it sold to Madame Roussell?'

I thought, for one awful moment, he was going to die. His skin literally turned white in front of me. He withdrew his hand and leaned back into his chair as if his belly was giving him pain. I glanced across at the red cord dangling by his bed, wondering if I should pull it, but he rallied with a huge sigh.

'It was her, everything was fine until she came,' he said quietly. The colour was returning to his face, pink rising in his cheeks. 'It was her, she was the one who destroyed our lives, smashed everything to pieces. I found it all out, I went there, to Paris, you know. I uncovered the whole story bit by bit. Evil, evil woman, she nearly finished me.' He turned to regard me, his eyes earnest in a face edged with pain. 'She made me think about doing myself in.'

'I'm sorry,' I said, straightening up. 'I shouldn't have disturbed you, Mr Carrick. It's clearly bringing back awful memories for you.' I made to go, standing up and reaching for my bag, I'd put it on the end of his bed.

'Open that cupboard,' he said, indicating with a crooked index finger to a wardrobe on the other side of the room. 'In there.' I did as I was bid and, on the shelf, following his directions I found two thick notebooks. 'Pass me the top one,' he instructed. The cover and spine were held together with aged Sellotape, dark brown and barely doing its job.

'Read that first line to me please,' he said.

I opened the book and saw that each page showed the most beautiful handwriting, his, he had written his name on the inside front cover. It was in faded blue ink, line after line with hardly any amendments or breaks in the format. I read it to him. "Inevitably, the subject turned to Cécile Roussell as I knew it must. There was intrigue in his voice something quite unfamiliar to me."

'That's the one,' he said. 'Take it home with you and

read it, then, if you have the heart for it, come back and I'll give you the next one to read. I always swore that I'd give that to somebody one day and it would be someone who needed to read it, for one reason or another, and here you are.'

I felt the most tremendous rush of gratitude. I sat back down and squeezed his hand. 'Thank you, Mr Carrick, I am indebted to you for trusting me.'

He looked suitably pleased. 'I want you to know that sometimes the answers lie elsewhere.' Having rallied and been quite loquacious, he suddenly looked very tired and I knew I had outstayed my welcome. I would be better prepared next time. With his eyes beginning to close, he said, 'Just one more thing before you go.'

'Yes, anything.'

His eyes closed and yawning, he said, 'Bring that dog of yours next time.'

57

As the door slammed closed on the following Monday morning, the sense of relief was enormous. Steve was still being cold with me. I have become used to the sullen silences over the year, those tortuous hours of non-communication, but I felt this one was unreasonable.

I called Rory's number, but it went to answerphone so I rung off. I just wanted to talk to him and tell him what had happened so he would stay clear but the thought that he wasn't there was unbearable and I felt completely numb. Then I imagined him meeting someone in Spain and sipping cocktails in some beach bar without a thought for me. I could see them there, she'd be Sarah's age, long swinging blonde hair, perfect skin, honey-kissed with bright white teeth. I despised her.

The landline rang and everything in me willed it to be him.

'Hi Mum, it's Sarah.'

There was a fraction of hesitation before I replied. 'Oh, hi love.'

'Sorry, is it a bad time?'

'No, no I'm fine, sorry.'

'Is everything okay, you sound a bit flat?'

I resolved to tell her nothing, but I found myself saying, 'Dad and I have had a fall out.'

'What about?'

The room was growing cold around me and I shivered involuntarily. I checked myself. 'Something and nothing, it doesn't matter. Anyway, how are you? That's the main thing.'

'I'm fine. I was just checking in about coming over to you for the weekend, perhaps the seventeenth?'

'Yes, that's fine, we'll do something nice. Do you fancy going to Gifford's Circus?'

I could hear the childish delight in her; 'Oh yes, I'd love to, but, Mum, I'll be bringing my new man, Garry.'

'And how old is this one?'

'Oh Mum, for God's sake, I just knew that would be the first thing you asked.' I sighed heavily, hoping she'd hear it. I knew this would make Steve even more angry. 'He's sixty,' she said resolutely. I could picture her lips pressed tightly together, holding back because she was speaking to her mother.

'Oh Sarah, your Dad will go mad. Another sixty year old, really?'

'He's my boyfriend, please don't pigeon-hole him until you've met him.' I listened as she told me about him: handsome, clever, hardworking, wealthy, everything a girl could want.

As I replaced the receiver, I could only speculate on what I was going to tell Steve. How on earth was I going to tell Steve?

I looked over at Mr Carrick's book, sitting by my

armchair, its cover a smooth blue leather, the edges of the pages a faded gold, an expensive notebook. I wrapped my shawl around me and tucked up my knees and then I began to read his words and the next thing I knew it was one o'clock and my stomach was rumbling.

I had reached the end when Steve came home to find me sitting in the still blue twilight, the book closed on my knee. I had a crumpled tissue in my hand and my eyes felt raw. He and I were lost, Carrick and me. He had recognised it in me too.

Steve took off his jacket and was beside me in two strides when he saw me sitting in the half dark.

'Martha, darling, what's wrong?' He threw his arms round me. 'I'm so sorry, I've been horrible, I shouldn't have been so nasty. I am really sorry. I've upset you, haven't I?'

'No, honestly, it's not you, well it is a bit, and Sarah.'

He leant over and switched on a table lamp. 'Sarah?'

'She's bringing an older man home to meet us.'

'Oh good God, no.'

'Yes, she rang this morning.'

'Shit.'

'That's what I thought, but she says we have to be reasonable and not pre-judge.'

'I'm going to be responsible for my own judging,' he said sitting back on the edge of the chair, his arm still round my shoulders. 'Bloody hell.'

'Perhaps we should just hold back, meet him, do the nice parents bit and–'

'And then I'll take him in the back garden and punch his lights out,' he said.

'I think we must put Sarah first, it's her life after all, perhaps reserve the punching bit for when she gets hurt?'

'And that she will, an old man like that, it's not right, it's just not right.'

'Let's not rush to judgment,' I said with a sniff.

'No wonder you were upset,' he said, his voice softening.

'It wasn't that so much, it was this book.' I showed it to him, he opened it staring blankly at the first page.

'What is it, some sort of diary?'

'A memoir. That old chap I told you about, Maxwell Carrick, he let me read it, it's about Lapston.'

'That bloody house again.' Steve shoved the book back at me, then stood up and stalked off to the kitchen. I took a deep breath and followed him, I wasn't looking for another argument and I should have kept quiet about the book, but I so wanted to share what I was doing with him and, ultimately, to be open about it.

'It's fascinating, a real insight into the people who lived there. There was this French woman who–'

'Not interested, Martha, not anymore, if it has to do with that house it has to do with him and I'm just not going there.' He grabbed the dog's lead from where it was lying on the work surface. 'I'm going out for a walk.'

I watched as he slipped on his walking shoes and Barbour jacket. Inca's tail was thumping against the Aga, her eyes bright and alert. This was a highly unusual thing, an early evening walk with her master and she was over the moon.

'Come on, girl, let's get out of here,' he said as they left by the back door and disappeared.

58

I was outside Rory's house watching the river rushing beneath me as I perched on the low wall. The swirl of grey and blue water was churning up white foam. The stones that were once the millrace were slick with wet spray. It was June, but it was damp and cold.

I had thought about going to Lapston. I wanted to see it again and picture them all sitting in the lounge or having dinner in the panelled dining room, to see their ghosts; Alice and Henry. They had died in France, did ghosts travel across water?

I pulled my coat around me, the spray in the air all about me cold.

No, that wasn't it. Was it vampires who couldn't cross water? Then I told myself to stop being so silly, I didn't believe in ghosts or vampires, in fact nothing supernatural. I was being stupid but I couldn't resist the draw of the old house, it was calling to me, wanting me to hear its secrets. Would I be trespassing if I went up to see it? I wished Rory were home, but his house was in darkness with the curtains drawn.

'Hello Martha!' The voice was so loud in my ear, I jumped out of my skin. It was Norman Fry, his eyes smiling at me from under his flat cap. 'How are you?'

'Norman, I'm fine, thank you. I'm afraid I was daydreaming.'

'Was it about our Mr McBride?' Norman pushed my arm playfully. 'I bet you're missing him something chronic. What a shame you couldn't go with him, but a business trip is a business trip I suppose, though what would I know, eh?'

'Norman,' I said evenly, 'there's something I should tell you–'

'Oh no, is he dead?'

'Who?'

'That's what I was dreading, that you'd get to Mr Carrick's place and he'd have passed on. He's a ripe old age, must be on his way to his telegram, makes me feel very young.'

'No, no, he's actually very well, I saw him on Saturday. I had a lovely visit with him. He's a very nice man though he was disappointed that I couldn't take my dog.'

'Oh, he would be. He loves dogs, does Mr Carrick.'

'He was very helpful indeed and I learned a lot of stuff about Lapston.'

'I'm glad to hear it.' Norman shook his head. 'Though it was all so sad, my mum told me it broke her heart how everything fell apart.'

'Yes, you said. Do you have any idea at all what happened to George, or Madame Roussell?'

'Russell,' he corrected me. I let it go.

'Or even Grant?'

'No, Mr Carrick's the one for that sort of thing, but I doubt you'll get a lot out of him, he's a very private man if you ask me, keeps it buttoned up in that old fashioned way, respectful like, not like today when it's all over magazines and those red tops.'

'He's actually let me have quite a lot of information, things he wrote about, in a book.'

'Really? Well I never, would you like a cup of tea and you can tell me all about it?'

'Thank you, Norman. I would have loved to but I must get back, I have a lunch appointment.' I was lying but I suddenly found I didn't want to share Carrick with anyone, not Norman and not even Rory. I wanted to hear Mr Carrick's story, the conclusion of it and I was going to go and see him, before the end of the week, whether it upset Steve or not.

59

He was gazing out of the window, a blanket wrapped around him, tucked in under his arms. He looked serene, as if a peace had come upon him. Inca barged through the door wagging her tail, and he was reaching out for her instantly, feeling for her head. His eyes watered up immediately.

'Ah now, this is a fine lady you've brought to see me,' he said with a big grin. 'What's her name?'

'Inca.'

'Lovely,' he said as he ran his hand over her back. 'Lovely girl, nice ears.'

Inca, for once, behaved immaculately as if she could sense that he could not move very easily. Instead she pressed against his thigh, looking up at him with soulful eyes.

'You'll have to remind me of your name,' he said, finally looking towards me. 'I'm terrible for names now.'

'Martha Nelson,' I replied, perching on the edge of his bed. 'I came a week ago and you very kindly gave me your memoirs.'

'Did I? Yes, I remember, you were the lost lady. I've waited a long time to meet you.' He held my gaze for a second and I his. I could see in his eyes the Carrick I had read about; the damaged man, the hurt man, the forlorn man. I have no idea what he saw in me, but we had connected. 'So, what did you think?'

'Did you eventually find them?' I asked. 'George and Cécile?'

'Oh yes, depending on how you define found.' He sniffed and fumbled for his handkerchief. 'I'm getting a cold I think.' I handed him a tissue from the box on the sideboard.

'Where they married?'

'No.' He turned back to the window, he was still fussing with Incas' ears with one hand. 'I didn't do the right thing at all.'

'What do you mean?'

'Have you come far?' he asked, still avoiding eye contact.

'I've come from the village where you used to live, at Lapston.'

'Really?' he met my eyes. 'What is she like now? I'd like you to say someone's done her up and returned her to her former glory.'

'I'm afraid not. She's a ruin. It's very sad.'

'She was beautiful. But she was sad too, at the end.'

I reached forward and put a hand on his arm. 'Mr Carrick.'

'Call me Carrick, they all did. She used to, never called me Captain, no one did, quite glad; I wasn't a good soldier.'

'Can you tell me what happened to everyone, to George and Cécile? How did Lapston pass to her?'

The look he gave me was unsettling, as if he was seeing me for the first time, and I leaned back unsure about what to do.

'In there,' He indicated towards the wardrobe. 'The second book.'

I stood up, knowing where to look. The wardrobe smelt old and musty as I opened it, the clothes were messy, thrown in there without care. No one thought about how his things were stored. The book was black, a leather bound notebook with gold-edged pages like a bible. It was his second journal.

'You'll find it all in there, take it,' He said with a sigh. 'I knew you'd come, it was only a matter of time.'

'How did you know I'd come?'

'I've been waiting for you. Everyone has to account for themselves, to purge themselves. I've been waiting for you to come for a long time.'

I opened the book. It was the same even hand, the ink black, foreboding.

'Do you really want me to read this, Carrick?'

He nodded. He had stopped stroking Inca's head. She raised a paw and placed it on his leg, her big eyes half-mooning. No one could resist her and she knew it, but Carrick was wiping a tear from his eye.

'I did what I had to do,' he said at length. 'I don't regret any of it, but I made the wrong decision about Alice. I killed her.'

'Killed Alice?'

'No, not Alice but as good as, I broke her heart, she wouldn't have put herself in danger if she was coming home to me. She volunteered for that flight, knew it was a dangerous mission. One of the last acts of war in France and my Alice was on that plane. One of the last acts of war, my Alice.'

I knelt down beside him, his head was tilting to the left. I had tired him out. He nodded and said finally, 'I killed her.' I drew in a sharp breath and stood over him as he slumped into a deep sleep.

Who had he killed? I knew the answer was in the book I was holding and I desperately wanted to start reading it. A chill ran through me, so many secrets, a past that was being unlocked by an imposter.

I left his room, closing the door behind me with a soft click. I so wanted to take a seat in the small visitor's lounge and read the first few pages of the journal, but I reckoned that if I left for home, and beat the rush hour traffic, I could make dinner for Steve and spend the evening reading.

I slid the book into my handbag and headed for the car park.

I tapped in "Previous Destination" on the satellite navigation system and the name of my village came up. As I reversed out of my parking space, I was wondering what I was doing and if I should be doing it at all. I had no idea what I was going to read in Carrick's book. Part of me said I should take it back and leave it there with him, but the journalist part of me was desperate to find answers.

I released the handbrake and left Lady Cormer House behind me, a retreating reflection in my rear view mirror.

PART THREE

60

The letter arrived at the end of February. Mrs Hall was waiting for me as I returned from visiting Peterson.

'It's from Mr George,' she said. 'I know the hand.' There was a tremor in her voice as she passed it to me. Naturally, she was still worrying that there would be consequences in her leaving Lapston so unexpectedly.

I turned the envelope over but there was nothing to suggest where it had been posted. The postmark itself was smudged, no return address on the reverse side.

'Oh, do open it, Mr Carrick, do,' she implored.

I ripped open the top.

"My Dear Carrick,

I have come home to Lapston for the final time.

By the time you read this I will be gone, I have nothing left. She has taken everything. I could not face what I must do now without telling you that you were always my trusted counsel and greatest friend. What I have done to you is terribly, terribly wrong, but it has been like a sickness, I was not in control of my own mind.

I am so very sorry.
Yours ever,
George."

'Oh good God!' I stumbled backwards, knocking against a bookshelf and dislodging whatever was upon it. Mrs Hall grabbed my arm to steady me.

'What is it? Mr Carrick, what is it?'

I held out the letter and she grasped it, reading it in seconds. She bit the back of her hand to stifle a scream. 'No!'

We stared at each other, our eyes mirroring the horror.

'Mrs Hall, go to the telephone box at once, try Lapston, then the doctor or police, whomsoever answers first.' I took the key to the house from its hook where it hung a sad, solitary relic. A glance at my watch told me I could make the four ten if I ran for it so I grabbed my Macintosh.

Mrs Hall was pulling on her coat when I had a complete change of heart. What was I doing? If the letter was sent even yesterday, I was too late. To inform the police or the doctor would be opening it up to the public and to scandal. I couldn't bear it.

'Come with me,' I told her, picking up her handbag and passing it to her. 'We need to deal with this.' She paled but nodded, she understood what I was doing immediately. Gripping her handbag tightly to her chest, we left at a pace, I'm not sure we even locked the door.

The house was unlocked and the front door opened with ease into a dim and chilly hall, our footsteps echoing on the chequerboard tiles.

'George!' I called. 'George, it's Carrick and Mrs Hall. We're here.'

Silence.

I told Mrs Hall to go to the kitchen, but she refused and instead followed a pace behind me. Our breath misted the air as we proceeded to the lounge. The double doors creaked open to reveal a silent, empty room. The fire had been lit, but had obviously failed to catch, for the sticks and screwed up paper that had been used to get it going were only half burnt.

I could feel the pulse in my head, the pain of a migraine rooted in my neck, and I could smell everything, the ash, the charcoaled twigs, the dampness of the furniture under the ghostly sheets.

We checked in the library but there was nothing there, no sign of habitation, and the dining room was locked. 'On account of the silver,' Mrs Hall told me in a whisper. We were both acting like sneak thieves working our way through a stranger's house.

When we took the stairs, my legs felt leaden, as if they were trying to hold me back.

He was on the bed, in Reginald and Augusta's room, now of course his own. The four-poster was hung with blue and gold hangings but one of the curtains had been torn away from its fastenings. A small brown bottle lay on its side on the floor, a handful of bright yellow pills had spilled across the rug. He was lying on his back, chin tilted upwards, eyes glassy and unseeing. He looked awkward and unnatural but still I wanted to touch him gently and say, "Wake up, George, old man." His skin had the pallor of death. Unmistakable. Collins. The endless corpses in ditches, mouths open, hollows where eyes had been before the crows had pecked them out. I'd seen it all before.

There was a sharp slice of pain in my head and a hot flush overtook me and, in response, I loosened my tie. Mrs Hall gripped my arm to support us both but I fear I was useless to her, paralysed. I could only stare at him, unable to rationalise it. George, my best friend George. I couldn't associate the warm, charming, kind man I knew with this terrible thing before me, this empty husk.

'I'll go and fetch the doctor,' Mrs Hall said.

'Only him,' I said with urgency.

She nodded and left.

I knelt on the floor next to George as I heard the door bang shut below us. He looked terribly old and drawn, not the George I had last seen in the library with her. He had had a haircut, there was a bloody mark, a scab on his cheek but he had not shaved, and ginger stubble was growing around his chin and neck. He looked like his father had in that dreadful year after we had lost Augusta. I could remember the very life-blood draining from him and the plates of food returned to the kitchen, bringing forth the worried sighs of Mrs Hall as she scraped them into the dog's bowl.

On his bedside table was a drained glass, whisky. I picked it up and saw a small telltale ring of amber in the bottom.

'George,' was all I could say as I broke down heaving great sobs. My forehead rested on the edge of his bed, the ice cold cloth of the sheet bringing instant relief to the now fierce pain in my temples. I so wanted to feel his hand reach out to me, to place his big bear palm over my head and say; 'Carrick, come on, old chap,' but he remained still, the room enveloping us in its chilly shroud.

The doctor and Mrs Hall returned within half and hour. I heard his car pulling to a halt on the carriage circle, the gravel crunching beneath its tyres.

Mrs Hall was at my side in an instant and I had my arm around her as we clung together. It took mere minutes for Doctor Beascott to assess the situation.

'I'm so sorry,' he said, stepping back. He looked terribly upset, but then I knew full well that George was his friend of many years. 'I cannot understand why he would do such a thing. It's a terrible business. He was married only a few weeks ago, wasn't he?'

'We don't know,' I replied as I led Mrs Hall to a bedroom chair and sat her down. She was weeping, mopping her eyes with a small handkerchief, a daisy embroidered on it, one of Alice's. 'We have not been in contact for some time, you see. He, they, went to France, as far as I know.'

Dr Beascott shook his head. He took out a notepad and wrote something down. Then he scratched his head with his pencil. 'I had no idea. I haven't seen George for months. I recall that I looked at his hip back in the spring. From what I have gathered since, I had the impression everything was going so very well for him personally, a bit of happiness after all the sadness. It simply must have been too much, Henry then dear Alice.' The doctor sighed heavily. 'A bad business it is.'

'What happens now?' I asked.

'To begin with we will need the undertaker to come and the coroner will have to be informed, there will have to be an inquest.'

'I don't want any of that,' I said coldly. 'I don't want any of this to be known. It is a slight on his memory, a terrible thing.'

'But Mr Carrick,' Mrs Hall protested from her chair by the fireplace. I could see she lacked the strength to stand up.

'I want him left to rest here. Mrs Hall and I will do what is necessary. I must insist that no one is told. As far as everyone is concerned, George is in France and he has chosen to stay there.'

'But there will be people who must be informed, an estate to administer.' The doctor mopped his brow with his handkerchief. 'I must–'

'You must let me deal with it.' I interrupted him rudely. 'I will pay good money to the coroner, the undertaker and whoever else might be involved, but George will be dealt with behind closed doors and he will be buried in the church in the grounds. I will not have his death to be the subject of gossip. Do you understand?'

'Carrick, a coroner will not be bribed!' The doctor raised his eyebrows, his manner changed. 'I can assure you of that, despite what you think, money cannot buy everything,' He was losing patience with me, but his professionalism kept his voice even and controlled. I, meanwhile, felt he was being impudent and unhelpful, but it was clear I needed him to do as he was bid without defiance.

'See that it is done, everything is to be kept as quiet as possible, out of respect to the family, and I will pay whatever needs paying, and more. It simply cannot be allowed to become public knowledge.

The doctor nodded ruefully. He could tell both by my voice and my fierce expression that I was not to be challenged. 'I will explain your request to the coroner and you can rest assured everything will be handled with the utmost sensitivity but it will be up to him, ultimately, how he proceeds.'

I could bear it no more. My head felt like it was splitting open with pain. I turned to leave the room. 'I will make sure I get to the bottom of this if it is the very last thing I do,' I told them and I swore in my heart that I would hunt down Cécile Roussell, even if it killed me.

61

As I settled down to read Carrick's book, it became clear Steve had other plans.

'I thought we could go out for a meal,' he said.

'Tonight?'

'Yes, that's the idea,' he replied as he shrugged off his jacket. 'It's such a lovely evening, very warm and I left school early specially.'

I glanced at my bag, where the book was peeping out of the top and calling to me but, with a sigh, I agreed and went upstairs to change. I was very disappointed and I still did not feel happy with Steve but, as we left the village, I hit on an idea.

'Steve, turn left there.'

'What?'

'Just here.' I pointed to the lane leading to Lapston.

He swung the car into it and dark trees overhanging the road swallowed us up. As the light changed, we were cutting through fields of sheep.

'We haven't got time to–'

'It'll only take a few minutes. I want to show you something special.'

He wasn't happy, his grip tightening on the steering

wheel, but I was determined that I would make him understand.

We pulled up outside the entrance to Lapston and, taking his hand, I led him down the path to the church and the gate.

'Kissing gate,' I told him but he wasn't interested, glancing at his watch.

As we pressed through the narrow path between the yew tree and the wall, he was huffing loudly. 'Here,' I said. 'Just through here.'

'Are we allowed to? I don't want to be shot for trespassing.' He was hanging back.

'Oh Steve, we're only going to see the house quickly, don't worry, it's fine, honestly.'

As we stepped through the gateway the path rose up before us, winding through the grass that had grown wildly to each side. There were poppies flowering through the fresh green, splashes of bloody red.

'How far is it?'

'Not far. It's worth it, I promise.'

I took his hand but he didn't grip mine, his fingers were barely connecting with me. We climbed up and past the bench until the tops of the ochre chimneys appeared.

'Here it is.' I sped up, striding purposefully.

It had been a warm evening, pleasant with the promise of sitting at a table outside a country pub, but as we reached the edge of the lawn, a swell of black clouds moved in and the air changed. I shivered.

We were looking across the lawn, the bobbing heads of

grasses in the fresh breeze before us. The house looked low to the ground, as if she were hunkering down under the darkening sky. She looked smaller, almost fearful.

'Is that it?' Steve was standing, hands on hips. 'Doesn't look as big as I thought it would be.'

I stood in silence. Why couldn't the light have remained a little longer and thrown a golden haze on those mellow stone walls? Why did everything seem so different and such a disappointment?

We traced our way back. I might have stayed on had I been alone but Steve was already making his way down hill. I watched the back of him. He didn't fit here, he brought no magic, no magic at all.

'Stop,' I called to him. 'Just there, on the bench.'

He looked at me as if I were very odd.

'We'll be too late for a table at this rate.'

'Only for a second.'

I took a seat and pulled him down beside me. The bench felt rough and uncomfortable under my thin skirt. I shifted my weight and took his hand in mine. 'Isn't it beautiful?'

The river was empty, save for a lone coot dabbling at the water's edge.

'I wouldn't say beautiful,' Steve replied flatly. 'It's pleasant enough but very overgrown, I would have preferred to see it as it was, more cared for.'

I sighed as I realised that it was all so pointless.

'I do love you, Steve,' I said after a while, as droplets of rainwater splashed on the path and quite suddenly, the clouds hung heavy and pregnant with rain above us. I leant against his arm but there was no yielding to me, his muscles feeling taut and strained.

'We should go; it's going to piss down in a minute,' he said and, rising stiffly, he walked away.

I followed him, struggling not to slide on the uneven patches of gravel.

Eventually I gave up and slowed down, letting the distance grow between us and then, absentmindedly, I plucked a piece of grass. I crushed the florets in my palm until I could feel the pain of my nails slicing into my skin.

62

I was at school with Charles Ellis-Pryce but, unlike me, he had thrived and prospered in his chosen career and now he sat before me bewhiskered, rotund, weak-chested and breathing with a rattle as he studied the papers I had given him.

'I'm sorry, Carrick,' he said calmly. 'I cannot help you. This former version of the will is null and void; It is superseded by the new one.'

'We cannot allow it,' I protested. 'George was obviously not in the right frame of mind when he had it drawn up.'

'The house, and its estate are owned, in their entirety, by Madame Roussell, and I am to act on her wishes and her wishes alone.'

I stared at him, unable to think of the appropriate words.

'She has no right, she has been duplicitous.' The words faltered on my tongue and I stumbled over them.

'Not according to the documents that have been drawn up by Messrs Horne and Son,' Charles said. 'In fact, it is quite the opposite. George states that he is of sound body and mind and is freely declaring that everything be left to his fiancée.'

'Fiancée?'

'Yes,'

'Not wife?'

'No, they never married.'

I scratched my head. 'I don't understand.'

'Nor do I, but the documents are incontrovertible.'

'I will have them countermanded. I will object.'

'Carrick, you are in no position whatsoever to do so. You have no bona-fide connection to the family and have no legal rights at all. I have to tell you that had Alice survived, even she too would have found it impossible to overturn this, a will is a will.'

I sat before him, listening to the sound of a bus engine idling outside the window. 'She has come into our lives and torn them apart, this woman of whom we know absolutely nothing, and now George is dead. I will not let this happen, I will seek her out and make her give it all back.'

'To whom?' asked Charles. 'To you?'

I shook my head again in disbelief. 'I would give it all to a charitable trust, the church, a convalescent home perhaps, anything but her.'

'Carrick, may I speak plainly with you?' Charles laid his fingers over the round dome of his paunch. I did not respond for I felt numb, as if some chemical had been used on me. 'Rise above this. This has been George's affair, his wishes. I'm afraid it is obvious to all.'

'We don't know that,' I replied sourly. 'That is just it, we do not know. Why would he leave the entire estate to her, not having married the woman? Something is terribly wrong. And then this dreadful thing he's done.'

Charles heaved himself up from his chair and walked around the large desk to my side. Instinctively I stood up.

'Carrick, take the advice of an old friend, there is nothing to be done. George made his wishes perfectly clear, we have no idea why, but the documents are watertight and there really is nothing to be done. And—' He put a hand on my shoulder where it felt condescending. 'You have no need for money, not with your private income, don't waste your life chasing the past. Use this chance to start again, old chap, find a new way for yourself, a new direction.'

I turned away and, picking up my Macintosh and hat, I left his offices. The High was shrouded in a thick blanket of fog. The dark, swirling mists around me may have clouded my way, but my mind was clear.

63

Garry had gone to the loo. I collected together the plates, not daring to look at Steve. Sarah was biting her lip, always a bad sign. As I stood up, I could feel the tension rising between them. I heard Garry moving about upstairs, the creaking floorboards underfoot.

'I'll fetch pud,' I said, feigning cheerfulness.

'Don't bother, we're not staying.' Sarah stood up, the chair scraping on the wooden floor. 'I'm not inflicting any more of this on Garry.'

'Of what exactly?' Steve was acting innocent. I flashed a look at him but he ignored me. 'What's the matter?'

'Oh, come on, Dad. I'm not stupid. You've been at it all morning. "We both remember the Beatles, Garry," and, "Have you got a good pension, Garry?" I know what you were doing.'

'Sarah,' I said sharply.

'Don't defend him, Mum. He couldn't have been more rude and he knows it.'

'I simply wanted to find out about him,' Steve replied, being unbelievably obstinate. 'That's all. Calm down.'

'Don't you tell me to calm down!' Sarah had raised her

voice and now I was wincing in case Garry could hear, but neither of them seemed to care.

'I'm not going to act like I'm happy about this, I don't do two-faced,' Steve said crossly. Inca stood up and slinked away from under the table where she had been sleeping.

'No, you couldn't pretend to like him just for me, because I'm happy. Mum's been trying, so why can't you?'

I placed the plates back down on the table. I was shaking.

'Please don't argue, you two.' I urged them to stop, conscious of Garry coming down the stairs.

'I won't. Dad's been too rude. What did you mean by "we old blokes must stick together"? You didn't even use that in context, just stuck it in for spite.'

I had never seen them arguing like this, their faces reddening, making their family resemblance more noticeable.

'Sarah, stop it!' I hissed.

'I'm not standing for any more of this.' She slammed her hand on the table, making everything rattle, and a knife slid to the floor.

'I think you're the rude one,' said Steve flatly, adding fuel to the fire whilst Garry was hesitating at the foot of the stairs. 'Maybe you've been misconstruing what I said.' That was Steve's first attempt at reconciliation.

'No I wasn't.' Sarah was turning to call for Garry just as he appeared at the door, squirming with embarrassment.

'What's wrong, love?' He looked very uneasy as he saw our expressions.

'Please can we go?' Sarah was fuming. 'I want to leave now.'

Garry looked completely thrown. He was shorter then her with thinning hair and thick-rimmed glasses. I couldn't imagine her with him, even with them standing in front of me, they seemed so completely unsuited.

'I'm sorry, Garry,' I said nervously. 'I'm afraid it's–'

'It's all about Dad,' said Sarah interrupting me. 'He obviously doesn't like the thought of us being together, and while you've been oblivious, he's been making snide comments. Like when he said you were "two old blokes" that was a jibe.'

Garry, bless him, tried to be conciliatory. 'I'm sure that's not the case, darling. Your dad was just being funny, weren't you, Steve?'

Steve said nothing.

'See, you don't know him like I do,' said Sarah.

I had to sit down because my legs felt weak and there was a churning feeling deep in my belly, I felt terribly sick because I hate conflict. 'Sarah, please don't say these things, let's all calm down a bit.'

Steve was staring ahead of him like he does when he's really angry.

'I knew he'd be like this, Mum.' Her voice was getting louder. 'He's so unreasonable.'

'I'm not,' Steve said. 'I'm allowed an opinion about whom my daughter chooses for a partner.'

'Most people would act politely but not you, you have to say what you think and not only that you make weird jokes. You have no social intelligence at all.'

'Sarah!' I finally raised my voice because she had gone too far. 'Don't speak to your father like that.'

'Mum, you're too soft, you let him say all these things and you never fight back. It's no wonder you've found yourself another man, for God's sake.'

It was like a guillotine had dropped home.

The silence was unbearably awful; it felt solid like a thick glutinous substance expanding to fill the space between us. The whole horrible moment was happening in dreadful slow motion. Sarah put her hand over her mouth, Garry's dropped open at the same time, and I heard Inca whimper from her basket.

Steve pushed the table away sharply. It shuddered like a boat being pushed into the sea from the beach and, as it did so, my mother's crystal sugar bowl shivered and fell to the floor. It smashed into tiny pieces, but no one noticed because we were all looking at my husband and the white-hot anger in his face.

He slammed the door so hard as he left that flakes of paint drifted from the woodwork like snow and littered the hall carpet with a sprinkling of white dots.

64

'Carrick, I have no idea.' Lewis looked at me blankly.

'It would be too much of a coincidence,' I told him earnestly. 'Your friend brings home a French woman, I meet her and then poor George falls foul of her too. It must be the same woman.'

'I do not think we can make assumptions, old man,' Lewis looked bemused. 'What do you mean, George has fallen foul of her?'

I realised my mistake instantly. No one must know, and for a moment I hesitated. Surely I could confide in Lewis? But no, no one must know I told myself.

For a moment, my mind drifted and was back at Lapston on that drear March evening, the rain sheeting down around us as we lowered the coffin into the grave. The vicar recited his words and the seven of us watched as George was lowered, bit by bit, into his anonymous dark hole.

I thanked the three undertakers and paid them well for their silence. Ogden and Jim looked at me from under their oilskin coats, hair dripping with rain. They each shook my hand and I knew I had their loyalty. I donated a large sum of money to the church and the vicar played his roll too. They didn't like to bury suicides inside the village churchyard, he was glad to be let off the hook.

Mrs Hall clung to my arm as we walked back to the house, whatever she thought, and I knew she didn't agree with my actions, she kept her own counsel. Money it seems, can buy you anonymity in death, it is good for something.

Early the following morning, as the sun rose over the house, casting a bright gold light on the lawns after a turbulent night, I walked down to the little church and stood over the freshly turned soil. I had with me a sapling, a yew tree. I planted it at the head of the grave, next to the wall. Yews, they say, prevent witches from entering churchyards and disturbing the sleep of the dead. I wished that George would sleep easy in that silent, secret grave.

I stood back and looked at the small insignificant little tree, imagining that it would grow steady and true, and that its roots would curl around that coffin and keep George safe.

'Carrick,' Lewis was concerned. 'Are you quite well?' I was dragged back into his office, the colours around me sharp, the smoke of his cigar pungent in my nostrils. 'Only, just for a second there, I thought you might be about to... you know...'

'I haven't been unwell in a very long time,' I reassured him. 'I have had too much to deal with, there has been no time for illness.'

'I'm glad to hear it. What did you mean about George falling foul of the Frenchwoman?'

'I simply don't like her,' I replied. 'She and I did not see eye to eye from the start.' I told him. 'She moved on to George and he was taken in by her, that is all.'

'I see. And where are they now?'

'I have no idea. There was talk about the south of France, but I have lost contact with them but no doubt they will soon be in touch.' He looked puzzled but unperturbed. 'I need to get to Paris, Lewis. How can I do it?'

'No one wants to go to Paris,' he said, tapping his cigar. 'Last time I was there they were starving, pitiful. I had cabbage soup three nights running at my hotel.'

'I need to go.'

He shook his head slowly, then he looked very thoughtful, considering something, but not convinced about it I could tell. He reached for a foolscap file, unwound the cord that held it together and opened it. There was a pause whilst he read the first page and then the next.

At length, he clasped his hands together in front of him and spoke slowly and deliberately. 'Look, old man, the thing is, I could use you in Paris.'

I leaned in.

He continued, still looking like he was uncertain of what he was about to say. 'I don't want to raise your hopes; it would be dashed cruel if you thought this to be true and it simply wasn't.'

I had no idea what he meant.

'We have a number of men and a women unaccounted for in France four are in Paris itself. We simply don't know if they are alive or dead or even somewhere in between.'

There was a prickle of sweat in the back of my neck.

He took a deep draw on his cigar, still looking dubious about what he was going to impart.

'What are you telling me?'

'As I said, it's absolutely imperative that you do not allow your hopes to be raised, but one of those who we cannot account for is Henry.'

I let out an audible gasp. 'Henry?'

'Yes.' Lewis placed his cigar on the ashtray in front of me. A flickering of ash spread across the leather and he brushed it away with his hand, a thick gold signet ring on it. All these things I remembered as I let the words settle into my mind.

'Not dead?'

'We simply don't know, we've had contradicting reports.'

'But they told us he was, he was...' My words drifted away, a great stillness overcame me, swamping me and I couldn't move. If he were not dead it was too cruel that Alice and George didn't know before they... I couldn't produce a single linear thought. I felt again the unsettling feeling, the shapes shifting in my mind. I thought of Collins – was he dead, or did I imagine it?

'We have a man over there tidying up, but our energies must be used elsewhere, as you know very well we have a big push on Germany underway. Things are desperate over there, Carrick, make no mistake. If you want to go, I can aid matters if you will help find Henry, or what trace remains, but I think any chance of him being alive is slim. I will organise that you meet our operative, Alec Trevise who has volunteered to stay out there until he's completed his task. He will help you.'

I wasn't actually taking anything in. Lewis's mouth was moving but I wasn't hearing a word. Henry might not be dead. The words were repeating over and over in my head. Henry might be alive. I swallowed and gripped the edges of my chair.

'If you are still… unwell… I cannot, in all conscience, send you,' said Lewis.

Finally, my brain was homing in on the importance of what he was saying. I sat up straight. 'No, I'm absolutely fine now, I will go. You can send me whenever you like.'

'You may be hurt all over again when you uncover the truth,' said Lewis. 'You must be prepared for that.'

'I am,' I told him. 'I am.'

65

I sat on the wall by the millstream with my arms wrapped around my knees as I watched the rushing waters below, the powerful force that once moved the large iron wheel. I had seen a picture of it in one of the files. A tangle of weeds and shrubs had grown over the years to camouflage the steep bank, and I could see a plastic carrier bag had been blown amongst the foliage. The Tesco logo looked so out of place and offensively wrong amid the greens and golds. Then I saw the Lucozade bottle half hidden in the soil and an oily rag, and my mind fixated on these three imposters in what should be a perfect, untouched place of natural beauty, but I couldn't reach any of them, it would have been dangerous to try.

I'd worked out Rory was coming home that day, but I didn't know what time. I had slept so badly in my empty bed, Steve had left me and not come back and I had no idea where he was. I had phoned him numerous times, left messages, texted him and now I hated him for making me worry. I also hated him for imagining that I wasn't faithful, that I didn't love him.

I also hated him for not being Rory.

The hamlet was quiet, no sign of life. I imagined what

it would have been like in Carrick's day with the mill a hive of activity. The carts queuing up to take grain to the station, or would it have been trucks? Petrol was such a scarcity, I decided it would have been carts.

I raised my hand to shield my eyes, but the road was empty, the line of trees on the hillside a thick ridge of green, verdant and full of life. The same trees Carrick and his sad family had known.

Inca yawned and made the cute squeak I loved. She was sitting looking up at me, telling me that we were wasting time when we could be walking. It had been a long walk there and my legs were stiff as I stood up; I was getting old.

'Come on, Inca, let's go and see if he's home,' I said and she wagged her tail pulling instinctively towards her friend Scooter's house, but I yanked her lead and pulled her away. 'Not today, your mate's not here. I meant let's go home.' I felt my heart sigh.

We retraced our steps back past Norman's house and then up the lane, the mottled purple shadows latticed with green light. It was a cool and very pleasant place to be after a hot day and I was soon back in my stride as Inca and I walked up the hill.

The pickup turned into the road at the junction and Rory saw me immediately and waved. He pulled in and, through the windscreen, I could see how tanned and relaxed he was, he was wearing sunglasses.

'Well, hello stranger,' he said as the window lowered. 'What are you doing in my neck of the woods?'

I was overcome with embarrassment, like some stupid

schoolgirl caught waiting for the boy she fancied at the school gate.

'Hi, I was just walking, it's such a lovely day.' I knew I sounded terribly false, like we barely knew each other.

'You okay?'

I couldn't meet his eyes so I looked away.

'Martha?'

He was out of the truck in an instant, leaving the engine running, and the driver's door open. Before I knew it, I was in his arms, the strength of him enveloping me. He kissed the top of my head and then my forehead and then my lips. The taste of his mouth was divine, the roughness of his chin against my face and the tang of sea salt in the crevices of skin in his neck.

'Rory.' I felt like every muscle in my body had weakened as if, at that moment, I gave in to it all; my broken marriage; my angry daughter; my terrible retirement; my increasing lack of self worth, and yet, at the same time, I was so lucky compared to Carrick. I was suffering so little compared to that old man who sat day after day at his window staring out at that little bird table.

'What's the matter, sweetheart?'

'Everything,' I told Rory as I pressed my face to his chest, the firmness of it comforting against my cheek. I needed him so much right then.

'Come on, back to mine, I'm seeing a very great need for a cuppa here.'

He helped me to climb into the pickup and then lifted Inca into the footwell. Her tail was wagging madly and it was obvious she thought it was all a very fine adventure.

As we drove, I wrapped my hands around myself defensively, self-hugging, as if it might protect me from my own feelings. Rory glanced over at me but said nothing.

In two minutes, what had been my walk of nearly quarter of an hour, we were back at his house. He didn't bother with his luggage, instead we walked straight to his door and I noticed he fumbled as he slid the key in the lock.

In his hallway, I stood like something washed up on the seashore, a piece of debris that had no earthly use, just a faded memory of a past.

He led me to the sofa and, instead of kissing me and making a move on me which he could so easily have done, he put his arm round me and held me to his side, pressing my head to his shoulder as you would a child who needed consoling.

'Tell me,' he said. 'What is it?'

'Steve's gone, I don't know where. He won't answer his phone, though I'm pretty certain he's at his mother's place. Sarah and he had a bust up, she's got herself a man who we don't really like and he's too old for her and I feel completely lost. I don't know how anything works anymore.'

'Works?'

'You know, me. I don't know who I am, or Steve for that matter, and I thought I knew who Sarah was but she's got no taste in men and she hates us.' I sniffed, tears forming in my eyes, the room blurring.

'I see,' he said, a finger was stroking my temple, rhythmic, soothing.

'And I missed you,' I said. At that point the tears

flowed. I wiped the back of my cardigan sleeve across my face. 'And I shouldn't do.'

'No,' he said, kissing the top of my head. 'You shouldn't.'

He was silent, as if waiting before speaking, then after a moment or two, he continued. 'And I shouldn't have been pining away in Spain, staring into every glass of San Miguel and trying to see your face in it. I couldn't stop thinking about you, not for a single moment. I'd have given anything to have you with me.'

I was motionless, the sound of my own breathing seeming to fill the whole room.

'So there were no hot Spanish floozies fawning over you then?'

'Yes, of course,' he said nonchalantly. 'Loads. I kept batting them off saying "Go away Spanish floozies I've met a lovely lady who makes me feel all fuzzy inside." It didn't stop them of course, but it held them off for a while.'

I smiled, I turned towards him. 'Fuzzy?'

'Yes.'

I was looking directly into his face. He was tanned, his eyes were bright and even his teeth looked whiter. He looked so healthy and handsome and so alive. Rory was not trapped; he was a free spirit, and not a bit like me.

I leaned forward, pushing myself up a little and kissed him. He turned and pulled me to him until I was on his lap then he kissed me again. I could hardly breathe as his hand curled around the back of my head. There was an urgency between us, a feeling of time rushing in and forcing us together, making it happen. He slid his hands under my shirt at the back, unfastening my bra, so that it was loose under my clothes. I felt my nipples harden under his hands as he cupped my breasts. It had never felt like this, the absolute truth. It was as if I'd asked the question all my life and here he was, right here, answering it. I pulled off my clothes uncaring that the big windows made me visible to anyone outside. I was woman in her sixties and I didn't care.

He kissed my shoulders, my arms, my breasts, and then he ran his fingers down my back setting off sparks in me, small at first and then bigger, brighter until my body was alive with them. He pushed me down onto the sofa, the cracked leather cold against my back and then he was undoing his jeans, and before I could take it all in he was kissing and licking my stomach.

His hands were caressing me, moving across my tingling skin making my back arch with pleasure. It was then, right then, I could have said no and I should have said no. I had my chance but I didn't. I didn't want him to stop, I wanted everything he was: his mind, body and soul I was greedy for him, jealous of anyone who had ever touched him. He eased into me and the sparks ignited all over me and I was his. I gave my all to him. Everything that was Steve and me was a far away distant thing, Sarah ceased to be, and my life, before Rory, withered and died.

In the corner of the room, Inca moaned and put her nose between her paws with big soulful eyes, as she watched me with abject disapproval.

66

Alec Trevise was thin. He had a mop of sandy hair and a faint Cornish burr. I imagined that, before all this, he skippered a boat around Fowey harbour and brought home fish for his rosie-cheeked wife.

'Carrick?' He extended a hand to me. 'Knew it would be you, fattest person in Paris!' I smiled, because I was the lightest I'd been in my life. 'Bloody war,' he continued. 'They tried all the ways they could to kill us and now we're dying of post Liberation starvation.'

'I brought food.' I placed my case on the table in the café. 'Cheese, two slices of bacon, eggs and a fruitcake, made with eggs too I'll have you know, by my housekeeper. Lewis told me how bad the situation was here.' I went to click open the latches, but Trevise stopped me.

'Not here, old man, don't want to cause a riot.' I glanced over at the café owner who was watching me suspiciously from behind the bar. 'Deux bières s'il vous plait, Claude.' Trevise diverted the man's attention with a wave of his hand.

'I saw someone skinning a cat yesterday, a small cat, not enough meat to feed a single child let alone a family.' My eyes widened in disbelief. 'There used to be birds in cages everywhere, the French let them sit in windows, très charmant, but it's been silent for months. No birdsong anywhere.'

'London is the same,' I said. 'Hardships like I could never have imagined. These are dark days.'

He nodded. 'Still, here we are experiencing Paris. Lewis briefed me, said you had it bad in Italy. Came up through Africa?'

'Barely touched Africa, sent straight on to Sicily, was fighting hand to hand for the hill villages, but at least we were getting somewhere, well eventually.'

'Lewis said you and George were badly injured, George's hip done in.'

I nodded. 'We were luckier than most; they brought us home. George was assigned a desk, but they let him off, he can't sit for long and then his company started some engineering lark, so they needed him.' I cocked my head to one side. 'So you know George?'

'Of him,' replied Trevise, 'through Henry.'

'Really?'

'Yes, Henry and I trained together at Roughwood, and before that I knew of him through friends of friends. Over here we became quite close, as one does when one's arse is permanently on the line.'

'And what do you know of him?' I asked.

'Well, he was caught by the Jerries after a raid. We were all four scattered: north, south etc. Just ran for it. Lost the other two and Henry looked like he'd got away with it as well, but they shot him and dragged him off. If he hadn't been special ops, they would have polished him off there and then, but they liked to give us the special treatment. Thing is, they had wounded him, so they had to operate before they began to kill him all over again.' Trevise half smiled. 'Jerry logic, very efficient but also highly ironic.'

'So they tortured him?'

'We don't know. The next thing is we hear the Yanks are advancing on Paris, then they're not. We send out a couple of Resistance to make contact with the Americans, but no one hears back from them. You have to have been here to experience the chaos. Jerries moving one way then bedding in. French advancing from the south; snipers taking potluck shots from windows; barricades being built in every street. German High Command was talking about razing the city to the ground, but something or someone stopped them. They bombed a circus, you know. All the animals were running wild all over the Champs-Elysées, lions and the like. Bedlam.'

'Lions?'

'Camels, horses. French ate 'em.'

I stared at him as he sipped the warm flat beer.

'Carnage. And during all of this, Henry is somewhere, supposedly in a building in the eighth arrondisssement, near Gestapo HQ.'

'What did you find there, when they'd gone? Did anyone know anything about him?'

Trevise shook his head. 'Not a thing. We interrogated a Jerry who'd worked there, but he was useless, a bloody coward. The Gestapo had long gone by then and our lads still in there were done for.'

'But no Henry?'

'No, no sign of him. The Jerries were fanatical record keepers, but they destroyed everything before they scarpered so they couldn't be incriminated. The Resistance sent word he'd been finished off by firing squad, three of them taken out at first light, shots fired and all that.'

'So what now?' I asked.

Trevise swallowed down his beer and threw some coins onto the table.

'I take you back to my digs and we eat that cheese and bacon.'

Two of the eggs were cracked, in spite of Mrs Hall's best efforts to protect them by wrapping them in straw and a robust box, the ten hour journey had taken its toll.

Trevise emptied them into the small frying pan, shells and all and began whistling as he cooked them on a blackened old stove. The bacon smelt divine.

We were in a small bedsit apartment on the Rue Galande, a medieval building, painted green, with a set of impossibly narrow stairs leading up to a cramped attic room. A small gable window let in some light, but it was so dirty, it was impossible to see out of it. A low row of grimy panes ran along the back wall and a line of chipped and broken terracotta pots sat on a narrow wall outside, all the plants dead and shrivelled.

'Home Sweet Home,' said Trevise cheerfully as he made space for me to sit down on a defeated old armchair.

'How long have you been here?'

'In Paris or this flat?'

'The flat.'

'Five months, since hostilities finally ceased. Up until that point, a chap could lose his head to a sniper just queuing for bread.'

'Who was shooting?' I asked.

'Everyone who believed in something: Resistance; Communists; Free French Army; Fascists; stranded Jerries, the mad, people with a grievance, you name it. Bullets were far more common than food, still are.'

'And how long have you been in Paris?'

'Off and on two years,' he replied. 'Arrived with a pair of Russians on one occasion. Absolutely useless.' Trevise's face twisted. 'Caused mayhem. She was a liability and was snapped up immediately, then spilled. Lost our pianist thanks to her blabbing and then the other coward legged it back to Moscow, never to be seen again. Waste of time.'

'Pianist?'

'Radio op, bloody good she was too, pretty girl.'

'What happened if they caught you?' I asked, not really wanting to know.

'At first they are soft, they strip you, hang you by your arms until it's unbearable then they try to crack you. If you give in, like that stupid Ruskie, you get off more lightly, but if you hold out, it's anything they can think of. Drowning; electric heaters; wire; electrodes, they didn't hold back. Most of our crew held out, we were trained to withhold for twenty four hours to give our colleagues chance to make a run for it.'

I felt bile rising in my gullet. My head was starting to throb. I focussed on the smell of the bacon to stop myself fading. To this day, I think of Trevise, and that dirty little apartment, when I smell it.

'Henry?' I asked weakly as Trevise shared out our meal equally. (I insisted he took all the bacon, he needed it more than me.) 'What do you think happened to him?'

'Our sources inside the Gestapo, who we had tamed by then, said he was operated on immediately. They had a crazy old doctor who would pop in and do repairs with a kind smile, just before he signed you off to be tortured. Bizarre.'

Trevise and I were seated each side of a small table, him perched on the arm of an old chair. He tucked into his eggs, relishing the taste, a trickle of yellow ran from the side of his mouth and he wiped it with a finger, then licked it off. Clearly for him, manners were a thing of the past.

'We heard he had been tortured having failed to smuggle him an L pill. Things were a mess by then, the Gestapo were very nervous knowing, I'm sure, that their time was up. The Resistance managed to cause them a lot of trouble, but we failed in trying to free prisoners.

'So what happened?'

'In late August the FFI got into Avenue Foch and then Rue des Saussaies in the eighth arrondissement. The poor sods they'd tortured had been kept in small dark damp cells, shivering, whimpering, crying for their mothers. I was told it was pitiful. I asked everyone about Henry, but there was no sign. We have no ID, we're ghosts, they call us The Spooky Boys, you know. It was hugely dangerous. One moment the streets would be filled with people then a volley of shots would send them scattering into doorways and behind pillars and such. FFI men with old pistols and

German rifles would start firing at what they thought was the source of the attack.

'I met an American, an agent who had been in there. He told me there were scratchings all over the walls, the unfortunates sending last messages to relatives and one said, "Life is Beautiful." Can you imagine that? Life is beautiful. And that made him weep, he told me it was that moment he cracked. He said he walked outside took a deep breath of fresh air and vowed to marry his girlfriend back home in Boston. And he was as tough as they come.'

I rubbed a round clean patch in the window with my handkerchief, and looked out as the light changed across the city. A mellow peach sky was resting above the dark shadows of Notre Dame and the Île de la Cité.

I could just about make out their shapes. It was noticeably warmer than in England and all at once something occurred to me. 'If Henry was captured on the twelfth of August and operated on, he may just have made it until the Liberation. Surely it is possible that he was still alive.' I felt a quickening in my heart.

'Twelfth of August? What makes you say that?'

'Oh, I should have said this by now, I have met his fiancée, she told us.'

'Fiancée?'

'A woman called Cécile Roussell, she–'

'Cécile Roussell?' He looked absolutely thrown. He stood up abruptly, dislodging the table as he did so, almost tipping it over. 'Where is she?'

'I have no idea.'

'When did you see her?' he demanded. It was as if he

had been taken over by the devil. 'When?' His face was flushed with an angry red.

'Just before Christmas.'

He paced back and forth in the small space between us. 'Where? Come on man, answer me!' he shouted, his fists white-knuckled and I seriously feared he might strike me.

'At Lapston, Henry's house.' I am almost certain that I leaned away from him in case he went for my throat.

'Bitch,' he spat the word. 'Bitch.'

'What did she do?' I could feel the heat from his body, the anger.

'She married me.'

67

I looked into his eyes as we lay side-by-side in his bed, and I realised I was totally in love. Not the vain, desperate love of teenage years, not the expected settle down and get married love of my twenties, this was a full-bodied, ripe, passionate love of the all consuming sort. What terrified me was that I saw it reflected in his eyes. It was a huge burden to carry and my mind was not up to it.

He reached out and pushed a strand of hair back from my face, then touched the end of my nose tenderly.

'Rory, I...' The words failed me.

'It's best if you don't think about it all, just let it settle. You might panic and run off and I'll never see you again, and that I could not bear.'

I lay back, head against the pillow. A house martin swooped past the window and landed on the crossbar of the frame. I could see its beady eyes assessing us and then it was gone on tiny beating wings and I was left thinking of Simon and how he'd caught us.

'I need to get home,' I said, almost matter-of-factly. 'I saw Rory's expression was laced with disappointment as I kissed him and moved across the bed. He didn't watch me as I dressed. It was that strange thing when you've been intimate with someone, but still feel shy of them seeing you naked.

'I'll drive you. I need to pick up Scoot. I told them I'd be there at three.'

He made it sound like dropping me off was only an option because it was convenient, as if I could have walked all that way home. 'That sounded bad, didn't it?' he said immediately. 'The truth is, I don't want to take you anywhere, I want to spend the night with you and hold you, I never want to let you go back.'

I raised an eyebrow. 'Now you do sound a bit creepy,' I told him. He returned my smile. 'I have to go.'

'I know.'

'But I will come back,' I promised.

He left the bed and walked towards me, naked. Dark hairs spread across his chest but his tan ended at his hips, pale skin above the dark hair. I took a deep breath. It was almost too much to bear.

He kissed me once more and I felt a bond so strong it was as if he had coiled it around me like the fingers of the Gorgon holding Jason. All at once, I remembered watching that old part-animated film as a child terrified that Jason was snared and done for.

That was me. I was done for, and I knew it.

68

'Married? When?' I asked.

'Here, in August last year, the bitch. I knew it, I was played.'

'She actually married you?'

'Yes, organised a ceremony with a priest in a church near here, then she scarpered, late that night. Couldn't find her anywhere, bloody priest acted like he couldn't remember anything the following day.'

'So it was never consummated.'

'It was never anything, no record of it; she took the paperwork.'

'And you haven't seen her since?'

'Not a word.' He tried to run his fist under cold water but the puttering tap struggled to work and it was little more than a trickle.

'She turned up at Lapston, saying she had been Henry's fiancée, she wanted to see where he had lived.' I couldn't describe the feeling inside me, the insane need to cheer and shout; I was vindicated. Yet, at the same time, I felt I was crushed under the weight of this new intelligence.

'She barely knew him.' Trevise was shaking his head. 'Barely knew him.'

'But they had met?'

'Yes, but you know Henry; he was mission first, didn't let his head be turned, not like me. I was reeled in, I was overwhelmed by her.'

I could feel the darkness at the corners of my mind encroaching; creeping in on me. Images flashed before my eyes. The creamy white skin, the cocktail dresses, the silver feather on its thin chain.

'I don't understand,' I said perplexed. 'I don't understand what she was doing.'

'I do,' Trevise cut in. 'I was her meal ticket, I organised for her to leave Paris, made it easy for her, gave her the safe passage she needed. I realise now that if he'd lived, it would have been Henry's name on her paperwork. Instead she had to resort to me. One of us was always doomed to fall for her in the end.'

'So you knew she was leaving? She didn't run away?'

'We were both going initially, a few days after the wedding. I had all the papers, I'd booked a hotel for us in Oxford, The Randolph. Lewis sorted it all for me, he even arranged for someone to see us safe through, an escort.' Trevise looked mortified. 'I didn't see it coming.'

'Didn't you try to go after her, what stopped you?' I could feel the anger rising inside me. If Trevise had got his act together, he could have stopped all this, everything.

'I received some information that day that I simply had to act on.' He was running a hand through his hair, his eyes tight shut as if he was recalling something painful.

'So you let her go?' I was shuddering, the darkness was crushing the sides of my head. In that stark and dreadful moment, I found myself wondering if this "thing" came on when I was angry. How could I be sure? I tried to take a deep breath for I was determined not to let Trevise see this, this unmasculine weakness. I had not been ill for months, just a sharp headache in the temples from time to time, not the blackness, not this.

I realised he was looking at me, so I repeated myself. 'You let her go?'

'I was tipped off by someone reliable that one of our boys was still alive. I had to look into it; I was convinced it was Henry.'

69

'Sarah?'

'Mum.'

'I'm so sorry. I... I didn't mean to say those things.'

I felt that grip of pain, the conflict in my mind between how wounded I felt and not wanting to cause any hurt to my child, a tearing sensation deep inside me. I tightened my grip on the phone. 'It's okay, it's fine,' I lied.

'But it's not,' she said. 'I said some things and I–'

'It's fine,' I snapped. 'Just leave it.'

'But Dad.'

'Dad's fine about it, just forget it, Sarah.'

'I saw him.'

'Who?'

For a dreadful moment, I thought she was referring to Rory.

'Dad. In Oxford. I was there at a seminar and I bumped into him. He's staying at Grannies.'

I didn't know what to say.

'Have you split up?' she asked, blunt as ever.

'No, we're just having a bad time that's all,' I replied. I could feel a knot in my throat, and tears welled up in my eyes, but it was Rory I wanted to go to and not Steve.

'Sarah, I'll have to call you back, there's someone at the door.'

'No there isn't,' Sarah retorted quickly, outwitting me and being bloody difficult.

'I've got to go, I'll phone you tomorrow.'

I could hear her protests as I slammed down the phone and stood, palms flat, on the kitchen work surface, as if they might support me and stop me from shrinking into the cold stone flags beneath my feet.

70

'What did you find out?' I wasn't sure I believed Trevise. There was something about the man, some unnerving edge to him, yet he had given up on his new wife to search for Henry. I was still feeling below par, but I was willing myself to fight on regardless. I had promised Lewis I would and I was not going to let him down.

'I came across a Jerry in hiding, he was holed up in a boarded-up shop in the Marais. I caught sight of him behind the shutters and he must have guessed I was English, the hair dye was growing out and I was auburn again. Anyway, he let me in and I had two choices, kill him or throw him to the Resistance, but he had other ideas. He asked me if I wanted to know the whereabouts of an English spy. No name. The man was seriously injured, might even be dead by now, he said, but if I wanted to know where the agent was I needed to fetch him some food and water.

'I brought him some rice bread and coffee the next day. I had struggled to find anything at all. He told me the English man was in an old beamed house in the eighteenth arrondissement, told me it was a small street where Dali had once lived, near the patisserie. I knew where the shop was.'

'Was it true?'

'No, no such house there. I went up to look but it was just another false lead.'

'What did you do?'

'I checked it out, then came back to where the Kraut was and cut his throat. I like to think I did him a service; he didn't stand a chance in Paris, he was finished, he was a waste of bread and coffee.'

Cut his throat. Collins. The room was becoming airless.

'Strange thing to say all the same,' I faltered a little. 'And he hadn't gone when you returned? If he'd been deceiving you he would have moved on, surely?'

Trevise sat down heavily in his armchair. 'I don't know, I searched for Henry, asked questions, left messages, but I turned up nothing.'

'Let me try,' I volunteered, although I did feel terribly ill; there was a heavy pressure on the back of my neck. 'I'd like to try to find Henry for myself.' I stood up as if I was going to grab my coat and leave, but in truth I was trying to evade the onslaught of what was coming.

The thick, heavy feeling engulfed me, the familiar rapid pace of my heart and the inky blackness. I pressed my hands to my cheeks and pressed the nails into my flesh, but it was too late. I hit the floor and felt the harsh crack of my head against something solid and I was gone.

71

I was reading Carrick's words. It was three in the morning and I felt the dampness of tears on my cheeks. It probably wouldn't have affected me so much if I hadn't met him, the old man, in the home. He was speaking to me, words written so many years before, telling me things no one else knew. They talk now of Post Traumatic Stress Disorder but then, seventy years ago, no one would have known what it was. They would have written him off as mad. I closed his book and stared into space, then I picked up the bedside phone and dialled Rory's number.

'Hi,' I said.

'Hey you.'

'I don't know what to do.'

'Sleep would be one option.' I could tell he was yawning, he would have been fast asleep when I phoned.

'I'm sorry if I woke you.'

'No, I'm glad you did, I keep thinking about you and wondering what you are going to do, but if you don't want to, you know…'

'I haven't got a clue what to do, Rory, I've never been in a situation like this, I feel terrible and–'

'And frightened?'

'Yes.'

'And excited?'

'Yes.'

'And in love?'

I hesitated. Was I? What is love? What is infatuation? What is lust?

'I can't...'

'I love you,' he said with all honesty. 'I have it bad. Please tell me you feel the same way.'

'I can't...'

There was an ugly silence broken only by a slight crackle on the line. When I began to speak again, I realised there was no point; he was gone.

72

It was Henry. He was alive! His face swam in and out of my vision. He was obviously worried about me, for his eyebrows were knotted together in concern, but it was Henry. I was right to come to Paris, to have taken so long to get here: the discomfort; the endless miles and begging for lift after lift; paying for American soldiers to drive me along countless broken and damaged roads. It had been worth it, I had found him.

'Carrick, old man,' his voice was strange, inaudible, his eyes the wrong colour. I was lying on the floor as he patted my cheek to bring me round. He helped me up onto my elbows and, tilting my head towards him, let me a sip from a glass of cloudy water. It was Trevise.

'You took a bit of tumble there, old man, may have walloped your head.' He helped me to my feet. 'What is it? Epilepsy?'

'No, no, must have been exhaustion, long journey.' I stumbled towards the cot he had under the eaves. 'If I could just lie down.'

'Could be the flu, old chap,' Trevise offered. 'Lot of it about.'

When I awoke again, Trevise had gone. There was a slicing pain in the base of my skull where I'd banged my head. I washed my face in a dribble of water, pulled on my overcoat and, as I headed down the steep stairs, my footfalls caused doors to open ajar in my wake and thin curious faces peeped out timidly.

Trevise was coming into the building with a brown paper bag in his hands as I opened the front door.

'Croissants,' he said. 'Fresh. Quite a rare treat. Feeling better?'

I pushed past him into the dark dirty streets where a scruffy child was staring at me, wide-eyed, as he sucked on the cuff of his jersey.

'Where are you going?' shouted Trevise after me.

'To look for Henry,' I replied, turning up my collar to stave off the cold.

'Good luck!' he shouted after me, but if he said anything else it was caught on the wind.

Montmartre was full of artists plying their trade but it was obvious, post occupation, for a fraction of the money. A man with a long thin moustache beckoned me over to his easel. 'Monsieur your portrait, five hundred francs only.' I shook my head. 'Three hundred?' he offered. His eyes were sad, his face skeletal. I gave him the five hundred, but waved away the offer of a sketch.

'I'm looking for an Englishman, undercover agent. Have you seen him?'

He shook his head.

'No, sir, I cannot help you. I have seen no one.' He

looked genuinely upset. 'We owe you English a great deal, sir.'

I had spent the day asking for help in all the shops and cafés around the steep and unnerving streets of Pigalle and the Goutte d'Or where suspicious eyes watched me from darkened doorways. I found myself looking over my shoulder on more than one occasion.

By the time I threaded my way up through the cobbled streets of Montmartre, to the top of the hill, I was exhausted. I shuffled along the narrow uneven streets, my feet sore and my back aching, but wherever I asked heads were shaken regretfully and apologies were offered with great sadness but there was still no information. Not a glimmer of hope.

It was late afternoon when I turned the corner to be faced with the magnificent Sacré-Cœur itself, its imperious edifice rising up to a gunmetal sky. Two verdigris horsemen stood guard before the magnificent white dome, their faces looking out across the entire city.

When I turned around, halfway up the steps, there was before me a vista with no equal. A thin haze of purple mist had descended upon the city, the sky above dark and threatening, but every so often, across the cityscape were pinpricks of golden light, the low winter sun catching in glinting windows. No camera in the world could ever reproduce the breadth or beauty of that sight, and even the most talented of artists could not have portrayed the splendour of that moment. Paris was finding her inherent beauty once again, rising phoenix like. There was hope for London and Coventry, and those sad dockland cities up in the north of England too.

As I slipped inside the cool darkness of the Basilica, I had an overwhelming gush of emotion for the fact that that magnificent building had survived in an occupied city. Trevise had told me about the threat to lay waste all the great buildings of Paris as the Nazis retreated, but the Sacré-Cœur stood defiantly intact, still remaining in her stately beauty long after the hate, fear and terror had receded.

A funeral mass was underway inside, a nun singing incantations. The smell of incense was rich and intoxicating. All eyes were fixed, if not on the nun, then up at the towering figure of Christ that emerged from a backdrop of gold, silver, purple and crimson high above us, his arms wide open in risen glory. The singing of the lone nun was mesmeric as it soared up into the cupola, she had a quite angelic voice. Then the other sisters and the organ struck up, the exquisite blend of everything made my head swim and, all at once, I was swept away with regret. I was thinking of George in that cold wet English soil back at Lapston. What on earth had I done? I had denied him all ceremony and due respect. I had deprived him of a history and a true remembrance. What madness had overcome me and what did I think I was doing?

I rubbed my fists into my eyes, grinding them into the sockets to cause myself pain. Nothing was right, nothing. Everything was gone, all of it.

'Sir, are you quite all right?'

The French was spoken in the softest accent. It was an old woman, her face wizened, her back bent and her eyes a translucent blue. She was dressed in widow's weeds.

'I'm fine, thank you,' I told her, but when I went to stand up there was no strength in my thighs and I gave in to it.

'Can I help you, sir?'

I felt I was reaching the end of my search with no conclusion at all and I was so very tired. I rattled off the sentence I had used on other people earlier, but it came out part whispered. 'I'm looking for someone, an Englishman, possibly injured,' I told her. My French accent has never been all that passable, not like Henry or even Alice, but she nodded and rested her hand on my forearm.

'Wait here please.'

She returned ten minutes later with a priest. He was young, fresh-faced and willing to help, so very young. It fell to these children to find a way now. 'May I help you, sir? Madame Jellis here tells me you are looking for the Englishman.' I noted the word 'the,' it lifted my heart.

'Yes, Henry Amsherst, a British agent, missing since the Liberation. Do you know anything of him?'

'Come with me, sir.' He half bowed and led me to a side door, though first we had to wait for the priest and his entourage to proceed down the nave. I can still recall every detail of that captivating sight: the incense, the coloured smoke, the glittering silverware, and the nuns passing me with absolute serenity in their devout and quite ethereal faces.

Finally I had a breakthrough! When I thought it impossible to go on and at the point of giving up entirely, I was going to find Henry.

73

'Please meet me @ Knot Garden. Come thru church g8.'

It was a text. The ping of my phone had broken my concentration. I was reading Carrick's book and wanted to know if Henry was alive. It was nine o'clock in the morning and I was still in bed. Inca was curled up next to me, her head resting on my leg. I had found huge comfort in her being on the end of the bed at night, even if it broke all the house rules, and the counterpane bore a circle of muddy brown where she lay.

Outside, a bright sunny day was pushing through a hazy mist. Finally, after three weeks of heavy driving rain, "the wettest July on record," the sun was making an appearance. I rubbed my hand across the cover of Carrick's book. So much pain and loss, and all of it so typical of war, all those silenced histories consigned to the grave.

Inca moaned and licked my hand. She needed to go out and I had to see Rory.

I set off for the Lapston at ten, the bright beautiful day

belying the butterflies in my stomach and the weakness in my jelly knees.

As I made my way through the churchyard, I stopped at the yew tree, Carrick's yew tree, the one that marked George's sad forgotten grave. What did Emily Brontë call it? "Unquiet slumbers... in that quiet earth."

The gate in the wall was stiff and took some pushing and, although I managed it, I couldn't make it close behind me. It was wedged against a tussock of grass then, as I took the path up to the house through the whispering gold grasses, my mobile rang.

'I'm coming home to talk, I'll be there in an hour.' Steve, despite the brevity, sounded kinder and more himself, but even so my heart sank. He would have to call at that precious moment. 'Are you in?'

'I'm at Lapston, but I'll be home soon.' I wanted to be truthful. If we were going to talk I was determined to tell him everything.

'I won't ask if you're meeting him.' His voice remained even, no trace of anger or resentment, and then I wondered if he was reconciled to our parting and if it really was all over. The lurch of sickness in my guts felt hot and raw as I realised I might have lost him.

'You've come.' Rory was standing in the middle of the knot garden his face so full of relief it nearly crushed me. He threaded his way towards me and Scooter, who had been chewing sticks on the grass border and making a complete mess, leapt to his feet and began his wagging twisting dance, barging between my knees at one point so that I nearly fell over.

'Scooter, no! Stay down!' Rory shouted as Scooter jumped over the low hedge. He grabbed the dog and made him lie down though the flat-coat was visibly trembling with excitement.

When Rory hugged me his strong arms were like a sanctuary, a safe harbour.

'Oh Martha, I'm sorry,' was all he said.

I felt very weak, tired and, if I'm honest, frightened. 'You don't need to be sorry,' I said, my voice muffled by the fabric of his shirt.

'I put pressure on you, it was silly of me, I know I rushed it, I just thought...' He took my face in his hands and looked into my eyes. 'You look terribly tired.'

'Thanks.' I pulled away because I was scared he was going to kiss me.

'Come over and sit here on the wall.' He took me to the side of the house, to the cool shade, and to where, whilst we were talking, Scooter had scooted on his elbows and was now lying flat out on the gravel path, his pink tongue flopping.

'He could really use a swim to cool down, but the river has deep currents here, I worry about him. It's better further back under the bridge.' Rory sat on the low brick wall and indicated for me to sit next to him. I did so, but not too close, not touching.

I looked up at the house, Carrick's bedroom above us. I could visualise him now, looking over the knot garden and watching George and Cécile walking there that morning. Before it all began.

'Rory, I can't do this... us.' I spoke softly. I was looking down at my legs, they looked aged, white, unattractive. I told myself that I should stop wearing shorts, I was getting too old. It was such a stupid thought to have at that moment, the very moment I was about to let go of a man I adored.

'Is it something I said?' he asked. 'Because whatever it was I would un-say it in a heartbeat.'

'No.'

'Have I upset you?'

'No.'

'Was I no good in bed?'

I felt the corners of my mouth turn into a smile that didn't quite reach my lips. 'No, you were… '

'Phenomenal?'

'Yes.' I looked up at him and, on seeing the expression on his face, I had to smile, but I also noticed that he had dark rings under his eyes. 'I've never known anything like it truly, it was like every stupid metaphor in every book I ever read.'

He smiled kindly but the joker was gone, he knew we had shared something special. 'But you love your husband?'

'I do. I have done for forty odd years. He and I, it's… we are a good fit.'

He sighed. 'My loss,' he said, and as he did so, I noted a quiver in his voice and that pinched my heart.

'I'm sorry,' I told him. 'Really, truly sorry.' I reached up and touched his face. There was rough stubble around his chin, he'd had a sleepless night and come up here early without shaving.

Just for a moment, I was looking into his eyes, the deep limpid pools of brown, and he was holding my gaze.

It was I who broke the contact and stood up because I simply didn't trust myself, not one bit. One touch would be all it needed for me to cave in. 'I hope something good happens to this house,' I said, clumsily changing the subject. I leant a hand against the warmed stone. 'Because it holds some good memories of good and honest people.'

'How do you know?' he asked turning to look up too. 'Have you been ghost hunting again?'

'Yes, and I'm close to laying some of them to rest.' I didn't want to tell him any more than that. I had not told him about my meeting with Carrick and, in a strange way, I felt the separation of them in my mind was a good thing.

'I'll walk you back to the car.' He took my hand and called to Scooter who had fallen asleep. 'Then, I'll try to let you go.'

As we reached the bench, midway down the path, we turned and looked back at Lapston.

'There's a letter in there, trapped behind the mantelpiece in the library, I'd like to have found it, but I know now I never will.'

'Martha.' He paused for a moment before speaking, as if he wanted to save me from hearing something painful. 'Martha, I'm sorry but they are going to start knocking it down next week. I just heard, I had no idea up until now, and I'm going to lose my knot garden too.'

'No!' I was so alarmed and upset for him, I knew how much he loved the place and he looked absolutely devastated. 'I am so sorry, I wish I could buy it for you, if

I had the money I would,' and I meant it, I'd do anything I could to save his garden, his pride and joy.

We were hugging each other, standing perfectly still and facing that lovely old house. The gentle breeze was tugging at my hair, the warmth of the sun on our backs, a perfect day for our desperately sad final moment.

Then I heard my name being called. It was like being woken up from a pleasant doze. The sound was sharp and loud as it carried on the light wind and Scooter on hearing it too looked up wagging his flag-like tail.

A tall figure was coming up the path towards us.

Steve.

74

Sister Evangelina was diminutive, her pale face heart shaped and framed by her starched wimple. She was standing in the small whitewashed visitor's room of the nunnery behind the Basilica. I would never have found the tall brick built house, nor made it through the locked iron gates without the help of the young priest. She had her hands pressed together as if in prayer as I entered through a plain wooden door. I have never met anyone so fragile or more birdlike. When she turned to me, her large eyes were a window to the sadness in her soul. They spoke of excruciating things, of pain and suffering witnessed and born in silence.

I extended my hand but she didn't take it, instead she indicated that I should sit on a small wooden pew that was leaning against the wall.

'I am Maxwell Carrick,' I told her. 'Henry Amsherst is my dearest friend, did you know him?'

She nodded. 'I did.'

Did.

'How? Where is he now?'

She took a deep breath and laced her fingers together in her lap. Small white fingers.

'We found him at the side of a street leading out of the city, back in August. Everything was very bad and we were all frightened. He was semi-conscious and bloody as if he had been hit on the head.' She touched the top of her head, her fingers lightly indicating where the wound had been. 'He was moaning, some people thought he was German and would have nothing to do with him. One man even tried to kick him, but thankfully they pulled him away.'

The sister was speaking in an unbearably slow and measured way. It was all I could do to stop myself telling her to speed up. To this end, I interjected rudely.

'Is he–?'

'He was very badly injured; his legs were severely damaged. We took him into a house where there was a bed for him. We tried to find help but there were snipers and mobs rampaging through the streets. The Americans were coming, but no one knew when. The family were so good, kind people and they tried to help, but they had no food and they themselves were starving. I dressed his wounds with material from old shirts. The smell, the smell was terrible, like nothing I'd come across before. I knew it was gangrene.

'One of the men who had helped me carry him into the house managed to find some bandages and iodine from outside, but there was very little I could do. Henry had a fever and he was delirious. When he spoke, it varied between English and French... and sometimes he screamed. He would yell "no, no, no" and push me away, I couldn't calm him at all. I did search, but there was no identification, no papers on him.'

I felt sick to my stomach. Henry.

'I mopped his brow and held his hand, I'm sorry but it was all I could do. Then, at one point, he was calm and quiet, it was like he was drifting towards the end and I asked him his name and where he was from. He whispered the name "Lapston." Then I realised it must be a village in England so I told him I imagined there were trees, hedges, green pastures and spires of churches, everything I could picture of your country, even though I've never been. These were the things I had heard about when I was growing up.

'There was a time when I thought he was going to improve a little. He smiled when I came into the room and told me I was beautiful, but it was fleeting, his face would crease with pain; he had a much weakened voice.'

She hesitated and searched my eyes as if she was wondering whether or not she should proceed.

'I hate to tell you this, and I don't have to if you would prefer it, so...'

I indicated that she should continue even as my blood seemed to freeze in my veins.

'His body was covered in welts and burns, but worst of all were his feet, there was no skin left on them. Someone had wrapped them in cambric and as we pulled the material away his skin came with it. His legs were burnt.' She dipped her eyes and looked away. How old was she? Twenty? A young beautiful girl, she was no age at all. 'I am so sorry, I couldn't keep him alive, I had nothing and though we all tried, we couldn't find anything, nothing for the pain. We were told to stay inside. You should know that the family were so good and gentle and caring, given that they were so desperate themselves.'

'He died.'

'Yes. I was with him and I held his hand. Towards the end, he kept repeating the same name over and over again, he kept saying Alice George, Alice George. I asked him which part of England he came from and he said Oxford, but it was barely a whisper. I wasn't sure if I even heard it correctly, you see, I only speak a very small amount of English I'm afraid.'

I stood up and turned away from her for fear she would see me on the brink of tears. My dear friend was dead. It broke my heart to think that he was calling for his brother and sister whilst dying in agony in some grim anonymous house and in a foreign city. I leant against a screen, a carved ornate thing with angels carved crudely into it. My hands grabbed hold of one of the figures and, although the wood was hard under my fingers, I felt I could crush it such was the anger that surfaced in me. The nun didn't move she sat quietly, back ramrod straight, and perfectly still whilst I took it all in.

'How did he get there, in the street?' I was seething inside at the thought of it.

'We think it was Nazis trying to escape the city, that they took him with them to bargain with. We think this because they took others, important people. As they retreated, they were stopped and burnt out of their vehicles by the mobs. Some of them died, on fire… in the streets, screaming.'

'Is that what they did to Henry? Was he set on fire?' I asked, my heart pulsing in my chest.

'No. These were the well-known wounds of SS torture. We had seen these many times before at the convent hospital when we treated people who were rounded up and suspected of resistance.'

The angels carved into the wooden panel were surrounded by rough-hewn grapes and curling leaves and, as I stood before it, the panel faded in and out before my eyes. Meanwhile she continued to talk, placid, calm and sotto voce.

'During the war, we had all the right supplies and sisters who knew how to nurse well but, in the last weeks, it was all so very desperate.'

'What had they done to him?' I felt morbid for asking, but I needed to know.

'They had roasted his feet in a fire.'

I thought I might throw up. The room was swimming around me, my head so heavy, pulling me down to the ground like it was made of lead. When I spoke, it was through a cracked and broken voice. 'What did you do with him, with Henry?'

She turned away and clasped her hands, her veil shielded her face from my view. She couldn't speak.

'Where is he?'

Again silence.

'Where is he?'

'You have to understand we were all very scared, the streets were dangerous, the only time the men of the house could risk going out was to try to find food, was at night.

We had Germans in the next street holed up in a hotel just shooting at people, anyone.'

'And?'

'We dragged him outside during the night and left him on a patch of empty ground. We left him there. There was nothing more we could do.'

I took a deep breath. I could feel the flickering in my eye, the edge of darkness. I must, at all costs, keep focussed, I must not let the demons in. 'Did you report this to anyone?'

The French family promised me they would tell the Americans when they arrived; they assured me that they would. I had to leave Paris then, I had work to do with women who had been punished for collaborating and so many orphans. Your friend was only one, only one of many who suffered.'

She stood up, her habit rustling as she moved towards me. She curled her small fingers around my hands and gripping tightly said, 'I did what I could. Later on, I wrote a letter, to Alice George, Lapston, Oxford, England in the hope it would get there. I have no idea if it ever reached its destination, but I prayed each night that it would.'

I knew it had reached its destination, with God's speed, but I now knew that the devil had intercepted it.

75

'I knew I'd find you here!' Steve's face was puce with anger and I knew he'd been getting himself worked up as he drove over. I should never have told him where I was.

'And you, you bastard, what are you doing with my wife?' Steve was standing in front of Rory, until he realised he was lower down and was much shorter. He compensated and went further up the path to gain extra height. As he passed me, I tried to grab his arm, but he pulled away. 'No, Martha, no!'

'Steve, we were just leaving,' I said, trying to be as assertive as I could, I wanted him to just walk away with me.

'So this is him. The demolition expert and part-time gardener. Do you realise you could have killed my wife taking her inside that wreck?'

Rory moved so that he was standing between Steve and me. It was a bad move because he looked possessive. 'I knew what I was doing, Steve. I can assure you that Martha was perfectly safe with me,' he said calmly.

'Don't you Steve me, you bastard, I don't want anything to do with you.'

Steve was angry but next to Rory he looked small and

weedy, the pale-faced indoorsy maths teacher facing off against the landscape gardener who had powerful arms and, I suspected, a powerful right hook.

'Steve, leave it, please, let's go.'

'There's nothing to worry about,' said Rory. 'We were just close friends.'

'Friends don't sleep with each other.' Steve was spitting out the words. 'I know all about it.'

Neither of us could say anything because there was simply no way of denying it.

'Martha loves you,' said Rory. 'Do yourself a favour and take her home. You should appreciate that she's an amazing person, she's gentle and very beautiful... and so very easy to love.'

I looked up at him, the straggling hair, the six o'clock shadow, the dark circles and those loving eyes that fell on me, even then, as our brief affair was coming to an end. I nodded and acknowledged his words, but I couldn't speak.

Steve looked like he was in two minds, fight or flight, but he snapped his fingers around my wrist and pulled me away. Then he jerked me down the path, more roughly than he intended to, I'm sure, as he dragged me towards the gate. I managed to shake free, but when I looked over my shoulder, Rory was staring after me, a silhouette against the sunlight, and he was shaking his head.

'Leave me alone.' I was disgusted with my husband, with the way he was treating me in front of Rory.

'I'm ashamed of you,' Steve said angrily. 'This is totally humiliating for me.'

'No one knows,' I said miserably. 'No one knows anything.'

'Except that Simon guy at the church, and everyone he's told, bloody gossip.'

'He won't have said anything, he doesn't even know.' I was struggling to keep up with my husband as he strode on long legs down the uneven path. 'Oh but he does you stupid cow, he asked me all about your boyfriend, told me he'd seen you out and about together and how you must be "good friends" because you seemed "so close."'

'He doesn't know anything, nothing, he's just nosey that's all.' I pleaded a defence but it fell on deaf ears.

'Do you know how that makes me feel?' Steve shouted as we reached the gate. 'Do you know how embarrassing it is to have your wife shagging another man?'

And suddenly I felt utterly dreadful. I had made him feel this way, I was cuckolding my husband. I was all the people you read about, a duplicitous cunning two-timer who had chased excitement and lust, and I had made a huge calamitous error.

I was about to grab his arm to pull him towards me and hug him. No, I was going to cling to him, because suddenly I wanted to promise him the world and tell him how much I loved him, but just as I reached out for him I heard a loud, urgent shout from over by the river. 'Scooter, oh my God, no!'

76

I was sitting in a café bar when Trevise located me.

'You found out?'

I nodded.

Trevise ordered drinks and as the barman placed a Ricard in front of me on the table he paused and asked my companion if I was unwell. Trevise waved him away impatiently and then turning to me said, 'Bad?'

I nodded again.

I couldn't shake the image of Henry, his legs burnt, his skin peeled off, lying there abandoned on the side of a road. Surely someone would have done something, taken him somewhere. Perhaps if I asked around, if I paced the streets, talked to everyone, if I put up notices...

I felt the tight blistering pain behind my eyebrows, damnable pain and the Ricard smelt overwhelming, a thick aniseed that filled my nostrils. I pushed past Trevise and threw up on the cobbled street outside. A passerby, a woman, only just avoided my vomit as it splashed into the gutter. Her brown court shoes topped with a delicate silver buckle, scurried away from me.

For a moment, my world was the uneven cobbles and those feet. The pain tore through me, a great heaving ripping pain and I was with Collins. He had no face, then he did, it was Henry's face. He was laughing, throwing back his head, his green polo shirt, then he was screaming. He was not laughing, he was screaming I was completely wrong and–

'Come on, old man,' said Trevise grabbing my arm. 'Let's get you home.'

Trevise was asleep when I woke up, soft morning light falling on the floor from those low dirty windows. The shadows of the dead plants outside, ghost plants, twisted and untended, fell across the linoleum floor.

I watched for a while, making the random elongated patterns and shapes into pictures. Another day, in another time, I might have experimented with painting the dark greys onto a patterned background of a similar tone. But not now, nor ever again. I would never paint, nor even sketch, and I would never find happiness or contentment, of this I was certain. These were my friends, my family and all of them dead and sickeningly I knew I was the unifying factor. I was the bad omen, the spurious link between their fates. Except of course I wasn't. I had been a bystander, a unwitting spectator, this whole situation – Henry, Alice, George – this had been the result of a catalyst. Blue, green, red, blue, green, yellow... I remembered the experiment at school, the litmus test.

I was hoarse with thirst, but the rusted tap had run dry. Trevise had placed a pail of water in the corner from God knows what source. I drank a little but didn't risk too much.

He was in the armchair, head lolling backwards, mouth open. I shook him awake and I'm afraid I startled him. He pushed me away before he realised who I was and was all set to lunge at me. Then he collected himself, shaking his head, and apologised.

'Sorry, old chap, I do that every time. Can't get used to life being normal again.' He rubbed his eyes and ran his fingers through his auburn hair. 'Thought you were Jerry coming after me.'

'Do you have a gun?'

'Three,' he replied. 'Why?'

'I need one.'

He reached under the bed and pulled out a small tattered box. Resting on top of the box, which was full of bullets, was a Luger. He passed it to me. 'What are you going to do?' I think he seriously thought I might be about to top myself.

My mind made up, I had reached the point of no return.

I was going after Cécile Roussell.

77

I ran back up the incline and reached the riverbank, so dense with nettles and shrubs I could hardly see the water. Rory's voice alerted me to Scooter whose long sleek body was submerged under the eddying brown water. There were cloudy swirls of muddy water churning up around him. He was paddling, his head just above the surface and he was making frightened snorting noises.

'Come on, Scoot, come on.' Rory was standing on some sort of wooden promontory, part of an old bridge or boat launch. He was leaning out over the water coaxing his dog and acting like he had something in his hand. 'Come on, Scoot, see here, come here lad, a Bonio, look here.'

The current of the river was barely detectable but it was stronger than the dog could cope with. He paddled faster, his paws broad and webbed, making no difference at all. For all that he swam against the current, he was getting nowhere.

'Rory, throw a stick.' I pointed down river. 'Throw a stick and make him turn side ways, towards us.' Rory tore away a piece of the old wood from the bridge and lobbed it into the water. As it splashed, Scooter looked over his shoulder, but it was obvious he couldn't move, and was spluttering and coughing.

I knew Rory couldn't swim so I unstrapped my sandals. I reckoned I could wade in, if I could find a way though the vegetation, and grab Scooter's collar then I could pull him towards me. I weighed it up, making the presumption that the river could not be so deep where there were reeds. There was a small fallen tree I could cling to as well, but even before I had time to think about it, Rory had jumped in, there was a splashing sound and he was suddenly up to his chest in the frothing water.

'No, Rory, no!' I shouted. 'Let me.'

He looked shocked as the cold hit him. 'Scoot!' he called but he lost his footing and water filled his mouth. He coughed and spluttered, flapping his arms about. It was like a film, watching a man drowning in slow motion, his hands scrambled back towards the rotted wooden structure but he didn't reach it, he sank under the water and then, when he emerged, his face was white and he was utterly terrified.

I tried to make my way through the foliage, but great fronds of hogweed were stopping me and nettles with nasty sharp prickles were spiking into my calves. My blouse ripped as I slid down a steep muddy bank. I was hurtling down towards the water, my hip grinding against a protruding rock, and my feet were losing all purchase in the mud.

At that moment, I heard another splash and between the shouting and the dog, who was now whimpering mercilessly, I could hear the sound of strokes cutting through the water, rhythmic, strong. I scrambled back up the bank, using holes in the craggy surface for purchase and managed, feet slipping and sliding away from me, to grab hold of a thin tree trunk and haul myself back up.

Then I could see the water again, coursing between the reeds and under the overhanging trees, but as I ran along the side of it there was no sign of anyone. Then I saw Scooter, who had been swept further down. He was struggling to stay above the water and his snout and black eyes were all I could make out. Even further along, two shapes were splashing and creating undulating waves in the middle of the widening water: Steve and Rory.

Rory was flailing. He looked like he was fighting Steve off, then I realised he was panicking. The river was very deep and he was dipping under the surface and reappearing as he struggled for breath. Steve was trying to grab him and he too was losing strength. I ran down the edge of the river, hampered by the rugged rise and fall of the bank. Then the river turned a corner and I had to run around the swimming pool, its glassy waters rippling from edge to edge.

'Martha!' Steve had grabbed Rory from behind and he had him safe, cupping his chin with one hand and pulling him backwards towards the bank. He was in the widest part, the silent current buffeting him. He was finding it almost impossible. With all his might, he raised a hand out of the water and pointed. There, on the top of the next bank, was an old life-saving ring, orange and a dirty grey, hanging on a rotted post. I ran to it, my ankle giving under me as it hit a divot, but I limped on and grabbed it.

When I looked to see where they were, somehow they had separated again and Steve was looking everywhere for Rory, he was spinning around in the foaming water. Rory was behind him, the two of them were trying to find contact with the riverbed, but it was just too deep. I threw the ring as hard as I could and it hit the water with a thudding splash. The force of throwing it made me lose my footing and I fell, crashing heavily into the tangle of reeds and nettles, and my ankle buckled with a loud crack as I hit the ground.

78

It was a "dreich day" as the Scottish Amshersts would say, a great bruise of a cloud hung low over the city as I looked down at the address on the scrap of paper, Trevise's writing was spider like.

The road was narrow, widening only slightly at the midway point, and there I could see a small turret above a deserted café. Opposite was a large door with the carved head of a man set high above an arch. To each side were a handful of apartment windows and two had window boxes. I identified the one I was looking for, white and ornate. It was quiet in the anonymous street, and when a woman appeared from a small doorway to my left, I took her by surprise. Her eyes were haunted and full of trepidation, she looked at me uneasily. Even then, months later and long after the occupation, fear was ingrained in her everyday existence.

There was a huge wooden door, a blue that had been sun-beached to grey. I pushed it open as Trevise had instructed and slipped inside. There were doors to each side of a dirty cobbled courtyard and more above my head. I took the metal staircase slowly, it was not sound, and it reverberated under my tread. As I reached the gantry,

I caught a glimpse of a curtain moving top right, and a sallow face dipped back out of view.

Her flat was number four. Unlike the others, the brass numeral was gone, but there was contrasting paint where it had been.

I knocked.

There was no answer.

I rubbed away a layer of dirt in the small side window and peered in but it was in vain, I could see only the blurs of a room through a thick, dusty net curtain.

I tried knocking again, even though I knew it was fruitless. Trevise had warned me. "She's long gone, old man, ran off ages ago." His words were ringing in my ears as I leaned over the balcony wondering what to do next.

The door to my left creaked as it opened and the sallow-faced woman, dressed in black, was looking at me.

'What do you want?' she snapped. 'What are you doing here?'

'I am looking for Madame Roussell.'

'Madame! Ha, that's a laugh. Madam more like.' She was a rough sort, something akin to a kitchen maid or cleaning lady.

'Did you know Madame Roussell?'

She threw back her head and laughed again, a nasty bitter sound.

'Oh yes I knew her, tart that she was. I saw what she did to that Englishman too.'

I stepped closer to the woman and she backed away a little, not someone of great nerve, but a weasel woman made desperate by war.

'I'd be able to tell you more if I had a few francs to aid my memory.'

Close up her teeth were black, rotted holes ringed her gums. I felt inside my trouser pocket and pulled out a handful of coins. She snatched them from me, feeling some of the rims with dirty fingers as if she didn't trust their worth.

'Yes I knew her. I saw it, what happened. It was a late afternoon, August, the sun still fierce. There was shouting, in German, and soldiers were coming from both ends of the street, I could hear them. The man came careering round the corner, I thought he would fall and he nearly did, but he balanced himself somehow.

'She was on her balcony, like I was. I had been watering my window box and the water was dripping down into the street, that must have been why he looked up. He didn't take any notice of me but he saw her and there was a connection, but they said nothing. The noise of the footsteps was nearer, bearing down on him. She raised four fingers to him and he ran across the street and crashed through the doors beneath us. Then he was taking the stairs two at a time, I heard him. I closed my balcony windows, but I didn't close the shutters, it would have made me look suspicious.

'I watched through the small window next to my door. He was banging on that door, her door, number four, but she didn't let him in.

'They were coming see. It was too late. They poured into the courtyard, four, six, eight grey helmets, those terrifying uniforms, heavy boots stamping on the walkway.

He had his back to them when they shot him. He was wearing a white shirt and the blood it was everywhere. Red. Bright. Glistening. Yet he wasn't dead.

'They carried him down the stairs with his feet dragging behind him. He was limp, like a rag doll. It was me, of course, who swilled down that blood; she'd never have done anything like that, that's how she was, pompous, above herself, like a duchess she was.

'Have I seen her, you ask? No, and I hope I never see her again. She was a magnet to men, and very dangerous, yes very dangerous.'

79

I opened the terracotta pot and shook out the pale grey ashes. They caught on the breeze and splayed in an arc around me, then fell across the petals of the fading roses. It was the very least I could do for him, in the garden he loved.

Steve was standing a couple of yards away giving me a few moments to myself. He didn't need to be with me, I was well aware he could have played no part but instead, in spite of everything, he had helped me.

My ankle was stiff and the strapping felt too tight, I had to hobble to turn around and look up at the house. There was a dense colourless cloud descending on it, a mantle of gloom shrouding its pale, ochre frontage.

'Do you want me to make a marker or something?' Steve asked as I limped back to him, clinging to his arm for support.

'No, there's no point,' I shook my head sadly. 'Before long, this will be a housing estate, and it will all be gone. But Scooter will be in Rory's knot garden forever and that seems so right somehow.'

I felt the tears welling up in me, the hard rock-like feeling in my throat seemed to have been wedged there since the previous week and I could not swallow it down. It corresponded with the pain in my heart that was sharp in its intensity. I didn't tell Steve that, there was a lot we would never discuss now and much between us that we would both never understand.

'Are you going to see him?' Steve asked. He looked so sad and so incredibly forlorn. It was as if we had both lost our point of reference, there was so much to rebuild, a long road ahead of us.

'Yes,' I said. 'I am.'

80

'You'll want to see inside, no doubt,' the old crone said as I stood looking at the metal steps where they had shot Henry and dragged him away. What did she say? A rag doll? Thoughts ran around my head like hot rods, red hot, searing into my brain. I was gripping hard on the iron balcony as I turned to face her.

'You can gain entry?'

'I have a key.' The woman nodded. She reached back inside her doorway and dangled before me a set of keys. 'I was to hand these keys to a man called Laurent Ducas if he ever came here. He was allowed to stay here, but he was the only one, no one else. I presume you are not him.'

'No,' I replied. Ducas was a lover no doubt, in on the scheme, someone who knew she had gone to England and would be using her apartment in the interim. Another victim no doubt, waiting for her return. My mind was racing.

'I suspect Mr Ducas would have paid handsomely for this key when he turned up,' said the old woman with a repulsive smile.

I took out my wallet and peeled off some notes. She

grabbed them and hugged them to her chest as, with the other boney hand, she handed me the key.

The door didn't open fully; it was wedged against the mat. I bent down and moved it and, as I did, black beetles scurried in all directions. The three doors, left right and centre, were closed. I glanced over my shoulder at the crone who was watching me with great interest.

'Thank you. That will be all,' I told her.

The central door opened into the salon. Two tall windows graced the room, shutters half closed. The light, dull and insipid, flattened the shadows and shapes around me. In the places it fell, tones of grey, muted colours and dark shadows met the eye. Every stick of furniture was worn and dirty, the armchairs full of slits in the tattered fabric. There were a few cheap pieces of wooden furniture but they were dilapidated and damaged. There was no carpet square, only bare wooden floorboards. At the other end of the room there was a table, a makeshift desk. I picked up a book, it was a woman's novella, I forget its title. There was a writing pad, some stamps, and a number of letters wedged into a metal rack. I pulled them out, and yes it felt wrong, but I would answer to the gods later.

The first was a letter from her bank. It was telling her that no more funds were available in her account and she must make good her overdraft. The language was to the point, not a polite request. There was another, a bill from a costumier for a suit and a black evening gown, to be paid in full within seven days. Another was from a hat shop.

There were two more notes of no consequence, but at the bottom of the pile was a small folded piece of thin paper. From what I could see, it had been written in a hurry, in French, the lines of writing sloped upwards at the ends. There was a date, 6th September then it read: "Confirm that I have brought the date forward and I will be escorting you. All arrangements are as discussed with Trevise, but I've made sure it is just you and me. This is fate, my darling."

It was signed with a cross for a kiss.

I slid the letter into my pocket.

The bedroom led from the salon. It was compact and contained a single bed pushed up against the wall and a small armoire. The few clothes left inside it were worn and, as I touched the hem of a white blouse, I saw that it was frayed. On the small table next to the bed was a picture frame. I lifted it up and saw the face of Cécile Roussell, her hair glossy and swept into a high pompadour, a pearl necklace at her throat. Seeing her gave me a chill. She was in a bar, rows of bottles behind her Dubonnet, Ricard, Absinthe, and the bar man was standing behind her left shoulder, a thin pencil moustache topping off his broad grin. Then I saw the mirror behind him and in its pale reflection was a man with a camera, his face obscured by it, but behind him, the street outside, was a way of tracing her.

81

'I am so sorry,' Rory was lying in the hospital bed, the tubes and wires gone, the blankets folded neatly over him, recently straightened. 'I couldn't stop him, he just jumped in.'

'I know. Perhaps he fell, dogs do know these things. I'm sure they can tell if the water isn't safe.' I was fishing for words – I had no idea if that was true.

'Not him, he was more of a "do or die" kind of a dog. I guess this time he...' Rory's pallor was sickly, his voice rough.

I pulled up a seat and placed my hand on his. 'We spread his ashes in the knot garden. It seemed the right place.'

Rory nodded. He gazed out of the window and I suspected that he was fighting back a tear, but I couldn't tell. 'I loved that garden. Thank you for doing that, I'm glad he's in there before they start...' His voice trailed away again.

I wanted to tell him then that I loved him, that in other circumstances, in another time or place, I would be with him for the rest of my life. I was thinking about this when he suddenly coughed and his head tipped forward so that I could see the shaved patch and stitches in his scalp. He had been unconscious when they'd brought him in. I suspect he had nearly died. How I wanted to look after him because I couldn't bear that he would be in that house on his own and he had no one.

'My oldest is coming to stay with me,' he said, his voice rasping a little. It was as if he knew what I was thinking. 'She's on her way over. I'll be fine.'

'Good,' was all I could say.

I leaned over and kissed his cheek, taking in the smell of him, the fresh outdoors scent was replaced by disinfectant and medical smells, but he was still my Rory.

'Take care of yourself, Rory.' I withdrew and, as I looked over my shoulder, he raised his index finger. It was a simple, small gesture that meant the world to me.

82

I had ripped the photograph from its frame and I was staring at it, studying every part of it. There, reflected in the mirror behind the photographer's shoulder, I could see familiar arch of the Cour du Commerce Saint-André, the famous street where Joseph Guillotin practised how to kill victims cleanly. I knew exactly the location; I remembered the narrow cobbled passage from a school trip. One of her hauntings. The memory made my blood run cold.

I locked her apartment, and on handing the key back, I asked the woman if she knew anything of the whereabouts of Cécile or the man Ducas, but if she knew she was not telling. I made my way through the narrow streets of the Latin Quarter and as I reached the café, the heavens opened. My hair was dripping wet under my hat, water running down the inside of my collar for I had no scarf.

The boy behind the bar was young, a scrawny neck and thin red scar across his cheek. I ordered coffee and wiped the water from my face and neck with my handkerchief. It was only a second or two before I caught sight of the man with the pencil moustache, he was wearing a white apron, just as he had been in the photograph.

'Garçon!' I called him over and he was soon at my side.

'How can I help you, sir? Would you like a towel perhaps?'

His humour, on other occasions, might have garnered a smile from me but I was otherwise occupied.

'Do you know of a Madame Cécile Roussell?'

He looked right, then left, suddenly shifty. 'Who asks?'

'I am looking for her. I owe her some money.'

'You are English?'

'Yes.'

'Related to Henri?'

'You know him?'

'Yes, he was our friend. We owe him everything.'

'How so?'

The bartender pulled out a chair and sat down. He opened a packet of cigarettes and when he offered me one, I took it.

'Henri was working undercover with the Resistance. We knew him as Charles Rainier, but he used other identities. We were a safe house for him – he slept in our cellars from time to time. There were others, a woman, Florence and an older man, but we didn't know his name. They were helping us overthrow the Bosches.'

'What happened to him?'

'They came one night. He was in a townhouse, boarded up, not so far from here, a Jewish family had owned it. The Bosches were tipped off, it seems, it was of course common in those days. Collaborators. Anyway, he escaped and was looking for somewhere to hide. Cécile had met him a few days before and they had struck up a friendship. I trusted her, I've known her off and on for twelve years in here and round and about. He was here at about eight that morning and I told him to make it to her apartment, the streets are like warrens, narrow alleyways and the like. Sadly Cécile said he never made it, she never saw him.'

I looked into his eyes, there was no deceit that I could see in them, he seemed honest enough. He was working on hearsay, her words. Her lies.

'You say they had known each other for only a few days?'

'Yes, sir, she had another man, English too.'

'Trevise?'

'I don't know his name. I never met him.'

'Do you have any idea where she is now?'

'Yes, she's living with a friend who is ill, in Saint-Michel, just along from here.'

83

Steve had forgiven me. We promised we would never talk about it again, even though I had things I would have liked to have said. If he thought I was going to broach the subject, he would find something to occupy himself or suddenly take Inca for a walk, even if it was bucketing down.

I felt absolutely lost, as if I was in uncharted waters and I simply didn't know where I was from one day to the next. Worst of all, I no longer felt safe, as if the ground might open and swallow me up at any moment.

Then came the day of the summer fête. The village green was alive with sound and music. Small children were running around, faces adorned with ice cream moustaches and amid the noise and colours, there were people dressed up as animals. A giraffe was moving amongst the crowd, its long neck was sticking up comically above the mass of people. Camilla Crocket was running the tombola and the dog walker, the one I saw back in the spring, was buying tickets. Her Pomeranian was tugging away from her, trying to reach a discarded hamburger. Angela was serving cakes and next to her was Simon chatting and laughing with people as he took the money.

'Martha, darlin'!' Angela had caught sight of me and was motioning for me to come over to her stall. 'How are you?' Simon saw me but looked away, the turn of the shoulder obvious, cold. 'You do know I missed you at our meetings, don't you?' Angela continued. 'You brought a lot of kudos to our project. I didn't want to drop you, you know that, don't you?' I nodded and mumbled something in reply. 'Only I was out-voted. Maybe you could come for coffee some day. I'd like to get to know you a little better.'

I was about to say how nice it would be to see her when Steve tapped my elbow. 'There's no need to buy any cake,' he said humourlessly. 'I think you've had enough of that lately.' He nodded towards my stomach.

'I beg your pardon.' I stepped back and stared him down, horrified by what he'd said, and in front of Angela. 'What do you mean?'

'Nothing.' He turned away and began rifling through a box of graphic novels on the bookstand.

'Ooh, that was sharp,' said Angela. 'Are you okay honey?'

I was dreadfully embarrassed. What had he meant? I looked down at my tummy. I wasn't overweight. It was so completely out of character for Steve to say something so cutting that I was having trouble taking it in. I tugged on his sleeve, as he fingered the spines of old books set out in large crates.

'What did that mean?'

'What?'

'That jibe about me not needing cake.'

'Oh that. It was just a joke.' He didn't even look at me as he spoke. But it wasn't a joke, it was a barbed comment, something that was happening more and more often. They were insidious, none too subtle digs at me and I had just chosen to ignore them and not react.

I waited for him to move around to the other side of the bookstall and then I turned away and walked towards the church and the quiet refuge it offered, but why I imagined it would be empty, I do not know. In fact, it was full and busy with people looking at the cascading flower arrangements designed by a famous florist who had recently moved into the village. People were gazing in awe at a massive display in reds and blues that dominated the chancel.

A small group of people were singing godly songs, shaking tambourines and clapping, whilst an earnest bespectacled man accompanied them on guitar. Other people were dotted around the pews, some of them munching their way through tea and cake.

I saw that the small doorway to the secret room was open and a handwritten sign said: "Open Today Only, Careful Steep Steps." I slipped inside to perch on the cold stone treads, which meant I was out of sight behind the tapestry. When the shadow fell across the doorway I thought it was Steve, but instead it was Simon.

'Are you all right, Martha?' He was using his kindly voice, the tea and scones voice.

'No,' I said bitterly. 'I'm not, Simon, and frankly it's all thanks to you.'

'What did I do?'

I studied his face for a moment, the thinning hair, his pale brown eyes looked perplexed, but he was faking it.

'Making comments to my husband; being judgmental. You could have just kept yourself to yourself and stayed out of my business.'

Simon looked bruised and his expression clouded over, as if I'd really hurt him. 'I didn't mean to, it just slipped out.' The tambourines were getting louder and louder and the audience, scant as it was on the front pews, sang along and then clapped in time to the music. 'Go up a minute, I'll explain where it's a bit quieter.' He nodded towards the monk's room.

'No, it makes me feel claustrophobic.'

'I want to show you something, something I found that will help you.'

I took a deep breath and went up the two or three remaining steps. I was bristling for a fight and I was determined to warn him off, to tell him to stay out of my way. The room was airless, the window closed tight shut. Someone had laid a monk's habit and a bible on the bed as props for visitors to see.

'What is it you want to show me? What do you want to say?'

'You know, Martha,' he said as he reached the top of the staircase behind me. 'I actually did you a favour... well, more your husband if the truth be told.'

I was incredulous. 'What on earth–?'

'I know you aren't a churchgoer, but for all your lack of belief you cannot deny that it really is a sin to commit adultery.' He levelled an accusing look at me, a cold expression framing his face. 'This is the problem, you people have no moral compass.'

'We people?' My mouth fell open.

He picked up the bible. 'You'll find it in various parts of the good book and, of course, it is one of the Ten Commandments.'

'Simon, I–' I moved carefully towards the steps because as he reached for the bible he left a space for me to squeeze past him to the door. He flipped open the book, the gold-edged pages reminding me fleetingly of Carrick's journal.

'Here for example, Leviticus 20:10. "And the man that commits adultery with another man's wife, even he that commits adultery with his neighbour's wife, the adulterer and the adulteress shall surely be put to death."' Simon turned his eyes to me, the whites showing beneath the auburn pupils. 'So, you see, much as it behoves me to ignore what you did from, shall we say a more modern social standpoint, from a biblical perspective, that's another story.'

'I really think–' I moved to go past him and down the stairs. I could hear songs being sung in rounds: 'In my heart there rings a melody… In my heart there rings…' I began to feel the constriction in my throat, a rise of heat in my neck.

'I just wanted you to know that God is there for you. You only need to knock and he shall answer…'

'Simon, I'd like to go now, please let me pass.' I felt the air thinning around us. I needed to go back downstairs.

'If you ever want to talk, do come and see me, won't

you? That's what I wanted to say and that goes for your husband too. It's him I feel for.'

I half pushed, half squeezed past him, I felt my breast press against his arm and his smile, by return, was deeply unsettling, but he gave no quarter.

'My wife was an adulterer, Martha. She left me to pick up the pieces.'

I could feel his breath hot and salty on my cheek. I placed my foot on the top tread of the stairs with its solid reassuring stone, but it was only half the depth of a normal staircase.

As I began to descend, my head dizzy and my heart thumping against my rib cage, I felt Simon move behind me and then there was a sudden sharp jolt in the small of my back and I fell straight down the steps.

My ankle, the one that was still lightly strapped up, buckled beneath me as I hit the floor.

84

I was on the Rue Danton, close to the Fontaine Saint-Michel. I had positioned myself diagonally across the street and was observing a very fine Haussmann building. I was hidden from view under the awning of a closed down shop and in front of a fading ghost sign that advertised Cinzano. A tower of discarded crates gave me the cover I needed, but already the strength in me was sapped.

I had been standing for what seemed like hours and the tension in my body was making me feel rigid with cold. There was also a hunger growling in the pit of my belly and the ever present darkened corners of my mind were weakening me, but I had resolve. I would bring this to an end and it would be today.

I could have knocked on the front door of the building and forced my way inside, but I didn't know who else was in there and the waiter had told me that someone in there was unwell.

It was just after eight o'clock when the door opened and above her, at that moment, a shutter was unfastened and it caught my attention. A small hand, possibly that of a child, fiddled with the catch then withdrew inside. When I looked back at Cécile, she had turned in my direction and was walking straight towards me. I leaned back, aware that the slats in the crates allowed for her to see movement, but her eyes were fixed resolutely ahead. She was so close I could smell the soft scent of her perfume as, heels clicking on the pavement, she passed by, heading for the river. She was wearing the smart blue suit and the fox stole. A man passing on a bicycle gave her a surreptitious glance; they were all of them moths to her flame.

When she was a safe distance away, I followed, moving in and out of shadowed doorways or blending with other pedestrians whenever possible. She never once looked over her shoulder. At the bridge she stopped to light a cigarette and taking a long drag on it she exhaled a curl of blue-grey smoke into the evening sky.

A majestic sunset had spread wide across the horizon and the windows of the elegant buildings on the opposite bank reflected the sun in brightest gold, a Tintoretto backdrop to enhance her singular beauty.

I observed her for some five minutes, taking cover behind an advertising kiosk like a spy. Throwing the stub of the cigarette to the pavement, she ground it under her shoe then, after rummaging in her handbag, opened her compact. She applied lipstick, a harsh red, and then smoothed down her hair. In the peach glow of the sunset, she looked exquisite. Then she walked a few yards before turning sharp right, down some steps, to the quayside.

I followed. It was difficult to see over the wide parapet, but I saw her make her way under the bridge where she stopped, and I got the impression that she was talking to someone who was not visible from my position. She had her back to the deep cold waters of the river as the first vestiges of dusk were lying thick upon the air, the heavy mottled light that deceives the eye.

As I watched a man's hand held out a cigarette, but she was refusing it. I saw the sparks of a struck match light up her face, making her seem ethereal and phantom-like, and then I strained, on my toes, to see more and in doing so, caught her eye.

I pulled back immediately and walked away knowing that, in the dimming light and at that distance, it would have been hard to make out my identity. I stopped at a pillar and waited a few moments, then walked back, retracing my steps and onto the bridge itself. From there I could see her, and from my new position, I could see him too: Trevise.

85

I was sitting on the couch, my leg resting on the arm, elevated, as the doctor had advised me. The whole thing had been embarrassing, a church full of people saw me fall and then everyone was fussing and talking about calling an ambulance. When I had tried to stand up the person whose hand was under my elbow, taking the weight, was Simon.

'Let us through, I'm afraid Martha here has taken a tumble.'

'I've always said that those steps are dangerous,' said a small beady-eyed woman.

'Thank you, Mrs Pratly. We'll see to this.' A tall, mop haired man with a deep voice had taken over. 'Thank you, Simon, I'm the first-aider here. I'll take care of this.'

Simon was squeezing my elbow, maintaining contact with me, controlling things.

'Well, if you're sure, Gordon, only it was rather a nasty fall and Martha hurt her ankle recently, that's probably why it gave way so easily.' He left his hand on my back – a little too long – as Gordon took over, leading me to a nearby pew.

'Thanks, Simon. Someone's gone for Dr Braun, could

everyone move along please, give this lady some space.' I could see Simon hovering at the edge of the crowd, a sea of eyes were watching me, and the beady-eyed lady was holding my hand with warm fingers.

'There there, dear,' she said. 'Does it hurt?'

I nodded as I watched Simon head towards the door of the church. My throat was still constricted, my head dizzy but I saw him clearly as he slipped through the archway. He glanced over his shoulder, stopped for the briefest moment, and smiled.

Later, on the couch, as the clock in the living room struck six, the whole stupid thing seemed days away, yet it had been only hours. I was pretty certain that shock had taken me over and I couldn't think straight and my ankle was throbbing mercilessly.

As I went over and over it, I could see that horrible smile on Simon's face and something else, had I felt the pressure of a push in my back? I was confused. Was it possible that he'd pushed me? Surely I imagined it. Did I tell Steve? Most of all I wanted to tell Rory; he would have sorted it out.

'Here you go.' Steve placed a tray of tea next to me and he'd arranged some biscuits on a plate too. It was okay for me to have biscuits, but no cake I thought to myself.

'Thank you.' I shifted my position, wincing as I did so. My foot was throbbing under the bag of frozen peas that were slowly defrosting, and thin rivulets of icy water were now running down my leg.

'What were you doing up there?' Steve sat back heavily

in his armchair. 'I mean you don't even like tight spaces, do you.'

'Simon asked me to go up, he said he wanted to show me something.'

'Oh that old trick, mucky sod.'

'Steve–'

'What? He's known for it, always trying it on with women.'

'Are you kidding me?'

'No, Gordon told me.'

'Gordon who?'

'The tall bloke, runs the fête, nice chap. He said Simon's always skating on the thin ice between chatting women up and getting a bloody nose from their husbands.'

'I think he's a bit more dangerous than that,' I said weakly.

'What do you mean?' Steve looked incredulous.

'He told me he doesn't like women who commit…' the word nearly stuck in my throat, '…adultery.'

Steve snorted. 'Who does?' He was levelling a stare at me. 'I feel very much the same.'

I was snookered. I'd walked right into the trap. It had been set a week earlier, the empty snare, the conversation waiting to be had.

'You're never going to let it go, are you.'

'Probably not.' He reached across to the coffee table and opened the large book on National Trust properties that I had bought him for Christmas.

'I'm never going to be forgiven, am I,' I said and, all at once, I felt a rage rise inside me, a frustration, the feeling of being caught between two lives, the one I had now and the one I could have had.

Steve slammed the book shut with a loud thud.

'No, I don't think you are, Martha,' he snapped. 'You see, what you don't know is that I have questions going round my head all the time, every single bloody day: What would have happened if…; Why did she shag him?; What did I do to deserve that?'

I closed my eyes and pressed my lips together. This was a raw unreal pain in me, something I had never experienced before, and my head seemed to go into lock down, everything inside it a thick fog. 'I'm so sorry…' I whispered. I was going to say more, but I couldn't verbalise it.

'And then there's the question that gnaws away at my mind night and day.' He leaned forward so that his eyes were level with mine.

'What?' I asked.

He closed his eyes, a tremor on his bottom lip, it was so unlike him.

'I keep wondering which one of us you wanted to be drowned.'

86

'Carrick!' She looked astonished as if I had caught her completely unawares, her eyebrows arched, eyes wide beneath them. 'What a surprise.'

Trevise stood in the darkness with his back to the wall, his red hair a soft grey in the light of the flickering gas lamp on the wall above us.

'Cécile, how strange to find you here,' I said calmly. 'And with you, Alec. I thought you said she had, what were the words you used, "run off"?'

Neither of them reacted. Trevise drew on his cigarette and breathed out the thick smoke from his nose, a heavy cheap tobacco: Gauloise. She spoke first.

'Carrick, I can–'

'Can what? Explain? Oh Cécile, that's exactly what you are going to do. I want to know everything, every sordid little detail of it.'

She dipped her eyes and, for one tiny second, I felt that whatever she said I could forgive her, that haunting beauty, the pale skin, but I told myself that she was a dream, an image and no more. I realised right at that moment that most of who she was I had created in my mind.

'Carrick, old man, let's have a talk, we can sort

something out, let you in on it.' I had paid no attention to Trevise, so his voice trespassed on my thoughts.

'On what?' I replied without regarding him, my eyes were fixed on her.

'The money of course.'

'What money?'

'The sale of the house, of Lapston. We have it, in cash.' It was her speaking but it was as if her voice was a fading echo from a time long gone.

They say a red mist descends when a person is angry and I saw it, like gauze, before my eyes as I comprehended the words she had just spoken. The two of them stood to each side of me, Trevise with a pistol in his pocket I was certain of it, but all I could think was that they were ghouls.

'So it was all planned?' I said evenly, trying to act as calmly as I could. 'All of it.'

I was staring at Cécile but she could no longer look at me, instead she focussed her attention on Trevise as if she was willing him to speak. He threw the stub of his cigarette into the river where it floated for a second, a red spark lying impossibly on the surface of the water, before it was extinguished.

'We didn't bank on you,' said Trevise. 'Or your tenacity. We thought you would give up on it, go and live elsewhere, make life easy for us.'

'And I almost did. I nearly got out of your hair, didn't I?'

Trevise had a steely look about him. 'You made life very difficult for us.'

'No, it was she who made life difficult,' I asserted, raising my voice. 'She has ruined everything.' I was pointing at her, but still she couldn't look at me. 'What did you do to George? How did you prise Lapston from him?'

'Don't tell him, he doesn't need to know,' Trevise said sharply. 'He can't do anything now.'

I pulled out my revolver, holding it at waist height. I had it levelled at her as I said, 'You will tell me.' The thing that surprised me was their mutual lack of reaction to my gun, they looked completely unmoved.

'Very well,' she said taking a step towards me, 'but put down the gun.'

'No, stay where you are,' I said, 'and start talking.'

Her unwavering eyes were fixed on me above those perfect red lips, the fox stole, a rich burnt sienna, was caught in the dim light of the gas lamp. The details are still so sharp in my mind, every last second enhanced.

'It was Alec's idea. He told me about Henri and I made our meeting happen.'

'You only knew him a few days.'

'I did, but we did become friends in those few days.'

'Not lovers.'

'No.'

'And when he was arrested? You saw your chance, knowing the Gestapo would carry out the job of getting rid of him.'

She nodded.

'But they didn't finish the job because the Americans arrived.'

A barge slipped past us, a dim light at its prow, the

slap of the waves against the riverbank alerting us to its proximity, the engine was all but a gentle hum.

'So you were dicing with death, Henry's death, yet you suddenly realised that he could still have been alive, you heard rumours, didn't you? You were fearful of his return and what would you do then? It would have caused your filthy plot to fail, wouldn't it?'

'The war office had declared him missing in action,' Trevise said coldly. 'No one could say any different... I had reported it in.'

It felt as if the ground had shifted underneath me, I swayed on my feet. This was deceit of the highest order, one comrade against another.

'You bastard.'

I fingered the trigger, the metal cold on my skin.

'Fog of war, Carrick. You of all men know that.'

As the words settled between us I felt the churn deep in my belly, Collins. I tried to keep focussed. 'And George?'

'George was the easiest part,' said Cécile, there was a chill in her voice. 'Easy to charm, malleable, stupid, and craving an heir for his failing estate.'

'But he loved you,' I said.

'Everyone does,' she replied icily. 'It's how everything happens. Trevise here knows that, you know it. I make sure it happens that way. And, make no mistake, I could have chosen you, Carrick, after all you're the most attractive of them all. You have striking good looks and a guaranteed income with an inheritance to boot, but who wants a man who is so pitifully damaged? Who wants a madman to father a child, a man who collapses like a bent reed every time he feels troubled? Not me. I went for the easiest target, I always do.'

I saw Trevise flinch. He looked uneasy, he was uncertain of her I could tell and now I could see his hand was in his coat pocket, resting on his gun, but I cared not. I neither cared if I lived or died, all I wanted was the truth from them.

'What did you do to him?'

'I saw his weakness, his Achilles' heel. He was in love with someone else, tortured by it, living a complete lie.'

That threw me. I was at a loss.

'Who?' I could think of no one, a stupid idea passed through my mind about Fillie and whilst I was still trying to make my scrambling mind make sense of it, Cécile said the name I least expected, or ever could have expected.

87

The problem was I couldn't give him an answer, not reflexively. I was just staring at him and he had his eyes fixed on mine. I knew he could not bear it, I could see the glistening of wet tears in the corner of his eyes. He looked so old sitting there and so completely wounded.

I remembered a documentary I'd seen years before about wolves and the devastating close up of the pack leader wounded in a fight. He had fought the young usurper valiantly but he had been defeated, tooth and claw and had limped away, stricken with pain. The commentator, probably Attenborough, told us he would go away to die. That's how Steve looked.

'Come here,' I said, holding out my arms to him, and he knelt down beside me, pressing himself into my body. I rested my chin on the top of his head and held him tightly.

'I thought I'd lost you, I told Sarah I thought we were finished, and as I said the words I found the thought unbearable.' He was pressed against me, supported by my body. 'And I know I'm not a good husband,' he said sitting back against the sofa, on the floor. 'I'm not exciting and I'm grumpy and I don't send you bloody flowers, not even from the dog, but Martha, I do love you so much.'

I put my arms around his neck and hugged his head to mine.

'I know,' I said. 'I know.'

88

'Grant.'

I swallowed hard.

'Grant.' Cécile repeated with a snide curl of her lip.

'I...'

'You never knew,' she said with a self-satisfied smile, a victorious challenging sneer that said, "I win." 'Grant and George were lovers for years, no one knew about it, but I found out.' She nodded towards Trevise. 'He knew about George, didn't you?'

Trevise looked down at his feet, ashamed.

I felt my heart race. Images raced through my mind, but not one element of them, not one smile or gesture or furtive look had given anything away to me. I realised I had let the gun drop to my side. The images of George and Grant were swimming in my mind, blending together then tearing apart like ripped paper, then I remembered London and that sordid little man in that dirty shop, a front. Grant had gone in there. I felt sick.

'A man is easy to bribe when you find his weakness,' she continued. 'Lord of the Manor, a member of parliament in the making and a queer, it only takes a short time of being acquainted with a man to find the weakness, if you search hard enough.'

I felt the bile rise in me, the nasty bitter taste of it in my gullet. I was sickened by all of it, but I needed an advantage at that point. I would not let George down.

'There was another man, in Oxford.' As I spoke, she was steadfastly holding my gaze, but Trevise turned from looking at me to her. 'Or did I imagine it, Cécile?'

'A man?' Trevise's face betrayed his surprise. He was a sap, like the rest of us; she had used him just as much as me, or George.

'Oh yes, Trevise, another link in her chain of deceit. You haven't been as clever as you think.' I took out the note from my pocket and handed it to him. My eyes never left hers as we spoke. 'The poor fool who works for Lewis, wasn't it, Cécile? Your escort and organised by you, Trevise. Was he called Ducas?'

She shook her head. I was showing her my hand, what I had found out, and she knew I had been in her apartment.

'You all have your uses,' she said flatly. 'It is how women have survived the war, it takes nerve and cunning.'

'You were never married you two, were you?' I said it not knowing if it were true or not. I fully suspected that it was a smoke screen and ill conceived lie to put me off the scent, to make Trevise look innocent. Neither of them replied. He was staring at the piece of paper in disbelief. I turned away. I was looking down on the water, a ragged line of debris was being dragged down the river's edge, a child's toy, a doll was lying amongst it faded, dirty, grey.

George and Grant it was unthinkable.

A click of heels and Cécile was suddenly standing beside me, her lips at my ear, her scent overwhelming me. 'You can still have me,' she whispered. 'You and I. Alec is of no importance to me, he simply made things happen. Think of it, you and I, with the money from Lapston. Just my half is enough to make something of ourselves, it would improve your health; there is a life after all of this!' Her lips were almost brushing my cheek. 'We can go to Italy, India, South Africa, Cape Town. Carrick, think of the jacaranda trees, purple flowers, we can see them together. You and I, you have nothing to lose.'

The mist before my eyes had thickened into a wall of fog, and the water in the Seine took on another life, a swirling scarlet like a river of blood. Henry's blood, Alice's blood, George's blood. I turned sharply and thrust my gun into her belly.

There was a tremendous bang, a reverberation in my head, and the feeling that the world was suddenly a tunnel swallowing me up. She looked shocked, then her eyes bulged. She was there for only a second and then she was gone, her neck spattered in blood; was it my blood? Collins. I didn't know.

She fell away from me, backwards into the Seine. A surge of colourless water closed over her and the swirling mass of it engulfed her. It seemed to happen in slow motion, her fox fur dragged behind staying on the surface for a moment, and the glassy eyes of the animal in its wretched face were the last thing I saw. Then it was gone.

Trevise had shot her. My finger was still curled around

the trigger at the point of firing, but he had beaten me too it.

'Best that way, old chap,' he said matter-of-factly as he slotted his gun into his belt. 'You would be committing murder whereas, for me, it's all part of the job.'

I was incredulous. 'What the hell do you mean?'

'Simply that I was meeting her for this very reason, to end matters.'

I glanced at the river and then back at her murderer. 'Why? I…'

'We never found out for certain but we think she betrayed our side, some suggested she had lured Henry to her apartment, set a trap, but we can't be sure. Either way, this morning I woke up to the fact that I can't trust the woman.'

'But her plan, you assisted her, you reported his death. The money…'

'Outcomes, dear boy, outcomes. War changes everything, everybody. Before I met Cécile I had nothing, now I have something, a future. A word here, a detail there was all it took and…'

'And making sure Henry was dead and stayed dead.'

'It was highly unlikely he was alive, you had to know what they did to them. The fact he was found elsewhere was purely timing, fate. His death opened up an opportunity that's all, you can't blame a chap for seizing the day.'

'You sold yourself to the devil,' I told him through gritted teeth.

'You may see it that way, old man, but I see it differently. I have given everything to this bloody fight. My very existence has been erased along with my scruples and my ability to feel pain, real or emotional. I have another plan for my life, my new French self, I'm going to live a long way away and try, with every fibre of my being, to forget that these.' He held up his hands as if in supplication, 'that these can snap a human neck in seconds.'

With that, and with a last look into my eyes, he turned away from me and walked along the quay. I knew he half expected me to shoot him, but I was past the stage where I could. As I watched, the shock and horror of it all taking root in me, he vanished into the night.

89

Carrick was in a small lounge, sitting in an uncomfortable looking armchair, a fire safety label dangling from the headrest. There was patterned rug at his feet and a glass-fronted bookcase next to him with no key in the lock. It occurred to me that hundreds of lives had passed through this small lounge with its fire-regulated furniture and unopened bookcases, and not one had left a trace of personality. It was little more than a soulless waiting room.

The French doors opened onto a faded lawn and beyond a squabble of blue tits was flying backwards and forwards to a birdfeeder, tiny wings thrumming.

Inca pushed up against Carrick and nudged his hand, but he was in a deep sleep. I watched him as he snored softly, and noticed that the heavy grief in his face had receded and there were the traces of a younger man; a handsome face, high cheekbones, smooth skin.

'Why did you give me your journals to read? Why did you say we were so much alike?' I asked him. I wanted so much to know, but his was head tilted towards the crevice of his chest, he wasn't hearing me.

My thoughts were interrupted when a woman stepped through the doors from the garden. She was slim, with short dark hair and dressed sharply in expensive jeans and a crisp, white blouse. I guessed she was about my age, perhaps a bit younger.

'Oh, hello, I didn't see you there,' she said.

'I've just arrived,' I replied as Inca left Carrick's side and waggled over to her.

'Hello there. You're lovely, aren't you?' The lady squatted down to stroke Inca's round head. 'I do love labs.'

'That's Inca,' I said.

'Ah, now that make's sense. If this is Inca, you'll be the "nice lady" who owns her. I've heard a lot about Inca but not too much about you. I'm afraid I don't even know your name!'

I smiled. 'Martha,' I told her, extending my hand towards her.

'Alice,' she replied as we shook hands. Her touch was light but her eyes were warm, a smile in them.

'Alice?'

'Yes, Alice Carrick. This is my father.'

'Oh.' I was shocked because I had immediately assumed she was a health professional working at the home, I hadn't imagined that Carrick had relatives. 'I didn't realise…'

'He didn't mention me?'

'We have barely talked. It's so nice to meet you, he didn't write anything about his life after the war.'

'Ah, you've read the journals…' she said, spotting the one I was carrying in my left hand. 'My parents separated and so it's been a struggle to maintain a father-daughter relationship. Despite appearances, strictly speaking I'm Indian! I was born in Bombay. My father left England after the war and went to stay with his father, but that all

435

went pear-shaped. He found a job and he met my mother working in the same office. She was what they call a "Deb" but she resented being paired off with an aristo, so she applied for a job with the Foreign Office. Anyway, they had me, but it didn't last because of...' she nodded towards the book, 'because of his illness. You know all about it, it's called Post Traumatic Stress Disorder now but of course they didn't know that then, they just called it shellshock.'

'What happened to him?'

'He was put into therapy. They made him write those journals, the idea was to expunge everything and throw them away afterwards but, sneaky as he was, he managed to keep them. His doctors thought he made most of it up.'

'Really?' I was taken aback.

'Yes, they didn't believe all that espionage and that woman, Roussell. They said she was a figment of his imagination.'

'But the house? She owned the house, she took it off George.'

'That's what his journals say, but you know sometimes it's easier to cover your tracks with a fantasy version of history than face the actual truth. The family was on its knees, almost bankrupt. They probably lost the house that way, it would explain George's... demise.' Alice was looking at her father. 'The war shattered that family, they were all killed by it in one way or another, and my father has suffered the most, but his has been a slow death.'

Carrick moved and arched his back slightly then his eyes opened. He took a moment to gather his thoughts before he focussed on the dog.

'Inca, my lovely girl!' He was beaming. 'My lovely girl.' Inca bent almost in two, wagging. 'Good girl,' he said as she licked his gnarled hand.

'Papa,' Alice leaned forward. 'Martha's come to visit you.'

'Who?'

'The nice lady, Inca's mum.'

When Carrick turned his head and saw me, his face visibly brightened. 'Did you read it?'

I reached over and touched his arm. 'I did.'

Alice was watching and she may have felt a little uncomfortable, I wasn't sure, but I was invading her space and I was, after all, a complete stranger. 'I am very grateful to you for sharing it with me.'

'I'll go and get us some coffees,' Alice offered. 'Leave you two to chat a while.'

When she had gone, I pulled a chair up to Carrick's side.

'I understand everything,' I told him. 'You wrote it all down so people would know what really happened.'

He looked at me through rheumy, watery eyes and smiled. 'I did. I knew that one day someone would come along who understood. Someone who knew what it was like to search for answers. That was you.'

I felt humbled.

'What do you want me to do now?'

He sighed and played with Inca's ears, but his head was drooping and his bottom lip was protruding. I was losing him, he was drifting back to sleep.

'Carrick, what do you want me to do?' I shook his arm gently. 'Please tell me.'

He twitched and shook his head. 'What did you say?'

'What do you want me to do?'

He looked disorientated for a second then he said, 'I'd like you to take my books and write down my story, tell them it is true, the Amshersts deserve better, not their fault.'

All of a sudden, a lone blue tit flew in through the French doors and hit the glass of the window as it tried to escape. It crashed onto the sill, dazed, its tiny eyes half closed. I picked it up and felt the weightless bones and feathers in my hand. 'I walked over to the doors, almost tripping over Inca who was desperate to see what I was holding, then I held out my hands and the little bird took off and was gone in a second, twittering in protest.

Carrick was watching me. "Good job" he was telling me through kind eyes, I smiled in return.

'I loved animals,' he said. 'I loved my Jester. 'She nearly had him done away with, but I stopped her. They don't believe me because of my head, but you do, don't you?'

'I do,' I reassured him. 'I know it's all true.'

He smiled and as he leant his head back against the chair, it was a smile so satisfying I felt I had done something really worthwhile, something deeply good. I had taken the time to study his words and bring everything to a conclusion. I had finally brought him peace at last.

90

I closed the door on my little arts and crafts house in Oxford for the final time and waved goodbye to Mrs Hall, who was standing in the front window dabbing her eyes with Alice's handkerchief. She would be happy here and I would make sure she was provided for, she and her girls.

It was a bright fresh summer's day, the swifts were swooping overhead and I was reminded, as I so often was, of Lapston and the countryside around it brimming full with wildlife. I missed Jester but he and Beau were assured a happy retirement with grateful new owners in Charlbury. They were in a paddock by the station and I had made a special trip to see them a week earlier Jester came when I clicked my tongue, lumbering across the field in his familiar way. He let me rub his big, broad face over the gate and I felt sad but content in the knowledge they would both be well cared for.

'Farewell, old chap,' I whispered to him. 'Look after yourself, my friend.'

There was time to spare before the train departed Oxford and so I alighted at Handborough and dropped in on Lewis at Blenheim Place. He was sitting, looking overwhelmed, surrounded by teetering piles of boxes and copious brown coloured files, stamped confidential, and all ready to be transferred back to London. He puffed on a big cigar, his face more jowly by the day.

'It's all over, Carrick,' he said as he poured me a whisky. 'I kept this for the big day and now I'm polishing it off out of a sense of duty!' He laughed, his face free of the heavy burden of war and his unenviable responsibilities.

'How long before it's completely finished? Japan?'

'We're all hoping for autumn at the latest. Thank God.'

'I can't help wishing God had acted a little sooner.'

'Mysterious ways, old chap, we don't know what His plans are.'

'Well, we seem to have an idea what his plans were,' I said regretfully. 'A hell of a lot of devastation and loss is all I can see.'

'And bravery, sacrifice, acts of heroism, unvanquished human spirit and all that. One can only hope that lessons will be learned.'

'I hope so,' I said without enthusiasm because I had cause to doubt it. How long before the next ill thought out conflict? World War Three; they say things always come in threes, don't they?

'Anyway, you're off now, to America no less. What are you going to do there?'

'They have new ideas about treating...' I still found it hard to find the words. 'Difficulties like mine.'

'Good show, I think that's a capital idea, and you have the money, Carrick. Use it, learn from what they tell you, the Yanks are always so much more open to these things than us.' He tapped his cigar on an ashtray. 'Then where, India?'

'Yes, I plan to meet up with Father. He says he can find me a career behind a desk, some sort of planning operation, I'll be good at it apparently.' I didn't realise, until I spoke about it out loud, just how ghastly it all sounded.

'Did you ever sort out that problem with that French woman?' Lewis asked innocently. 'I don't think I ever saw you brought so low as when you told me about her, seems like she really got under your skin.'

'I dealt with her. She won't be breaking any more hearts.'

I picked up my briefcase ready for the off. 'By the way, was there any news of Trevise?'

'No, last heard of in Spain, heading south. Fair play to the man. He stayed on longer than he should have done, volunteered for it, trying to bring together those loose ends and, as you told me, he found out about Henry in the end. One of our best operatives, deserves a medal if you ask me.'

'Yes,' I said flatly. 'One of your best.'

I shook hands with Giles Lewis for the final time, I would never see him again; he would be retiring into the Sussex countryside and taking his secrets to the grave. Then, as I was about to exit his office something occurred to me.

'Lewis, have you ever heard of a Laurent Ducas? In Paris.'

He looked thrown for a second.

'What yes, that was one of Henry's covers, Ducas, that's right. Rainier and Ducas.'

91

Alice returned with the coffee after a short while. I had been sitting, quietly reading the last pages of Carrick's journal again.

'He tries to give them to people to read, you know, the nurses, doctors, the vicar and everyone pretends they will read them, but they never do, they just put them back in the wardrobe.'

'He's asked me to have them,' I told her. 'Is that all right with you? I would really like them.'

'I suppose so, I don't want them,' she said, 'and I'm his only living relative.'

'I find it all fascinating,' I told her. 'And, I think you'll find, from what I have researched, that it is true.'

'If you say so. If it is true, it's a sad story and, if it's a product of his imagination, then–'

'It's a good story,' I said with what sounded like sarcasm, but it was unintended. 'I will research more and maybe offer what I find to a military museum to archive, there is one in Woodstock.'

I squeezed Carrick's hand and stole a kiss on his forehead. He was almost completely asleep, but I heard him say softly; 'Goodbye, Inca.'

Alice and I walked together to his room, passing bland watercolours of roses that were lining the corridor, and I found myself thinking about all the lonely fading lives that were living out their last behind the walls of this place. It was so sad.

Alice found the first journal amongst the untidy belongings in the wardrobe and gave it to me with no visible sentiment. In truth, I found her quite cold and not someone I could become friends with.

'Are you going to write them up, adding in what else you find out?' she asked.

'I don't know, I'll have to think about it. I'm not sure how everything is going to pan out with me. You see, I'm going through a difficult time myself.'

'Marriage?'

I nodded. 'I'm the archetypal retired woman who's lost her way and who discovers she might have missed out on another life whilst she was busy making other plans.'

Alice raised her eyebrows. 'You don't look the runaway sort to me. Sometimes in life you have to settle for what you've got and make the best of it. I broke up a long-term relationship a while back. I miss him every day.'

I sighed and shook her hand politely as we parted. She was right; it's about being sure, having a foundation and knowing your ground. Dreams are for dreamers. I crossed the car park of the old folks home and looked back at the nameless, faceless windows and the blotchy yellow turf of its sun-bleached lawns. The shrubs and annuals had gone over, having borne their flowers, and they all had started to die back, tinged with brown. They were rusted and spent of their life force. Autumn, the time of decay, was on its way.

The car was too hot, the smell of plastic pungent and strong. I opened the windows to let the cool air in before I began fiddling with the sat nav.

I had my home address set as "previous destination" but, as I went to press the button, something stopped me. I leant back, letting my head clear for a moment. I thought of Carrick and I thought about how his life was wasted, damaged irrevocably making him nothing but the debris of a cruel war. Alice had called it a slow death. And what had she said about me? I didn't look like "the runaway sort." Was she right or was that the other me? The spent and rusted me.

I turned the key in the ignition and released the handbrake, but as I reached the exit I pulled up and took a deep breath, because I realised quite suddenly that I did have a choice. My future was in my own hands and I felt a peace coming over me, a moment of complete clarity. I reached forward and cancelled the 'previous destination' on the sat nav, then typed in the name of the place I really wanted to go to instead.

As I arrived at the edge of the Cotswolds, a brooding sky sat darkly on the horizon, threatening a storm and trees were shivering in the wind. I felt a moment of absolute fear and a tremor of guilt ran right through me but, as I breached the top of the hill where the chequerboard fields of the valley lay before me, a bright shaft of sunlight emerged from behind the iron-grey clouds and lit up the road in front of me, bright as gold.

Epilogue

The great hulk of the Gray Ghost was waiting in the docks, towering above us all. I'd never seen a ship like her and down below, in the shadows and crammed into every square foot of the dockside were, in their countless thousands, GIs in worn and dirty ochre uniforms. They were playing cards, throwing dice, smoking, laughing, relieved it was finally all over. They were on their way home, at long last, to the people they loved.

I observed them from a distance, an invisible watcher, set apart as I was in my suit and tie. Relief was writ large upon the face of every man but, in the midst of them, in the gaps between uniformed limbs and piles of worn out kitbags, I saw the faces of those who suffered like me. The bloodshot eye, the trembling hand, or the wary haunted look I recognised in myself.

We blended into the masses with nothing physical to give us away and we were, all of us, individually, trying to disguise our pain and erase the torture of our memories.

It was going to be a long road, but we had to face the future and believe that one day, on some dim and distant horizon, we would come to know ourselves once again.

Acknowledgements

As a writer, you hope that people might like your first novel, but it's impossible to predict how it will be received by its readers, so *The Seven Letters* being so very successful has been tremendously rewarding for me. I have saved every kind comment, read and re-read each treasured review and I have been very honoured to hear that the book has so many loyal fans.

There were highs and lows. I had moments of great joy and soaring hopes that were equalled by deep disappointment and dreams that didn't quite come true, but throughout the whole experience I learned a lot.

My husband Paul supported me to the full and without him, neither of my books would be published. Sarah Fitzgerald listened, advised and cheered me on as only a true friend can. Nina Smith showered me with her experience and insider knowledge and Annette Rainbow picked me up, dusted me down and set me off again on many an occasion. Thanks go to Liz Ringrose for moral support. For those special words of praise for the book that meant so much to me I must thank my great friend, Oggie Arathoon.

The Madhatter Bookshop in beautiful Burford

deserves special mention for not only getting behind *The Seven Letters* but selling countless copies and championing it right from the outset. The independent bookshop is king and this is one of the very special ones.

So many people helped me with research for this book: Nancy and Ken James, Robert Waller, Ingram Murray, Dr Bill Larkworthy and Françoise Jellis, to name but a few. Also there were the many people of Paris who, often although completely bewildered, answered many an author question with such unceasing grace.

My readers Mike, Nina, Liz, Sarah and Mandy are owed special thanks for giving *The Slow Death of Maxwell Carrick* the green light. Your comments mean the world to me.

I must thank Troubador Publishing for being so brilliant. Jeremy, Stephanie, Rosie and Alexa have been wonderful to work with and I should also give Chelsea a mention for the two amazing cover designs that have received so many plaudits. Thank you too to Morgen Bailey for the copy editing.

And finally, to my readers, bloggers and reviewers you have given me so much support and I appreciate everything you have done for me, truly. I hope I have brought you another novel that you will cherish as much as *The Seven Letters*.

Jan Harvey

About the Author

Jan Harvey has made numerous trips to Paris to research her books. The City of Lights has been a source of inspiration for her and provided her with many an adventure.

Jan is also an artist, working in acrylics, watercolour and glass. Her artwork has been sold worldwide.

In her spare time, Jan enjoys listening to jazz, walking her flat-coated retriever, Byron, who is every inch as naughty as Scooter, and watching old black and white films.

To receive updates about Jan, please do visit her

website and follow her on Facebook – she loves to hear from her readers.

www.janharveyauthor.com
Facebook: www.facebook.com/AuthorTheSevenLetters

Book Group Questions

Carrick suffers from PTSD and possibly a head injury. **Does this make him an unreliable narrator, or was he telling the truth?**

What were Cécile Roussell's motivations for her actions? What did you make of this sentence: 'A small hand, possibly that of a child, fiddled with the catch then withdrew inside.'

Why did Cécile tell her neighbour to let Laurent Ducas into her apartment?

If you were Martha, would you have stayed or would you have left?

If you enjoyed *The Slow Death of Maxwell Carrick* you will probably want to read *The Seven Letters* and you can buy a signed copy directly from the author at:

www.janharveyauthor.com

Book club notes are available there too.